KT-502-194

A brand new family could be the
perfect present…

Baby's First
CHRISTMAS

Two all-new heart-warming
baby stories that will make your
Christmas sparkle!

Baby's First
CHRISTMAS

FEATURING

THE CHRISTMAS TWINS
BY TINA LEONARD

SANTA BABY
BY LAURA MARIE ALTOM

DID YOU PURCHASE THIS BOOK WITHOUT A COVER?

If you did, you should be aware it is **stolen property** as it was
reported *unsold and destroyed* by a retailer. Neither the author nor the
publisher has received any payment for this book.

All the characters in this book have no existence outside the imagination
of the author, and have no relation whatsoever to anyone bearing the
same name or names. They are not even distantly inspired by any
individual known or unknown to the author, and all the incidents are
pure invention.

All Rights Reserved including the right of reproduction in whole or
in part in any form. This edition is published by arrangement with
Harlequin Enterprises II B.V./S.à.r.l. The text of this publication or any
part thereof may not be reproduced or transmitted in any form or by any
means, electronic or mechanical, including photocopying, recording,
storage in an information retrieval system, or otherwise, without the
written permission of the publisher.

This book is sold subject to the condition that it shall not, by way of
trade or otherwise, be lent, resold, hired out or otherwise circulated
without the prior consent of the publisher in any form of binding or
cover other than that in which it is published and without a similar
condition including this condition being imposed on the subsequent
purchaser.

M&B™ and M&B™ with the Rose Device
are trademarks of the publisher.
Harlequin Mills & Boon Limited, Eton House,
18-24 Paradise Road, Richmond, Surrey TW9 1SR

BABY'S FIRST CHRISTMAS © Harlequin Books S.A. 2010

The Christmas Twins © Tina Leonard 2006
Santa Baby © Laura Marie Altom 2004

ISBN: 978 0 263 88822 5

010-1110

Harlequin Mills & Boon policy is to use papers that are
natural, renewable and recyclable products and made from
wood grown in sustainable forests. The logging and
manufacturing processes conform to the legal environmental
regulations of the country of origin.

Printed and bound in Spain
by Litografia Rosés S.A., Barcelona

The Christmas Twins

TINA LEONARD

Dear Reader,

I love Christmas stories! They are one of my favourite things to write because, for me, the underlying themes of the season are family, friends and tradition. And a Christmas story is a chance to relive all of those wonderful emotions!

I hope you'll enjoy the story of Zach Forrester and Jessica Tomball Farnsworth, two very different personalities from opposite walks of life. I believe that Christmas works its magic on the most stubborn people, and magic in even the most challenging of circumstances can bring love to the most impossible situation. May your holiday season be lit by this very special spirit of love, charity and fulfilment.

Best wishes and much love,

Tina Leonard

Tina Leonard loves to laugh, which is one of the reasons she enjoys writing. In another lifetime, Tina thought she would be single and an East Coast fashion buyer forever. The unexpected happened when Tina met Tim again after many years—she hadn't seen him since they attended school together. They married and now Tina keeps a close eye on her school-aged children's friends! Lisa and Dean keep their mother busy with soccer, gymnastics and horseback riding. They are proud of their mum's "kissy books" and eagerly help her any way they can.

Tina hopes that readers will enjoy the love of family she writes about in her books. A reviewer once wrote, "Leonard has a wonderful sense of the ridiculous", which Tina loved so much she wants it for her epitaph. Right now, however, she's focusing on her wonderful life and writing a lot more romance! You can visit her at www.tinaleonard.com.

"I've tried to be perfect. I've lived in a world. Imperfect is a lot more fun."
—Jessica Tomball Farnsworth.

"I've tried to be perfect. I've lived in a world that wants perfect. Imperfect is a lot more fun."
—Jessica Tomball Farnsworth

Chapter One

Zach Forrester freely admitted that boredom was his worst enemy.

He didn't mind living in Tulips, Texas, on the Triple F ranch, but he wanted to do more in his life than just take care of a family property. He had plans to build a new elementary school in the small town, a challenge he would enjoy.

But now it was time for a different challenge. Maybe the late September moon was getting to him, but excitement seemed to be a hard-to-find commodity.

One thing was for certain, he wasn't giving up his life the way Duke had, to diapers and a wife and a round-cheeked baby. He loved his little nephew, but a baby put a certain stop to one's life. Nor would he ever let a woman lead him around by the nose as Liberty had Duke. She had left the altar with Duke standing at it, then made a surprise return with his baby, finally marrying Duke in a wonderfully romantic ceremony.

Of course, Duke was insanely happy with his new wife and child, but it had been hell on Duke getting there. Zach had to admit it had been fun watching his older brother struggle mightily to get his woman. *Everything always seems to come easy for my brother and sister and harder for me.*

He was enjoying his pity party as he drove, until he saw the hot pink convertible T-bird and the madwoman standing next to his favorite bull, which she'd clearly hit. She was talking on her cell phone as if it was just any old piece of meat she'd struck. But Brahma Bud was his best and finest!

Hopping out of his truck, Zach stared at the imperious woman with whiskey-colored hair. "What the hell do you think you're doing?"

She snapped her cell phone shut. "I am *trying* to get this beast to move, Cowboy. He seems to think he has the right of way."

"He does!" Zach stared at his poor bull, which gazed back in return, not bothered in the least by the annoying woman who had hit him.

"Well, he's been having his way for an hour,"

she replied, her voice so haughty it belonged in New York. "Do you think you could move his plump hide?"

Perhaps Brahma Bud had only been lightly tapped, because the bull didn't seem any worse for wear. He did, however, seem quite mesmerized by the pink T-bird, and as Zach forced himself to calm down, he had to admit the car—and the woman— were definitely worth second looks. "What's the rush, City?"

"I have a life," she told him. "I just can't stand here and watch the grass grow."

Well, hell, Zach thought, wasn't she special. Of course, she certainly looked special in her tight dress. When she spoke, she emphasized her words so that all of her bounced in the right places. "He might move tomorrow," Zach said. "Once he gets to a spot he likes, he tends to stay there."

"You have *got* to be kidding me!" she exclaimed, enunciating and bouncing, to Zach's delight.

Ah, city folk. So much fun. He leaned against her T-bird and gave her his best leer. "When I get to a spot I like, I tend to stay there, too."

"Cowboy, I know all about guys like you, and believe me, the words are bigger than the deed. Just take your cow and go home, okay? And I won't charge you for the dent in my fender. Not to mention I think he used his antler to lift my skirt when I tried to make certain he was all right."

"Yeah, that would be the easy way out," Zach said slowly, suddenly realizing what he wanted more than anything was to shake things up, and this gal was a smoking-hot challenge even if she didn't know horns from antlers. "I'll do two things for you—one, I'll ask my prize longhorn here to move, if you're nice. Two, I won't ask why you're trespassing on my private drive, if you're nice. I won't even be mad that you hit my livelihood, here," he said, dropping a casual hand to Bud's horn. "However, I do insist upon a kiss."

She gasped. "I consider kissing to be sex. Why would I have sex with a stranger?"

He laughed out loud. "Make it a brotherly peck, then."

"No. You're weird. It might be catching."

"I think you're the weird one." Crossing his arms, he decided this exceptional woman was his next challenge. "So, I noticed you didn't protest that you had a boyfriend or were married or something."

She wrinkled her nose. "I just broke up with my boyfriend. He was too possessive."

Zach raised his brows. "Possessive?"

"He thought he owned me."

"Boyfriends will act like that sometimes." He wondered if he'd feel the same way if she was his girlfriend. *Nah.* He'd never felt that way about any woman. *Safe!*

Her back stiffened. "Being possessive is bad and being bossy is worse. But if you'd like to boss someone around, why don't you tell that cow to move so I can get back on the road?"

He shook his head. "You're not going anywhere."

She put her hands on her hips, prepared to give him a nor'easter full of cold sass. "Why not?"

"It's not just the fender you damaged. It's hanging off." He pointed to the front of her car. "And you have a flat tire. I notice you didn't respond to my offer of a kiss, by the way."

Jessica Tomball Farnsworth looked at the cowboy. He was hunky, to be sure, but so was her ex-fiancé. She'd learned that a man that hot was usually firing more than one pistol at a time—just as her possessive ex-boyfriend had. He'd found a more available set of female arms while she'd been away on business, traveling with her cosmetics company.

That thought led her to consider dropping straight into this willing man's arms and slathering his face with kisses since he wanted kissing so badly. After all, revenge was sweet.

But she felt a stronger desire to get as far away from men as possible. She wasn't bitter; she was simply willing to acknowledge that either she was a poor judge of character or all men were louses.

Until she had that figured out, she wasn't kissing this cowboy, or any male. She narrowed her eyes at him. *Make that hot cowboy.* "Smooth come-ons like yours put me off." Taking a deep breath for bravery, she gave the large animal a push on his rump to encourage him to move.

He swished his tail in response.

"We could be here all day," the cowboy said.

This seemed, unfortunately, to be true. She had places she needed to be. With her heart beating too fast, she rose on tiptoe and kissed the cowboy full on the mouth, more than ready to get the hell out of wherever she was.

He looked at her when she sank back to ground level.

"You call that a kiss?"

"Yes, I do," she said tartly. "Do you keep your promises or not?" A delicious zing of wonder had struck her when she'd brushed his lips, along with a wayward desire for more, more, more.

He took a peppermint from his pocket and let the giant bull smell it before tossing it into the winter-touched yellow meadow. The bull casually strolled after the candy treat while the man inspected the broken fence, which had allowed his beast to escape and wander the roadside. Never in her life had she seen an animal that big up close. But then its kind, curious eyes had stared over the hood at her, and she'd been grateful it didn't appear to be hurt.

"Why do you keep animals like that?" she asked. "He deserves to be wild and free."

The cowboy laughed. "He is wild and free, City. This is my best friend. He lives in the lap of luxury."

He was clearly amused by her lack of knowledge of his world. Jessica sniffed, not liking his attitude at all. "I suppose you think it's cute to give him candy. What happens when he gets a cavity?"

He sent a slow, amused grin her way. Shaking his head, he went to inspect her car.

Jessica ignored him, keeping her gaze on the bull, which appeared to be just as happy inside the meadow as out.

"What's your name?"

"Jessica," she said, unwilling to share more.

"Mine's Zach," he replied, though she hadn't asked. "I can help you get on your way, Jessie."

She turned, staring at him.

"Or you could kiss me again," he said conversationally. "I know you liked it as much as I did."

She gasped. "No. I didn't."

He smiled, the expression in his dark eyes registering disbelief. It made Jessica mad that he knew better, and madder to know she was so easy to read.

"So," he said, drawing near to her, "was it good sex?"

Not as good as it could be. "I'll thank you to not make fun of my sense of decency," Jessica said. "Thank you for stopping and moving your cow out of the way. Now please tell me where I can get this tire fixed."

"You certainly have issues, lady," Zach said, catching her hand in his, "but I'm not afraid of issues. In fact, I look forward to helping you solve yours, Jessie." He ran a thumb over her bottom lip. "Tell me your full name."

"Jessica Tomball Farnsworth," she whispered, wondering why she bothered to answer. "I don't have as many issues as you do, by the way." She backed away, knowing full well he was messing with her senses.

"Sure I do, City," he said, moving closer. "Where I come from, a man's not a man unless he's got a full plate of issues. Sins." He gave her a wink and slid a hand around her waist. "We're born with issues, and we use them to lure women 'cause they think they can save us from ourselves. Then we die with our issues, knowing we've enjoyed them every step of the way."

"You're crazy," she whispered, unable to make her escape because of the way he was pressing her against the car.

"And you like it," he said against her neck, shifting his hands under her Versace skirt.

"I think I do," Jessica said, closing her eyes. *What the hell. I was never cut out for boredom.*

And Jessie T., boyfriend-dumper and responsibility-escaper dragged the bad boy into the back seat of her hot pink T-bird, embracing sins and issues and everything else that came with the sinfully hot package.

Chapter Two

Two hours later, Zach stared up at the sun in the Texas sky from the back seat of the T-bird, glad his ranch was off the beaten path and that he'd had enough privacy to enjoy this wonderful surprise gift from the city.

Who said you couldn't find a city girl worth wasting country on, anyway?

He examined the blanket he'd found in the back seat. The label read Saks Fifth Avenue. "So I'm guessing you're on the pill," he said idly, wondering if he could talk the beautiful stranger into staying at his ranch for about another day. Only his sister, Pepper, was ever around the ranch anymore, and she pretty much kept to herself. "Ow!"

He rubbed the spot on his cheek where City

had slapped him. It had actually been a light tap, but it was enough to get his attention.

She stared at him, angry again, reminding him that her spirit was one of the many things he liked about her. "So are you?" he asked, thinking with some trepidation about Liberty and Duke and their unplanned pregnancy.

"You are not a gentleman!" Jessie exclaimed.

He nodded, and said, "We already established that. Let's get to the answer."

Her cheeks pinked. "I use a method of control."

He glared. "Don't they discuss birth control where you're from?" He glanced at the blanket label again. "Saks Fifth Avenue?"

She ignored him.

Okay. She obviously didn't want to talk about it. A faint trickle of unease slithered through him.

"I have to go," she said abruptly. "Please get the hell out of my car."

He frowned. "Not until you tell me about your 'method.'"

"You should have asked before," she said. "No matter what my method is, if it's not any good, it's too late."

He digested that, realizing she was right. Had he lost his mind? His gaze ran over her tight, smooth skin. The luscious curves had bewitched him, and all of her attitude set off raging emotions inside him.

Duke must have felt just this way about Liberty.

He had never wanted to be like Duke, despite the fact that, to him, his sheriff brother was pretty much a hero in all ways. If not a hero, then a major example of what a good man should be.

But he'd never wanted to be out-of-his-mind wild over a woman, and he sure as hell had never wanted to get one pregnant out of wedlock.

That would spell commitment for certain, and he hated everything about the sound of that particular word.

"I've been seeing twins," he murmured, going for jackass and making it pretty well, he thought. That should run her off quicker than wildfire, which he needed her to do if he was going to escape this growing dilemma and the future his brain was imagining.

"I don't care," she said, laughing, "if you're dating triplets. Or quadruplets."

He scratched his chin, noticing she wasn't leaping out of the back seat. In fact, they felt rather companionable together, their legs stretched out along the soft leather. She fit him very well. "Got a sister?" he asked, trying to save himself.

She gave him a thorough eyeing. "Really working those issues, aren't you?"

She wasn't falling for it. Women always fell for his routine! Jessie got out of the car, fixed her skirt and hair and pulled a huge carpetbag-sized purse from the front seat. She rummaged around in it, fishing out a pair of red panties. "Close your eyes."

"I can't," he said. "Watching you is the most fun I've had lately."

She shrugged, reaching under her skirt to shimmy her lacy panties into place. He felt himself wanting her again. She had impossibly long legs and nothing he didn't want to see. She was an intriguing beauty, tempting his eyes. Silently, he handed her the panties he'd previously removed and tossed to the floor. She snatched them from him, stuffing them into the carpetbag.

The panties went into the carpetbag. He realized with a pang and a worrisome erection that she was used to traveling or undressing because most women didn't carry a change of underwear in their purse. "Don't suppose you're going to change your bra, too?"

She shook her head at his hopeful tone. "Hand me the one you took off."

It was soft and silky, like her. He wanted her where he could enjoy her for hours, without the top and skirt, which had been left on out of necessity. He'd been lucky to discard her bra and panties, actually, because he'd discovered she had a cute shy side despite her projected carefree attitude. "You're beautiful," he said, knowing she was that way without trying to be.

"It's my business," she said. "It's all a mirage."

There, he thought, *that's an answer to scare the hell out of even the baddest, bootwearing hardass around.*

Jessie was thinking through the birth control issue, more concerned than she was letting on. The truth was, she'd been fitted with a vaginal ring when she and her boyfriend had gotten serious enough to discuss marriage. But they hadn't had sex in the past couple of months, as he'd claimed to be working late—an excuse she was to learn was code for: *Your chief business rival and I aren't just discussing the latest spring palette after-hours.* So she hadn't been wearing the ring when she'd left the city and the man behind.

Babies had been the first thing on her agenda,

following a wedding. But there was no reason to tell that to Zach. He seemed like the worrying type. Any other man would have simply let her drive off into the sunset. Then again, he had issues, as he'd calmly and proudly admitted. She decided to keep her desire for a baby a secret. "I've got to go, cowboy," she said.

"My name is Zach," he said, sounding a bit cross about it.

She nodded. "I know."

"No, you didn't," he said. "Jessie T., you're not a good liar. You forgot my name."

She looked at him.

"You're not even on birth control, are you?"

He *was* going to be difficult. "Are *you?*" she asked, stalling for time. "Maybe you were wearing a condom and I didn't notice." She would have noticed, definitely, because it had been skin-on-skin passion, nothing between her and him in the most wonderful connection a man and woman could share.

His jaw set. "Great. This is my worst nightmare."

She didn't usually have a temper but irritation crept into her. *More like raging than creeping.* "It's none of your affair."

"Well, now," he said, his voice a stony drawl,

"that's where you're wrong, Miss Jessica. One thing about us Forresters is that we make everything our business. After you've been in Tulips for a while, you'll know this to be true." He snagged her car keys from the ignition. "Come on, city girl. No doubt you're going to make me crazy for the next month, but there's always a little hell to pay for a little pleasure."

She grabbed for the keys but he held them above her head. "You can't keep me here."

"I'm not keeping you," he said, scooping her up to deposit her into his truck bed. "Your car is out of commission."

"No, it's not," Jessie protested. She'd bitten off more than she could handle with him. Zach was nothing like her ex, a man easily led by his groin and whichever way the wind was blowing at the time: Blonde, brunette, redhead. "Look, you were a great fantasy, but—"

He stopped her in the act of crawling out of the truck bed. "If you're going to be easy about this, you can ride in the front seat. If you're going to be difficult, you ride in the back and I've got some throwing rope to make sure of it. But you leaving is not an option. It's one of my issues, you see."

He grinned at her. Jessie pressed her lips together. "I have a business convention I have to attend. It's really important. We're presenting holiday looks for the upcoming season. This being September, I've got to get the wares on the road."

"I sympathize." He nodded. "But you can clearly see that your car is leaking something."

Jessie stared at the ground in horror. Something was leaking from her precious T-bird!

"I can't have you running off around the world to Saks Fifth Avenue and the like if you're carrying my child."

"I'm not!"

He leaned against the truck, crossing his arms. "Let me share with you the problem. My brother fell in love with a woman, and they were supposed to get married. They were in the middle of getting married, in fact, but she got cold feet at the altar, and before we knew what was happening, Liberty went running off faster than a greased piglet in a pig race."

"That has nothing to do with me," Jessie said, trying to sound like she didn't care. However, she could see where Zach would empathize with his brother.

"Well, it turned out Liberty was pregnant," Zach continued, ignoring her, "though she didn't tell Duke. She was afraid to, and then the little old ladies in our town, and the men, too—you'll meet them all soon enough—well, the Tulips Saloon Gang got involved—"

"Gang?" Jessie whispered.

"Gang." Zach nodded. "You don't know anything about issues until you meet the Gang."

She blinked, not wanting to get drawn into this sexy man's loony life. "I'll call you if I'm pregnant."

"You wouldn't," Zach said. "And then I'd be like Duke almost was, with a son of mine wandering around out there, never knowing that his daddy was a caring man who wanted to play football with him and teach him to hunt and shoot beer cans. Budweiser beer cans only, which is how my great-horned beast out there got his name, Brahma Bud. I keep my life simple, as you'll learn."

"Oh, no," Jessie murmured, the impact of her flyaway good sense dawning on her. "Where is the rewind button on my life?"

IT WASN'T HEROIC of him to do what he was doing to the flitty woman who'd blown into town, but it wouldn't be fair if he had a son that never knew its father. Zach was quite satisfied that he'd made the best possible decision considering the circumstances.

His sister, Pepper, would tell him he should have kept his pants zipped, and he should have, but he didn't regret making love to that little firecracker out there staring sadly at her car, which had been towed to the drive of the Triple F Ranch. He watched Jessie through the window, smiling when the family dog—who was supposed to be Duke's dog but couldn't be trained to one person—greeted Jessie with a big doggie smile and a wave of a golden plumed tail. Her name was Molly, or Jimbo if other members of the town of Tulips were asked.

Zach grinned. Jessie knew nothing about issues until she met the citizens of Tulips. It was time to introduce her, even though he'd be painted as the black villain of the piece—a part which he'd relish, much as Duke had.

Actually, his older brother had suffered under the good-hearted critiquing of the town's elders. But Zach was prepared for it. He knew what he'd done—and he was prepared to pay the price.

He would take his critiquing in stride, because every time the elders tried to point out the error of his ways, he'd just think about Jessie's partially nude body and smile like Molly-Jimbo with a new bone.

"Oh, my," Pansy Trifle said when Zach walked through the heavy glass-and-wood doors of the Tulips Saloon.

Helen Granger stood, her hands on her hips. "This is Ladies Only Day, Zach."

"I know," he said, with a most regretful tone, to the room at large, "so I've brought you a lady." He tipped his hat to all of them, and gave Jessie a gentle push. "Take good care of my friend from Saks Fifth Avenue."

He left, a broad grin on his face. Very soon he would be in big trouble with the elders of the town, and he was going to enjoy being the cause of all the uproar.

In the meantime, he had a T-bird to "hide," just in case Ms. Saks decided to take a fast hike, à la Duke's wife, the cagey Ms. Liberty Wentworth.

History would not be repeating itself.

Chapter Three

Helen and Pansy stared at the newcomer with surprise, sympathy and curiosity. Nervously, Jessie said, "I'm not really from Saks."

The ladies in the room laughed.

"Sit down here," Ms. Pansy said, patting an antique chair. "Zach must want us to get to know you better or he wouldn't have brought you here."

"Which makes him even nuttier than we'd previously surmised," Helen said. "I'll get you a cup of tea while Pansy introduces you to everyone. Then we'll be more than happy to advise you on whatever problem that Forrester male is giving you."

Following some brief introductions, Jessica told her story. "Well, you see," Jessie said, after being introduced, "I hit his steer. Or maybe it was a bull. I'm not certain of the proper terminology."

Pansy looked at her. "Not Brahma Bud?"

"I'm afraid so."

"Oh, my," Helen said. "I do hope Bud's all right. Zach's had him since he was a child. Won't part with him."

Jessie blinked. "I didn't realize it was a pet."

"Well," Pansy said, "it was a gift from his parents. So it's a link with the past, you might say."

"I might have been a bit callous," Jessie said. "I might have called Bud a hunk of steak or something. I don't remember. I was very angry."

"Why were you angry, dear?" Pansy asked gently.

"I was in a hurry to get somewhere," Jessie said, "and the bull—do you call it a bull or a steer?"

"Not important," Helen said, dropping a lump of sugar into her teacup. "Continue, please."

Jessie sighed, realizing they didn't want to have to explain something to her that was plainly obvious to everyone in the room. "There are places I need to be. Bud stopped me. He wouldn't move. I thought maybe he was hurt or in shock, but I really barely tapped him. In fact, he did more damage to my car than I realized, because Zach said my car was leaking."

"Hmm." Pansy put some cookies on a plate for her. "We're so glad you've come to Tulips, dear."

"But we understand you want to be on your way." Helen smiled around at all the ladies in the gathering. "Are you staying with Pepper and Zach?"

"I don't want to," Jessie said. "Is there a hotel in town?"

"We'll have one in the future, I feel certain," Helen said. "Or at least a bed-and-breakfast."

Jessie shook her head. "My family isn't used to me being anything other than right on schedule."

They perked up. "Do tell us about your family," Pansy said.

"Well, my mother and father own a cosmetics company called Jessie's Girl Stuff. I have two brothers. They're lawyers," Jessie said.

"Lawyers," Pansy said, glancing at Helen.

Helen smiled at her. "Did you call them, dear?"

"I let them know where I was. And I told them I'd be on time for the convention in two days." Jessie took a deep breath. "Zach says I can't leave, though."

"Until your car is fixed," Helen said.

"Until…" Jessie paused, not about to admit her plight.

"Oh, my," Pansy said, "I do believe our Zach is developing feelings for you, Jessie."

Jessie's eyes went wide. "Just the opposite. He's quite pigheaded."

"Aren't they all?" Helen said with a smile. "Do you like him?"

"No," Jessie said. "Bossy men are not my thing."

"We completely understand." Pansy nodded. "So what we want you to do is call this number." She scribbled a number onto a tulip-printed pad and handed it to Jessie. "We have a few men in our town, very few, mind you, but the ones we have are mostly useless. I mean, *useful*."

"Yes," Helen agreed. "Ask to speak to Bug Carmine. He'll be more than happy to taxi you wherever you want to go. Where is this convention of yours, dear?"

"California," Jessie said. "Do you think it will take that long to fix my car?"

"You could call roadside assistance," Pansy said. "They'd probably be out here lickity-split and fix you right up."

Jessie straightened. Of course they would! "You ladies are marvelous! I never thought about that! I don't know why I didn't, except that I never hit a bull before—"

"And Zach swept you off your feet," Helen inserted.

"Yes, and that's never happened before, either. I mean, how many people hit a poor sweet animal like Brahma Bud… But roadside assistance is the perfect answer! Shame on Zach for saying you all had issues," Jessie said. "You're clearly as smart and capable as anyone I've ever met."

Helen sniffed, reaching for a cookie off the tray Pansy had set down. "Zach said *we* had issues?"

"Oh, yes," Jessie said, nodding. "He said I didn't even know the meaning of the word until I'd met 'the Gang.'"

"Well." Pansy smiled brightly. "Helen, dear, why don't you hand sweet Jessie the phone so she can make her call? I'll telephone Sheriff Duke while you're doing that, and let him know his baby brother needs his brotherly supervision."

Helen grinned and gave Jessie the old-fashioned, floral-painted phone.

"And if they can't fix your car today," Pansy said, "you're welcome to stay at my house for as long as you like." She and Helen shared a secretive and satisfied glance as Jessie dialed.

FAR FROM BEING SUPPORTIVE and helpful, Zach learned that the Gang wasn't going to be as conniving about him and Jessie as they'd been about Liberty and Duke. Much to his chagrin, they'd ratted him out to his brother about Jessie's presence at the ranch, earning him a lecture on propriety and a babysitter in the form of Pepper.

Pepper was the soul of responsibility. A hard-working student and now a much-lauded doctor, she was well respected not just in Tulips, but in the medical community. With Duke and Pepper on his case about his houseguest, Zach was certain he'd never feel the glory of Jessie's skin again.

But what had he expected from the Gang? They never operated the way one suspected they might. Now he understood why Duke had been so miserable as the object of their machinations.

Secretly, he'd hoped that they would try to encourage some type of romance between he and Jessie. He'd been looking, in fact, for some matchmaking by the little old ladies, and perhaps a bolstering of his worth in Jessie's eyes.

Something had gone terribly wrong. Jessie was now staying with Pansy, and Helen wouldn't speak to him. Duke was breathing down his neck, and even Molly hesitated to allow him to pet her.

He was in the proverbial doghouse, and it was a very uncomfortable place to be.

But a man had to stand firm. When the roadside assistance fellow came out to the Triple F ranch, Zach told him the car had been repaired and that he could leave. It was lucky he'd thought to hide Jessie's car in one of the outlying barns on the ranch.

"It's hard to be the villain," he told the chickens that were checking out the white-walled tires of Jessie's T-bird. "Being dishonorable is not fun. But if I let that gal out of my sight, I could very well end up worse than Duke."

He and Duke and Pepper had grown up in a traditional family. Liberty had been raised by parents who mainly ignored her, but luckily she'd lived nearby and had been befriended by Zach—who had always looked at her as a brother would—and by his parents. But her sad upbringing had hurt her all her life. He could never do that to a child of his own.

He sat on the bumper of Jessie's car. "I wish I could say I shouldn't have done it, but I liked being with her," he told Molly as she sat beside him, her golden fur soft and reassuring under his touch. "I liked being with Jessie more than I ever liked being with a woman in my life."

Molly barked at him.

"Yeah, it's crazy." He got off the bumper. "I just hope she's not as fertile as she looks, because as hard as it's been to keep her in Tulips, I'd likely never get her to the altar!"

JESSIE PUT her carpetbag away in Pansy's guest room, glad she always carried makeup and a change of clothes. She had a secret, one of many, only this one was a big one, and the cowboy had made her realize how much she didn't like hiding it.

She was afraid of settling down. She'd simply wanted a baby, and her ex-boyfriend had been the way to achieve that.

She'd come to the unhappy realization that she'd probably never been in love with him, which probably meant she was shallow and vain. Her family was successful; she shouldn't have needed to conjure up a relationship in order to validate her goals in life.

Maybe she was lacking a fundamental building block in her personality, like patience or strength of character. "Trust a relaxing jaunt through the country to give me more time to think and be hard on myself. Just what every second-thoughts bride needs."

She heard the doorbell ring as she put away her belongings. A second later, Pansy called, "Jessie!" up the stairwell.

Jessie walked down, surprised to see Zach sitting very properly in Pansy's living room. "Hi, Zach," she said, trying to ignore the excitement rushing through her.

Pansy sat down in a nearby chair and began to knit, a quiet chaperone. Jessie sat in a floral chair across from Zach.

Zach looked at her. "Settling in all right?"

Jessie nodded. "Yes, thank you. And I sent roadside assistance out to repair whatever was leaking on my car."

Zach shifted on the sofa. "Would you like to take a walk?"

Jessie shook her head. "I'm pretty tired. It's been a long day."

"Okay." Zach stood, nodding to Pansy. "See you all later."

He departed, surprising Jessie. She looked at Pansy as the door shut behind Zach.

"Oh," Pansy said. "I do think he likes you."

Jessie knew what was really on Zach's mind. "I don't think so. I just think he's very protective."

Pansy put away her knitting. "You know, it's been difficult for Zach. He's the middle child, and was often pushed to the side. Not quite the man of the house, and not the baby. Sometimes I thought he was never certain whether he wanted to follow in Duke's footsteps or be a role model for Pepper. He tried to do both and somewhere along the line, he became a bit arrogant and somewhat overly determined."

"I can see where women would be attracted to that trait."

"Yes," Pansy said with a smile, "but he's never bothered to ask any of them to take a walk."

Jessie shook her head. It didn't matter. She was leaving as soon as her car was fixed. There were enough stray matters in her life to occupy her time. "Thankfully my car might be repaired tomorrow. Good night, Pansy. Thank you for everything."

Pansy waved a hand as Jessie stood. "I'm enjoying having you here, Jessie. Plan on staying as long as you like."

Until the morning, Jessie thought. *And then I'm out of here.*

Before she was waylaid by the temptation of an attentive, opinionated cowboy who had "bad for you" written all over him.

JESSIE SLEPT WELL. In the morning she showered, ate breakfast with Pansy and Helen—scones and hot tea—packed her carpetbag and hitched a ride in Sheriff Duke Forrester's truck to the Triple F.

"If my brother gives you any more trouble," Duke said, "you just let me know. I'll give him a pounding he'll never forget. Or better yet, just tell Pepper. Zach hates it when Pepper gets on to him."

"That won't be necessary." Jessie smiled. "My car should be fixed by now, and I'll be out of everyone's hair."

"Well," Duke said, "if you ever want a place to visit, I know the ladies would love to have you back. They're always trying to entice people to settle here."

"Oh." Jessie looked out at the passing countryside. "It's pretty here, but—"

"Not your kind of place," Duke said kindly. "I understand completely."

"You do?"

"Sure. Liberty has a wedding shop in Dallas, as well as one here. I go into town with her from time to time. There's a lot to offer folks in the city. Here in Tulips, we live life at a snail's pace."

"The Gang doesn't seem very snail-like to me," Jessie said. "They seem rather lively."

He grinned. "Be careful. They'd just love to figure out a way to bring you into the fold. Wait until you meet Liberty. Together, they got me to the altar."

She heard the pride in his voice. "I rather like the single life."

"I did, too, for a while. But Liberty had other plans." He laughed. "Actually, that's a small-town big tale. It was hard to catch that little girl, and I did all the chasing."

Jessie smiled as they pulled into the Triple F. "I think I may have heard that from Helen and Pansy."

"You watch those two. If they decide Tulips would be better off with you on the census rolls, here you'll remain. All I do as sheriff is make certain everyone behaves."

Jessie got out of the truck. "Thanks for the ride, Sheriff."

"Sure." He glanced around. "Where's the pink Caddy I've heard so much about?"

"T-bird. Maybe the roadside assistance person moved it."

Zach walked out on the porch, waving. "Good morning."

"Where's her car?" Duke asked.

"I sent it over to Holt's to look at. The roadside repair guy was terrible. Didn't know his hat from his ankle."

"Holt's our town hairdresser," Duke said to Jessie. "It's in good hands now."

Jessie's eyes went wide. "I don't see how hair relates to automobiles."

"Oh, he can fix anything," Duke said easily. "Don't worry about a thing."

Jessie felt her teeth grinding. "Did Holt say how long it would take for him to fix it?"

"No," Zach said. "Come on in and have some breakfast. Pepper's cooking."

"Don't mind if I do," Duke said, striding toward the porch. Jessie hung back.

"Is there a problem?" Zach asked.

"Yes," Jessie said. "I can't seem to get my car back into my possession."

"It's Saturday," Zach said. "What's your hurry?"

Jessie took a deep breath. "I don't trust you. I want away from you, and this town. I feel like I've fallen into Peyton Place, or maybe even Brigadoon, and I want back into the twenty-first century—my life as I know it."

Zach nodded. "You can borrow my truck to get wherever it is you need to go."

Jessie's breath left her for an instant. "Really?"

"Of course." Zach frowned at her. "You're not a prisoner, Jessie. For Pete's sake!"

"I—" She narrowed her eyes.

He shook his head. "You're not being a drama queen, are you?"

Jessie put out her hand. "Keys."

A moment stretched long between them as he

stared at her. Reaching into his pocket, he tugged his keys out and handed them to her.

Jessie looked at him another long moment, clutching the metal pieces of freedom.

"It's over there," he said, pointing. "Happy trails, Jessie."

Chapter Four

Giving Jessie his truck was the fair, manly thing to do. After all, he was hiding her car. This way, he wasn't exactly kidnapping her, as Duke had claimed, threatening to put him in the jail until Jessie left town if he didn't behave. Zach was wisely keeping a bargaining chip. Something precious to her for which she would return. When she came back after the convention, perhaps there would be some light shed on the subject he was most worried about.

He looked at Jessie as she considered his offer, dismayed to realize he was envisioning her in a maternity dress. Liberty could whip Jessie up a beaut.

Shoving that thought from his mind, he shrugged. "The truck's got a full tank of gas. Hit the pedal."

"I don't know," Jessie said. "It seems unfair to take your truck after I hit your livelihood."

"Call me a gentleman," Zach said. "I don't want you in trouble with your boss."

Jessie glanced over at the truck. "My family owns the company. I'm the president of Jessie's Girl Stuff."

He couldn't help smiling. "I sensed you might be a bit of a princess. Tell me more."

"In case I'm the future mother of your child?"

"It's an intriguing thought. I'm not as put off by it as I probably should be, under the circumstances."

"And what are those?" Jessie asked.

"You're a highly excitable female," Zach said. "But I was looking for some excitement so I'm okay with that."

"Funny," she said, "you don't seem like the type to like a high-maintenance woman."

"True. There's a difference between high-maintenance and excitement. I love independence in my women."

"Excellent." Jessie jangled his keys at him and headed toward his truck. "Thanks for the wheels."

"No problem." He headed after her, getting into the passenger seat. "My wheels are your wheels. It's the least I could do for a lady who gave me an afternoon I'll never forget."

She barely glanced at him as she switched on the engine. "Wow. Listen to all that *vroom*."

"Yep," he said happily, putting his arms behind his head. "It's a lot of horses."

"And won't I just look sophisticated when the valet parks my truck at the convention?" She glanced at him. "You can get out now. I've turned on the amazing vehicle without incident."

"Oh, I'm not getting out." Zach grinned at her. "My stuff's all packed and in the truck bed. I like your style of traveling, so I tossed my change of clothes into a hefty bag."

"This hefty bag of mine," she said, holding up her carpetbag, "is a Merada Fine. It cost one thousand, nine hundred and fifty-four dollars. Please do not refer to it in the same breath with a plastic garbage sack, as convenient as one is at times."

"That much money and it doesn't even carry itself. Gosh, you'd think it could run by remote control or something. Or voice activation. 'Purse open,'" he said. "'Purse close.'"

"Very funny. My girlfriend makes these purses, so I'll thank you not to make fun of them. I'm supporting her efforts."

He touched her cheek. "Meradas are actually a respected breed line of horses in Texas. So it's interesting that you're carrying something that's a little less urban than you're used to."

"Coincidence. Nothing more."

He grinned at her stiffness. "We actually have the same sense of humor if you'd ever let yourself smile."

"I smile. Just not around annoying men."

He laughed. "I don't annoy you that badly. Do I?"

"Need you ask?" She backed down the driveway. "I'll take you with me, simply because you're such an excitement freak. This is going to be the most boring thing you've ever done in your life."

"Lots of women there, though." Zach pulled his hat over his face, preparing to snooze while Jessie drove. "As long as my eyeballs are busy and excited, that pretty much takes care of my brain's need for activity."

"It's nice of you to trust me to drive your truck."

"No trust involved. I'm right here, overseeing the whole adventure." Assuaging his conscience from the front seat of his truck was no difficult task, but she didn't know that. Although he tried to drift off, Zach could smell Jessie's fragrance, making it entirely too difficult to relax.

Possibly his senses were overstimulated because he'd been thinking of the upcoming holiday season, which Jessie had mentioned after their glorious afternoon together. He'd always loved winter holidays, most of all when he was a child.

He might have a child one day to decorate the house for, bake for and share stories with. A longing burst inside him that he'd never before recognized. "I never thought I'd want children," he said slowly, and Jessie nodded.

"You've alluded to that."

"If I had kids, though, I'd have a reason to hang candy canes. I like to decorate at the ranch." Zach frowned. "Duke tells me I'm being childish because I love Christmas."

"Didn't you say he's just had a baby? He'll probably beat you to the decorating this year."

Zach grinned, enjoying the thought of the tables turning on his big brother. "I'll be at his elbow every time he puts one raisin on a gingerbread man, every time he hangs an ornament, to tell him how childish he is."

"Probably one reminder of a person's mistakes is enough," Jessie said. "I sure wouldn't want anyone belaboring me over mine."

He raised a brow. "Story time."

"I'm busy driving."

He sent an assessing look her way. "Try one on

me. I know nothing at all about you, except that you have a strong sense of adventure."

"Change has been my downfall. Really."

"Not from my point of view," Zach said sincerely, "unless you count T-bird sex as a pastime."

"I don't," she said, and he grinned.

"Maybe I'm the catalyst for change in your life. I'd count that as being a positive influence."

"Maybe just a pain in the ass," she said, a trace of irritation in her voice.

"Hmm." Zach thought about the sheets of plastic he'd dragged over her pretty T-bird to keep the chickens out of it and decided not to push his luck. No one ever knew what the future would bring. "So did you love him?"

"Who?"

"The ex-boyfriend who cheated on you."

She turned her head to look at him briefly. She'd put on big black sunglasses with gold *G*'s in the corners that made her look like a reclusive movie star, and she had on way too much red lipstick for kissing, although it did look porn-star sexy on her. When they got to know each other better, he was going to tell her that all these girly enticements she was using to subconsciously lure him were not necessary. He liked his women plain and natural.

"I did not," she said. "If I'd loved him, why would I be sitting in a Ford?"

He mulled that. "Perhaps you said Ford in a slightly disdainful tone."

She laughed.

He noticed irritation slipping into his comfort zone. "Fords are the kings of the road, I'll have you know."

There was no response to his allegation. No argument, no comment, *nada.* He rolled his eyes. "If you're going to have my baby, you're going to have to understand a few things."

"I am not having your child," Jessie said. "As much as I wanted a baby, I would not want to make one with you."

Rubbing his chin, he said, "So you're not going to claim your pregnancy is a result of wanting to catch me?"

"I don't think so. And who says I'm pregnant?"

She'd become so saucy. *Snooty,* even.

"I wouldn't even be talking to you right now if you hadn't stolen my car," she said. "Never mind claiming you as the father."

"Aha! You admit it! You wouldn't have told me if I'd given you a baby."

"I would have told you," Jessie said, "but it

wouldn't have mattered to me. I wasn't trying to catch any old guy just to get over my broken heart."

"I thought you said you weren't in love with him."

"Oh." She glanced at him, her lovely eyes hidden by the dark glasses. "My ego was bruised like any normal woman's would be."

"That's code to mean you did love him." Zach thought about that. "So you slept with me on the rebound. Revenge lust."

"Oh, hell no," Jessie said, laughing. "I just—"

He waited, watching the smile slip from her face.

"Well, it's one or the other," he said. "Either you slept with me to subconsciously avenge your boyfriend's treatment of you, or you are, in fact, attracted to me."

"Maybe I was just having a bad-girl moment?"

He rubbed a light finger down her arm. "I don't think so, Jessie T. You're possibly a case, but I also think you're a damn sexy woman who just needs the right man to unlock all your secrets. And I have to warn you—I'm pretty darn good at knowing just how a woman likes her lock picked."

SEVERAL HOURS later it was time to stop for gas. After Zach had bragged about his prowess with women, Jessie turned on the radio and lost herself in her thoughts. Much of what he'd said bothered her—though she would never admit that she'd simply slept with him to avenge herself on her ex. The thought had crossed her mind, of course, but she didn't have to do that to make herself feel better. The simple act of walking away from him had washed away any need for salving her hurt feelings.

The truth was, attraction had surged inside her fast and hot the second she realized Zach had every intention of seducing her. Her answer had been *yes, yes, yes*. The focus of her body had been entirely in the here-now-*more* with Zach.

Her desire for a baby with her ex had been a misplaced sense of emptiness she'd been trying to fill. She knew that and more about herself now. Thanks to the cowboy, she could move past all those feelings of confusion and concentrate on growing as a person and as a woman.

"I don't need change as much as I used to now," she said. "I don't have to beautify everything."

"Yeah, you do," Zach replied, his voice muffled by his hat.

"I was always afraid of letting people down, so I learned to fake everything. I'm never faking again."

"I have to worry about a woman who admits to being a fake. I'd almost worry about our sex life except I know for damn sure you weren't faking anything then."

He didn't have to sound so proud. "You never know. A woman who's had as much practice as I have at faking might be very good at it. Super-convincing."

Grunting, he shoved his hat off his face. "Want me to drive? You've been driving for four hours solid."

"I like driving this beat-up Chevy," Jessie replied, happy to tweak him.

"Jessie, there are certain things I would never do in my life," he began, his voice full of that pompous confidence she had begun to recognize and maybe even admire. "Drive a Chevy is one."

"Really?" she asked, as if she hadn't known he was going to get crazy over her remark.

"Second, I would never let a woman annoy me." Zach took her black sunglasses from her face. "I'm damn tired of not being able to see your big baby blues."

"Give me those."

"Nope," Zach said happily, sticking them inside her carpetbag. "Take you a week to find those now that they're safe inside the loch."

"The loch?"

"A deep, mysterious lake. This purse is symbolic

of the loch in your life. You could hide a baby inside this bag, actually," he said, holding it up with wonder, "and lots of other secrets, which is how you operate your life, I'm betting. You know what, I've had saddlebags smaller than this handbag."

"You're obsessed with my purse."

"But the question is, is it a purse or a suitcase? For the woman who's always prepared to run from the first sight of danger?"

She pursed her lips, fully aware he was probing her for information. "Zach, I'm a simple girl. You're making this too hard."

"How old are you?"

"Twenty-eight."

"Just a baby."

She conducted a mental eye roll or two to allow herself to stay calm. "How old are you, grandpa?"

"Twenty-eight."

She laughed. "And Duke?"

"Thirty. Pepper's twenty-seven. She's the pistol of the family."

"I liked meeting her. She seems very level-headed. And somehow sad."

"Sad? Pepper's not sad. Pepper's the smartest one of the family."

She had definitely picked up on some wistfulness in Pepper's personality. "Zach, while we're at the convention in Los Rios—"

"Which I'm looking forward to, by the way."

"Maybe you could find something to do locally."

"Nah. I know one of the convention speakers and I'm hoping for a front-row seat."

She didn't think that was such a good idea. "There aren't as many women at the conventions as you think there are."

"Oh." He touched her hair. "I had a horse once with hair the color of yours. Very shiny."

"I suppose that's a compliment."

"But you've got all this stiff stuff in your hair today, and your lashes suddenly look like spider legs," he said, drawing near to inspect her. "And there's a lot of red gloss on your lips."

She frowned. "So?"

"So it bugs me. You look like you're hiding the real you. Like you're in costume or something. So is this convention for the grand poobahs of fakers? Because I thought you were giving up on that stuff."

He was in for a big surprise. "Zach, you should call and check on my car."

"I'll do that when we get to the convention. I'm sure I'll have time between seminars."

She shook her head. "You're not going to any seminars."

"I'm not?"

"No," she said, knowing she didn't want Zach that much in her life. There needed to be a fine line between what she did and who she knew. Not every family was homespun like his, not every community was apple-pie sweet. "Here's where you and I part ways." She parked the truck outside the hotel, handed him the key and grabbed her carpetbag. "Happy trails, Zach."

Chapter Five

"Zach decided to accompany Jessie at her convention," Pansy told Helen. "And Pepper just called to tell me that she abandoned him—left him high and dry in Los Rios."

Helen cocked her head. They sat inside the Tulips Saloon, the spot of many a cozy meeting and many a scheme. It was a wonderful second home for the women of the town. They were proud of the tea shop they'd created. Once a lackluster cafeteria with few customers, they'd overridden Duke's objections to calling it a saloon and decided to make a gamble for the tourist trade. "I knew that girl had spunk. I knew she was right for our town the minute I laid eyes on her."

Pansy dusted off the chairs with a tea towel. "She's a bit fancy."

"Zach needs fancy. It will be good for him."
Helen smiled. "Those Forrester kids always liked
whatever was completely opposite from their own
personal experience."

That had been true in Liberty and Duke's case.
Duke was stubborn, and Liberty was…stubborn…
Helen pursed her lips. "Or maybe they like their
own mirror image."

"Then that would make Jessie all wrong." Pansy
got a fresh tea towel and began polishing silver
sleigh-shaped vases. She'd bought pretty red flowers
to go in the vases for color and to spiff up the
ambiance of the Saloon. "There's definitely something going on between those two that is different
from Zach's usual pattern, and I suspect he's interested in her or he wouldn't have gone with her."

"Yes," Helen said thoughtfully. "But if she left
him in Los Rios, what's he going to do now?"

"He's on his way home, according to Pepper.
And not happy about it, either. She said he was all
set to learn about the life of a princess."

"It sounds like there's an edge to those words,"
Helen said. "I found Jessie very down-to- earth."

"Yes," Pansy agreed. "But still, she's definitely
not the type to settle in Tulips, Helen."

Helen frowned, unwilling to concede that point

and yet wondering if her good friend was right. She'd taken a shine to Jessie, she had to admit.

"Remember the goal is to grow Tulips," Pansy said gently. "Duke says it has to be done organically. No bachelor cattle drives."

"Oh, what does Duke know?" Helen had given up on the idea of the bachelor balls when Duke had decided to go along with Zach's idea of building a new elementary school. Zach had wanted to bulldoze the Tulips Saloon, and Duke had saved her precious tearoom from that fate. Zach had gotten his way about the elementary school—a very good idea but Helen only admitted that secretly—and in return, Helen had to give up her schemes for bringing men to Tulips.

But with so many single women in the town, it was hard to grow Tulips without males, and doing it organically might not be possible. Certainly not quick. Zach had dated most of the appropriate females around these parts and none of them had gotten him as far as Houston, much less Los Rios. "We have to work with what we have sometimes, Pansy." She considered her words for a moment. "Do you remember the first rush of being in love?"

Pansy put down her tea towel in surprise. "I remember madness and delight and anticipation."

Helen's cheeks pinked. "So do I. I also remember that the wonder of love was that it didn't have any rhyme or reason to it."

"Yes," Pansy said, "the emotions were simply there. They existed no matter how much I couldn't believe them or understand them."

"Which would perhaps point to why a woman would leave a handsome man stranded in a strange town."

"Not stranded," Pansy said. "She left him his truck, after all."

"True. We may not have gotten the whole story."

"I'm worried about her car," Pansy admitted. "Something seems fishy about Zach sending Jessie's car to Holt, our lovable hairdresser."

"Holt is wonderful with mechanics. He loves cars! Particularly vintage and special cars. He'll do a wonderful job for Jessie."

"Yes," Pansy said, sinking slowly into a Queen Anne antique chair with cherry blossom design. "Except that Holt never got the car."

Helen blinked. "Holt doesn't have Jessie's T-bird?"

"No." Pansy raised her chin. "I asked him what was wrong with Jessie's car, and he said he didn't have a pink T-bird, nor had he ever met a Jessie.

Nor had Zach called him about fixing any kind of vehicle."

"Oh, my," Helen said. "This is not good."

"I only gently suggest that we mind whom we claim is leaving whom high and dry."

"Point taken. This is a tasty dilemma," Helen said. "Poor Jessie."

Pansy sighed. "I do believe so."

"We're going to need the boys for this one," Helen said, and Pansy nodded.

"As inept as they are, they are the perfect ones to ferret out the male dynamic for us."

"And Jessie's car, to be sure," Helen said. "We must always fortify the position of the female." She reached for the phone. "I will call in the spies, such as they deem themselves."

Pansy smiled. "I love living in Tulips."

BUG CARMINE, self-annointed parade master of Tulips—if they could ever talk Duke into letting them have a parade—and Hiram, who lived in the cell Sheriff Duke presided over by choice, stared at the fancy pink car hidden in one of the Forrester's barns.

"That's some set of wheels," Bug commented. "Mrs. Carmine would like to take a spin in that."

"Looks like a sin-mobile to me," Hiram said.

"In my day, girls that drove something like that would have been the ones you wouldn't take home to Mother."

"Yeah." Bug placed the cover carefully over it again. "Now that we've found it, we have to make a decision. Either we tell the ladies it's here and they bust Zach, or we say we didn't find it, and let matters really get hot in Tulips."

"Can't put 'Here Lives A Car Thief' on a town billboard." Hiram shook his head. "Still, I like the idea of putting one over on the TSG. What crime has Zach committed anyway? It's good that he likes a girl enough to steal her car."

Bug sniffed. "In my day, we sent flowers as a token of our affection."

"These are different times," Hiram said, "as you should know from what the Tulips Saloon Gang regularly put us through."

"There is that," Bug agreed. "We can't tell on Zach. Bringing the TSG down on his head—well, I couldn't stand to see that happen to him."

"Yeah, they're still mad at him for his idea to bulldoze the saloon and make an elementary school out of it." They walked out of the barn and closed the door. "As far as I'm concerned, I never saw a thing," Hiram said.

"Nor me." Bug shook his friend's hand.

"My conscience is clear," Hiram said with satisfaction as they walked away. "I do love keeping secrets from the gals, and tonight, I'll sleep like a baby with my conscience for a blanket."

TO ZACH'S SURPRISE, days passed without any word from Jessie. When the weeks slipped into December and he still hadn't heard a word from her about her beloved car, he knew he had a big problem on his hands.

A tulip-pink convertible land yacht wasn't easy to hide. It was only a matter of time before Duke or Pepper went into that outlying barn for something. Duke was busy with Liberty and the new baby, and Pepper was busy doing whatever she was doing, but time wouldn't be on Zach's side forever.

He couldn't believe Jessie hadn't returned for her car. He'd thought he was being so smart, so in control of the situation.

Of course, he should have known better when Jessie asked the convention security to have him blocked from the site under the guise of it being for women only, a trick she had eerily in common with Pansy and Helen and the other TSG members. He'd hung around until the convention was over but he'd never caught another glimpse of Jessie. The people at the checkout desk had been supremely unhelpful, but he'd finally bribed a young clerk into telling him that the entire mascara-and-lipstick crowd was long gone. The president, the clerk had told him in a whisper, had left by helicopter.

No wonder he hadn't seen Jessie escape. He'd only been patrolling the glass-and-brass hotel doors, not the rooftop.

Maybe she'd never return and he'd have a lifetime souvenir of the one golden afternoon they'd shared. He'd forever remember how he'd worried that she'd give him a child, and she'd given him a vehicle instead. Not to mention that it was a completely inappropriate ride for him to be seen driving, so she'd cornered him in a lose-lose situation that would do nothing except color his reputation pink or get him in deep brown with Duke.

"Okay, you win," he muttered under his breath. "Just come get your damn car before Duke finds it."

JESSIE LOVED spending the weeks leading up to the holidays on the road. Her job was glamorous and fun. She loved to travel. Meeting people and helping women to look their best was her favorite part of the job, especially at this time of the year. This was her moment to help ladies shine, like ornaments that stayed in storage all year and came out radiant for the holiday season.

Hopefully, what she taught them stayed with them the rest of the year, too. That hope of helping women was what she'd built her position on at her company, and was the driving factor behind its success today.

Hot pink was the color of her life.

Her parents had known that when they'd chosen her car, her promotion gift. No mere heiress's job, her father had said that her vision held the direction the company needed.

She looked at her best friend as they sat in the living room of her suite at the world-class hotel her parents owned. Fran Carter was also her secretary and together the two of them had cooked up this year's special holiday look. It had almost been glittering and fabulous enough to keep her mind off a certain cowboy, but Jessie hadn't forgotten him despite the miles she'd put between them.

It would be impossible to forget Zach.

"So, Jessie T.," Fran said, curling up on a coffee-colored suede sofa, "we know all about how to cry so your mascara won't run and your fakies won't fall off, and how to make things look a helluva lot prettier than they really are. But I don't know a makeup trick for what you need."

Jessie shook her head. "The thing is," Jessie said slowly, "I think I would have fallen for Zach no matter what. He was pretty smooth for a man who grew up far away from sophisticated surroundings."

Fran nodded. "You could call him."

"I really can't," Jessie said. "If I do, he'll think I'm just looking for my car."

"It *was* a helluva calling card you left him," Fran said. "Eventually, he'd understand that your call wasn't completely about your vehicle."

"I'd never met anyone as stubborn as Zach. I'm afraid I didn't exercise good judgment in leaving him behind. My feet seemed to take flight of their own accord." No man had ever made her feel that nervous before, and escape had seemed the logical and only action.

"You've always put your job first," Fran said. "Don't be so hard on yourself. So you had a fling. It's completely understandable." She giggled. "Although out of character, I'll admit."

Jessie looked out the window at the skyline of the city. It was beautiful in Dallas, and she loved living here. But… "This is not where I want to raise a child," she said quietly.

"I know," Fran said. "Which is the real reason he'll know you calling is not about the car."

"His worst nightmare," Jessie murmured. "He told me so more than once."

Fran nodded. "We all have nightmares eventually."

Jessie touched her stomach. His nightmare was actually her dream come true.

At least part of her dream.

Chapter Six

It was a cold December this year, with gray twilight skies leading into dark nights. Zach hung candy canes on the Christmas tree in the Forrester living room rather morosely, thinking that Duke's child was too young to appreciate the decorations, and nobody but him seemed to carry on the holiday spirit.

Only this year, his holiday spirit had been flagging. Even a visit from the ghost of Christmases past would have livened things up a bit for him.

The ghost he'd least expected to appear got out of a yellow taxi and turned toward the house, catching him gawking out the window at her. His breath completely left him as Jessie waved hello.

She's come to get her car, Zach thought, squashing the relief rushing through him that Jessie had returned to Tulips. The doorbell rang. Zach dashed a hand through his hair, wished he was clean-shaven and decided he didn't care what had brought her back. He just thanked his lucky Christmas stars he was going to get to lay eyes on her one more time.

She'd scared him by leaving his pink ransom-mobile so long without even a call to check up on it.

He jerked open the door.

She looked at him silently.

"Do I know you?" he asked, trying to be funny. So many emotions rushed through him that he lost his place in his be-cool script.

"In the biblical sense," Jessie said, strolling into his living room. "Neither of us knows each other in any other sense, of course."

He'd forgotten how his wit never disarmed her—she could come right back with her own zinger. "I'm surprised you could find your way back here without a trail of bread crumbs or something."

She pulled a checked cashmere scarf from her neck. "The taxi driver didn't have any trouble finding the Forrester ranch."

She wouldn't even admit that she knew exactly where he lived—er, where her car was. He narrowed his gaze on her. "Make yourself at home, I guess, since you're here."

"Thank you." Sitting gingerly across from the tree, she studied his efforts. "Just getting started?"

He'd been at this chore all afternoon. "Yes. I suppose your tree is up and looks like Mrs. Claus decorated it personally."

Jessie blinked. "I never did ask you how Brahma Bud was. I hope he didn't suffer any effects from hitting my car."

Zach crossed his arms, taking in the delicate bones of her face and the gentle lines of her features. "*You* hit *him,* as I recall. He was minding his own business, entirely unaware that females driving pink cars might be bad for his health."

"So he's fine."

Zach sighed. "Yes. Thank you for asking."

She nodded. "I was worried about him."

"So worried that you called. Say, did you know that some people actually leave a building by helicopter when they're avoiding someone?"

Jessie stood. "I've come at a bad time. If I could just have my car keys—"

"Certainly." Reaching into a cabinet in the living room, he pulled out the keys and handed them to her. "And now that you have what you want, let me show you to your car. I think you'll find that it's been kept in the very best possible condition."

"Zach—"

He turned. "The car is this way. I'll drive you to the barn. I'm sure your schedule doesn't allow you much time to sit and chat."

She looked at him for a long moment. "No. It doesn't," she finally said. "And I'd like to pay a visit to the ladies before it gets any later."

He raised a brow, surprised. "Pansy and Helen?"

"Well, yes," Jessie said. "I don't expect to be coming this way again, and I'd like to say hello."

Of course she wouldn't come through Tulips again. His heart began a restless pounding as he considered his options, which appeared few and unfortunate. As in none. He couldn't keep her here: he'd already tried that and she'd shown a remarkable ability to outwit him. He'd tried romance, but she hadn't been exactly banging down his bedroom door to throw herself into his den of sexual pleasure again. *A normal woman would,* he told himself sourly, just to keep his pride from ebbing away. "Are you hungry?" he asked suddenly. The silence had stretched long, he was out of options and blurting anything, even the offer of a hamburger, was his brain's desperate appeal to keep her with him another moment or two.

"I am," she said solemnly. "Are you?"

If she was hungry, he was hungry. Whatever it took. "Ravenous," he said. "I could eat a horse. And the barn."

Jessie looked at him. "I seem to be eating more lately."

Her eyes widened. He glanced down the length of her body, admiring her pretty red coat, her winter boots and pantsuit of some soft fabric which went well with her whiskey-colored hair. "You look great to me," he said. "If you're eating more, it's certainly going in the right places." Her breasts looked great, he thought. Her figure was curvaceous, perhaps a bit curvier than he remembered, but heck, at the time he hadn't been paying as much attention to the form as the opportunity to…his gaze shot to hers. "Everybody seems to eat more during the holidays."

She nodded slowly, her eyes holding his.

His heart began to beat hard in his chest, nearly stealing his breath, almost painfully choking it from him. "You wouldn't be trying to tell me in your refined way that you're…eating more because you're eating for two, would you?" he asked, his whole body tensing as he watched her eyes.

Her gaze dropped for just an instant, but in that instant he knew that he had followed in his brother

Duke's footsteps. "I'll be damned," he murmured, trying to sort out how he felt. Delighted, devastated, shocked, scared—

"Actually, three," she said quietly, her eyes moving back to catch his.

He blinked. "Three what?"

She shrugged. "I'm eating for three. Me, and the twins. Merry Christmas, Zach."

JESSIE WATCHED as Zach sat heavily, his gaze locked on hers. Helplessness washed over her.

"So much for your method," he said. "I could have said no, I could have worn a raincoat, but I fell for you like a starving man for food."

She walked out the front door, keys in hand.

Catching her hand, he turned her toward him. "What's your hurry? Looks like we're going to be spending a lifetime together, City."

"It's so annoying when you call me that," she snapped, wishing she felt more relieved now that he knew but only feeling guilt. "My name is Jessie."

"And a wonderful name it is, gorgeous." He kissed her on the lips, surprising her so much she didn't pull away. "We'll be naming the twins together."

She hadn't thought that far ahead. Names had not been high on her list of priorities—figuring out how to tell Zach had been first. "You could take one, and I'll take the other."

"Nah." He gave her stomach a mischievous eyeing. "Two? How are they both going to fit in that little tiny tummy? Two of my big, strapping sons?" He put a hand on her still-flat stomach. "If they're anything like Duke and me, they're going to be fighting for space constantly."

"This topic just doesn't feel as light to me as it seems to be for you," she said. "I'm still trying to make sense of it. Just the stress of having to tell you—"

The last two weeks of planning, worrying and stalling had finally worn her down. Tears burst out of nowhere, running down her face before she could compose herself.

"Uh-oh," Zach said. "That's the main difference between pregnant women and pregnant cows, I guess. Emotions."

She wiped at her face quickly. "I could tell you were a sensitive male the first time I met you."

He wiped her tears away with his thumbs. "You're cute when you spring a leak."

Jessie moved away from him. "Could you direct me to my car, please?"

"I could, but you'll probably tell me a few more

things you're keeping from me. You're kind of like a firecracker that way. If I wait long enough, information just explodes—"

"Zach," she said, "are you in shock?"

"Yes."

She sighed. "I thought so. I've been a bundle of nerves because I knew how mad you'd be."

"Well, I am mad," he said, "but I'm not going to be upset in front of the children."

"The children?"

"Yes." He put a protective hand on her stomach. "They need to know from day one that they're loved, anticipated and cherished. Our family is very close, in our own oddly special way."

She looked at him. "So the reason you're acting so nonchalant is that you're faking it for the children?"

"Faking it doesn't sound right." He touched her carefully constructed eyelashes. "From now on, I don't want you wearing any more of this goo around me."

"I make my living with this goo," she said, and he nodded.

"I make my living with bulls and things, but I'm not going to make you look at them all the time. I prefer natural skin on my woman."

"Zach, I am not your woman. I will never be your woman," Jessie said. "I don't even know you."

"That's going to be a problem," Zach said, "since I am your prince charming. Your knight in shining armor."

"I don't need the platitudes of fairy tales," she said hotly, making Zach laugh.

"Okay, we're stuck with each other for life," he said. "How's that for relationship lingo? When we're at the boys' soccer matches, we'll introduce each other as 'this is the person I'm stuck with forever.' People won't talk, I'm sure. Not in Tulips."

He wasn't going to make her life easy. Racing ahead into the future, thoughts of Zach made her brain whirl. Ever since the thin blue line had shown up on her pregnancy test, and the super-shocking news of a double pregnancy had been confirmed by her doctor, Jessie had been holding her breath. Trying to think how to tell a man she barely knew that he was going to be a father. She hadn't thought of baby names, nor soccer games, nor what the two of them would be to each other. She'd dreaded having to tell him, but since she knew his worst fear—that he'd be a father and his children would never know him—she wanted him to know as fast as she could tell him. Dealing with all the other consequences she'd put on the back burner.

He had the pot on the front burner, turned to full boil. Strangely, he didn't seem to mind the heat. "I thought you'd be scary about this."

"I'm going to be scary in a little while," Zach said easily. "When I have to tell Pansy and Helen, I'll probably be at my worst. They're going to be so pleased." He gave her a wry glance. "My brother the sheriff says he wants the town to grow organically, which is not quite what the Gang wants. They're going to love the fact that they're getting two little organic sprouts out of one Forrester. They'll say it serves me right, and then smile into their fragile little teacups."

"I don't understand."

He shook his head. "Just be prepared for the Gang to give you a very large baby shower."

"I don't want that," Jessie said quickly. "Can't we come to an agreement about this?"

A frown crossed his face. He stared down at her, his brows knit tightly together. "Agreement?"

She swallowed. "Um, a custody agreement?"

"No," he said, his gaze like dark glass, "and never talk like that in front of the children again. Ever."

ZACH WAS MORE SURPRISED than he let on to Jessie about his impending fatherhood. But he wasn't surprised this was happening. The moment he'd seen her, he'd known she would change his life—and she had.

They didn't even know each other, and what he did know about her signaled a bumpy road ahead. She was flighty. He was methodical. She was spoiled. He was hardworking.

Those differences were just the beginning. He looked at her, imagining her with a big, round belly, and wanted to rub his hands with glee. Twins! It was a Christmas miracle as far as he was concerned, and he wanted this new phase in their relationship to start well. He wasn't saying one thing to upset her. "Were you planning on telling Helen and Pansy? Is that why you really wanted to go into town?"

"I...don't know." She put her keys into her purse and sat back down. "I know I was planning on telling you. That's all I knew."

"So you're moving out here with me," he said, leaning against a wall, quickly trying to devise a plan. "Or I'm moving somewhere with you."

"No," Jessie said. "We're not moving anywhere, at least not together."

He frowned at her. "Look. We're not throwing

away what we did as just an afternoon of freebie sex. We need to become closer."

She appeared to shrink into her coat. "I don't understand you. I know that this is your worst fear come true."

"Yeah." He scratched under his hat. "Funny how it doesn't seem that bad now that it's happened. If that was my life's biggest fear, maybe I never had anything to be really afraid of."

She smiled. "You're not going to say that I tried to trap you?"

"Did you?"

"No!"

He laughed. "Oh, come on. Leave a guy with a little ego."

She stood. "I'm not interested in your ego. I would never cling to a man, or trap him, or—"

"Jessie," he said softly, reaching for her hand to calm her down, "when I met you, you were hotfooting it away from a boyfriend or ex-fiancé or husband or something. You're clearly not the kind of woman who lets men influence her life. I know you're a big shot in your company and that you're more likely to wear pants than panty hose. I get it, okay? Don't keep worrying that I think you're some thimble-brained woman who can't take care of herself."

"Thimble-brained?"

"Those things Pansy and Helen are always using to sew with and stuff."

She nodded. "Nice analogy."

He gave her a wry look. "I know you're not ready to walk down the aisle with me. You can relax. The electric fence you've got up around you is shooting sparks at me."

She sighed. "I don't mean to be so uneasy."

"Well, don't get too comfortable, either," Zach said, grinning. "I don't want to be taken for granted now that you've gotten what you wanted from me."

"Zach!"

He crossed his boots and stared at her. "You did say you had planned to get pregnant as soon as possible after the wedding."

"Yes, but my fiancé was not a stranger." She gave him a haughty look. "Wanting children is not unusual inside a marriage."

He shrugged. "I should hire myself out for stud. I have bulls that don't perform so successfully."

She rolled her eyes. "I'm leaving to tell Pansy and Helen. I need female advice. Yours isn't worth a damn."

"That's what I hear," he said cheerfully. "It comes from being middle child."

"Whatever," she said.

"I'll drive you if you promise not to steal my truck."

"You have no worries," she said, and he nodded.

"Good. We can break the news together. First we have to tell Duke, of course. Pepper we can tell by phone because we hardly see her anymore."

Jessie backed up a step. "You can tell your brother by yourself."

He grinned, liking that she was feeling a little bit nervous. It made him feel big and strong and protective. "Duke won't throw you in jail."

She stiffened. "Of course not! What charges would he have?"

"You were trespassing," he reminded her.

"I was lost," she snapped.

"You did assault my livelihood with a deadly weapon. Poor Brahma Bud."

She sniffed. "Any other charges?"

"You did steal my heart," he said, trying to be light but realizing the moment he said it that he'd made a serious error. Jessie's eyes went dark.

"I stole nothing worth keeping, then," she said. "Consider it returned."

"Whew, prickly," he said. "Did you know you have a habit of being prickly when you're nervous?"

She stared up at him, her gaze very serious. "Did you know you have a habit of trying to be funny when you're nervous? It doesn't go over very well."

"Why would I be nervous?"

"Impending fatherhood, a woman you only met once, your worst fears realized, telling your brother—" She paused. "I can't decide which of those nerves of yours is most rattled."

"You may have a point." He rubbed his chin. "I don't know how to act. Mainly, I don't want you to go away before I get to know you better. That's my biggest worry now."

He meant it, even if sounded silly. How could he do the right thing for her, and for his children, unless he knew who Jessie Farnsworth really was?

"These kids of mine are going to matter to me a lot," he said gruffly. "I know you've got a busy life, but…marry me, Jessie."

Chapter Seven

An offer of marriage from Zach was the last thing Jessica had expected from him. Her heart took a dizzying leap. *If only it were that easy.*

"I know you're not the marrying kind," he said, "but we could probably work out a satisfactory arrangement."

She blinked. "Arrangement?"

"Yeah. I don't know what. But something we could both live with."

The front door opened, and they moved away from each other. Duke walked in, sleet spilling off his hat. "Howdy," he said to Zach. "Well, hello, Jessie."

"Hi, Duke," she said, sending a worried glance Zach's way. Her composure had deserted her with the marriage proposal. Surely he hadn't been serious!

Yet a secret part of her wondered what marriage to Zach might be like.

"Hope I'm not interrupting anything," Duke said. "Liberty says she needs some bolts of plastic covering she stored in one of the barns. I'm not sure which one. Hellish weather to search four barns but at least you made it in before the storm, Jessie. I heard the roads were freezing up just east and north of Tulips. It's on its way here."

Zach frowned. "Plastic covering?"

"Yeah. There should be several rolls of it. Big enough to cover the carpet in a wedding chapel."

"I never saw bolts of plastic," Zach said.

"You don't go into all the barns regularly," Duke said. "Jessie, you look well. Are you in for a couple of days?"

She shook her head. "I wasn't planning on it."

Duke looked from Jessie to Zach. "Well, good to see you all the same. I'm off to root around out there."

"No!" Zach crammed a hat on his head and pulled his keys from his pocket. "I'll look. You stay here and keep Jessie company."

Duke looked bemused. "I don't think I should do that, Zach. I believe she came to see you."

Zach nodded. "That's true. So I'll just head off now and do that looking around for you. I'll call you if I find any of the plastic. In the meantime, grab some soup off the stove and try to warm up."

Duke looked at him. "Hell, Zach, you wouldn't have even known I was at the ranch if I hadn't walked in. Just pretend like you don't know I'm on the property and go on doing what you were doing." Duke turned to leave. "You're acting nuttier than a Christmas fruitcake, which, by the way, the ladies whipped up for us. Full of pecans and things. Be sure to stop by my office and have a bite, Jessie. The Gang can cook for certain, and this is the time of year when they really get their aprons on. Our neighboring-town baker, Valentine, has challenged them to a poppyseed cake bake-off, and that's a holiday snack I look forward to."

Zach slid out the door while his brother was completing his polite goodbye to her. Jessie looked at Zach's retreating back, surprised. "He definitely doesn't want you to get chilled," she told Duke.

"He is one strange apple that fell off our family tree. If I didn't know better, I'd think there was something in one of the barns he didn't want me to see."

"Oh," Jessie said. "I thought strange was his normal behavior."

"I can see why you'd think that." Duke sighed. "Come on. I can't leave you here alone, though my brother has no manners. You can sit in my nice warm truck while we search. Who would want to get married the first week in December, anyway?" he grumbled, holding Jessie's elbow as she walked so she wouldn't slip.

Jessie shook her head. "Liberty's brave to handle gowns and wedding details. I'd be too worried to have brides as my clientele."

They got in Duke's truck. "Zach says you do makeup for conventions of women. That sounds just as challenging as brides. Women in search of beauty would terrify me."

Jessie smiled. "Female dreams aren't scary. Really, they're not. Females want what males want."

"I've only been married a couple of months and haven't figured that out yet," Duke said with a chuckle. "What the hell?" Stopping the truck, he shone the brights into the barn, which Zach had obviously reached at a breakneck speed.

Jessie squinted into the darkness. "Looks like a whole lot of plastic wrap covering something big." She got out of the truck and followed Duke.

Zach was busily tucking the plastic onto a large roll, while diligently keeping his back to whatever object he was removing the plastic from.

"What the hell?" Duke asked. "You didn't use Liberty's wedding aisle-covering stuff, did you, Zach?"

"Quite by accident," Zach said. "You two go on back to the house and get warm. I'll be done in a jif and bring this plastic with me."

"Yeah, but what the hell you used it for is what I want to know," Duke said, approaching Zach. But Jessie already knew.

"My car!" she said. "You jerk, you never got it repaired." Anger flooded her. "Which means it was never broken in the first place."

"Well," Zach said, and he would have said more, but Jessie turned away so she wouldn't slap the excuse right out of his mouth before he could tell her any more lies.

She got into Duke's truck without saying a word. Duke also got in, leaving the plastic wrap behind, and silently started the engine. Unable to stop herself, Jessie peeked at Zach. He stood forlornly in front of her car, which was still half-covered with wrap. Sleet began pelting the roof of the truck and bounced off the barn roof.

"Storm's coming in," Duke said gently. "I'm sure not making excuses for my brother, but you don't want to drive that pretty car in this weather, anyway. It's not good for a convertible."

She was too mad—and too hurt—to speak.

Duke sighed. "I'll drive you into Pansy's. One of the old gals would just love to put you up for the night. Or longer. They'll pamper you thoroughly."

She nodded. He turned the truck around, leaving Zach.

"I'd like to say something good about my kid brother—"

"You should arrest that car thief, Sheriff." The words came out a whole lot more bitter than she wanted them to sound.

"I never considered that," Duke said. "You have a point. But you don't really want him locked up, do you?"

She sighed. "He'd just get on your nerves while you tried to work."

"Are you sure you don't know my brother very well?"

Well enough to be having children with him. "Better than I'd like to, at this point."

"When the weather clears and it's safe for you

to drive out from the ranch, I'll make certain Zach gets your car to you, in complete working order."

"Thank you."

"I have to be honest, I'm a bit surprised by my brother's behavior. Though I'm trying not to rush to judgment, I'd like to apologize on behalf of the Forrester family for my brother's prank. I really am surprised by him."

Duke would be more surprised if he knew he was going to be an uncle.

He pulled into a driveway. "But these three houses are friendly territory. Miss Pansy's, Miss Helen's and then Liberty's house, which she's also converted into a wedding shop. We still stay here when we need to be closer to town, though. When bad weather comes in, I like being near my office. I can walk from here."

The houses were small and quaint, certainly not like anything Jessie had ever lived in. "Are you sure I won't be putting anyone out?"

"The ladies will be delighted to have company. I promise." He waved to them as they came out on their respective porches, and Jessie smiled, delighted to see the ladies again. Duke came around to her door just as Zach's truck pulled up behind them in the driveway. He got out, slamming his door.

"I can take over from here, Duke," Zach said.

"I don't think so," Duke said with a scowl. "You have a lot of explaining to do, and I don't know that you're operating honestly where this woman is concerned."

"I'm trying to marry her," Zach said.

"That might have nothing to do with honesty on your part," Duke snapped, but Jessie's eyes widened. Pansy clasped her hands together, and Helen's mouth puckered.

"That's no proposal," Helen said, coming forward to shoo Jessie toward her house. "Pansy, be careful coming down those steps. Come on over and I'll make us some tea. It's so good to see you again, Jessie. We wondered when you'd return."

"Yes," Pansy said, giving her a hug. "When is the baby due?"

Duke stared at her, surreptitiously shooting a glance at her midsection, which was concealed by her red wool coat. "Baby?"

"How did you know?" Jessie asked Pansy.

"You glow, my dear. You simply glow. And you've put on a teensy bit of very flattering weight."

Duke put his hands on his hips. "Is that why you stole her car?"

Helen gasped. "Stole her car?"

"Yes. It's hidden in one of our barns."

Pansy gave Zach's arm a light slap. "Shame on you, Zach. Your parents would be so disappointed."

Zach sighed. "You people are not helping."

"I bet those rascals found the car and never told us," Helen said to Pansy. "I'm going to give them what-for when I see them."

Pansy nodded. "Jessie, we sent out a search team to check on your vehicle. But they failed us." She gave a haughty sniff at Zach. "You can't hijack a lady when you want to get to know her better, even if she's having your child."

"Children," Zach said.

"Children?" Duke repeated, glowering at his brother.

"We're having twins," Jessie said.

Duke grinned. "Way to go, Bro! Nice shooting!"

The women groaned. "Come on, Pansy," Helen said. "We've had enough excitement for the night, and Jessie needs her rest."

Pansy wiped the delighted grin from her face so she could level a stern look at Zach. "And no climbing through windows or any other shenanigans to talk to Jessie. She'll talk to you when we're good and ready. You just go cool your heels, Zach."

Jessie was fine with that. She was stunned to find that Zach had lied to her. "Thank you for the ride, Duke," she said, allowing Pansy and Helen to lead her away.

"Hey! How about my marriage proposal?" Zach asked.

"We never heard one," Helen called over her shoulder as they walked away. "We heard a stubborn man trying to get his way with little effort, though."

"Thank you," Jessie said as the door closed behind them. It was nice to be out of the cold, and even better to be inside the welcoming doors of Helen's cozy house. "The only bright spot in this is that when Liberty finds out Zach used her precious wedding floor covering to protect my car, she's going to be annoyed. I don't know that it can be used now for the purposes for which it was intended."

"It'll be good for Zach to have a bunch of females peeved with him," Pansy said, taking Jessie's coat. "Hopefully, it'll smarten him up."

"That's for certain." Helen set the kettle on the stove. "He's been quite spoiled since we have so few males in town. So few reasonably intelligent males."

Pansy giggled. "So much for our spies. They're either terrible at their job, or conspiring against us."

Jessie looked at the women. "Why would your friends not tell you if they knew my car was perfectly fine?"

"To be on the boys' side," Helen said simply. "This town has always been about the battle of the sexes. And we girls always win."

Pansy giggled as the three of them sat at the table together. A pretty lamp with a cut-out shade sent warm light around the kitchen. Jessie relaxed, feeling like she was home for the very first time in her life.

Chapter Eight

Zach cooled his heels for as long as he could stand it—approximately ten hours—and despite the bad weather, drove over to Helen's. He just had to see Jessie. Okay, she'd shocked the hell out of him. He hadn't reacted appropriately—heaven only knew he hadn't done *anything* appropriately.

But there was a lot of history in his life that forced him to seek appropriate action where Jessie and his kids were concerned. He'd had a major Christmas present tossed at him, and he was determined to learn how to keep it.

Fortunately for him, he was a Forrester, and so far, the Forrester family was one-for-one on figuring out when to keep their hands on their pregnant significant other.

Pepper would be too smart to let herself get

ahead of the romance, he thought sourly. Younger sisters shouldn't be so calm, cool and collected about everything—only the men in the family seemed to have a hard time with relationships.

"It should be the other way around," he muttered, thinking about last night's impromptu proposal which had brought him no credit whatsoever with Jessie, Duke or the Gang, either, for that matter. As much as they adored hearing about proposals, they'd barely paid his any attention.

They hadn't taken him seriously—which seemed to be a theme in his life. He stared at Helen's house, wondering how to approach the puzzle his world had become. Should he try romance?

"Little late for that." Jessie wouldn't take him seriously on the romance issue. He had to be very careful with his pursuit because she possessed a natural-born wanderer's foot. She could take off any time, in any method of transportation, and it might be months before he laid eyes on her again.

Perhaps help was required in this matter. He pulled out his phone and dialed Holt, investor and civic-minded counterpart to the Gang. Holt sided with the ladies, but he also sided with the men sometimes, and was guaranteed to give a rational and unbiased opinion.

"Holt," he said when he heard a brisk hello on the other end of the line.

"Yes, Zach," Holt said. "I already know why you're calling. I heard your little lady is back in town wanting her car, and that you told her I was supposedly fixing it. I don't like being in the middle if I don't know what's going on."

Great. Life wasn't good when the only hairdresser in town was in a tizzy with him. "Sorry about that. It seemed like a good excuse at the time."

"It didn't work, though, did it?"

"No," Zach said, sighing.

"So now she's returned, and she wants her car, and you want some visitation. That's what I hear through the grapevine," Holt said.

"Grapevine's right," Zach replied. "I want custody of my kids if Jessie won't marry me."

Holt sighed. "The only way you can achieve that is through the courts, Zach."

"I was thinking flowers, maybe some time alone together—"

"You called for my opinion," Holt said. "Becoming a father with a woman whom you've greatly aggravated is not a position of equanimity, you know."

He wasn't sure what equanimity was, but it

didn't sound like he was in a good place with Jessie. "But if you met her—"

"I did." Holt sniffed. "Not that you brought her by. Helen invited me to come meet the newest Tulips citizen."

Zach frowned. "I doubt you'll ever be able to call Jessie a citizen of Tulips."

"At the rate you're going, no."

Everybody is a critic. Zach said, "Do you have any advice, or are you just going to ride the Zach's-A-Louse bandwagon?"

"Legal documentation. And remember she has two legal eagle brothers. The deck may be pretty well stacked in her favor."

"Legal eagle brothers?" Zach listened to the dial tone in his ear. "That was so helpful."

Drumming his fingers on the steering wheel, he looked at the three small, two-story houses that so delicately hid the strength residing within them. Jessie did fit in with that group of strong women, he realized. He had been attracted to her strength from the moment he'd met her. She wasn't the kind of woman who flirted. She didn't put on airs around a man. With Jessie, he'd learned that what he saw was pretty much what he got, straightforward and honest.

That was some small comfort, but he couldn't help mulling the rebound factor. She'd been in a vulnerable time in her life when they'd met.

He conceded that he might have come across as a bit ham-handed and perhaps even a bit horny. Those might be reasons she hadn't taken his marriage proposal seriously.

"Like I just jump on every cute girl I meet." He stared at Helen's house through slivers of sleet bouncing off his windshield. He owed it to his children—and he and Jessie—to present himself and his plan one more time, even if he had to do it in Miss Helen's living room.

He got out of the truck and went to the door. On the door hung a piece of paper that read, "At Liberty's." He went to the middle house and rang the doorbell. Duke answered, shaking his head at his brother. "Next door," he said, while Molly-Jimbo barked a welcome at Zach. Duke closed the door. Zach headed to the final house, finding the front door open and about ten women standing in the entryway of Miss Pansy's.

"Did I miss a party?" he asked, wondering how he could have missed seeing the parked cars or commotion or something.

The ladies went quiet. In front of the fireplace

sat Jessie. At her feet were small gifts of welcome, ranging from knitted baby booties to decorated cloth baby diapers. There was even a stack of recipe cards.

Pansy came over to give him a hug. "We're having a very tiny, most last-minute welcoming party. Holt's been by as well."

"I heard," Zach said, not feeling too happy that he was left out of the fun.

"Well, it's a wonderful day for hot tea and cookies," Pansy said. "And who knows when we might get another chance to introduce Jessie to some of the girls? Thankfully your brother didn't mind rounding everybody up in his truck and bringing them over. It couldn't have been more fun if it was a sleighing party! Duke even wore a Santa hat."

Jessie watched him, her eyes wide and somewhat worried. Since some of the "girls" were between sixty and eighty years of age, Zach realized his audience was one of romantic souls.

He decided to play to that audience. "Hi, Jessie."

"Hi." She barely glanced at him.

Whew. Frosty as the cold air outside. "Hope you'll forgive me about the car," he said. "I got carried away."

A murmur went around the room.

"You certainly did," Jessie said.

"Though I kept your car in excellent shape," he said.

"Yes," Liberty said. "You owe me for plastic—"

"I certainly do," Zach said quickly, before the subject could move from his intentions to his sins. "Jessie, I know I asked you to marry me too quickly—"

The murmur went around the room again, this time with more excitement. Jessie watched him, her gaze suspicious.

"But I want you to know I'm willing to wait," Zach continued, "a long time, if I have to, to get your 'yes.'"

The ladies turned to look at Jessie, whose cheeks had gone strawberry-pink.

"Thank you," Jessie replied, "but my answer must remain no. You lied to me, Zach Forrester, and I'd never be able to trust you. Plus, it was a silly scheme, if you ask me. I should send you a bill for all the travel inconvenience you've caused me."

This wasn't going to be easy. "I'd pay that bill and any other," Zach said. "You could have come to get your car anytime. Why didn't you?"

The audience turned to look at her again. Jessie shifted on her chair. "I didn't want to see you again."

The room went so silent a teacup could have cracked and no one would have noticed.

"By the time Thanksgiving passed, I realized I was expecting," she said, lifting her chin. "I decided this was something I needed to do myself. Of course, at the time, I thought something was terribly wrong with my car and you were honestly trying to get it repaired. I had no idea you'd simply hijacked it."

The ladies leveled frowns on him.

Miss Helen stood. "Well, I must say, perhaps this isn't the time or place for this discussion," she said gently. "But all the same, Jessie, I must speak on behalf of Zach."

Zach blinked. Was one of the town's most sturdy pillars going to put in a good word for him?

"Zach has ever been the more impulsive Forrester," Helen said, with Pansy nodding in agreement. "And yet, he has a heart of gold so that one must love him in spite of his foibles."

Jessie looked surprised to hear that, as was Zach himself. *Go on. Now we're getting somewhere,* he thought gratefully. He wanted to be loved in spite of whatever that thing was she said he had.

"His brother spent a great deal of time trying to

derail our best plans," Helen said, "but Liberty's tamed him now so there's very little chance of that."

The ladies laughed. Jessie shifted again, not meeting Zach's eyes.

"Pepper is her own woman. Very independent, much more so than her brothers."

"Hey," Zach said, "can Duke and I vote on that?"

"It's true and you know it," Pansy said. "If you'd but admit it. She went off and got a medical degree. She is trying to grow the town with the clinic she wants to start."

"Well," Helen said, "Duke's idea of growing the town is to just hope and pray the sky rains interested newcomers who want to settle a fair piece from city life."

"He's becoming more broad-minded," Liberty said.

"Only because you have a shop in the city as well as here," Helen said. "He's learned to admit that there must be something that draws people to a place. We had no railroad and we're no port city. Big industrial farms have changed the livelihoods for many of us. We missed some opportunities to show that our light could shine brightly," Helen said. "But along comes Zach, and he disagrees with his brother, and has a big idea."

Zach nodded, liking the way Helen was making him look smart and important, all very necessary to be the man he thought Jessie might want. She began packing the welcome gifts into a sack, looking at him askance.

"I'm starting to see a theme here."

"What?" Zach asked.

"Good ideas, wrong follow-through," she said.

"Possibly," he said, "though I really believe my ideas are just bigger in scope than other people are willing to comprehend at the moment."

She pursed her lips at him, a gesture he very much appreciated. Made him want to kiss those red cherry-puckers again—this time for hours. No more quickies for him! Next time he got his hands on Jessie—

"It's better than Duke's idea," Helen told Jessie. "He just wants us to grow the town organically. Like every person here of child-bearing age could either adopt or become pregnant with the amount of children we'd need to grow this town. I'm so sick of the word organic I could scream."

"What would you do differently?" Jessie asked, and Zach was amazed that she was so interested.

"We suggested matchmaking balls and dances

and all kinds of things, but Duke was being selfish and didn't want other men around Liberty," Pansy said.

Liberty laughed. "I brought my business here, and that definitely brings customers to the saloon. Then we try to keep people by showing them the beautiful countryside and down-home warmth we offer."

Jessie looked at Zach. "Twins will definitely help, but it's no population explosion."

Was she suggesting more children? "No, it's not," Zach said, his mind working rapidly. "I'm willing to work on a population explosion with you."

The ladies giggled, but Jessie sent a frown his way. "You have all been very kind to me," she said, and the ladies smiled. "I'm sure you appreciate why I will probably not live here full-time with my children—"

"What?" Zach exclaimed, and the ladies began a nervous rustling. That pronouncement had to be worse than anything Duke had ever heard from Liberty! Maybe Holt was right. Although legalities were certainly something to be avoided… He'd much rather romance Jessie into seeing matters his way.

Jessie ignored his excitement. "Maybe my

family's company could have the next convention here."

The ladies looked at her, their faces wreathed in hopeful delight.

"No," Zach said. "I don't like makeup and cosmetics and face creams. Natural is the only way to go. But thank you for trying to help." He sat down heavily. "Our problem isn't women, we have plenty of those. There are few eligible bachelors, so the women have to look outside the town. Eventually, they move." He looked at Jessie. "Bet you thought I'd say yes just to keep you here."

She raised her chin. "I do not plan the conventions. I oversee them and give lectures."

"You're being hasty, Zach," Helen said. "Remember, we're all about commerce here, and commerce is commerce, even if it comes out of a bottle."

Zach blinked. It would never work. "This town is about women," he said slowly. "We need to showcase our women."

Pansy and Helen smiled, and the other ladies looked at him with appreciation.

"We have more to offer here than anywhere." He looked at Jessie. "You could do it. You could fix them up and make them beautiful, and we could be the most beautiful town in Texas, women-wise."

"They are beautiful," Jessie said. "Every woman here is unique and I've enjoyed meeting them."

"But most men, unlike myself, like the package. They like the bows on the package, too, the red lips and the fancy hair."

Jessie shook her head. "Zach, you don't understand."

"Tell me."

She got up. "I'm awfully tired all of a sudden, ladies. Thank you so much for your lovely gifts."

Somehow, he'd lost her attention. "I'll help you carry them to Helen's. The sidewalk is probably getting more slick, and I don't want you to fall. Now for the rest of you," he said, "is Duke coming back, or can I play taxi for you ladies?"

"You just take care of Jessie," Pansy said. "I'll call Duke to finish his driving duties. That means I get to watch the baby." Grinning, she went to the phone.

"Good night," Jessie said, hugging everyone in the room as she left. "Thank you so much for everything." Beside her, Zach carried out the gifts that had so warmed her heart. He'd completely surprised her by showing up, and then by basically offering himself in front of the ladies.

She'd learned a lot about him that she hadn't known, too.

But they were too different, they had different goals, and he'd lied to her. That reminded her very much of her ex, and she'd made a vow to herself that, if a man lied to her once, there were no second chances. She couldn't afford to make that mistake again.

She'd trusted Zach, and learned that he, too, told convenient fibs. She couldn't cut him any slack just because he'd lied to keep her in Tulips. "I've proven that I'd stay here willingly if I could," she said as they went through Helen's front door.

"Sensible of you," he said. "We're good people here."

She set her things down and took off her coat. "The jury is still out on you."

"Are you mad?"

She gave him a quizzical look. "What would you be, if our circumstances were reversed?"

"Hey, you hit my prize longhorn, and I didn't hold a grudge."

"Because the longhorn was still standing," Jessie said. "And we had sex."

He frowned. "We didn't have sex. We created children."

"I don't think you can be particularly sentimental about sex in the backseat of a car."

His frown grew deeper. "I damn sure can. I am very sentimental about that car! I've had it in storage for more than twelve weeks, a monument to the best sex I ever had!"

She blinked. "Really?"

"Well, hell yeah," Zach said. "Why? Didn't you think so?"

She tied her long hair up into a ponytail and pulled off her shoes. "I never did that in a car before, so I have no frame of reference."

"But you'd do it again? Wouldn't you?"

She glanced up at him. "With you?"

"You're sure as hell not ever making love to anyone else, Jessica T. Farnsworth," he said, "so don't waste your time considering your options."

She straightened. "That did not sound like a marriage proposal. It sounded like an order."

He nodded. "You didn't accept the proposal, so I have to declare limitations some other way."

"It's not going to work." Jessie moved into the kitchen, looking for Helen's teapot. "Marriage would make both of us crazy."

"We'd get to know each other better," Zach said, "and that's my whole goal."

"That's it?" She took down two teacups from the cabinet. "Shouldn't Miss Helen be here by now? You should check on her. It's very dangerous to be walking on the wet cement."

"See," he said, "you're starting to care about us. You're starting to take on Tulips' ways."

She shrugged. "I do care about Miss Helen and Miss Pansy. And some of the other ladies I've met."

He cleared his throat.

"Liberty, for example," she said. "And I'm pretty sure I'd like Pepper if I got to know her better."

He helped her put out cookies. "So, about this get to know us better thing," he said. "It probably works just as well for me as my sister."

"Maybe," she said, "but your sister isn't trying to tie me down."

Stubborn. But she had a point. "What if I didn't try to tie you down? What if I merely tied myself to you?"

She looked at him suspiciously. "I know you didn't mean that the way it sounded."

"I don't have Duke's handcuffs, if that's what you're worried about." He sat in the chair she pointed to. "How about if I move into wherever it is that you live?"

She shook her head at him. "Your ranch is here.

You would not enjoy my lifestyle. It's all travel, and you're a homebody."

He sensed an angle and perhaps an advantage. "So you can't take twins on the road with you."

"I can."

"Well, at first, maybe. But later on, they'll need stability. They can't get any better stability than here in Tulips." He took a slow sip of the hot tea, thinking how much he liked sitting here with Jessie, just the two of them talking about their future and their goals.

He'd get her to see his way eventually.

She looked at him. He sensed a struggle.

"Kids need schools and balance and ties to heritage," he said softly. He gazed at her, his fingers reaching out to cover hers on the table. "The girl who has everything ought to know that."

Chapter Nine

Jessie shook her head. "It's not quite like that. I've worked hard for everything I have. And I've always felt quite 'normal.'"

"I'm not sure that's the right word for you." Zach grinned. "Maybe 'exceptional.' There's the word I'm looking for."

"Well, it definitely seems exceptional to be having children with you," Jessie said, feeling uneasy. "This is probably not going to be the most graceful relationship between two people, considering how we've started out."

"I'm good with it," Zach said. "You'll be a great mother, I'll be an awesome dad. The babies will have interesting and varied lives." He gave her a slow, sexy grin. "You've definitely made my life interesting."

She nodded. "Still seeing the twins?"

He grinned again. "You're the only woman in my life now."

Her brow lifted. "How do I know you're not telling me a fib?"

"You can trust me. But because you think you can't, I'll tell you a secret no one in this town knows."

"Part of me is curious, and part of me says knowing anything more about you could be detrimental." *Mostly to my heart.*

"That suspicious streak of yours is going to interfere with our closeness," Zach said. "I'm sure you wouldn't want that to happen, for the sake of the children."

He was going to use that angle every chance he got. "Go on," she said, "tell the monumental secret."

"I have to trust you," he said.

"You're stretching our boundaries," she said. "All we've learned to do so far is distrust."

"Okay," he said with a mock frown, "but I don't share secrets with just anyone."

"I won't dignify that with a show of curiosity."

"The twins live in Dallas. They're writers."

Jessie blinked. "Interesting, if you like to read in bed, I guess."

"So suspicious," he said, laughing. "You're almost no fun to share a secret with."

"I never said I was fun," Jessie said. "I'm just learning to embrace stability."

"I write western romance," he said proudly. "They're my critique group."

She stared at him. "That's your secret?"

He nodded proudly. "Yep."

"It's a good one." Zach with a creative, cerebral side? It was almost hard to imagine. "You know, the Gang would love to know—"

"Hey!" He sat up. "You promised not to say anything."

"But it's so juicy and scandalous," she teased. "They'd love to know your mysterious side."

"We're bonding over secrets," Zach said. "The Gang is not to know."

"But they'd figure out a way to use your hobby to grow Tulips." She grinned at him. "Imagine your face on a billboard at the entrance of the city 'Tulips—Home Of Zach Forrester, Western Romance Writer.' You could turn this town into a haven for aspiring artists."

"It's not organic," Zach said.

"Maybe Duke doesn't get everything he wants.

And I might remind you, we are doing our part in the organic growth department, twice over."

"I should have known you'd go for the dramatic tie-down of my bachelorhood."

She shrugged. "So back to the billboard—"

"I notice you care about our town." Zach smiled. "You seem to be thinking deeply on our dilemma. This gives me hope for our future."

"Don't," Jessie said. "I could never marry a moody writer."

"That's a cliché." Zach bit into a cookie. "Just as much a cliché as women having moody times of the month."

Jessie opened her mouth to say she probably did, then closed it. She wouldn't be having one of those for a while, so there was no point in scaring him.

"You were going to say you had no moody times," Zach said. "I'm glad for that. Only one of us can be moody."

"What good does it do to write if no one knows you do it?" Jessie asked.

"I need that outlet for my soul. I can't not create. I started out with cowboy poetry, and one day, I realized my poem went on and on. It had taken on epic proportions but wasn't as good as

The Odyssey, for example. I feared, in fact, that it was pretty much lengthy dreck. I took it to a workshop and I met the twins, and they suggested a romance, and we've been together ever since."

Jessie tried not to be jealous of other women having a piece of Zach she would never share. "Should I read some of your work?"

He looked surprised. "Would you want to?"

"It would be a sampling, wouldn't it? Of your style?"

"You're trying to cheat," Zach said with a grin. "It won't work. You're going to have to learn about me through one-on-one communication."

They looked at each other for a long moment.

"Besides, I don't think western romance is your cup of tea," Zach told her. "I'll tell the babies bedtime tales of cowboys and Christmas carols, though."

"I never heard those."

He nodded. "I know. I sensed that the girl who had everything might not have experienced some of the best parts of life."

She leaned back in her chair. "I've always believed that people who make lasting bonds with each other are best suited if they have similar backgrounds."

"We're not exactly dissimilar. We're both the rogue elements in our families."

"I wish I could refute that," she said slowly. "Unfortunately, I only lately came into the family's good graces."

Zach grinned. "The old ladies can pick a winner every time."

"What does that mean?"

"It means," he said, "that they seem to know how to find diamonds in the rough."

"They did not find me," Jessie said, "I drove through this town. I don't want to believe that my future is based on my bad sense of direction."

He grinned. "I'm really looking forward to this."

"It's not going to work, Zach," Jessie said honestly. "My bad sense of direction applies to maps *and* men. They say once bitten, twice shy, and you've already proved yourself to be less than trustworthy. No bonding between us, no cajoling and teasing, can change the way I feel." She looked at him, wanting him to understand. "Everything I know tells me you're not a good bet for my life. While I realize nothing is a safe bet, now that I'm going to be a mother, I'm going to be making the best choices I possibly can."

Zach left Helen's house, knowing that he and Jessie were further apart than ever. It wasn't easy on a man who was afraid of being an absentee father.

He went home to the Triple F, wondering how he would ever convince Jessie that he was a good man, a man she wanted and needed in her life. All the lights were on at the house, which surprised him since it was quite late.

Pepper tugged an overstuffed suitcase out the front door as he walked onto the porch.

"Going somewhere?" he asked. "I can't advise it. The roads outside the ranch are slick."

Pepper shook her head. "I know. I'll be all right."

"I could drive you," he offered.

"No, thanks." She slid the heavy suitcase down the steps and then almost slipped.

"Pepper, this isn't your best idea. The most educated Forrester should know that."

Sighing, she stood upright, facing him as he stood at the top of the porch. "All right. You have a point."

"A damn good one," he said gruffly, going down the steps to retrieve the bag. "This is heavy! What the hell, Pepper?"

Once he reached the top of the stairs and set the case inside the door, she tugged it down the hallway. He followed her, bemused. "I suppose it's possible you're heading for a warmer place."

"Zach, could you mind your own business?" she snapped.

"Not usually," he said mildly. "It's a flaw in my personality, particularly where my sister is concerned."

She burst into tears. Zach blinked. "Damn, Pepper, is something wrong?"

"No. I just need to get out of here."

She was acting a lot like Jessie. "What the hell's the matter with all the females around here, anyway?"

"We all have lives that you men can't exactly comprehend," Pepper said, "because we're not being good little apron-wearing, dinner-fixing feetwarmers."

"Whoa," Zach said. "I only know five words in the female language. 'Let me get the kettle.'"

"That would be nice," Pepper said, sniffling as she finished dragging her suitcase off like a protective animal.

"It's the weather," Zach mused. "It's making everyone stir-crazy." Setting the kettle on to boil, he set out two teacups the way Helen and Pansy would. He felt proud of himself, and got a little more fancy by putting some chocolate chip cookies on the saucers. Whatever was ailing Pepper would surely go away when his sister saw his handiwork.

She came into the kitchen and sat at the table, grateful to let him handle tea-duty.

"It's the Christmas season," Zach pointed out. "We should be feeling tidings of joy. Not panic and stress."

Pepper shook her head. "I can't talk about it, so don't ask."

He poured the hot water into the teacups, setting one in front of her before he sat down. "I can talk about my dilemma, if you're in the mood to humor me."

"Shoot," Pepper said. "One of us might as well abuse the sibling privilege."

"Right." Zach burned his tongue, not paying attention to the heat in his cup as he sipped. "Last chance to spill before I grab the spotlight."

Pepper shook her head. There was no way she could talk about her secret. It wasn't time. Eventually, perhaps she could. But not now. Zach would be shocked. Duke would be stunned. Despite their own out-of-wedlock pregnancies, they would be beside themselves to learn of her own children.

She couldn't second-guess her decisions now.

The die had been cast long ago. "I am positive that if we spend this cold, rainy evening getting your issues addressed," Pepper said, "I'll feel better empathetically."

Zach hoped so. A less-selfish brother would insist that she let big bro shoulder her burden, but Pepper wasn't the type of girl who could be pushed.

"My problem is Jessie," he said. "She's having my children."

"I know," Pepper said. "I took a gift by. I look forward to having her in the family."

He frowned, completely startled.

"Well, I do," Pepper said. "She'll be a wonderful sister, just like Liberty."

"Do you know something I don't?" Zach asked. "Because when I left her forty-five minutes ago, she didn't want to have anything to do with me."

"Not you, maybe, but she's fine with me. And I'm the auntie. I'll occupy a glorious place in those little babies' lives." She smiled, pleased by the notion. "It's a wonderful Christmas present. I'll have two little Forresters to spoil and coddle, and when they turn into brats, you won't be able to blame Aunt Pepper because they'll love me too much."

Zach frowned. "They need to be Forresters."

"They'll be Farnsworth-Forresters," Pepper said. "Doesn't that sound pretty?"

"It's a mouthful," he said unhappily. "Pepper, I don't want to be a father who isn't married to the mother of my children. I want us to live under one roof. Does that make sense?"

Her brother touched a nerve inside her. But she doubted her teenage love would have shared Zach's sentiments. No one wanted to be tied down by children at that young age. "It makes sense," she said carefully. "I'm not really a good person to talk to about this."

"You're the best."

"No," Pepper said, getting up from the table with her teacup. "Believe me, you should talk to Helen and Pansy or Holt. I am no expert on anything except medical matters."

Since she'd just been on her way out the door to catch a redeye to visit her own twins, Toby and Josh, her advice was probably the worst Zach could receive. Far better for him to talk to someone with a success rate, like Duke.

She had to concentrate on her children and Christmas and the medical clinic she was starting, and how she was finally going to bring the boys home to Tulips without everyone she knew being completely ashamed of what she'd done so many years ago.

IN THE MORNING, Zach got up bright and early and went outside to the barn to check on Jessie's car. Molly-Jimbo slept in the back seat, so he shooed her out, not certain how she'd sneaked into the garage and gotten in. "You are the wiliest dog I ever met," he told the golden retriever. "Why can't you act like you're Duke's dog?"

Molly barked at a chicken and ran off, not bothered at all by Zach's lack of praise for her cunning.

He inspected the car, certain Jessie never had a long-haired dog sleeping in her precious land yacht. The best thing to do would be to take it into town, have it vacuumed and polished, hang a wreath on the grill and take it to her with an apology and a goodbye.

"But I'm a stronger man than that," he said, starting back toward the house. "I'm not going to let her scare me off with a wee little 'no.'"

After talking to Pepper last night, he'd realized he couldn't give up so easily. Not this time. Duke had hung in there until he won Liberty's heart—surely Forrester grit counted for something.

He had babies counting on his grit.

He felt good about deciding that determination would be his guide. The doorbell rang and his heart leaped—maybe Jessie had come to get her car at last. Or even better, perhaps she'd come to say that their future together, in whatever form or fashion, would be a bright one.

He hoped so. He was becoming quite fond of that sassy girl from the city.

Opening the door, he looked at the two tall, big-shouldered strangers on his porch. A faint sense of alarm trickled through him. Strangers didn't pass by this way often.

"Howdy," he said. "Can I help you boys?"

"We're looking for Zach Forrester," one of them said.

"I'm Zach," he said, and the men nodded their heads.

"Good," the other said, punching him square on the jaw.

Chapter Ten

Jessie heard a crack and a thump and realized her brothers had not been candid with their reasons for wanting to meet Zach. "You hurt him!"

She rushed forward and knelt beside Zach. "Are you all right?"

"I was better about five minutes ago," Zach said, rising to his feet. He looked at her brothers with a frown. "Settle your issues, boys, and move along."

"The issue is Jessie," one said, but Jessie put out a hand.

"No, I am not the issue. Apologize! Both of you. And introduce yourselves properly. Or I'm not leaving with you."

They shifted, glaring at Zach. "I'm serious," she said. "If you're going to be medieval about this, you might as well go home."

They took that comment in with frowns. Just when she thought this might be the first time her brothers didn't listen to her, they each put out a reluctant hand.

"Robert Farnsworth," the taller of the two said. "This is my brother Cedric."

Zach nodded. Jessie noticed he didn't touch his chin, which had to ache, judging by the redness on it and how hard Robert had hit him. "I am so ashamed of you," she told her brothers. "Zach, I do apologize. They've never acted like cavemen before."

"I'd invite you in," Zach said, "but you'd probably prefer to say your piece on the porch."

"Actually, we've said all we have to say," Robert said.

"Excellent." Zach nodded, handing Jessie's keys to her. "You know where your car is, Jessie. Glad you have someone to accompany you home. I won't worry about you."

He closed the door.

Jessie's jaw dropped. "Zach!" She wouldn't reduce herself to banging on a man's door to get his attention, but her heart jumped wildly inside her. "You did not help the situation," she told her brothers.

"I wasn't thinking," Robert said. "I'm sorry, Jessie. I've just been wanting to do that so badly ever since you told me what he did to you."

"He did exactly what I wanted him to," Jessie said between clenched teeth. "Oh, Pepper! I'm so glad you're here."

Pepper glanced up in the process of hauling a big bag out the door with her. "Hi, Jessie." She locked the front door and stood. "I'm Pepper Forrester," she said to Jessie's brothers. "You must be the reason I had to put a cold cloth on Zach's face."

"We should apologize," Robert said.

"Well, I don't think it'll matter." Pepper lugged the case down the steps. "He's not in a listening mood. Kind of funny and temperamental that way."

"Can I carry that for you?" Cedric asked.

"Oh, no," Pepper said. "We Forresters stick tightly together, so I'll have to forego the niceties you're offering. Goodbye, Jessie."

"Pepper!" Jessie exclaimed.

"This is kind of an odd bunch," Cedric said, watching Pepper wrestle with her huge bag on the way to her truck. "I feel like I'm on a set of *Gunsmoke*. Jessie, I don't know what you saw in that cowpoke."

Jessie whirled on her brothers. "Let's just get my car and go. You've quite destroyed any credibility with me and worn out your welcome in Tulips."

Robert walked down the porch. "I saw a saloon in town where we could get a bite to eat before we go back—"

"Don't even bother," Jessie said tightly. "You'd probably be served arsenic."

"Surely they don't get their feelings hurt that easily," Cedric said. "It was just a tap on the chin. A big strong cowboy can take a tiny knock."

Robert shrugged. "How do you expect us to feel? If it wasn't for him and his lack of polite gentleman's equipment—"

"Condoms," Cedric said.

"You'd be back with your—"

"No, I wouldn't," Jessie said. "Whatever came before Zach doesn't matter to me anymore."

"Jessie," Robert said, "this can't possibly work. You don't even know him. You come from different places. I can't see you living here."

Jessie shook her head. "Zach is a good man."

"He lied about your car. He took advantage of you. There's no good in that," Cedric pointed out.

"You're a lawyer," Jessie said. "Lies are something you've been known to—"

"Jessie," Cedric said, "we don't like him."

"That's tough," Jessie said. "I want you both to get back in the car you came to town in, and go home. I'm staying to fix this with the father of my children."

"Mom and Dad will be upset," Robert reminded her.

"I'll deal with that later," Jessie said. "Goodbye."

Robert and Cedric stepped off the porch. "Call us if you change your mind. We'll be here—"

"I have a car. I'm not a prisoner." Jessie raised her chin, a sisterly thought coming to her. "On second thought, be certain you stop in at the Tulips Saloon on the way out. You just can't beat their coconut cake."

Cedric perked up. "I love coconut cake."

"This one is so heavenly and light that you barely taste the coconut. It's more like fluffy sweetness you can't describe."

Robert nodded. "I'm hungry."

"Good. You'll like it."

"What if he doesn't let you in?" Cedric asked.

"Oh, Zach will let me in." Jessie looked upstairs. "Don't worry about me."

Grumbling about leaving her behind, her overprotective brothers got in their Lincoln Town Car and drove away. As soon as they were out of sight, she turned to knock on the door. It was snatched from her fingertips before she could, and Zach's strong hand pulled her inside.

He locked the door and kissed her passionately, his mouth all over hers, hard and searching. Then he pushed her away.

"Just in case you think I'm being a coward by not fighting back," he said, "I don't fight with relatives, even future relatives who behave badly."

"They weren't truthful to me. They said they just wanted to meet you," Jessie said.

"Now they have. I'll always remember my first Christmas holiday with your family."

"Hold that thought." She pulled her cell phone from her purse. "What is the number to the Tulips Saloon?"

He told her and she dialed quickly. "Pansy," she said, looking at Zach, "I was hoping you'd be there. No, I don't need anything, but I was going to let you know that two very handsome, very eligible bachelors are on their way to try your coconut cake."

She smiled as Pansy told Helen to make sure she had two large slices for the men. "I knew you'd take care of it. Thank you, Pansy."

Clicking off the phone, she smiled at Zach. "They're calling several of Tulips' most eligible ladies to visit the newcomers."

"Excellent revenge," Zach said. "Your brothers are about to get everything they deserve. I didn't know lawyers were such physical types. Maybe a lawsuit, a custody skirmish—"

"No," Jessie said, "there'll be none of those."

"Good," Zach said. "Holt suggested it, but it's been years since anyone in this town has practiced law."

"Was anyone in Tulips ever involved in the legal profession?"

"Duke has mostly been the town scales of justice," he said. "I believe I was in the middle of kissing you—"

Jessie put a hand on his chest to stop him. "No."

"Kissing is still sex for you?"

She gave him a wry look. "I think we're past that point. Kissing is the least of my worries. My brothers brought up an important point."

"This should be good." Zach crossed his arms.

"I'm very, very reserved around men I don't know, and I may have been under the opposites attract theory when I, when we—"

"I like where this is heading," Zach said. "I've

never been a woman's fantasy before. At least I don't think."

She rolled her eyes. "We need to shed the illusions."

"God, I hope so." Zach gave her dress a tiny tug. "I want you to shed a lot around me."

"I'm moving in," Jessie said.

"Tulips will be scandalized," Zach said with a grin.

"WHAT WE NEED," Pansy said, the next day when it seemed things were more quiet around Tulips, "is to help Pepper meet a man. This is where we're going wrong."

Helen and Pansy sat inside the Tulips Saloon, sharing a companionable cup of tea now that all the day's customers had left and the store was closed. This was home away from home, their very favorite place to relax and enjoy friendships.

"I thought perhaps Jessie's brothers might have been prime candidates," Helen said thoughtfully, "but the Tulips' ladies so fawned on them that their dance cards would be totally full should they ever return."

Pansy giggled. "They won't. They know what's

waiting for them if they do. Our girls would get them to the altar."

Helen nodded. "The problem with Pepper is that the only man she ever fell for was—"

"Highly inappropriate." Pansy stared down into her teacup. "I had so many hopes for Luke McGarrett when he was a child. He turned into such a rascal."

"Poor Pepper. So intelligent, such a model of responsibility, and the man who breaks her heart is—"

Helen shook her head. "Good thing he never returned to Tulips. I hear he made a fortune doing something nefarious. It's always the good that attracts the bad."

Pansy adjusted her spectacles. "I don't know where we'd find the man who deserves Pepper, anyway. So let's work on Jessie."

Two sharp raps on the window caught their attention. Hiram and Bug stood outside, waving urgently.

"They want tea," Pansy said.

"Of course they do." Helen got up to let them in. "It's cold outside, and we made cookies, besides."

She unlocked the door and the men darted in.

"What is it?" Helen asked.

"We've got news," Hiram said.

"Whatever it is, we've probably already heard it," Pansy said. "I do hope we haven't."

"We're going to throw an impromptu Christmas parade," Bug said. "I couldn't get over the idea of a parade. Me and Mrs. Carmine will ride at the front on our bays, and Hiram's gonna dress up as the fat white, whiskered man in the red cap and throw candy."

They all considered Hiram, who was thin as a rail and had no decent throwing arm as far as any of them knew.

"Okay," Helen said. "Did Duke approve this quilted plan of yours?"

"We're not going to ask him." Bug looked over his shoulder through the window toward Duke's office. "He'll just say no. We're going to have the parade, and when he asks why we didn't tell him, we're going to say we left him a permit request but perhaps he was too busy with the baby and his brother's T-bird-stealing ways to notice it."

"Forgiveness instead of permission," Pansy said. "I should have a problem with that, but I don't."

"And what's our goal?" Helen asked.

"To put Tulips on the map. To bring the outside to us. Heck, Duke's keeping us all in the Dark Ages,"

Hiram complained. "We need the light of progress to come to this town, at least before I expire."

"You are getting rather long in the tooth," Helen agreed, for the hundredth time. "Pansy, you could be Mrs. Claus, and we could ask Jessie to judge the floats. If she's still here."

"Floats?" Bug wrinkled his face. "What floats?"

"What was the parade going to be, Bug?" Helen looked at him. "You and Mrs. Carmine riding horses, and Hiram bringing up the rear with a tiny sack of peppermints to throw at...my stars, we don't have any children here. What would be the point?"

Pansy sighed. "As usual, there is no point. It'll have to wait until Duke's child is old enough to catch a piece of candy."

"A parade with no children would be sacriledge," Hiram agreed. "I hadn't considered that. I thought people might bring their youngsters and see what a nice town we have."

"But if no one came, then—" Pansy began, and they all fell silent.

"Is Jessie still here?" Hiram asked.

"Last I heard, she was visiting Zach. Apparently, her brothers went to help her pick up her car and gave Zach a little tap on the chin."

"So is the car still here?" Hiram asked. "We could take our parade into Dallas, if we borrowed her car."

They all stared at him.

"It'd be even better if she'd drive us. She could be our town princess," Hiram said. "Every town has a princess of something. Like a harvest princess, or a snow princess."

Helen blinked. "It's advertising."

"She looks all citified," Bug pointed out. "She's pretty, and her car is awesome."

"I don't think we should use someone for their car," Pansy said.

"We could use Duke's squad car," Hiram said, and they all groaned.

"Why don't you hold that thought, Hiram?" Pansy said, and they all smiled so he wouldn't have his feelings hurt. "Our first Christmas parade should be less formal-looking, and a pink car is very festive."

"It's just the right color for Tulips!" Helen exclaimed. "Why didn't I think of that before?"

"Because we never thought about taking our parade to the city," Pansy said, "and then we wouldn't need Duke's permission."

"We could decorate it all fancy, and put a sign on the side that reads 'Come To The Tulips Saloon For Christmas Memories And A Chance At A

Thousand-Dollar Santa Sack,'" Pansy said, which earned her three shocked expressions.

"Where would we get that kind of money?" Bug asked.

"Perhaps we'd offer donations in the sack. Like, maybe a wedding gown or services from Liberty's Lace, and maybe cookies from our saloon, and we have many talented ladies who can do all sorts of things here," Pansy said reasonably. "If all fifty of us chipped in four bucks, that'd be two hundred dollars right there."

They considered that for a few moments.

"I have four bucks," Hiram said.

"Who would be the one to ask Jessie?" Bug asked.

"We would," Helen said. "You keep Zach busy. He might tell Duke, or he might get weird on us about Jessie removing her car from his barn. So far, and through twists of fate, he's managed to keep her prized possession in his barn, which I suspect makes him very happy."

"So Jessie's would be the lead car, and there'll be no horses, which will make Mrs. Carmine sad, but she'll understand," Bug said thoughtfully.

"We can take Molly-Jimbo. We'll put a Santa cap on her head, and the kids will love that," Pansy suggested.

"And we'll pack the willing ladies from our town into trucks that follow Jessie's car," Helen said.

"It's crazy," Hiram said. "Wouldn't we have to have a Dallas permit?"

"For three or four cars?" Helen asked. "We'd be out of there so quickly, no one would think it was a parade. We're just leaving calling cards that advertise our town as a great place to live. Which it is."

"But men don't come out for wedding dresses, which is what you're giving away," Hiram said reasonably. "They'd beat a hasty path out here for land, though."

"Duke would not be happy about that," Pansy said. "It's not organic growth."

"Bachelor land-grabs." Helen thought over that a moment. "Someone call Zach and ask a member of the young set if they'd go for that."

Pansy picked up the phone and dialed. "Oh. Hello, Jessie," she said. "Didn't I dial the Forresters? Oh, I did. So, you're still in town. Ah. Oh, how nice. All right. Thank you. Goodbye, dear."

She hung up, looking at Helen. "We'll have to put the parade off for a year or so due to lack of car and Tulip Princess, I believe. Zach and Jessie are leaving town. They're eloping."

Chapter Eleven

"I wouldn't be doing this if my brothers hadn't been so heavy-handed," Jessie said. Zach drove her car and she sat beside him, enjoying the midnight ride out of Tulips. Because it was two weeks until Christmas, and the weather was still cold and rainy, they had the top up on the convertible. But she didn't care. She could see the stars in the sky and she was on a new adventure in her life.

Change always made her happy.

"They were heavy-handed, indeed," Zach said. "Right on my jaw. So I'm completely for whatever suits your bad-sister adventurous side."

"Thanks," Jessie said. "I think." She gave him a considering look. "Do you think you'll encourage our children to be wayward as well?"

"One of us will. It'll be a toss-up as to which of us will be the more steadying influence."

"Hmm." She sighed. "I don't see a future for us."

"Of course you don't. You left your crystal ball with your magic mirror."

"Were you trying to make a joke?" Jessie asked. "A pointed reference to my line of work?"

"Nah. I'm just saying we're probably not meant to be together, so we shouldn't worry about that part. Legalizing us for the sake of the children is a good thing, though, and it'll mean we won't totally scandalize the little old tyrants of Tulips."

Jessie laughed. "They're not tyrants, and you love them."

"Yes. But even you recognize that living to-gether under one roof without legal commitment would send them into plotting overdrive."

"Yes," Jessie said. "Our elopement should make everyone relax."

"Except you and me." Zach patted her leg, then tried to reach a sneaky hand under her skirt, which she expertly batted away. "I don't think I'll ever relax around you."

"Really?"

"You make me very crazy in an uncomfortable

way. I see you, and I want to kiss you. I smell you, and I want to hold you. I touch you, and I want to undress you. How's that for crazy?"

"Pretty much all in," Jessie said, secretly touched.

"So, you can tell me you feel the same way about me," Zach said, obviously hinting for attention.

She smiled. "I could, but I wouldn't be honest."

"Oh, man. I knew you were the kind of girl who wouldn't want to stroke my ego."

Jessie laughed. "You're right. I don't." Although she did have all the feelings he'd admitted to. She just wasn't ready to share those emotions. Her heart was still too raw; her pride wanted conviction that Zach wanted her, really wanted her.

For her children, she wanted to know that this man wouldn't change his mind on her, the way her ex had, and it seemed smart to make certain she was making a responsible choice.

"You're going to like being married to me, Jesssie."

"I am?" She raised a brow.

"Yes." He nodded. "We just need to make a covenant between us."

"Like what?"

"We agreed on a marriage compromise. I wanted the children to have my name, and be able to grow up in Tulips without everyone knowing they were the kids whose parents couldn't get their act together. And you wanted a trial period since we don't know each other."

"This is all very sensible," Jessie said, feeling very good about being orderly about her life for once. "Except I don't remember us covering the part about the children living in Tulips. My parents would be crushed, I think."

Zach was quiet for a moment. "I hadn't considered the parent factor. I need to meet your parents before we get married, even if it is only temporary."

Jessie hesitated. Zach in her world would likely not be a good thing. He'd already met her brothers, if that painful meeting could be called an introduction.

"Don't tell me. Your parents feel the same way your brothers do."

"I will admit that they're not exactly thrilled. They don't know you, and…"

"And I'm not from their social circle." He took his hand from her leg and put it on the steering wheel. "Maybe we're heading in the wrong direction."

"No. We're on the road to Las Vegas and the Elvis impersonator you said you wanted to marry us."

Zach shook his head. "We need to head to your folks, Jessie. It would be bad manners on my part not to ask your father for your hand in marriage."

Stunned, Jessie blinked away tears that rose unexpectedly. It was very sweet of Zach, very gentlemanly, to say such a thing. The veneer of realness he was trying to put on their situation stole her breath, and more significantly, pieces of her heart.

It was too much, too soon, after her recent breakup.

"Zach, I'd rather elope," she said quietly.

"Tell me why."

"It's hard to put into words—"

"Not really. I'm a guy who likes plain words and reasoning. Be honest about what you're thinking."

Be honest. Her whole career was spent on making things pretty, showing anything unflattering in the best possible light. "My parents were crazy about—"

"Yes, yes. Okay. The guy you left at the altar was their kind."

"I didn't exactly leave him," Jessie said. "I had a choice. He was having an affair with a woman from a rival firm. I could have glossed it over and married him and hoped for the best. But covering up my feelings isn't as easy as covering up scars, stretch marks and blemishes." She looked at him. "My parents advised me to marry him, that the affair was wedding nerves."

"No," Zach said quietly. "It was a guy being a jerk, wanting to have his cake and eat it, too, and getting away with it pretty well."

"That's what I thought," Jessie said happily, pulling out a bag of pretzels for them to share and cracking open a Coke for him and a bottle of orange juice for her. "So it seemed much more sensible to me to live through the humiliation of calling off a wedding."

"I like your sensible side."

"Which is why you have to listen to me about my parents. They're not going to like you. They're just kind of that way."

"Why? Because I won't sleep with your rivals, girlfriends or anyone else while we're married?"

She blinked. "Would you want to?"

"Hell, no. Why would I, when I've got you?"

"Are you perfect?" Jessie asked. "I have to tell you, I keep looking for your flaws, and you're annoyingly short of them."

"No, I'm not," Zach said. "I told you, the men

in our town live by the reputation of our sins. Remember that conversation?"

"Yes," Jessie said, "but I'm starting to not believe you."

"Trust me, you'll find plenty about me that is imperfect."

"Good. I'm much more enthralled by imperfect these days. It's safer."

"What's your parents' address?"

Jessie sighed. "You're right. You're not perfect."

She could see him grinning widely by the lights of passing cars. "We'll be needing an airport."

"I like driving. We can get to anywhere."

"We can't get to Bermuda in this mode of transportation," Jessie pointed out.

"No, we can't," Zach said. "I'll be the first man in Tulips who had to go out of the country to meet a bride's parents."

"Are you okay with that?"

"Yes, except I'm not a good flier."

She laughed. "That's why my parents gave me this wonderful car. I drive just about everywhere I can. I like to see the countryside, and I like to meet people."

"Okay." Zach nodded. "So we could get married in Bermuda, I guess."

"No. That's the one thing you have to promise me. We do this temporarily, with no pomp and circumstance, just like we planned, after you meet my parents."

"I agree," Zach said, "only because I want the mother of my children to be happy."

"Thank you." Jessie pulled her phone from her purse. "Where's the nearest airport?"

"We're approximately one hour east of Dallas. So I would say DFW."

She dialed numbers on her phone. "Hi, Mom. Yes, everything's fine. I'd like to bring someone home to meet you. That sounds wonderful. Thank you. Yes, I love you, too. Tell Daddy I love him." She hung up and looked at Zach. "My brothers had business in Dallas that they attended to, so the company plane is still at the airport. They're going to hold it for us."

"So I'm going to be flying on the same private plane with your brothers?" Zach asked.

She smiled. "You asked to meet my parents."

"Yes, I did. And I'm looking forward to it."

"I have to warn you, they're a little frosty at first. Definitely not as warm as the people of Tulips. But they'll be on their best behavior."

Zach grinned and didn't say a word as he turned

the car around. Jessie looked out the window, thinking that surely, on the road to the altar, the second time was a charm.

"MOTHER, FATHER, this is Zach Forrester," Jessie said to her parents, who stood tall and elegant in the doorway of their Bermuda home.

Zach had survived the plane trip with Jessie's two brothers without incident. He didn't care what they thought about him. But that was the easy part. He did want Jessie's parents to like him. Deep inside, he knew she was the girl for him.

Her parents didn't look so convinced.

"Hello, Zach," Mrs. Farnsworth said. Mr. Farnsworth merely nodded.

They weren't snobby, Zach decided, merely unhappy and perhaps surprised by the turn of events. He could understand that, so he gave them a chance to warm up to him.

They never did. Dinner was a quiet affair. He was seated across from Jessie at the table, though that was fine because he could enjoy looking at her. She'd dressed a little fancy for dinner, in a red dress with cleavage and glittering diamond earrings. He had only one change of clothes with him, since they'd planned on going to Vegas.

Jeans had probably never been worn to dinner at this table.

The brothers ignored him, as they had on the plane.

He shrugged all that off. Whether they liked it or not, they were going to be family for the rest of their lives. Like a bucking bronc, he would let them have their head until they calmed down. If the shock ever wore off and they did ease up, he'd be the first to extend a hand of friendship.

"What do you do, Zach?" Mrs. Farnsworth asked.

"A lot of ranching, mostly. My ranch is in a small town in Texas called Tulips."

"Jessie, I can't imagine what you were doing there," her mother said. "Did you take a wrong turn?"

"I think…I took the right turn for me," Jessie said, and Zach gave her a smile.

Mrs. Farnsworth laid down her fork, all pretense at gentility evaporating. "I just don't understand how this happened. How could you have gotten our daughter pregnant? She doesn't even know you. We don't know you. For heaven's sakes, Jessie, this man could be a…a—"

"Mother," Jessie said. "I'm going to go lie down. It's been a long day."

They all stood. Zach looked at Jessie, worried.

"May will take you to your room, Zach," Mrs. Farnsworth said. "The driver will take you back to the airport in the morning at eight o'clock."

All of Jessie's family merely stared at him silently. Zach realized he'd been dismissed.

"The driver will be taking me and Jessie to the airport," he said, his voice measured and quiet. "We're getting married. I came here to ask you for your daughter's hand in marriage, sir. Whether or not you give it willingly, I suppose, is up to you." He nodded to them and followed May down the hall with a last look at Jessie.

She'd turned very pale, a startling contrast to her red gown.

He closed the door, looked around the well-appointed room and sighed before pulling his boots off and sitting down in a chair to think.

IN THE NIGHT, Zach heard his bedroom door open. Squinting at his watch, he saw it was two o'clock in the morning. He lay very still, waiting to see who his visitor was.

The person quietly closed the door, then crept to the king-size bed. Luckily for him, he'd chosen to sleep on the side farthest from the door. He held his breath.

Whoever it was had a sincere lack of courage. They, too, seemed to be holding their breath.

He felt his blanket turn back, then something soft and warm slipped into the bed next to him.

Jessie.

"Zach," she whispered.

He felt his heart speed up. If her parents caught her in here with him, there'd be bad feelings for years. Maybe he should just fake sleeping, for her sake, and then she'd go away.

She slid up against him, curling her head against his chest. "Zach," she whispered, "Bermuda is a wonderful place to spend Christmas."

Chapter Twelve

Zach rolled over on her, pinning her beneath him. Surprised, she shivered.

"Are you asking, making a comment or have you been set up to lure me to stay here?"

"All of the above," she whispered.

"No," he said, kissing her. "We're sticking to the original plan. I don't like your folks, and they don't like me, and you knew that's exactly what would happen. I've done the right thing by meeting your father and asking for your hand. I never said I cared whether he gave me his blessing or not. Now we move on to Vegas, and then home sweet home to Tulips."

He kissed her hard and then softly, enjoying her lips and making her want him. She ran her hands along his back, shocked to find him naked.

"You have one last chance to run out of here, little Red Riding Hood," he said. "If you stay, we're really going to shock your family. I promise."

A shudder of delight tingled her body. "You're crazy."

"Yes, I am. You knew that about me, so there's been no surprises from my side. You, on the other hand, didn't exactly tell me your situation."

"I told you we were from different worlds."

"And luckily, you fit my world just fine, because that's where we'll be spending our time."

Jessie pulled him close. "Let's not talk about plans for the future right now."

He nipped at her lower lip gently. "Your brothers could rush in here any minute, determined to shoot me for dishonoring their sister in their home, and you don't want me tying you down?"

Jessie giggled. "My brothers aren't that bad." He was kissing down her neck to her chest, making her crave him even more. "Are you going to make love to me?"

"I can't decide. It would probably pale next to doing it in the back of your car in the open air under the sun. It's so stuffy in this house, I feel like I'm in a cage."

"It's not stuffy. It's—"

"I don't do stuffy, and neither do you, Jessie, which explains why you live out of a carpetbag, drive a convertible and stay on the road most of the time."

She went still. "I never thought of it that way."

"Because they kept you busy with a promotion? An atta-girl for staying in the family fold?"

"No, I really am good at what I do."

"I believe that. I just don't think you need all the family props to be what you are."

She pushed him off her. "What are you saying?"

"I'm saying you don't have to let them send you in here to plead their case for them."

"True." She sat beside him, and he knew she was staring down at him. "We have a lot to talk about."

He pulled her down next to him and held her tight. "We're going to shock May in the morning when she finds you in here. That'll be my answer to your parents—nothing is separating us. Not them, not the meatheads playing rough, which they didn't do very well, I'll have to say. I got hit harder on the playground."

"I must have missed your stubborn, determined side."

"Then you missed my best side," he said, kissing

her neck. "One day, Jessica Tomball Farnsworth, you're going to be glad my bull stopped your car from its speeding path to nowhere."

She pinched him. "My life has not been nowhere."

He grunted. "If you pinch me again, I'm going to take that as a call of the wild to make love to you."

"You could, you know."

"I could. But I'm not going to because we're not married yet, and I don't want you to want me just for sex. Now don't beg anymore, it's not ladylike."

She gave a backwards kick, hitting him squarely on his leg, but he just tugged her up against him closely so that she lay in the crook of his body. There was warmth, and hardness and affection wrapped all around her, it was giving and not taking, so Jessie closed her eyes.

This one is different.

In the morning, Zach and Jessie stood on the tarmac, preparing to board the Farnsworth jet.

"You need to be here for the holidays," her mother said.

"You need me to be here?" Jessie asked. "If last night was any indication of how happy the holidays would be around here, I'd be better off somewhere else." She hugged her mother. "Good-bye, Mom."

"We invited him," her father said as she hugged him.

"This isn't about you," Jessie said. "It's about me and Zach, and the life we're building together. So far, my brothers have punched him and you've treated him like he's committed a crime, when all he wanted was to come here and show you respect. I'm lucky he's still talking to me. Goodbye, Daddy."

"We'll come to the wedding," her mother said, but Jessie shook her head.

"It's better this way. We're having an Elvis impersonator officiate, and I don't think you'd be comfortable, Mother."

Her parents looked stricken. Jessie gave them a soothing smile. "It's going to be all right. It really is. This is going to turn out so much better than the future I had planned."

"But what kind of future do you have planned? Have you thought about anything beyond the children?" her father protested.

Jessie looked at Zach. "Not really. But that's the way we've planned our marriage, so we'd call that a success."

Zach helped her onto the jet. "Are you all right?"

"Yes," Jessie said, turning around to wave goodbye to her family. "I feel strangely grateful to you."

"Always a good thing," Zach said happily. "What do they serve on this flying turkey? I'm starved."

Jessie shook her head. "Just about anything you want. Ask."

"I could get used to traveling like this. Maybe I'll let my wife keep her job."

Jessie smiled. "Maybe I'll let my husband keep his."

Zach bit into an apple. "You make more money than me?"

Jessie laughed. "Money's not important in our relationship. We have enough issues to work out."

"Can this jet take us straight to Vegas?" Zach asked. "There's a woman I'm in a hurry to marry."

She blinked. "I never thought about it, but yes."

He tossed his apple core into a bag and leaned his head back, closing his eyes. "I feel like a kid on Christmas morning. I'll have a wife by sundown."

Jessie put her head back and closed her eyes, too, deciding napping was a good idea. She needed time to conceptualize actually becoming a bride. Not wanting to hurt Zach's feelings, she hadn't let on to how much her parents' disapproval bothered her. They were right: there was no future in their marriage. It was planned to be short and sweet.

Something inside her felt uneasy about that. A vague tickling of disappointment, and perhaps concern, made her stomach slightly nervous. "Oh. My father sent this along for you." She handed Zach a large brown envelope.

"What is it?"

"I have no idea."

He opened it, his face studious. "Papers signing away any rights to Farnsworth properties, businesses, monies, etc., etc."

Her heart stilled in her chest as Zach continued reading.

With a shrug, he pulled a pen from his jacket pocket and signed the documents. Shoving them back inside the envelope, he handed it to her and promptly went back to sleep.

Jessie's jaw went slack. He could have no idea he'd just signed a prenup that excluded him from millions of dollars. She stared at the envelope in her hands. A great part of her wanted to tear it to shreds; the other sensible part of her knew that her parents were being careful.

Zach didn't care about money at all. And while part of her admired his lack of fiscal greed, she knew he was merely sticking to their agreement to divorce after the birth of the twins.

He appeared to be completely prepared to keep his side of the bargain, which worried her more than made her happy—a surprising shift in her emotions, warning of a heart that might be broken a second time.

Jessie closed her eyes and tried not to think about Zach not feeling the same way about her as she was beginning to feel about him.

THE WEDDING was going to be short and sweet. They didn't have an Elvis impersonator because Zach had never really intended to do that. But he was aware Jessie might spook easily, so he'd fed her that story to make her try to see the marital mission in a light way.

This was a bride he intended to keep at the altar, and he'd learned the hard way by watching his brother's pain. Plus, he knew Jessie had a running streak in her, and after meeting her family, he sensed a reason for her to be headstrong.

"This is a good thing," he told her, gazing down at her as they stood in the chapel.

"I know." Jessie nodded.

"You can trust me," Zach said. "You're going to like living in Tulips."

Jessie shook her head. "I'm not living in Tulips."

The minister cleared his throat. "Are we ready?"

They stared at each other.

"We'll work it all out," Zach said. "Beyond the babies, everything else is just details."

"Major details." Jessie blinked back sudden tears, and Zach feared he might be losing her.

"Get a move on, sir," he said. "My bride suffers from cold feet. I intend to keep them warm for her."

The minister smiled. "We love a quick wedding in Vegas, but we also understand if you need a moment to collect yourself, young lady."

Jessie shook her head. "I'm all right. Thank you."

The minister cleared his throat, saying a lot of words Zach didn't hear, but what he did hear was Jessie's soft voice saying, "I do."

They were the sweetest two words he'd ever heard.

He kissed her to seal the deal.

But it was more than a deal, and his heart kicked hard in his chest to remind him of that. He was never going to get over falling for Jessie.

It was up to him to convince her.

THE MOMENTARY FEAR gripping Jessie as she stood beside Zach at the altar wouldn't go away. Even when the minister asked her if she needed a moment to collect herself, Jessie knew a moment wouldn't be enough to do the job. Considering what her family had put Zach through, she was surprised he still wanted her. This was not a man who was going to fall into another set of arms. He wasn't going to leave her. He'd said that in the beginning, and he was clearly a man of his word.

They flew back to Dallas in silence. Zach stared out one window of the jet, and she wondered about the man she'd married. Zach would never have wanted to marry her if she hadn't been pregnant, and that thought bothered her more than anything.

Her parents' worries worked in her mind.

Unconsciously, she touched her stomach, and the reasons why her life was changing much faster than it ever had before. "Beyond organic," she said, "another way to grow Tulips might be fish."

Zach turned to stare at her. "You have me hooked."

An unwilling smile tugged at her lips. "Impressed as I am by your clever repartee, I'm putting forth a genuine idea which may not be as good as building an elementary school, but one which draws men."

"Fish."

She nodded. "Fishing and needlepoint are two of life's most rewarding activities, as well as its greatest frustrations. Both require patience."

"We have little of that in Tulips, I'll warn you."

"In a town overpopulated by women? I doubt that."

He shook his head. "Please outline your plan for me."

"A Great Catch contest. Give away a fabulous prize for the biggest fish caught on the nearest lake. The twist is, every gentleman who enters has to take on board his boat one woman from Tulips to teach her to fish. She must be the one who catches the fish, down to putting the worm on the hook."

"That's almost cruel, and yet somehow genius," Zach said.

Jessie leaned her head back and closed her eyes. "That night, we have a fish fry on our land. Notice I said *our* land."

"I did, and I'm shocked." Zach shook his head. "The council of elders is going to give you a key to the city for that idea."

Jessie smiled to herself. All she needed was a key to Zach's heart. She'd leave the baiting and casting to the other ladies—she'd caught the man she wanted, at least for the next few months.

His approval warmed her and gave her hope for their coming family of four.

Chapter Thirteen

Four hours later, Zach took Jessie into his house, realizing they hadn't discussed sleeping arrangements. Setting down the suitcase she'd brought from the plane, he looked at his new bride. "Excuse me." Lifting her up, he went back out the door and carried her over the threshold.

"Nice," she said. "That was smooth, even for you."

"Just making sure I observe all the traditions. We're into traditions here."

She walked over to the Christmas tree. "I'll help you finish decorating this tomorrow. You never got past the candy canes."

"And no one else is going to do it, that's for sure." Zach shook his head. "I'll take the help, gladly. I suppose we should also discuss sleeping arrangements."

Jessie didn't look at him. "We can discuss it."

"I liked the one we had last night."

She turned to him. "The one where I sneak into your bed in the middle of the night?"

"That would work. Or you could start out there. It's up to you. We're married now, and I could even offer you the benefits of marriage."

She seemed embarrassed, and he liked it when she blushed.

"Do you realize we're a week from Christmas?" he asked softly. "And I've already gotten the best gift in the world." With one finger, he reached out to gently touch her hair.

"Sometimes your intensity is…unnerving."

A slow grin curved his mouth. "Ever since I met you, I've felt unnerved. This is not like me."

"I believe you." She hesitated. "When we agreed on a temporary marriage, it made sense to me to have the children born with your name. Not illegitimate."

He frowned. "It made more than sense. It was the only thing to do."

"I agree," she said quickly. "But if we share a marriage bed, it's going to feel a lot more real. Intimate. Not like we had an agreement."

"I see your point." He looked at her. "This thought must have occurred to you last night."

She nodded.

Holding her had been very intimate. He'd liked it. He'd held her as tight and close as he could— all night. "And you're not ready for that."

"It's hard when we barely know each other. And this time that we're married is our getting-to-know-each-other trial period."

"I do like sticking to agreements," Zach said. "A man is only as good as his word."

"It's more than an agreement. It's necessary. Everything about us is completely opposite."

"I hear your parents talking," he murmured.

"Maybe," she admitted. "They're a bit on the cool side, but they want me to be happy in the end."

"So do I." Zach nodded. "All right. Separate rooms it is, mother of my twins."

She stared at him. "Zach, I'm not going to say that my family was cordial with you. I'm embarrassed that they sent a prenup for you to sign." Uncertainty crossed her face, shadowing her eyes. "All the same, I'd like to thank you for understanding them."

They looked at each other for a long moment

before Zach shrugged. "I really couldn't care less about them or their money. I'm only interested in you."

She didn't say anything. There was nothing left to say. So he picked up her bag and carried it down the hall to a guest room. "You'll find everything you need in there. My room's upstairs, so…"

He'd been about to say "we basically have our own separate apartments," but the stricken look on her face stopped him. "So make yourself at home," he finished.

"Thank you," she said.

Nodding, he left her to settle in.

THEY WERE MOVING too fast. Zach recognized that. Or at least he was moving too fast to suit Jessie. If he were in her shoes, he'd probably feel the same, and since the goal was to keep her from freaking out, he'd decided to head upstairs to his bachelor bed.

They'd bought plain gold bands in Vegas. He thought that was the right decision, since she was determined to keep their marriage temporary. Diamonds would have said "I love you" and he didn't want to say anything she didn't want to hear.

There was nothing worse than someone forcing

emotions on a person that they didn't want to know about.

He'd have to wait to romance her. The two of them were alone in the house, so if he was patient, maybe he'd get a signal that she was beginning to feel secure in what they meant to each other.

Until then, he was going to be one hot and bothered cowboy.

THE NEXT DAY, Zach met Jessie at the breakfast table. Surprised, he saw that she'd set out two plates, each piled with eggs, bacon and steaming hot biscuits.

"Hungry?" she asked.

"Of course." Zach shook his head. "Did you do this because you like to cook or because you felt you had to?"

She turned to look at him, putting down the skillet she'd been drying. "Because I never get to cook."

"Oh," he said, sitting down to dig in. "Because I was hoping you were going to say 'I did it because I thought you'd like it,' and then I could say something manly like, 'Oh, you don't need to do that for me. I can cook for myself.'"

She raised a brow at him. "Can you?"

"Yes. Not as good as this, though." He began to shovel the food. "Much better than mine."

"I wouldn't have thought you were the kind of guy who could cook." She sat across from him.

"I can. Outdoors, indoors, it doesn't matter. I can gut a deer and get the venison ready for— Jessie, what's wrong?" He watched as she slipped from the room, putting down his fork in concern. The powder room door closed quickly, and he could hear Jessie being ill.

What to do now? If it were him, his mother would have offered him a cold cloth, or something, but he didn't know what to do except wait.

His stomach churned with worry.

A few moments later, she headed outside. He found her sitting on the porch. "Are you all right?"

"I am now. I shouldn't have cooked breakfast, I think. The bacon did it for me, and then, the story about the deer. I am a city girl, you know. I'm not going to be able to, you know."

"Oh, the g-word."

"Right. Some wives might be good with that, but I'm not going to be able to handle that stuff."

He reached to hold her hand, which was somewhat clammy. "I'm sorry. I've never known a pregnant woman before, except Liberty, and none of us knew much about her pregnancy until the very end."

"I'll probably stick to plain eggs from now on." She managed a wan smile.

"No, I'll cook breakfast," he said quickly. "Being ill like that can't be good for my children."

She leaned her head against his shoulder. "I always think I can keep going and going and never slow down. That's the first time I've been nauseated."

"Ugh, don't do it again," Zach said, his voice sympathetic. "I could cut fruit for breakfast."

"Fruit is my favorite," she said.

"Are you all right now?"

"I'm fine. Thank you."

An awkward moment passed between them. He desperately wanted to comfort her, and hold her, tell her she looked beautiful, tell her he was so excited that she was having his children—but he didn't know how she'd take that. He'd always heard pregnant women needed to be treated with care—that they could be *moody*. He wanted to avoid an argument. "Thank you for breakfast. Next time, my turn."

She smiled, relieved. "I plan to take you up on that."

"So, maybe dinner could be your thing. Something light. And I'll make you Pop-Tarts for breakfast. Or doughnuts. Fruit. Bagels. No cooking smells, maybe."

She nodded.

"All right," he said, glad they'd settled that for the moment. "I'm going out for a while."

"So am I."

He wanted to ask her where. His heart began pounding with concern, and he had to tell himself that they'd made an agreement and she would stick to it. "Let me know if you need anything," he said, heading outside.

He was living for the day when he could kiss her goodbye, like he wanted to do so badly. Although if he had his way, the goodbye kiss would last forever and move from the hallway to the bedroom.

I'm starting to scare myself.

"I've got to go see the council of elders," Zach said to himself. "I definitely need help on many levels."

JESSIE TIDIED UP, slightly embarrassed that she'd gotten ill in front of Zach. That's what she got for showing off, trying to be the good guest, the good wife-in-trial. She'd known her stomach had been queasy but put it down to wedding nerves. Relationship nerves.

It had definitely not been a Jessie's Girl Stuff-ready moment. For a woman used to making everything beautiful, she'd certainly been making messes.

Zach didn't seem to mind.

"I need help with this," she told herself, "before I make the biggest mess of my life." Packing her carpetbag, she left the house and hopped in her T-bird.

Twenty minutes later she was peeking through the windows of the Tulips Saloon. Shocked, she saw Zach was inside, talking to a woman she'd never seen. Having tea.

Backing away from the window, her heart pounding, she got back in her car, glancing around to make certain no one had seen her spying through the glass. She was chilled, and it wasn't because of the cold air blowing through the square. *Decorations,* she thought randomly, *the square would look so much better with Christmas decorations.*

"Stop," she said to herself. No more prettying things up. No more faking it. No more smiling when she felt sad or worried.

She got out of the car and walked inside the saloon.

Zach's face broke into a smile when he saw her. "Jessie, come meet Valentine Jefferson."

Jessie moved forward, putting a smile on her face.

"This is my wife, Jessie Forrester," Zach said,

and Jessie's skin jumped. Forrester. She'd almost forgotten.

"It's so nice to meet you," Valentine said. "I've heard so much about you, I feel as though you're my sister."

Jessie relaxed, and gave her a genuine smile. "Thank you."

"So you caught him," Valentine said. "Actually, I know better than that. The Forrester men remind me of the Jefferson boys in Union Junction. *He* caught *you.*"

"I did," Zach said, "and I'm keeping her, too."

Valentine smiled. "I can't believe Pansy and Helen let you get away with an elopement."

"That's what elopements are for," Zach said happily. "Not asking anyone's permission and getting the deed done quick."

Jessie blinked. "It's nice to meet you, Valentine. I'm looking for Helen and Pansy, actually."

"They're in the kitchen." Zach leaned back. "Valentine brought a load of new cookies over for them to try, and they're inspecting her wares."

"I will, too, then. Sounds delicious." She smiled at Valentine and walked into the kitchen, trying not to panic at the thought of Zach talking to the beautiful redhead.

Pansy and Helen rushed over to hug her. "Congratulations!" Pansy said, while Helen said, "You're a daughter of Tulips now!"

"You look beautiful," Pansy said, and Helen said, "Glowing," and they began talking all at once so that nothing was really reaching Jessie except their happiness. She let herself bask in it for a moment before saying, "I need help."

They stopped chattering instantly.

"Anything," Helen said, and Pansy nodded.

"You two are the only ones I can ask," Jessie said. "I need to save my marriage. Before I totally screw it up."

Chapter Fourteen

Helen, Pansy and Jessie sat down at a small table in the kitchen. "I would have voted you Most Likely To Succeed, Jessie," Helen said. "Zach seems very happy to me."

Pansy nodded.

"It's the babies," she said. "I think our marriage should probably be based on more than that to make him happy. And I'm kind of nervous. I don't really know him."

"No, you don't," Pansy said. "But you have to understand, Zach can't stand to be bored. What you two did is something he relishes. It's that different-from-my-brother thing that makes him feel like a maverick."

"Not to mention he tied you down in one," Helen said practically. "Duke had to go to the altar twice to win Liberty. That probably feels very good to Zach."

Jessie took a deep breath. "We have fundamental differences, and I've always known that even makeup required a good foundation or everything on top cracked."

Helen nodded. "You're savvy, I'll give you that."

"Men do thrive on effort of the right sort," Pansy agreed. "We're not exactly short on answers, believe it or not. We do have more in our arsenal besides platitudes."

"True," Helen said. "Let me look through the recipe box." She dusted some flour off an old recipe box, and Jessie shook her head.

"I threw up when I cooked for Zach this morning. I was trying to be so…housewifey or something, and I cooked and then sort of ruined the effect," Jessie said miserably. "It's embarrassing to throw up on your first day as a newlywed."

Pansy and Helen stared at her over their spectacles. Then they glanced at each other before looking back at Jessie.

"No more cooking, dear," Helen said. "Men aren't good with moments of female gastric distress."

"Yes." Pansy nodded her head. "They want to believe we're always dainty, bouncy and ready to hop naked into a bed, stream or back seat, which-ever place they happen to be at the moment the call of the wild hits them."

Helen and Jessie gazed at Pansy in silence.

"Well," Helen said, "let's just stick with you not cooking anymore for a while." She closed the recipe box. "We're going to need a little time to work on this, Jessie, but we promise we know how to help you. Don't worry about a thing."

"Yes. Although we gave up on giving advice a long time ago, we may have a recipe that's appro-priate for your situation."

Jessie stood. "Thank you for listening. I feel better already."

Pansy and Helen hugged her goodbye. "Don't worry about a thing. We're just glad you're part of our town now."

Jessie left the kitchen, truly feeling better. Zach passed her on the way into the kitchen.

"I'm going to snatch one of those fresh cookies," he said.

She replied, "They're delicious, see you later," and kept on walking until she reached her car and drove away without anybody seeing the worry in her eyes.

She didn't need a recipe. For the first time in her

life, she needed a map—one that would point her in the direction of lasting love.

"COOKIES," Zach said, walking into the kitchen. "Be still my heart."

Pansy smiled at him. "Your heart has always been drawn to sweet things."

"Jessie's pretty sweet," Helen said, and Zach nodded.

"She's a honey," he agreed, "and I just want to—"

"Congratulations again on your wedding," Helen said quickly. "I'm sure you were a handsome groom."

Zach shook his head, biting into a powdered chocolate crinkle. "Mmm. That is so good! I love Christmas. There's no time of year that the cooking is better." He gazed with delight over the trays of frosted reindeers, painted snowmen and sugared trees. "Are we having chocolate pecans this year? Or fudge?"

Helen began placing red hots on gingerbread men for buttons. "Just be glad for what we've got."

"Speaking of what we've got, Jessie had an awesome idea for a catch-and-release for men." Zach licked his fingers. "I think that's what she called it."

Helen looked at him. "Jessie thinks a lot, doesn't she? I don't believe I would have guessed she was a thinker when I first met her, but she really is."

"Yep," Zach said proudly. "Just when you think she's not thinking, she comes up with something I can't believe she'd think."

"Try to say that again," Pansy murmured, "if you *think* you can." She giggled.

"Okay," Zach said, settling into a chair, "so I was bragging a bit about her. But she's really special."

They smiled at him.

"Actually, I didn't come in here just to snitch cookies." Rubbing his chin, he pondered how to approach his two best Dear Abbys. "You know, Mom and Dad were happily married."

They nodded.

"Very stable. Real good parents. I want that for my kids, and for Jessie and me," he said. "But Jessie and I started our relationship so fast that now we're trying to slow it down, and it feels unnatural. I keep thinking Mom and Dad didn't seem to have any speeds, just an even keel of harmony and love and respect."

"Well," Helen said, "they were of similar backgrounds and goals."

"Yeah," Zach said, "I know the scales on my marriage are tipped toward short, and I want them to weigh in more toward long-term."

"I have to admit I didn't think Jessie was right for you in the beginning," Helen said. "She has certainly proven herself to be a wonderful young woman that Tulips can be proud to call its own."

"Yes. You were lucky," Pansy said, "in spite of her hitting poor Brahma Bud."

"Oh, Bud," Zach said. "She barely tapped him, and he barely noticed. How hard she's hit me is a whole other story, though."

Helen and Pansy gazed at him for a long time, gentle smiles on their faces.

"This from a western romance writer," Helen said with a sweet smile. "I thought you'd have all the answers."

Zach stared at his two dearest friends. "How'd you know?"

They giggled. "While you were gone with Jessie, two beautiful women stopped in on the way to your house. Naturally, we inquired."

"I'm afraid they told us your secret," Pansy said, not sorry at all, "and they left us something to give you." She pulled out a brown envelope. "We've been waiting for you to return so we could ask your permission to read it," she said hopefully.

"You haven't already?" he asked.

"Of course not!" Pansy exclaimed. "We're not busybodies!"

Zach laughed. "Tell you what—you can read my work-in-progress if you help me win Jessie for good. I really want her to be happy, and I sincerely do not want to screw this up."

"Now where have I heard that?" Helen asked, looking at Pansy with a grin.

"We'll need time to think about it," Pansy said. "Our best ideas come to us over tea." She put his manuscript in the drawer. "Although we don't think you need us. Any man brave enough to write a book is brave enough to win a woman's heart."

"But I want Jessie's," Zach said, "and that's a puzzle."

"We like puzzles," Helen said. "We'll get right on it."

They gave him a gentle shove toward the door, so Zach grabbed a couple of snowmen and reindeer and left the saloon.

It was Christmas, for Pete's sake. Surely there was one miracle with his name written on it.

Chapter Fifteen

That night Jessie walked into the barn to look for Zach. As much as it felt like Tulips was her home now, she and Zach had agreed to divorce following the babies' birth, and she had an international company to run.

She supposed she could always move her offices here, and she was essentially on break for the holidays. There would be plenty of time to look for a house.

Yet, she wondered if she'd ever really be a town girl at heart.

The air inside the barn was hazy, a strange type of smoky. Jessie held her breath, not wanting to breathe the smell. "Zach?"

"Back here," he called.

Some of the alarm ebbed out of her system at

the sound of his voice. "I didn't know if something was on fire or someone was smoking pot. It smells terrible."

Zach turned around. He'd been soothing a horse as another man worked on its hooves. "Pot? Does it smell like pot?"

"Well, pretty much," Jessie said. "I'm sure it's not healthy to breathe for long."

"It's the farrier. He's trimming the horses' hooves. It's got to be done every once in a while." Zach squinted at her through the dusty acridness. "Never thought about the smell of it before."

"Yeesh," Jessie said. "It doesn't quite have the aroma of Pansy's and Helen's bakery."

"You're right." Zach took her arm and walked her from the barn. "I forget what a sensitive city critter you are."

"I'm not!" she exclaimed, tugging her arm away. "Anybody would say that hoof business is stinky—you're just being stubborn."

"Calm down," he said calmly, rubbing her back. "All that upset isn't good for my babies. Not to mention they shouldn't know that their mother knows anything about marijuana."

"I don't personally," Jessie said, annoyed. "It's just there are some things one comes across at parties and concerts. But I wouldn't know it if I saw it."

"Well, I do," Zach said as he pulled Jessie down into his lap on a bench outside the barn. "Duke, Holt, Liberty and I got some weed from a high school friend who was growing it in his back forty where his parents wouldn't find his plants. We thought we were so cool, sneaking a smoke out where no one could see us, nothing around us but blue sky and dry grass. Liberty couldn't smoke worth a damn, and truthfully, I don't think she tried very hard. Holt had a coughing fit, and he didn't get more than a puff. Me and Duke, though, had to show off and act like we could smoke when we couldn't, and we ended up blowing out more than we took in. You wouldn't have thought being outdoors the smoke would cling to our clothes, but it did, and Mom smelled it."

"Uh-oh," Jessie said. "How'd she know what it was?"

Zach smiled at the memory. "Mom wasn't interested in what kind of smoke it was. It was smoke, and her kids had been out doing it, and we got the hidin' of our lives from Dad. Later on, the whole story came out, since Holt went home so sick. His parents told mine what we'd really been doing, and the folks grounded us off riding for three months. We also had to paint every building in the town square a fresh coat of paint over our summer vacation. That was a hardship," Zach said, shaking his head. "No swimming in the pond, no vacation, no nothing. Just paint, paint and more paint. Mom said if we wanted to be around stuff that would make our brains funny, we could get funny and do some good at the same time."

"Wow. I would have liked your mom," Jessie said.

He nodded. "If I'd known you then, I wouldn't have gotten in as much trouble, though."

She crooked her brow. "Why?"

"I would have known to say that the farrier had been out where I'd been, and that's what the smell was." He ran a hand through her long hair. "I wish I'd known you then, Jessie T."

"No," Jessie said. "Lying to your mother would have made you a dishonest person. Remember, you're already known to make a situation suit you when necessary."

"Now, Jessie," he said, "you've got to quit being mad about that. Not to mention, you're the one who makes ugly things pretty. Is that lying to a man if a woman's beauty comes out of a bottle? Isn't that trickery? The poor fellow thinks he's getting a show horse, then one night, he surprises his lady in the bathroom and discovers what he really got was a rack pony."

Jessie slapped him on the hand. "You're supposed to see my inner goodness no matter what."

"I do," he said. "I don't like the fakery and tricks women weave."

"*Pfft.* Zach Forrester, when some men say it's raining, a woman has to look outside to see if he's telling the truth."

Getting up, he tugged her toward the house.

"What are you doing?"

"I'm taking you inside and giving you a spanking," Zach said.

She pulled back. "Like hell."

He laughed. "I'm teasing. It's time to make your dinner. I can tell you get upset on an empty stomach, and I don't want my children going hungry."

"Stop." She dug in her heels so that their hands slipped apart. "Zach, I'm sorry, but it's either me or the children, as strange as that sounds."

A frown hovered on his handsome face. "Meaning?"

"You can't romance all three of us. We're not a family yet, and I...I need to feel like you and I have something in common besides parenthood."

He blinked. "We have nothing in common."

Ouch. "Okay. Then we need to find something. Before the children are born. Otherwise, I'm going to feel like one of your—" She stretched a hand out to encompass the barns and fields. "I don't know the proper word for female mother horse."

"Mare."

She looked at him, her hands on her hips. For the first time, she realized how important it was that they had some kind of connection that went beyond their pregnancy.

He stepped toward her, his eyes suddenly dark with a look she'd never seen before. "Zach?"

He kissed her slow and hot, his hands framing her face as he completely possessed her lips. Her soul seemed to melt inside her. Everything up to that moment between them had been fun and lighthearted. But not this kiss. He went for her heart and her fears and her secrets, and when he finally broke away from her to stare down into her eyes, Jessie had very little reserves left to challenge him.

"You," he said. "It's you."

Her fingers went to her lips, unconsciously touching the skin he'd set on fire.

"I'm done," the farrier called. "Is that the last one, or have you got more in the field?"

Zach gave her one last, silent look before striding toward the barns. Shaken, Jessie went inside the house, torn between happiness and being nervous. She'd never felt any of this with the man she might have married, and it was confusing that she hadn't.

She might have married a man who didn't make her knees tremble and her heart beat crazily fast. Was it a good sign that a man could make her feel this way with one kiss—or were her parents correct in believing that she'd lost her normal good common sense?

On the kitchen counter lay two pieces of mail: one, a brown envelope addressed to Zach in a flowing script. It appeared to have no postage. The other was a FedEx envelope addressed to her. She recognized Fran's handwriting on the label.

Wondering what business her secretary and best friend might have needed to forward to her that she couldn't have called her about, Jessie tore open the mailer. Inside was a white envelope addressed in her father's strong handwriting. She tore that open, finding a letter and an official document.

Jessie,
We know you're on your honeymoon or we would have called you about this, and yet a

simple phone call would not have sufficed. Given the circumstances of your recent decision to wed someone unknown to the family and our business associates, we feel it is best to terminate your position at Jessie's Girl Stuff and Farnsworth Enterprises. You will always be our daughter, but in the years to come, we are certain you will thank us for protecting you from your impetuous and, we feel, rash decision. Your mother, brothers and I are very sorry about this rift that has come into our relationship, but we know that one day the Jessie we know will return to us.
Dad

The accompanying document underlined her father's words in legal terms she knew the family lawyers had carefully chosen. Hot tears of devastated pain jumped into her eyes.

Zach walked in and she turned away so he wouldn't see her anguish, taking the envelope with her as she went to her room. She put it in a drawer, closing it tightly, putting off the shock until she could absorb it later.

"Hey," Zach said, knocking on her door. "You all right in there?"

No. "I'm fine."

He was silent for a moment. "Jessie, please open the door."

It was his house. Jessie waited for him to open the door himself, doing as he pleased in typical Zach fashion. But he didn't, and she realized she was holding her breath.

She swung the door open. "Yes?"

He gazed at her. "You've been crying, and I upset you. I'm sorry. I shouldn't have kissed you. It went beyond the boundaries of our agreement. I promise not to make you feel uncomfortable again."

He turned and walked away.

She wanted to go after him, to tell him that he'd misunderstood the source of her unhappiness and that with him, she was finally beginning to understand what she'd been needing in her life.

She went into the hall but he was gone, and he hadn't taken his envelope with him. It was a good excuse to go upstairs and see him, she told herself, egging her bravery to come forth. Picking up the large brown envelope, she put her foot on the stairs, wondering if she could take her first steps to going upstairs to the part of the house she never had set foot in.

Was it smart to cross a boundary they'd both agreed on?

She wasn't sure. It was too early in their marriage to know. She didn't want to shatter anything precious that might have built between them. Glancing down at the envelope, she told herself she didn't need an excuse to talk to him—she was married to him. Playing mail carrier wasn't the answer; strength of purpose was.

A note on the back of the envelope caught her eye.

Wonderful, wonderful, we knew you could do it. We just about rode off with the hero ourselves.
Love, Helen and Pansy

Zach's secret manuscript. This was precious, then, and certainly worth a trip upstairs, where she could apologize and then share the news she still couldn't take in. Zach was the perfect person to talk to. He understood family issues. He wouldn't get overwrought about it; he wouldn't offer advice she couldn't use. He'd simply listen—and Jessie realized that was a valuable commodity she liked in him. He simply never judged her. Teased her, yes, but never judged her.

It was sneaky, but she was dying to take just one peep inside the creative side of the strong man she barely knew. Just one small look, as Helen and Pansy and "The Twins" had gotten. Surely something he meant for publication wasn't a secret from his wife…his temporary wife.

Jessie slipped the front page from the envelope, her eyes scanning hungrily.

Bronson James would never have married the woman beside him if he hadn't known she was a gunslinger's daughter. The gunslinger's reputation needed no bragging. His daughter's reputation needed polishing. Bronson didn't give a damn either way because he'd married her for money, for protection and for the babies he intended to put in her belly. On the untamed prairie, there wasn't a better deal to be made than the one he'd just let the circuit preacher seal. The bitter fruits of bad decisions had brought him to this point of no return, but he wouldn't have turned back anyway. Not now. A man of conviction never retraced his bootsteps lest he know himself as a coward, and Bronson James was no godforsaken coward.

Jessie gasped. Her fingers trembling, she shoved the page back in. Glancing upstairs to make certain she hadn't been seen, she left the stairwell and hurried over to the entry table, returning the envelope to its place. Her heart thundered inside her chest.

Wild, hurt thoughts whirled inside her. She was in a strange place with few acquaintances and no Fran to discuss her sudden fears with. She didn't even have a company anymore. Her family had chosen to show their disapproval of her actions by voting her out of the company, which hurt more than she could have imagined. She didn't know her husband.

She jumped in her car and drove off the ranch.

Chapter Sixteen

"I liked Jessie's ideas," Pansy said. "She's got a quick brain."

Helen nodded. "How about a June fish catch-n-fry?"

"I like it," Pansy said. "June is for summer lovers, you know. If we're going to pick a month to throw out our lures, we might as well pick one with positive portent!" She giggled and sipped some tea.

"We just need to put the idea forward to the menfolk," Helen said.

"Duke," Pansy finished the thought.

"Don't forget Rocky and Bullwinkle." Helen sniffed.

"Oh, Hiram and Bug will be more than glad to help."

Helen sat up. "Where are we going to get bait?"

"Victoria's Secret," Pansy said blithely. "Our girls will figure that out, don't worry. And we'll be here for advice, and Liberty, too. That girl knows a little something about lace."

"I meant fish bait," Helen said.

"Oh," Pansy said. "Who cares about that? If the men are thinking about bait out in those boats with our girls, then we haven't done our job!"

"I like the way you think." Helen laid cookie tins on the table. "Valentine brought these by. She thought we could use a new look for Christmas in our cookie design."

"She's so talented," Pansy said, lifting up a decorated Christmas cookie shaped like a tulip. Illustrations were included with each new tin, so that they could see how to frost tiny tulips on tree branches, and even on snowman bellies.

A knock on Helen's front door startled them. "Must be the guys," Helen said, getting up. "It's always high-tea time around here for Bug and Hiram, and they have no qualms about hunting cookies."

She opened to door, surprised to see Jessie outside. "How lovely to see you, dear," she said, hugging her. "Pansy and I were just talking about you."

Jessie walked inside the softly lit foyer, breathing in the comforting aroma of baking. "I saw your tree was lit from outside," she said. "I hope you don't mind me stopping by this late without calling."

"I'd be upset if you didn't." Helen nodded at her tree. "Pansy and I just finished putting on the last touches."

"It's beautiful," Jessie said. Zach's tree still had nothing but candy canes on it. She'd meant to help him finish it, but now... Lovely sparkling lights of many colors lit Helen's tree, and silver balls hung from every branch. A pink tulip garnished the top, and filmy pink ribbons cascaded down the sides. She realized she'd always been traveling right before Christmas and had never put up a tree in her Dallas loft.

There were things in her life she'd sacrificed for her job, and now she wondered why. "I've always been on the go," she murmured.

"Yes," Helen said, nodding. "You're so talented and smart to get as far as you have in life."

"There's more to life than the corporate ladder. It's a lesson I've just begun to learn," Jessie said.

"Twins. You'll be surprised how your ladder is going to change from corporate to angelic. Come in the kitchen. We were hoping to see you soon because we have something for you. We just didn't want to bother you and Zach on your honeymoon."

Pansy enveloped Jessie in a tight embrace. "So good to see you. We've been trying to give you some time to settle in with your new husband."

Jessie looked at the tiny china plate Helen put before her, with a matching teacup. "I always feel so much better when I'm with you two."

"Now that doesn't sound like the voice of a honeymooner. Not to pry," Pansy said, "but is something wrong?"

It felt like she melted. Jessie told her friends about her parents' letter and reading Zach's book—which she shouldn't have done—and, worst of all, the tension between them. She told it without tears, but the tears stayed locked inside her like cold stones. "It hurts," she said, "more than anything in my life. I'm not sure how one day I was going down the road freestyle, and now my life is completely out of whack."

"Changes," Pansy said.

"But I always adapt so well. I like change."

"It's the people around you who are having to change, and they're not adapting well," Helen said. "Let us give you a wedding gift."

"Just a recipe," Pansy told her, "but it's worked for someone once. It may again."

Jessie took the slim light pink envelope. "Can I read it?"

"Not now." Helen smiled. "It's meant to be read in private, when you have time to sit and think about what you really want and what's most important to you."

"Thank you." Jessie tucked the envelope into her carpetbag. "I can't wait."

"This is all going to work out," Helen said. "The babies are the most important thing. You need to make certain you're getting good prenatal care, and take care of yourself. Think happy thoughts. Eat well. The rest will fall into place eventually if you focus on your children." She smiled at her. "You are happy about your babies, aren't you?"

"I'm thrilled beyond words." Jessie smiled, feeling the glow of happiness radiating inside her just thinking about the two babies she would one day hold. "It's more than I ever dreamed of."

"Well, then," Pansy said, "you just think about that, because they're all that matters besides your man, of course. But you have a recipe for that." She winked at her. "Now, dear, help us a little more with this idea of yours for a catch-n-release party.

We need to catch as many tourists of high quality as possible."

"I can take care of that," Jessie said. "Since I'm no longer employed by my family, I can use my client base to send out invitations. I couldn't have before, because of conflict, but now I can."

Pansy blinked. "How many?"

"Selectively, I have a client base of several thousand around the world. We could start small and focused, perhaps just the Texas corporations I deal with for our first year. This will be the time to figure out our mistakes and what we'd do different next year."

"Oh, my," Helen said, "we'd best get busy."

"How are you going to do this and concentrate on your children?" Pansy asked.

Jessie laughed, delighted just to be included in their dreams. "My babies won't be born for several months. I'll work on the invitations, and you marshal your troops. We'll need lots of volunteers come June."

Helen smiled. "We're so very glad you've come to Tulips, Jessie. You're just what we've been needing."

Jessie smiled. Maybe she would stay here in Tulips—whether or not she and Zach worked matters out. It was beginning to feel a lot like a real home to her, and her children would benefit from what they could learn from people with such good hearts.

"Christmas is such a wonderful time of year," she said, and Helen and Pansy beamed. "I never slowed down enough to enjoy it before."

She hoped Zach would be happy to know that Tulips was working its spell on her. "I'm going home now," she said.

Pansy and Helen looked at her.

"To the ranch," she clarified.

They just smiled.

ZACH WAS beside himself when he realized Jessie had left. His worst nightmare washed over him. What if she didn't come back?

She would. She had to.

He'd not really given her a reason to.

She will. She has to. I want her to.

Her bedroom door was open, so he walked in, looking around. She kept everything neat: the bed, the closet, her things on the dresser. The room smelled of Jessie, a light peachy fragrance he loved. He touched a lipstick she'd left out, picking it up. *Jessie's Girl Stuff.*

She was girly, but she was also strong.

He left the room, closing the door behind him. There was nothing to do but wait, and hope he got a chance to apologize.

Going into the living room, he sat across from the Christmas tree. The candy canes seemed lonely and lost in the branches, so he tried to envision the day when, not only would the tree be covered with glittering ornaments and perhaps a shiny star on top, but loads of presents for little children would lay gaily wrapped in paper underneath.

Goose bumps ran over his arms at the thought.

It wouldn't be Christmas without Jessie. Surely she'd just run to the store, the saloon, somewhere close by.

The phone rang, and he leaped for it. "Hello?"

"Zach, it's Pepper."

"Oh," he said.

"And a very merry, scintillating, overexuberant Christmas season to you, too," she said. "Heard you got married on the sly."

"I did." He sank back onto the sofa, staring miserably at the unadorned tree. "Where the hell are you?"

"Up with Aunt Jerry. She gets lonely this time of year."

"Yeah, me, too."

"You can't be lonely. You have a wife."

He snapped out of his piteous mood. "I meant I might have been lonely."

"But now you have Jessie."

Not really. "Exactly."

"Congratulations," she said. "I wouldn't have thought you'd be the Forrester to elope."

"Yeah, it could've been you."

She was silent.

"Well, I mean, if you had someone you wanted to marry," he said quickly, not wanting to hurt his sister's feelings.

She sighed. "Zach, take good care of Jessie, okay?"

He frowned. "Is something wrong?"

"No, and yes," she said. "Someday, I'm going to tell you something I should have told you a long time ago."

"Yeesh," he said. "You're not coming back to town?"

"Oh, I'm coming back. I've bought a building for my clinic and a place to live."

He relaxed. "Good. I've gotten used to you being around. Sometimes I even miss you, as much as I shouldn't swell your head by telling you."

"We have a lot in common. Merry Christmas, Zach," she said, hanging up the phone before he could say the same. He stared at the phone in his hand for a moment before clicking it off. "Women are so moody," he said, going back to thinking about how gloomy the house would be if Jessie hadn't ever hit Brahma Bud.

It seemed so long ago.

But he'd caught her, for the moment. He paced to the window, staring out in the darkness, looking for headlights. Turning to consider the tree, he thought about occupying his time by getting out a box of ornaments. The thought depressed him, and he decided he was being moody like Pepper, and Forresters shouldn't all be moody at the same time, so he got out some M&M's and amused himself for a moment by tossing them in the air and catching them in his mouth.

The challenge of that only lasted a moment before he realized he hadn't been bored since Jessie had come into his life. She was what he'd needed all along. "Come home," he said aloud. "I swear, I'll follow Prince Charming's blueprint and sweep you off your feet."

He couldn't take thinking about it anymore so

he put himself to bed. In the morning, he was going to go throw himself on the little ladies for help.

ZACH GOT UP the next morning to start his chores, nearly kicking his heels up with joy at seeing the T-bird parked in its spot. His whole mood improved instantly.

Unable to bear not seeing her, he went and tapped on her bedroom door. There was no answer, so he gingerly pushed it open.

She slept soundly, her arms curled around a pillow. *That should be me she's holding. I'm doing something wrong if a pillow is my substitute.*

Maybe that was the way she liked to sleep. Silently, he closed the door. "Either way it should be me in that bed with her," he said, hurrying outside to feed the animals and do his chores.

Then he cleaned up and left, determined to get some advice from the only people who could help him.

"Not that I'm helpless," he said, when Helen opened the door to let him in, "but this one matters to me and I'm kind of messing things up."

"You mean Jessie?" Helen asked with twinkling eyes.

"Well, yes, ma'am." He entered as she indicated and gave her a kiss on the cheek. "Where's your comrade?"

"In the kitchen trying to place decorations on sugar-cookie trees. It's not easy with her macular degeneration," Helen said. "The eyes play a few tricks on her."

"It's not getting worse, is it?"

"No," Helen said, "but it's dicey, of course."

His heartbeat slowed a bit. If there was one thing he wanted more than anything else in the world—besides Jessie and healthy babies—he wanted these two women and Hiram and Bug to see his children's faces. These four people had been his parents ever since his own had passed away, and through them he still had a connection to the warm love his family had given him and Pepper and Duke.

He walked into the kitchen and surprised Pansy with a big hug. "You're beautiful," he told her.

"Gosh," Helen said good-naturedly. "You've never told me that."

He winked at her. "I'll tell you again when you get me a glass of milk to go with my cookies."

She lightly rapped his knuckles with a wooden spoon, so he sat back, enjoying the smells of cinnamon and ginger. "Please teach me what I'm lacking," he said as Helen put a delicate plate of cookies within his reach. "I know you know."

Pansy stopped. "Oh, you made me draw a crooked line of dots."

"Maybe you should rest your eyes," Helen said and Pansy glared at her.

"Maybe I just need quiet to be creative," she said. "All artists work better that way."

"Tea…to soothe the savage beast," Helen said, and went to prepare a breakfast blend for her friend.

Pansy winked mischievously at Zach. "She fell for it. Jessie stopped by here last night, by the way."

He sat up to listen, Jessie being his favorite topic. "I wondered where she went. I didn't think about her coming over here." He'd been afraid she'd simply left town.

"Communication is the key," Helen said. "Jessie had gotten some bad news. She feels adrift right now and that's understandable."

"She's got me," Zach said, but Pansy shook her head.

"Does she?" Pansy asked. "She has to know that for herself."

"Maybe she doesn't know it yet, but surely she'll be able to figure that out in time," he said.

Helen shook her head. "Why do men never want to talk about their feelings?"

"Because we're afraid we'll insult the woman, or have our emotions left to dry in the wind when the woman rejects us. Those are the scenarios which keep a man's mouth closed." In his case, perhaps both fears were in play. He was walking on eggshells around Jessie, trying to keep to their agreement, and he was afraid she might decide he wasn't the man for her. "I guess I'm talking about men in general. My fear is that Jessie will decide she doesn't want to continue our marriage. I may not be able to convince her."

"Go see her," Helen said. "Talk it over."

"Do you love her, Zach?" Pansy asked.

"More than I ever thought possible," he replied. "It's hit me like a bat between the eyes."

The ladies giggled.

"We waited a long time to hear that," Helen said. "Now we have a little something for you." She handed him an envelope with his name on it and shooed him to the door. "Come back anytime. But right now, go home."

"That's good advice," he said, adjusting his hat for courage.

"Of course it is," Pansy said, letting him give her a peck on the cheek. "We've decided that's all we give."

ZACH WENT HOME feeling better but not in charge of the situation. Jessie's car was parked outside, so that instantly brightened his spirits.

But first perhaps he needed to read his letter, he decided. He needed a few tips on taming an heiress who didn't really need him. Pulling out the envelope, he impatiently tore it open.

A Recipe For Winning Your Sweetly
Stubborn Wife

Be Kind. Marriages are built on kindness and respect. Talk about pretty things and the future you will share together.

Be Thoughtful—as you are. Old movies and garden-picked flowers will show her your romantic side.

Call her parents and invite them to the ranch. Wealthy social people have feelings, too, that they don't know what to do with. As afraid as they are of losing their wealth, they're afraid of losing Jessie more.

He blinked. "Damn hard recipe," he murmured. But he had nothing to lose in trying. For Jessie, he would try anything, even if he was pretty sure the little old ladies were wrong about this recipe.

JESSIE PULLED OUT the pink envelope Helen and Pansy had given her, opening it eagerly in the privacy of her room.

How To Win Your Handsome, Slightly Chauvinistic Husband Who Doesn't Show His Feelings

Be patient. True love is experienced once, maybe twice in a lifetime. It's not like baking cookies with a recipe that comes out the same every time if you use the right ingredients. Zach hasn't experienced the ingredients before.

Be honest. He loves real and true things. Hiding feelings just hurts you both.

Remember what drew you both together and try a little more of that.

Call your parents. They love you. It's hard to go forward when you haven't made peace with the past—even if they're the instigators. They're used to having you all to themselves.

Jessie shook her head. There was more to following one of the Gang's recipes than she'd anticipated. But where Zach was concerned, it was worth a shot.

She shrieked when he tapped on her door. "Yes?"

"Can I bother you for a second?"

Her heart began a restless racing at the sound of his voice. She opened the door, overjoyed to see him. "You're not bothering me."

He removed his hat, and handed her a candy cane he'd put foil on to look like a flower. "Sorry. Garden flowers are out of season right now. Best I could do."

She smiled at him. "I didn't know you were so talented."

He nodded. "Neither did I. It was a stretch."

Putting the flower on her dresser she said, "I got a letter from my parents removing me from my position at the company."

"Whoa," he said. "Jessie, I'm sorry."

She shrugged, not wanting him to know how badly she was hurt. "They had their reasons."

"Yeah. Me."

"Which I don't agree with." She lifted her chin. "I'd rather have these children than the company."

She almost said, "You and these children than

the company," but stopped herself in time. Helen and Pansy hadn't said, *Throw yourself at him and see if he catches you.*

"You really are happy about the pregnancy, aren't you?" he asked.

"I've always wanted children. I just wouldn't have gotten them with my ex, which I now realize. It's ironic to me that I might have married him and had nothing, and I wasn't married to you and was given so much."

He shifted in the doorway. "I'm glad you're here," he said gruffly.

"I'm glad to be here," she said, meaning it.

"Even though you won't be spending Christmas with your folks?"

"I feel that they made their decisions. I'd rather be where I'm wanted."

His jaw tensed for a moment. "You're wanted."

They looked at each other for a long moment before he stepped inside the doorway and took her in his arms. "I know we agreed on temporary, but I'm pretty sure this won't be going away anytime soon," he said, kissing her, and Jessie's body sang an agreement her mouth was too busy to say.

They fell onto the bed together, reaching for each other's clothes at the same time. If her friends hadn't reminded her that what had brought them together was good and important, she might not be able to lose herself in the magic of this moment. She unbuttoned his shirt with speed equal to his as he undressed her, and then they lay in each other's arms, naked to each other for the first time.

"God, you're beautiful," he said. "I know that sounds like something any guy would say when he's about to score, but Jessie, you're beyond my wildest imaginings."

His hard body stirred her longings as well, and Jessie fought back the shyness to express herself by touching him first on the chest, and then lower, stroking and guiding him to her. "I was wondering if I'd imagined the way we felt together."

"No," Zach said, moving into her, "you didn't. It was good then," he murmured against her lips, "and it's going to be better now."

He carefully and gently rocked her to an incredible climax, and held her close when she cried out with pleasure as he shuddered with his own excitement. "Too fast," he complained. "I'm probably always going to be too fast with you. You get me the way I never expected to want a woman."

They lay in each other's arms, quietly enjoying the intimacy growing between them.

"I believe all good things happen for a reason," Zach murmured against her hair, and she nodded. She did, too. There was no other explanation for Brahma Bud to have stepped in her path, bringing her to meet her destiny.

"I called your parents," Zach murmured, and the cocoon of safety and joy was ripped from her.

She sat up and looked at him. "Why?"

He tried to pull her against him but she wouldn't unstiffen. "Because it's the holidays. Words were spoken in haste. I felt it was important to extend the olive branch."

She got out of bed and began dressing. "You conveniently didn't tell me that until after we'd made love. Zach, they fired me. Their only daughter."

"And I'm the cause of that." He reached to grab her arm. "Jessie, we're all family. And those babies need to know their grandparents."

"All the same," Jessie said, "in the future, please consider my feelings before you go off acting like Sam Houston fighting my battles."

Chapter Seventeen

Zach stared at his wife, confused. Pansy and Helen had specifically felt that he should make some effort toward her family, and though he'd rather not, he'd done it for Jessie. "Stop," he said. "You're not leaving this room." Getting up from the bed, he quickly dressed. Before she could get away from him, he reached out and grabbed her. "Oh, no, you don't, Jessie. You just ran out of run with me."

She let him hold her arm with a mutinous gleam in her eye.

"Now see, I've had horses look at me like that, and that's a sign to me that I haven't finished my work with you. You need me, beautiful, and I need you. So let's just take a deep breath together and talk this out."

"I don't need anyone's help with my family,"

Jessie said. "They're entitled to their feelings and I'm certainly entitled to mine. You have no right to butt into our private world."

He nodded. "It's like that, is it?"

"Yes! Of course it is!" She took a deep breath before saying, "Nowhere in our marriage contract did we agree to be anything more than temporary. And I certainly don't need you interfering with my corporate or family business."

For a long moment he stared at her, realizing that there were parts to him and Jessie that were wider than a gulf. He figured Helen and Pansy were right to encourage her family to come to his world, so whatever fears they had about him could be resolved. Resolution could only benefit Jessie and his children, he'd been certain.

Inviting her parents—and her brothers—to the ranch for Christmas hadn't been the easiest thing he'd ever done. But she didn't like the gift he was trying to give her. He shrugged. "Sorry. Next time I won't."

He left her room as a man who knew a little bit more about Jessie than he had five minutes before. She was serious about her space—and he was going to let her have all the space she could find.

It was a damn big ranch.

JESSIE REGRETTED the rush of angry words that came out of her mouth as soon as she said them, but it took her two days to find Zach so that she could somehow bridge the gap between them. He was in the attic, a place she would never have thought to look except that the ladder was down. For two days, he'd been a ghost, the only clue he was still in the house the smell of breakfast in the air, or coffee percolating in a pot with two mugs laid out beside it.

She climbed the ladder and poked her head through the opening. "Zach, can we talk?"

"I'm busy right now."

It was too close to Christmas to take no for an answer. Her parents' actions had made her angry and fearful and she'd taken it out on Zach. She'd needed a bit more time to assimilate how she felt about being pushed out of the family circle, but truthfully, it had made her realize all the more that Zach's family circle was the one she wanted: him, her and their two babies were a complete family. She stood before him, her heart anxious for forgiveness. "Zach, there've been a few times when you haven't let me run away from you, and this time you're not going to shut me out."

He glanced up, handing her a picture among

many he was looking at in a box. "Those are my parents. It's the closest you'll get to meeting them, I'm sorry to say."

She felt tears jump into her eyes. "Zach, thank you for trying to include my family in our lives. I should have told you that the other day. Instead, I spoke with the anger and bitterness that I was feeling for what they'd done. It's not the easiest thing that's ever happened to me, and I haven't taken it well."

"What they did was wrong, but it's their loss," Zach said. "But I don't want to come between you and your family forever. I figured Christmas was a time for forgiveness, and I still feel that way." He stood, looking down at her. "I feel bad that I'm the cause for this pain in your life, Jessie, and your family. I'd fix it if I could, but I can't."

There. Helen and Pansy would have to be proud of him for expressing how he felt. "I know this is our first challenge, but I have to say that I'm enjoying even this with you."

"Why?" she asked. "I'm afraid of disharmony."

He touched her cheek. "I'm not afraid of it if it means everyone understands each other better in the end."

"I don't know," Jessie whispered. "We have some very tough challenges facing us."

"As long as we make an addendum to our contract that says we always speak our minds and listen to each other, we'll just grow together, if that's what you want."

"I do," Jessie said softly, and Zach felt a piece of the wall between them crumble away. He ran a finger down a strand of her long hair, enjoying its silkiness.

"Never do we go to bed angry again," he told her, and Jessie nodded.

"In fact," she said, "it's high time you continue this theme of closeness in my bed every night."

He grinned. "You'll like my room better."

She looked at him. "Is that an invitation?"

Her face felt delicate between his palms as he cradled her. "You never needed an invitation."

Maybe she didn't, but that didn't mean she felt free to bridge that gap in their relationship. Especially not with the feelings she'd stored inside her from the words she'd read in his manuscript. "One day, then," she said, breaking away from him to scurry back down the stairs.

"Running?" he asked, watching her descent with a grin.

"It's important not to jump to conclusions," she

said, lifting her chin. "I'm merely leaving you to your cleaning."

He laughed, and Jessie decided to tackle a chore that she'd long wanted to finish. It was four days before Christmas and his tree was still barely decorated. The house seemed to be waiting, unnaturally empty of holiday spirit.

A box sat beside the tree, opened but not yet disturbed. Gently, Jessie took out an ornament, freezing when she saw the picture of Zach, Pepper and Duke as children set inside, all three of them dressed in matching candy-striped pajamas.

She had a picture like this of her and her brothers on her tree that by now Fran would have put up in her office. She gasped. "Fran!"

Running to grab her cell phone, she quickly dialed her best friend. "Fran, it's Jessie."

"And Merry Christmas to you, too," Fran said. "It's good to hear your voice. You've been a lot quieter since you caught that handsome cowboy. Congratulations on your decision to live forever in the sticks, by the way. I always said you worked too hard."

Jessie frowned. "What decision to live in the sticks?"

"Sorry," Fran said with a laugh, "I shouldn't

phrase it that way. Congratulations on your desire to make your home with your new husband and expected children."

"I didn't tell you that," she said, her blood running cold.

"I read it in the corporate memo. And also your parents mentioned your decision to me when they called to instruct me to forward to their corporate offices all documents pertaining to the job from which you'd resigned."

Jessie blinked back shock. "Corporate memo?"

"Yeah. Worldwide. All offices. Well, a position as big as yours would require an announcement to all offices, of course. It's not every day a Farnsworth gives up a prestigious family position."

She should have foreseen this, of course. "Lovely," she said, and Fran gasped.

"Don't tell me you didn't authorize this," Fran said.

"The company decided that it would be better in other hands in light of my unorthodox marriage," she said, the feelings of betrayal rising inside her again.

"Oh, Jessie, I'm so sorry."

"I don't understand it myself." Jessie shook her

head. "And yet, I somehow feel it's for the best. I'm certainly not losing on the trade-off."

"You're happy, then? In Tulips?"

Jessie hesitated, touching the picture ornament of Zach and his siblings she'd placed on the tree. "If you'd told me six months ago that I'd be without a job and living in the country, married to a cowboy and pregnant, I would have thought you were insane. Not in any way did this fit my plans for the future. But oddly enough, every day I change a little more, and it's all good."

"You're giving me shivers," she said. "I want that, too."

Jessie laughed. "But you still have a job."

"Actually, no," Fran said, her tone quiet. "Once I send the boxes of documents, I'm to close the office. Jessie, I promise I thought this was what you wanted."

Something snapped inside Jessie. At first she'd been embarrassed of how her family was acting. Then she worried Zach would feel cheated because he'd married a woman with few financial reserves at the moment, not to mention that he'd signed a prenup, guaranteeing his exclusion from any gains from their marriage.

But Fran deserved better. "First, I want you to

come to Tulips," Jessie said. "You're the most organized person I know. Come out here and find yourself a world of people who love newcomers."

"And employment?" Fran asked.

"Let's walk on the wild side," Jessie suggested. "Let's go into some kind of business for ourselves."

"Wow," Fran breathed, and Jessie nodded to herself. It was the right thing to do.

"What about Zach? Will he mind you starting a new venture?"

"No," Jessie said, "my man will applaud me for not buckling to pressure."

"Then I'll pack this office as fast as I can and head your way. Jessie, you're the best friend I ever had."

Jessie smiled, and hanging up, went back upstairs to the attic to talk to her husband. "Zach?"

"Yes." He swept a bunch of cobwebs from the eaves with a broom. "This hasn't been cleaned up here in years."

"I can see that," she said. "Is there a reason you're doing it right before Christmas and not, say, in the spring?"

"Hell if I know," Zach said, and Jessie nodded.

"Perhaps there's hidden meanings we should consider."

"I doubt it. I think the attic just needs a good cleaning."

"Zach," Jessie said, "I read a page of your manuscript."

He quit sweeping and put the broom down. "Payback for hiding your car?"

She looked at him. "No. Sheer nosiness."

He nodded. "I like an honest woman. Will you be making a habit of nosiness?"

"I must confess to finding my husband very interesting, and to being possessed of a desire to know him better," Jessie said. "But in the future, I'll be asking him before I snoop."

"That works for me." Zach looked at her. "I should be angry with you, though, right?"

"It was the twins. I admit to feeling jealous."

"They are beautiful," he said, tweaking her, "but just good friends."

"Still, they knew part of you I didn't."

"Ah," he said, "a jealous wife. I'll have to remember that."

"Please do."

"Good. Now get down. Pregnant women shouldn't climb stairs, and you seem to be making a habit of perching on my top attic step."

"Are you mad that I read it?" Jessie asked.

"No. You're my wife. Read what you like in my house. I have some *Playboy*s in the closet—"

"I'm tossing them," she said. "A pregnant wife does not want to feel upstaged by young, skinny women."

He laughed. "I'm teasing. My parents would have made us paint a water tower or something if we'd kept reading material like that on hand, even though the articles are good." He winked at her.

Jessie didn't know what to think about this playful side of her husband. "Thank you for not being mad at me."

"Thank you for being honest. Why'd you choose now to tell me?"

"I have attics of my own that needed cleaning," she said. "I want us to start fresh."

"Babe, we're pretty durn fresh. We just got married."

"I couldn't hide it from you any longer," Jessie said. "I'm beginning to realize how much considering your family members' feelings means."

"That's my girl. Although don't think that Duke, Pepper, and I don't get inconsiderate at times."

"I think you're avoiding your tree," Jessie said, and Zach raised a brow.

"I haven't been much in the mood," he admitted.

"Zach, when I read that first page of your book, I saw us in your writing."

"You couldn't have. It took me three years to write the damn thing. Or if you were there, you're clairvoyant." He came down the ladder and put it up. "Jessie, I'm too simple of a guy to be able to have a relationship and plot a book around it. I swear."

She felt so much better. "Because I thought, you know, the part about—"

"I know. Him marrying her because he had to, and he had all these deep reasons." He tugged her hair. "Do you think pregnancy hormones might be making you jump to conclusions?" Taking her by the hand, he led her into the living room.

"I'm sentimental by nature," Jessie said, as he stood her in front of the tree. "At least, I seem to be becoming more and more sentimental. But you have to admit cleaning a cold attic in the winter when there's four days till Christmas and a warm living room with an undressed tree seems a bit turned around. I thought it might be because of me."

"Oh, you have me turned around," he admitted, "but the tree thing has nothing to do with you. It's the fact that it's just me keeping the home fires burning, and Duke has always teased me about loving to decorate. Now that he's not at the ranch as much, I've lost the motivation of him tweaking me about it. I may have decorated just to get negative attention," he said with a grin. "I liked getting under my big bro's skin."

"I don't believe a word of it," Jessie said. "Look at these happy children."

Zach nodded, looking at the ornament picture. "That's why I was going through the boxes looking for old photographs. I want to be the kind of father my dad was to me. I want my kids to know the happiness we knew growing up." He took a deep breath. "I'm pretty nervous about being a father, to be honest. I guess I was just looking to the past for the right pattern."

She wrapped him in a tight embrace. "I think we're going to make it, Zach."

"Six months isn't that long," he said, and Jessie's heart fell. She'd meant forever, and he was talking about their original plan. It seemed so long ago that they'd agreed to marrying for the children to be born on the right side of the blanket, under his name. Jessie bit her lip. *Great. How honest can I be without upsetting our original agreement?* Would he feel deceived if she told him that she wanted more than what they'd agreed to?

How did you tell a man you'd fallen in love
with him if he hadn't told you?

The sound of caroling wafted into the living
room. She glanced up at Zach. "Carolers? Is this
a tradition in Tulips?"

"Not that I know of," he said.

They peered out into the darkness. Truck headlights illuminated the carolers' path, but they still
couldn't see who it was. Together they walked
onto the porch, grinning at Helen, Pansy, Bug and
Hiram all perched in the back of a truck, singing
at the top of their lungs.

"Merry Christmas!" Pansy called.

"Come take your cookie basket," Helen said,
holding one up with a big red bow.

Zach walked forward to take it from her. "Who
came up with this idea?"

They laughed, their faces aglow and their eyes
twinkling in the cold night. "We're starting a tradition," Helen said. "You're our first visit of the night."

"We like it," Jessie said, and Pansy clapped her
hands.

"Join us!" Pansy said. "The more, the merrier!"

Zach grinned. "Where are you going next?"

"Liberty's," Hiram said. "She'll have to tuck in
early because of the young'un so we want to get

her place out of the way next. But y'all were the honeymooners, so we had to bother you first!"

Zach looked at Jessie. "What do you think?"

"Well," she said, "I think there's no room in that truck for us. We'd have to follow you."

"In your tulip-mobile!" Pansy exclaimed. "We've got extra ribbon to put a bow on the grille!" She hopped out of the truck with ribbon. "Bug, you're finally going to get your parade."

"Hot damn, I am!" His face lit up even brighter. "Thank you, Jessie Forrester, I've always wanted a parade."

She blinked at the sound of her name spoken with Zach's last name, realizing she liked it.

Realizing she wanted to keep it more than anything.

"I'll get your keys," Zach said, and Jessie smiled.

"You drive," she said.

The carolers clapped, and Jessie fell in love a little bit more with all things Tulips.

Chapter Eighteen

Being part of a small-town parade was more fun than a cosmetics convention any day, Jessie thought as she sat next to Zach as he drove. They followed the truck in front of them, and Zach had put the top down so they could sing when they got to Liberty and Duke's.

"This is so exciting!" Jessie exclaimed. "Our first tradition."

Zach laughed. "I have to admit, you are not the woman I met. You were so fancy back then you would never have ridden in a pretend parade to make an old man happy."

Jessie shook her head. "Then I wouldn't have known what I was missing."

He reached over and put his hand on her leg. "There may not be much to miss out on in Tulips, but we do manage to stay fairly busy."

"I know." She liked that. Her parents would never understand this, and Jessie knew her life had changed too much for her to ever go back. She would call them one day as Helen and Pansy had suggested in their recipe, but right now, she needed her life to be about Zach.

She hoped he felt the same about her.

They stopped at Liberty's house and cranked up the volume on "Jingle Bells," their voices loud as they huddled together near the porch.

Liberty and Duke opened the door with their baby in Duke's arms.

"Ho, ho, ho," Duke said.

"Merry Christmas, Sheriff," Hiram called. "We're going to Holt's next. Wanna come with us?"

He shook his head. "Baby likes her bath and crib and Santa Mouse story about this time. Come in and let us give you carolers some hot chocolate."

"Mmm," Pansy said, quick to hug Liberty and head inside.

"Let me hold the tiny elf," Helen said, taking the baby from Duke. Liberty smiled at Jessie as she walked onto the porch.

"You look wonderful," Liberty said. "Pregnancy agrees with you."

"And I'm glad about that," Jessie said, laughing.

"Come on in out of the cold." She took Jessie inside and closed the door before following the carolers down the hall to the kitchen. "How'd you get caught up with the Gang?"

"It was easy. They came to our house first and we jumped at the chance to join in the fun." Liberty took Jessie's coat, laying it over a chair. "Zach and I needed some excitement."

Liberty smiled. "It sounds like you've been having plenty of excitement. I heard you sent back the diamond ring Zach got you because it wasn't quite what you wanted."

Jessie felt her smile turn unsteady. "Diamond ring?"

"Your engagement ring?" Liberty looked at her curiously. "You wanted something different, so you all decided to wait until after Christmas to pick one out together?" Liberty gasped at the astonished look on Jessie's face. "Obviously, I'm speaking out of turn, and I pride myself on not being a gossip. Jessie, I'm so sorry!"

Jessie felt weaker than she wanted to but she shook her head. "It's fine. Truly, Liberty."

"Oh, dear." Liberty looked at her, genuinely distressed. "All of us knew about it, so I assumed it was true."

Zach had never mentioned getting her a diamond ring. They'd chosen simple gold bands because they'd agreed on brevity and plainness for a temporary wedding. "I wouldn't send something back that Zach gave me," she said dully. "Liberty, please don't mention to anyone that I didn't know about the diamond."

"I won't!" Liberty promised. "I truly apologize for my runaway mouth."

"No, it's fine," Jessie said, following her into the kitchen. Zach had obviously changed his mind about something concerning her. Jessie's heart shattered into small bits, and when he put his arm around her shoulders in Liberty's cozy, warm kitchen, Jessie wanted to tell him not to bother to put on the good show.

No wonder he hadn't decorated the tree. He wasn't planning on them celebrating a Christmas with all the trimmings.

ON THE NIGHT before Christmas, Jessie placed three presents under the tree. She'd thought about what Liberty had said—a lot—and decided it was up to her to have Christmas.

Maybe the spirit of Christmas would work its wonders on them.

She'd bought a gift for each baby and made one for Zach. For the babies, she'd sentimentally bought booties.

Remembering the flower Zach had made her—and knowing how he had parenting worries—she made him a painted T-shirt that read *World's Best Dad* on the front, and *Love, The Christmas Twins* on the back.

She was pleased with her gifts. She hoped Zach would be, too.

She intended to celebrate Christmas as if this one were the first of many they'd spend together.

But for now, she had a difficult phone call to make and she couldn't put it off any longer.

ZACH HAD PLANS—big plans. He didn't know how Jessie would react to them, but it was time to find out.

He found her sitting with the phone in her hands. "What are you doing?"

"About to sweep cobwebs," she said.

He thought she'd never looked more beautiful, which made his plan all the more important. "Anything I can help with?"

She shook her head. "Not this time."

He sat beside her. "Want some company? Or privacy?"

She thought about that for a long time. "I really don't know," she said, so he kissed her to make her feel better. It was all he had to give her. She clung to him for a moment, and then broke away.

He missed her already. "Tomorrow's Christmas," he said, and she looked at him.

"I know."

"I'm glad you're here."

She nodded. "I am, too."

"I'm not going to ever submit my western."

"You're not? Why not?"

"It's not something I need to do anymore. I always wanted to write a book, so I wrote a book to see if I could. But the challenge isn't the kind of excitement I need. I've got you and that's enough."

"I wish that sounded complimentary."

He kissed her forehead. "It is. Should I dial for you?"

"I never thanked you for calling my folks. It means a lot to me, more than I expressed at the time."

He nodded. "I felt it was important."

Slowly, she dialed the number, and he sat down beside her. "Mother?"

He put his hand over Jessie's.

"Mother, I'm calling to tell you and Dad Merry Christmas. I'm sorry you don't trust me enough to make my own decisions and know my own mind, but I've accepted that. I love you, and I want you to be happy. So Merry Christmas, and that's all I called to say."

Zach held his breath. Jessie listened for a long time, her eyes beginning to sparkle with tears, so he handed her a tissue, and then she smiled, her whole face lighting up. "I love you, too," she said. "Zach will be delighted."

She hung up. "You're never going to believe this. My parents have had a change of heart, and they want to know if you'll mind if they come to Tulips for the birth of the children in May or whenever it happens."

He slowly shook his head, his eyes taking in Jessie's joy. "Of course not. Your family is welcome anytime."

"She said to tell you she was sorry. She and Dad panicked."

"I actually understand. I probably would have, too, had I been in their shoes."

"You have a big heart," she said, putting her arms around his neck. "The biggest in Texas."

"I don't know about that." He stroked her hair. "I'm glad you and your family worked everything out. It bothered me more than I can tell you that I was the cause of so much distress for you."

She pulled away to look at him. "Zach, I never doubted that you and I had made the right decision."

They sat together for a long time, holding each other and feeling the magic of Christmas wash over them. And when he got up and began to clean out her room, Jessie helped him, and together, they moved her up to his bedroom where she belonged.

ON CHRISTMAS MORNING, she heard Zach rustling around downstairs. She felt the bed beside her, where she'd slept snuggled up against him in his arms all night.

It had been so incredible, the best gift she could have gotten. He'd cradled her stomach in his big hands and she felt she'd come home for good.

But it was Christmas, and she wasn't going to let him start it without her. Hurriedly dressing, she flew downstairs and jumped into his arms. "Merry Christmas, husband!"

Zach laughed out loud, loving Jessie's spontaneity. She certainly wasn't a wife who would allow him to become bored. "Merry Christmas to you, too, wife."

Jessie gasped, looking at the tree he'd sneaked downstairs to decorate for her. "Pretty good, huh?"

"It's beautiful!" She smiled, delighted.

"You got me started." He pointed to the photo ornament.

"I'm glad. Have you finished? Or are there more?"

"There's a few more in that box. And this one," Zach said. "It's a special one. Please be careful when you open the box."

"Oh, I will." Jessie carefully unwrapped the family heirloom that had been kept in a red, velvet-lined box. She held up a gold carved heart-shaped ornament. "It's so beautiful."

"It even opens," he said, showing her how to unhinge it, and Jessie gasped when she saw the beautiful diamond ring inside.

He grinned, liking how he'd surprised her. "Merry Christmas, Jessie Tomball Farnsworth Forrester. Will you marry me and be my wife—forever?"

She threw herself into her arms. "Yes! Oh, Zach, it's beautiful!"

He held her close. "I love you, girl. I loved you the moment I laid eyes on you."

"I have waited so long to hear you say those words, so I could tell you I love you, too." Jessie kissed him softly on the mouth. "I love you more than I ever believed I could love someone."

"We'll have to have another wedding here, you know," Zach said, his eyes twinkling, "because the Gang felt slighted, though they tried to be supportive. Liberty wants to design you a dress, and the ladies want to get Valentine to bring a wedding cake over from Union Junction."

"And my family could come," she said on a hopeful breath, and he nodded.

"I already called your father and asked him for your hand in marriage, and this time, he said yes." Zach grinned.

"I bet Dad was impressed by your courage."

"I was more impressed by the fact that he tore up the documents he'd had me sign." Zach shrugged. "He said you had the brightest mind of any woman he'd ever known besides your mother, and if you chose me, then I was the man to make you happy."

Jessie began to cry tears of joy. "Thank you for being such a prince," she said.

"Thank you for being you," he replied, pulling her up into his lap. Together, they sat and watched the twinkling lights on the tree sparkling on the many ornaments, and the spirit of the season glowed like candlelight on them and the babies that had brought them together.

Epilogue

One Christmas Eve later, Jessie got the chance to relive her holiday miracle. She married Zach in a sweet ceremony in Tulips, allowing Pansy, Helen, Liberty and Pepper to celebrate her wedding the way they'd always wanted.

Jessie had been satisfied with their elopement, but as far as the Gang was concerned, if they hadn't witnessed the ceremony, the marriage wasn't completely perfect. And nothing could be more wonderful than a wedding surrounded by your friends and family, they explained, and so Jessie relaxed and enjoyed their surprise nuptials.

It hadn't been a surprise to Zach. These days, anything the Gang wanted to do he was amenable to. Liberty had designed Jessie a lovely wedding gown, and the ladies had decorated the parlor at the Triple F. They'd invited Jessie's family, and this time, even her brothers had shown up to watch her father give her away. It had been a very special Christmas wedding, and Jessie loved Zach even more for understanding how much it meant to her.

Her husband had turned out to be quite the conspirator, she decided, smiling at him as he cooed at baby Mattie lying in his arms. In May, when the babies had been born, he'd allowed the Gang to hang balloons and streamers all over the house as a baby welcome. Two giant wooden storks had been posted on the lawn, announcing the children's names and birth weights. The storks' faces had been covered over by photographs, one of Zach and one of Jessie on each. They looked ridiculous with human faces, and Jessie had laughed out loud when Zach drove her home from the hospital and she saw them for the first time.

"So, wife, our children are seven months old and look as if they understand there are presents under the tree for them," Zach said as he stood in front of the tree which, this year, had been decorated the day after Halloween. He said the children needed to learn about family, friends and holiday baking as soon as possible, though Jessie was certain Zach was eager to slip into his Santa role more than anything. He was wearing a Santa cap right now and was gazing at the twins like he'd received the most wonderful gift of all.

Jessie snuggled James to her cheek. "If they love the holidays half as much as their father, we'll always have a lot of excitement this time of year. I can't believe they're seven months old."

"Yes, a very important birthday," he said, kissing James's head and then Jessie on the lips. "But more importantly, it's our first Christmas as a family."

She smiled. "You're right."

"Next year, the babies will actually sing when we ride around caroling."

"I can't wait."

"I'm glad we got married again today," he told her. "The babies knew something special was happening."

She put her arm through his, and the babies looked at the lights glowing on the tree. "When I first met you that day on the road, I thought you were such a tough guy. And here you are, sentimental and sweet. I would never have guessed."

"You only thought I was tough because you'd hit my prize steer. If a woman ever hits your steer, James—"

"You'd best love her with all your heart,"

Jessie said, laughing. "Brahma Bud likes me better than you now."

"Only because you take him daily treats to atone for your poor driving skills."

Jessie laughed. "Mattie, if ever you meet a man who wants to seduce you in the back of your T-bird—"

"I'll not be buying my daughter a hot pink car," Zach said. "She'll be riding a bicycle for the rest of her life."

"You know," Jessie said, looking up at him, "when she falls in love, there'll be very little you can do about it."

Zach gazed down into Jessie's eyes. "If and when I allow my children to have a date with the opposite sex, I hope they're as happy as I am with you."

Happiness shone in Jessie's eyes. "I love you, Zach."

He kissed her lips and each baby flailed a fist, making their parents laugh. Jessie leaned her head against Zach's shoulder as they stood silently looking at the tree, holding their future in their arms, letting the magic of the holidays bless their marriage forever.

It was fairy-tale perfect, and only the beginning of their story.

* * * * *

Santa Baby

LAURA MARIE ALTOM

Dear Reader,

I'll let you in on a little secret… I want to go to Alaska so badly I can hardly stand it!

I'm not sure what it is about the place but it holds a special appeal for me. Trouble is, I don't just want to see tourist Alaska but the real deal. I'd like to experience winter in Atquask and summer in Akhoik. I'd like to earn my pilot's licence and land a float plane on a forgotten lake. I'd like to hike the Brooks Range and take ferry rides and pan for gold and fish for king salmon.

The version of Alaska that Colby introduces Whitney to has been somewhat softened. His lakefront cabin always has a nice breeze to keep big bugs at bay. In the true Alaska, men have gone down in planes, to die not from injuries sustained in the crash but from insanity caused by whining, biting mosquitoes. Yet the harshness of this vast place is balanced by unparalleled beauty. To any of you fortunate enough to live in Alaska or to visit—*any* part, I'm not picky—please drop me a note and let me know if it's as fantastic as it is in my dreams.

To fellow armchair travellers I highly recommend the book *Going to Extremes* by Joe McGinniss. I mentioned the book to the pilot I interviewed, saying that since it had been published in 1980, much must have changed. He laughed and said I'd be surprised how little has changed. Wow! Since in my neck of the woods, a new fast-food joint or strip mall seems to go up every week, Alaska sounds more intriguing than ever.

I do so hope you enjoy Colby and Whitney's story, as it holds a special place in my heart.

Best (and Merry Christmas!),

Laura Marie Altom

Laura Marie Altom began writing at the ripe old age of twelve when she penned a romance about a model falling for her photographer on a catalogue shoot in St Thomas. Up until page forty-two, she faithfully wrote at least a page a day, but gave up when following her own junior-high romantic pursuits became more fun than writing about someone else's!

Now, Laura spends her days contentedly writing and chasing after her twins and their menagerie of pets, ranging from a mutt named Sweet Pea, a mini long-haired dachshund named Cocoa, a black-and-white stealth cat named Domino and a yard full of ducks and geese who live in the pond but would like to live in the house! When night falls, Laura usually finds time to steal a few romantic moments for herself and her own hunky cover stud! Laura loves hearing from readers and may be reached via e-mail at BaliPalm@aol.com or snail mail at PO Box 2074, Tulsa, OK 74101.

Thanks so much to Alaskan bush pilot Dennis Whitesell. Your willingness to help a stranger all the way down in Oklahoma understand the Alaskan pilot's way of life makes you a hero in the truest sense of the word. That said, any research blunders are all mine, not his! Thank you to Mark at Budget Feed in Palmer, Alaska, for answering my cantaloupe questions.

Thanks also to my talented friend and fellow author Karen Crane (aka Karen Toller Whittenburg) who was so kind as to help with early drafts.

Chapter One

"You a virgin?"

"Excuse me?" Sociologist Dr. Whitney Foster glanced up from the Alaskan wildlife brochure she was trying to read. But her hands were shaking so badly from a wicked case of preflight jitters that the bouncing words, far from educating her, were making her nauseous. As hard as she'd been trying to learn about grizzly denning—and in the process, forget she was thousands of miles from home on Christmas Eve—she'd been trying that much harder to ignore her too-handsome-for-his-own-good pilot.

As well as being gorgeous, he also appeared to be clairvoyant. How could he tell just by looking at her that she hadn't been intimate with a guy in…well, suffice it to say it'd been a *loooong* time?

"You all right over there? Your cheeks look kind of pale."

Whitney shot the little plane's big pilot her most scholarly glare. "Sure. I'm, ah, great. After way too much school, I'm finally off on the career adventure of a lifetime. What could be better than that?''

His slow grin messed with her stomach even more than the clack of the plane's skis did as they skimmed over bumps on the lake's ice. ''Oh, I can think of a few things.''

''Which explains your interest in my virginity?''

''Ma'am…'' While she clutched the sides of her seat in terror, he pulled back on the yoke, then winked.

What did that mean?

''With all due respect to your bedroom experience or lack thereof, that comment was only my bumbling attempt at making polite conversation. You know, wondering out loud if this is your virgin flight in a small plane? If I ever ask a female passenger that question again, I'll rephrase it.''

''Oh. Yes. This is my first time.''

Whitney moaned inwardly. Where was a nice dark hole to climb into when you really needed one? Oh well, it wasn't like her pilot would ever get the chance to find out just how accurate his assessment of her had been.

While she wasn't technically a virgin, by the time she found a new Mr. Right, that old Madonna song ''Like a Virgin'' would definitely apply.

After aiming one more charming grin her way, he returned his attention to flying, thank goodness.

Oh, she knew his type.

Cornball-sexy Santa hat that made him look like a fun guy. A rangy build big enough to make a petite woman feel protected. Gulf-of-Alaska-green eyes with an entire tidal chart of perils. Thick dark hair perfect for running her fingers through. Square jaw sporting one of those all-day five o'clock shadows—just prickly-soft enough to tease a girl into thinking she'd been kissed by a real man, when in reality he was probably a snake.

Like another snake who'd coiled in the bushes, using her to pounce on her supposed best friend.

Ha! As if spoiled Marcie Hawthorne even needed another man—she was an heiress, for heaven's sake! And as for that no-good Rocco Stone—during her last weeks at school, Whitney had heard through the campus grapevine that Rocco wasn't even his name. His *real* name was Ralph Stanley. And he wasn't a senior in premed, but a late-night janitor pretending to be a student at Hillborough College.

After being sweetly courted by him for the better part of six months, after knowing deep in her heart that he was the one, Whitney had caught him sleeping with her roommate, Marcie—his new wife. She'd later found out through still more campus gossip that all along, Rocco had only been using her as an entrée to her rich friend.

Never had Whitney felt so foolish.

She'd thought she was in love with him. During particularly boring sessions of thesis research, she'd even practiced writing *Mrs. Rocco Stone* in flowing script.

Even worse, what with the less-than-stellar example her own parents had set with their love life, Whitney should have known better than to fall for a guy like him—or any guy for that matter.

Her dad, through his many conspicuous absences from the defining moments of her life, had proven that she would've been far happier never even knowing him. At least then she wouldn't have been so heartbroken when he hadn't shown up for her elementary-school Christmas choir concerts or high-school musicals or even her graduation.

Talk about leading by example. If she ever had kids, she'd darn well raise them on her own. She would've been much better off without a dad.

Her children would be, too.

And then there was her mom. Another great example of how *not* to lead your life. Her mom had long since shown Whitney that all males were dangerous with a capital *D*. Trouble was, Candace Foster-too-many-last-names-to-count didn't find men dangerous—she found them fascinating. She didn't just fall for every guy she met—she married him!

As a result, she'd become so reliant on men that she hardly answered the door anymore without asking her latest hubby for his opinion.

Whitney loved her mother dearly, and knew that when her father had left for greener pastures when she was ten, it'd really thrown her mom for a loop. But instead of figuring out how to make her own way in the world, Candace had turned to wedding rings for support.

Whitney, on the other hand—aside from her brief lapse of judgment in dating Rocco—had prided herself on being as self-reliant as they come.

Once the initial rocket launch into a gray winter sky evened into an only mildly bumpy ride, Whitney tried to relax by counting the plastic red berries on the silver garland lining the plane's curved ceiling.

Ceiling? Was that the technical term for the roof of an airplane? Who knew?

When that didn't work, she tried drawing parallels between this trip and the summer sociological field trip she'd taken with several classmates a few years ago. They'd been following up on Polly Wiesner's 1970s study of Hxaro gift exchange among the !Khung San in Botswana and Namibia.

Problem was, even on that remote trek, the bumpiest moments had been when their Land Rover caravan hit a treacherous series of mud holes. Sure, there might have been a few lions watching from the shadows for their chance to swallow her whole, but at least she hadn't had to sit beside them.

Up here, with only the width of her black down coat separating her from the pilot's worn brown leather flight jacket—the one filling the whole cabin with its rich scent—well…

The small craft hit a nasty sky bump.

Whitney instinctively grabbed one supple leather sleeve and the edge of her seat, trying to ignore the tingly-hot waves of awareness that flooded her system from that one simple touch.

"Uh-huh," the pilot said with another of his potent grins. "You're a virgin all right."

As if it had burst into flame, she released his sleeve.

Hmph. Who did he think he was? That hadn't been attraction for him making her fingers tingle, but an internal warning reminding her that just like so many men she'd met, this one was no good.

"Let's see if I can get us around the worst of this," he said, humming "Jingle Bells" while banking the plane hard to the left. But upon closer inspection of a towering gray cloud, he shook his head. "Where did that monster come from? I checked the weather twice, and this storm wasn't due for a while."

"If it's that bad," Whitney asked above the engine's raised pitch, "shouldn't we turn back? I'm okay with spending another night. The lodge I stayed at last night was charming. Crackling fire. Gorgeous Christmas decorations—even better food.

I had steak and a loaded baked potato. I didn't know you had sour cream all the way up here.''

"On good days we have satellite TV and bubble gum, too." He reached to the plane's dash for a purple pack of grape Bubble Yum. "So see? We're not all that uncivilized. Want a piece?"

Nodding, she took the packet from him and worked the foil free enough to take one of the four remaining pieces.

The plane hit another nasty bump, but this time, Whitney busied herself with the gum.

"Mind getting me a piece, too?" he asked after she'd popped her first bubble. "Smells good."

"Sorry," she said over the sudden pinging of ice against the windows. "I should have offered you some when I took mine."

Unwrapping his piece of gum, she tried not to notice how he'd tightened his grip on the yoke. Now she saw why commercial pilots kept their cockpit doors shut.

When it came to flying, ignorance really was bliss.

Bouncing, pinging.

Bouncing, pinging—then the engine launched into a whirring cough.

"Um, want me to rewrap your gum?" She'd only touched the paper.

"Wouldn't ordinarily ask this, but would you mind just popping it in my mouth?" Instead of his customary grin, he gave her a grimace. "With this change in the weather, I should keep my hands on the rudder."

"Absolutely." She nodded. "Sounds like a good plan. Excellent. Best I've heard in—"

"Gum?"

"Oh, right. Sorry." He opened his mouth and she popped it in, and instantly wished she'd kept her thick gloves on to perform the operation. The whispery brush of his lips and hot breath on her fingers caused more distress than the jostling plane. Her stomach flip-flopped, and that odd tingly sensation swept through her again.

Okay, what was going on?

No case of airsickness she'd ever heard of started with a gnawing, all-consuming—completely irrational—urge to touch one's pilot!

"Thanks for the gum," he said.

"You're welcome." *And thank you for being so darned hot that at least looking at you is taking my mind off this lousy weather.*

TEN MINUTES LATER, the icy assault had let up, and Colby Davis wondered if he should use the time to try calming his passenger. The flight and weather were routine to him, but judging by her wide-eyed stare, she wasn't likely to be a repeat customer.

"You know," he said, "back at the lake, I was in such a hurry to load your gear I didn't get a chance to properly introduce myself.'' Left hand on the stick, he offered her his right. ''I'm Colby.''

''Whitney,'' she said. ''Nice to meet you.''

His grip swallowed her slim fingers, triggering not only instant awareness and heat, but that infernal protective streak that had gotten him into more trouble than he cared to remember.

She's just a paying customer, he told himself as he released her hand.

Even so, he cranked up the heater to warm her icy fingertips.

Since she didn't seem all that talkative at the moment, he took a turn at tossing the conversational ball. ''You said you're a sociologist. What're you doing with those yahoos up at the oil site?''

''The company I work for back in Chicago performs employee evaluations for other companies. In this case, Global Oil. They have a high turnover rate at remote sites like this and want me to study how isolation affects the crew, then develop ways to counteract it.''

Colby nodded.

Sounded like a load of bull to him, but he wasn't about to tell her that. Alaska either made a man or broke him. If the state were equated to a woman, she wouldn't be kind or forgiving, but she was fair. As long as a man kept his wits about him, he'd be okay.

Colby happened to love Alaska.

His friend Tanner, on the other hand, was giving serious thought to chucking it all in. His plan was to somehow sell his failing fishing lodge and then head to the lower forty-eight to seek his fortune. At the first sign of trouble, his wife Jenny had bailed. Tanner probably thought he could chase her down and work things out, but Colby had seen this sort of thing happen more times than he could remember.

You either loved Alaska or hated it, and you sure as hell couldn't force a woman to love it any more than you could force her to love a man.

Colby clenched his jaw.

Damn shame about those two. They'd been good together.

"How much longer?" Whitney asked, tracing a pattern in the frost on the inside of her window.

"'Bout thirty minutes. Maybe longer with this head wind."

She nodded, and blew a bubble at the same time he did. They both laughed.

"Feeling better?" he asked.

"Yeah," she said with her first genuine smile of the day. "Never underestimate the calming powers of a good grape bubble."

Grape bubbles, hell. What he'd underestimated was the power of her grin, which was warming him way more than the plane's heater.

Colby had time for one last chuckle before all hell broke loose.

Ice pellets spattered the windshield like bullets, one of them cracking the glass. Ferocious winds buffeted the tiny plane like a moose swinging its rack at a gnat.

"Hold on!" Colby said as the plane lost altitude, dipping into a terrifying valley only to rise back up to a treacherous, turbulence-filled peak.

He risked a sideways glance and saw his passenger's teeth chattering. From fear? Or was it just the icy fingers of wind slicing through every air hole in the plane? The heater wasn't coming close to keeping up.

The ice pellets had turned to freezing rain, coating the windshield.

Whitney watched her pilot press a button that made some sort of de-icing liquid squirt from the windshield wipers. It helped a bit, but hardly solved the icy problem.

The engine struggled to outpace the wind, whining from the effort.

"You ever been in this tight a jam before?" she managed to ask past her dry throat.

"This?" His white-toothed smile held enough raw sex appeal to set her senses on edge again. The plane's every bounce jingled the bell on his Santa hat, distracting her even more. "This is nothing. You should've been here the time I—"

The engine coughed and sputtered, then died.

"Okay," he said, fiddling with knobs and controls. "Now, we might be in a speck of trouble. But just a speck." He held his thumb and forefinger barely apart, but that didn't do much to calm her nerves.

"Oh God," she said. Inside, she said a little more. She wasn't ready to die.

She wasn't anywhere near ready to die.

She'd really looked forward to getting out of school. Acing her first field assignment—a two-month gig. Renewing her relationship with her mom. While Whitney never planned to marry—her mother had done enough of that for the both of them—she did very much want to have kids one day. And as for what would *make* those kids—the sex—she wanted the chance to try it again.

"Oh, God," she wailed. "I don't wanna die. I *really* don't wanna die."

"Me neither, sweetie." He held the yoke so tight that his face reddened and a vein popped on his forehead.

"Mayday, mayday," he called into the radio, relaying their location.

No one answered.

"Think anyone heard you?" Whitney asked above the racket from the storm.

"Hard to say." He gave the dash a good hard thwack, then fiddled with more knobs.

And then a rogue gust caught them, aiding in their not-so-gentle glide to the ground.

"You filed a flight plan, right?"

"Uh-huh."

"So then just as soon as we land, someone'll be out to get us?"

"That'd be nice."

"But…"

"But, too bad for us, if I know this area as well as I think I do, we're coming down smack dab in the middle of some of the roughest terrain on God's white earth."

He radioed for help again.

Twisted still more controls.

Something scraped the bottom of the plane. Tree-tops? Rock?

The plane lurched, then continued its rapid descent.

Jaw hard and knuckles white from fighting the forces trying to rip the yoke from his hand, Colby said, "You the praying kind?"

"Not particularly."

"Now might be a good time to start."

Chapter Two

"Whitney?" Minutes after ditching the plane in a powdery-soft snow bowl angels must have guided him to find, Colby gave his fare a light shake.

He felt his way in the darkness to an equipment box he kept beneath his seat, reaching inside for a flashlight. He flicked it on, shining it her way.

No blood. Good. *Very* good.

Her complexion was waxy, but considering what they'd just been through, that was no biggie.

Garland had fallen on her right shoulder. He flicked it off of her.

Leaning back in his seat, he slammed the yoke with the heel of his hand. Dammit, how had he let this happen?

He knew the route.

Knew the weather.

His landing had been safe but sloppy. The left wing had been sheared, throwing the whole ride off balance, plowing them deep into the snow.

By his calculations, this storm should've taken at least another day to barrel through this part of the state. He should've had more than enough time to safely deliver his fare to the drilling site, then get himself back to a crackling fire, a bowl of Nugget's steaming beef stew and that special Christmas Eve Lakers game on ESPN.

His fare.

Gazing at her now, he frowned.

From the second she'd stepped off the snow-crusted dock and into his plane, Whitney had become his responsibility.

And now?

He raked his fingers through his hair.

Now, he could quite possibly be responsible for her death. He wished he had a keg of the best beer in the world—Moose's Tooth Fairweather IPA—to counteract that sobering thought.

"Hello? Whitney?" he asked, giving her another shake. He held his open palm just below her nose. Puffs of breath warmed his hand. Whew. She was very much alive. Breathing normally—or as close to it as could be expected.

Colby ran the light over her legs, finding them surprisingly long for her small frame. And straight—thank God. Her arms looked good, too. The last thing he needed was broken limbs. He would have enough trouble just figuring out how to keep her warm.

Well…one tried and true method of keeping warm sprang to mind, but while snuggling naked would certainly do the trick, it hardly seemed professional. "Whitney? Can you hear me?"

Her eyelashes fluttered.

He shone the light in her eyes and she winced.

"Sorry," he said, relieved to see her awake. "You all right?"

"Is this going to make me late for work?"

Grinning, he pulled her into a hug. "Ahh, one thing's for sure, your sass is still alive and well. You're gonna be just fine."

"Am I? I mean, are we?"

"Honestly?" He released her and glanced out the window at the white wall of snow curtaining the plane. Turning away from that unpleasant sight, he said, "I don't know. I've been in more desperate jams."

"But?"

"This one's looking worse by the minute. That's not to say we don't have a great chance of rescue. Our ELT transmitter's on. Course, the signal's operated by radio, so the odds of it getting out in this weather are slim, but I did radio our coordinates out on the emergency channel. And if we make it through the storm and the weather clears, I can fire the signal pistol if we see any search planes…."

"But?"

"Quit with the buts, okay?"

"Sorry. I'm a bottom-line kind of girl. Give me the worst-case scenario. We're going to be squeezed in here together for what? Maybe one or two days?"

His lips settled in a grim line.

"More like a week? I packed tons of snack food, you know, since I didn't know what provisions they'd have at the site. I've got Twinkies and three kinds of Little Debbie cupcakes and graham crackers and granola bars. And Snickers—lots and lots of Snickers. We should be fine for food. And jeez, with all that snow, we won't even have to worry about water."

She shivered. "Any chance of you fixing the heater? It's freezing in here." She tried making a smoke ring from her visible breath but failed. "What? Why are you quiet all of a sudden?"

He swallowed hard.

For a manly guy like him, she wasn't sure if that was a good sign or bad. "Does that look of yours mean the heater can't be fixed?"

He nodded.

"Okay, but we've got food and water. That's good, right?"

"I'm sorry."

"No, no, don't be sorry. Sorry is bad. Just a minute ago, when I said I was a bottom-line girl? Well, I lied. I'm really more the ostrich type. That's why I prefer flying commercial. Because that way flying is like a Disney ride. You know, magic. I just pop my window shade down, slip on my headphones and before you know it—poof—we're magically there.'' Even the tears streaming down her cheeks felt cold. She swiped them away to keep them from freezing.

Colby unfastened his seat belt and angled himself to face her. For a long time he just stared at her, and then he skimmed the warm backs of his fingers against her cheek. ''Whitney, I'm sorry. *Really* sorry, but the plain truth is that in these conditions, well…it's gonna be pretty dangerous for rescue crews to go out. If we make it till morning, and the storm clears, well, that could be a whole new ball game. I've got snowshoes and a hatchet. I could turn all Paul Bunyan and cut down a whole damn forest to keep us warm. Problem is, by midnight tonight, this high up, we could be facing temps of fifty below.''

''But you don't know that for sure, right?''

He dropped his stare.

''Oh, God, this *is* bad. I've got so many plans for the future.'' She looked to her lap, then at him. ''I'm sure you've got plenty, too. I'd hoped to spend next Christmas with my mom—just couldn't bring myself to do it this year. And my job…it was just getting good. I've always dreamed of becoming famous in my field.''

''I didn't know there were any famous sociologists—but, hey, what do I know? If they give out Nobel prizes for that kind of thing, I'm sure you're a shoo-in.''

His big grin started up that tingling again, and his words made her retract every comparison she'd earlier made between him and Rocco. This man was nothing like Rocco.

Colby was considerate and sweet and funny— just the sort of man only thirty minutes earlier she would never have believed even existed.

She licked her lips, realizing anew how close they were sitting to each other. Colby's face was only inches from hers—close enough that even in the dim glow of the flashlight resting on his lap, she could see the tenderness in his gaze. Even better was the way heat from his breath caressed her lips, teasing them into a smile as the grapey-sweet smell of his gum tickled her nose.

''If I didn't have this gum in my mouth,'' he said, ''I'd kiss you.''

''If you can reach behind my seat for my purse, I have some tissue.''

''Oh, you do, do you?''

Was that a twinkle lighting his eyes?

Her heart skipped a beat.

Here she was quite possibly on the verge of dying. How could fate be so cruel as to finally introduce her to the last living nice guy only to— maybe—snatch him away mere hours later?

He found her purse, and she dug through for tissues to dispose of their gum. For an instant, as she rummaged through everyday items like lip gloss and aspirin and the little sewing kit she never left home without, life felt normal. But then she glanced at the frosty window and the odd angle of their seats and knew Colby could very well be right.

This might be the end for them both.

At this very moment, they could be down to only hours to live.

Her breath caught in her throat.

Hours? That was it?

How was that possible?

She swallowed hard.

"Hey." Her pilot leaned even closer to brush away her tears. "What's with the waterworks?"

Looking away, she shrugged.

"You're not upset over my gloom-and-doom routine, are you? Because if anyone can rescue us, it's the guys in Kodiak Gorge. They're top-notch."

"Really?"

"Yeah. Oh, hell, yeah." He hugged her again. Never had she felt safer and more secure than in this virtual stranger's arms. His touch warmed not just her body, but her soul.

When she'd recovered from her latest bout of tears, she pulled back just far enough to look at him. "Thank you," she said. "I needed a hug."

"Ho, ho, ho…" He jingled the bell on his Santa hat. "I'm all about making the little—and big— girls happy."

She giggled, and then he was inching closer, closer, until the heat of his hands on her arms had nothing on the glorious blaze of his lips. His kiss started out soft, maybe even a little teasing with those sugary grapes still flavoring his breath. Then he increased the pressure and she found herself not just going along for the ride, as she had with the few other men in her life, but meeting his tongue thrust for spellbinding thrust.

Never had she experienced such a myriad of re- actions all at once, from fascination and ecstasy to brazen curiosity. If just kissing Colby felt this good…

He drew back. "Wow. Sorry. That wasn't very professional."

Shaking her head, she touched her fingers to his still-moist lips. "It might not've been professional, but it was very nice."

Cupping her face in his big hands, he murmured, "Just nice?"

"I said *very*."

"Oh, well, in that case…may I kiss you again?"

Teary-eyed, she nodded.

And he did kiss her. Again and again.

Whitney groaned, repositioning herself to sink more deeply into his welcome embrace.

An hour earlier, she hadn't thought feelings like this were possible. Her attraction to him was so intense it felt more like a beautiful, snowy dream than reality.

If she'd known relations between a man and a woman could be like this, maybe she wouldn't have insisted that men weren't for her.

He deepened his kiss and she arched into him, seeking comfort and warmth and a resolution to the unfamiliar pulsing between her legs.

After what felt like hours but was probably closer to minutes, she fought past the lump in her throat and tucked her mussed hair behind her ears. She took a deep breath. "You know how I got so huffy when we were taking off and you asked if I was a virgin?"

"Yeah."

"I practically am."

"As in a haven't-had—you know—virgin?"

She nibbled her lower lip. "Technically, I suppose I'm not a virgin. But that one time... Well, it wasn't very good. I'm not even sure if we did it right."

"If you have to ask," he said with a big, knowing grin, "chances are he fumbled."

"Yeah, that's kinda what I figured."

"So how come you never tried it again?"

She shrugged.

"Been saving yourself for marriage?"

"Not exactly."

"Then why?"

"I don't know. My girlfriends say I expect too much. That I'm looking for perfection in an imperfect world." She bowed her head, thrust her fingers into her long hair and pulled. "Some luck, huh? After all this *saving*, here I am, stranded on a mountaintop and maybe about to—"

"No." He touched his fingers to her lips. "Don't say it. Don't even think it. I mean, I'd be lying if I told you our rescue is guaranteed, but…" He curved his hand to her cheek.

Leaning into his touch, she shivered. He tugged her onto his lap, holding her and kissing her and telling her without a word that whatever happened, at least she wouldn't have to go through it alone.

Her whole life, she'd been alone. Her mom had always had her men. Her dad, his work and various other women. And there she'd been, all on her own, trying to convince herself that that was just the way she liked it. But here, with Colby, she was questioning that. For if going solo was so right, then why did being with Colby feel anything but wrong?

Laughing, she said, "I've never even had an org—well, you know."

"You mean a…oh." He coughed and, thankfully, didn't say the big *O* word out loud.

Good grief, what had gotten into her to even bring it up?

Maybe because the only thing Santa's going to bring me is frostbite?

Sobering, she nodded. "But listen to me, rambling on about something so unimportant in the grand scheme of things. If we don't make it off this mountain, the only person who'll miss me is my landlady—and that's not even because she particularly likes me, but because I'm the only one in the building paid up on my rent." She glanced to her hands, snug in his warm grip, then back into his eyes. "So? Who'll be missing you?"

"Besides my mom..." He squeezed her fingers. "No one special. I don't have a steady girl, or even pets. A lot of great friends, but that's about it." Leaning against his seat, he dropped his head back and sighed. "Mom sent me a plane ticket to fly down to New Mexico for the holidays. She didn't want me flying all that way by myself." With a sad laugh, he added, "What's that old saying about accidents always happening closest to home?"

Whitney swallowed hard. This wasn't happening. *Couldn't* be happening.

On the one hand, she was sharing great conversation with a fun guy. On the other, they might have only hours to live. The very thought didn't seem real, which was probably a good thing, otherwise she'd give in to the acid-tinged panic rising in her throat.

"I feel bad about not going to see her," he said,

gazing out the plane's side window at black fringed with white. "Even in hard times, Christmas was her thing. She always made a point of giving a gift to every single man, woman and child in this town—mostly cookies and homemade candies, but she didn't want anyone feeling alone or left out."

"She sounds like one of those rare souls who truly gets what Christmas is all about."

"Yeah. I miss her. I should've gone down."

"Why didn't you?"

He took his hand back, then used it to rub his forehead. "Long story."

"Unless the Marines show up, I'm not going anywhere."

Colby shot her a look. "I can't believe I'm this petty, but here goes. Truth? I didn't want to see my mom and her new husband because the two of them together—and his three daughters, and their husbands and happy, laughing kids—remind me how much I want to get married and have kids. They make me see what a cool grandmother my mom makes. How much better life would be if I had a family. Hell, seeing all of them makes me feel like less of a man. Like a failure."

"Oh, Colby, no. Not everyone has to get married. That's just what society wants us to think, but—"

"Look," he said, "I don't know about you, but

for me, having my own family isn't about recreating some sentimental magazine photo of a mom, dad and baby around a cozy fireplace. It's about how I feel—or lately, don't—in here." He patted his chest. "Dammit, I wanted a wife. Rug rats. I didn't plan on going out alone."

Whitney bowed her head.

You're not alone, Colby. You have me.

Obviously, though, she wasn't enough, and because it was Christmas Eve and she might not live to see Christmas Day, the realization hurt. Because, maybe for the first time in her life, she wanted more than just her career. That morning, she'd have denied it. But now, with the icy wind howling *now or never,* it was time for honesty—having someone all her own to love didn't sound half bad.

She closed her eyes, trying to find at least momentary relief from the stinging tears that seemed to have taken on a life of their own. After clearing her throat, she said, "You mentioned wanting a wife. Haven't you found the right woman?"

"Thought I had. Margot was up here on vacation. Her father's a Global Oil exec. It was a whirlwind thing. At the end of her two weeks, I asked her to stay. She asked me to come with her. Neither of us bent. End of story."

"I'm sorry," she said.

"Yeah, me, too. Now, I only date local girls."

"Are there many?"

"Sadly, no."

At another time, in another place, she might have found his comment funny. Now, it only seemed sad. Even in the short time she'd known him, Colby had struck her as a great guy. He deserved a great woman.

Like me.

The crazy thought hit as unexpectedly as the freak storm that had shot down their plane. But was the idea really so wrong?

Wouldn't it be just her stupid luck to meet the man of her dreams just before—

"What're you thinking?" Colby asked, illuminating her with the flashlight. "You've got a dangerous look in those big brown eyes."

She licked her lips. "My idea is only dangerous if we get rescued. But since you said yourself we probably won't—and you are the local expert in these matters—then..." She took the light from him and set it on a box that had gotten wedged behind her seat. Aimed outside, it gave the menacing snow an ironically romantic blue glow. Reaching for Colby's hands, she brushed the pads of her thumbs over the soft web between his thumb and forefinger. His skin felt rough but warm. So blessedly warm.

"Oh no," he said. "You're not suggesting what I think you are?"

She nodded. "Please, Colby. I might not even

get to live, let alone reach my destination. Please don't let me die alone. Even if it's for just one night, I want to feel…'' Out of her mind with fear, guilt, need and doubt, she kissed him, stopping only to slip off her heavy boots and scramble onto his lap. "Please," she said, ringing kisses around the small strip of skin above his sandy-colored wool sweater.

"Whitney…" Colby closed his eyes and sighed. This couldn't be happening—even though he had, very unprofessionally, been wishing it would. Hands lightly on her shoulders, urging her back, he said, "From what you've told me, maybe you are still a virgin. And we *are* going to survive. I can't in good conscience take that kind of gift from you. It wouldn't be right. You deserve better than this. A nice, soft bed and candles and romantic music and flowers and wine. I mean, here…the sheer logistics make it—"

She cut him off with another kiss—a seemingly innocent pressing of her soft, bubble-gum-flavored lips to his.

Initially, their lips were cold. Then came a torturous heat Colby knew he wasn't gentlemanly enough to deny.

He might be knocking on death's door, but until then, he was going to live.

Whitney groaned, words caught in her throat. Her pilot—her granter of last wishes—slipped his cool fingers beneath layers of wool and corduroy and cotton until he reached her warm satin bra. He circled his hand over her nipple, honing it into a sensation-filled bud.

Normally, with most men, this was about the point when she called it quits. It wasn't that she was a prude. She just never felt anything. But this time, here with Colby, her world was being transformed from an eight-color box of Crayolas into the giant sixty-four pack with the built-in sharpener.

Hand still teasing her breast, he dragged his lips from her mouth to her neck. Her toes curled with naughty pleasure. She closed her eyes, drawing him even closer.

"Wait." He pulled back again. "If we're going to do this, you should at least be comfortable."

After one more kiss, he gently coaxed her back into her own seat. Then he scrambled into the cargo area, rearranging her luggage and snacks to make room for a makeshift bed. Nestled between her suitcases was her down sleeping bag. He had one, too—an FAA requirement for Alaskan winter flying. Between the two of them, they had more than enough down feathers to line a damned cozy nest.

He took off his jacket and shoes. "Nippy in here," he said.

Teeth chattering, she nodded.

"Look at you," he said, clambering to the front.

He took her into his arms, trying to stop her shivering. When that didn't work, he released her and unzipped his coat. Tucking her warm curves against him, pressing her breasts against his chest, he told himself it was all about shared body heat. He fully planned to be a gentleman.

But then Whitney slipped one of her cold little hands up under his sweater, easing it along the wall of his chest. He wasn't sure who initiated the kissing—wasn't sure it even mattered who, so long as it never stopped.

Together they worked at removing each other's many clothes, and together they fell to the sleeping bags, slipping inside where the flannel was at first cold, but then soft and warm against bare skin.

He was half-on, half-off her, one of his legs between hers. She arched against him. "Now…"

Lips on her throat, he shook his head. "Later. *Much* later."

Gently, he swept a fallen lock of hair from her cheek and whispered her name, hoping both actions said quite plainly what his few words hadn't. *Later, much later, I'm going to make your second time—quite possibly, your last time—one you'll never forget.*

Chapter Three

Deep into the night, Colby had lost count of how many times they'd made love. Whitney had drifted into sleep eventually. Without her to distract him, the gravity of their situation hit hard. The air in the plane's cabin was so cold he could see his breath. A fine sheet of frost coated almost every surface. Already, his beloved plane—his most prized possession—was evolving from transport to tomb.

He moved to rub his stubbled jaw, but Whitney was using his right arm as a pillow.

Good Lord, what a night, he thought, giving himself an awkward scratch with his left hand. Whitney was an amazing girl—woman. Under different circumstances, who knew where things might lead?

Funny, when he'd first landed in this snow bowl in the middle of nowhere, all he could think about were the loose ends of his life that would now be forever undone.

And questions. So many questions.

Would his mom be all right? Who would get his stuff, since he'd never gotten around to drawing up a will? Who would fix Nugget's busted toaster or help him serve Christmas breakfast at the lodge? Who would gather old Henry's firewood when the snow got too deep for him to leave his cabin, and who would make sure he remembered his high-blood-pressure medication?

But now, nestled beside the sweetest curves he'd ever had the pleasure of embracing, his mind skipped to more important things. Matters of family and love.

His father had taken off the day before Colby's sixth birthday. Swallowing hard, he remembered his blow-out-the-candles double wish.

I wish Dad would come home.

I wish Mom would stop crying.

Twenty-five years later, his newlywed mom sported a perpetual grin. His first wish hadn't come true, but at this point, Colby didn't even want it to. As far as he was concerned, his old man was a bum. In every way possible—from overachieving in school to running a successful business while finding time to help anyone in need—Colby had strived to become the kind of man his father had never been. A man worthy of respect.

While Colby was growing up, his mom had waitressed at Kodiak Lodge. Having lived in Kodiak Gorge all her life, she'd often said she should have known better than to marry an outsider. She'd since married another, though, and become an outsider herself by moving to New Mexico with a retired CEO she'd met when he'd spent a week in Kodiak Gorge fly-fishing.

Colby used to wonder how she stood the desert heat, but right now an eternity of hundred-degree days didn't sound half bad.

As a kid, Colby had vowed that if he had a son someday, he'd never leave as his father had. Course, in light of his current situation, that was a moot point. From the looks of things, his dream of becoming a dad might never come true. Unless...

He glanced at Whitney. *Could* she be pregnant? No, he decided. And since they might both die, he wouldn't want her to be.

She rolled onto her side, snuggling her cheek against the coarse hairs of his chest.

Colby knew he was too rough around the edges for her type, but then that didn't matter much, either.

''Merry Christmas,'' she mumbled, the heat of her ice-fogged breath arousing him all over again.

''Merry Christmas yourself, Santa Baby. Although it's still dark and I don't know where you flung my watch, so I have no idea if it's really the big day.'' He kissed the top of her head, loving the clean scent of her shampoo.

"Who cares? With you, I'm guessing any day would be a big day."

"Thanks," he said, twirling a lock of her hair. "So? You ready for one more lesson?"

She grinned. "Sure, but after that, how about breaking for Christmas cookies and cocoa?"

"Sorry. I'm fresh out. But I do have something else you might like."

"HEY, GUYS, OVER HERE! I think I found 'em!" Working in near-whiteout conditions by the light of battery-powered headlamps near the top of Juneau Ridge, Brody Muldoon waved over the rest of his rescue crew. They operated much like volunteer firefighters, answering any nearby call for help. Hell, for that matter, most of them *were* volunteer firefighters.

Colby Davis would've risked his life for any one of them. For half of the adventure-seeking dimwits in Kodiak Gorge, he already had.

Now it was Colby's turn to be rescued, and by God, not a single man on the crew was prepared to even breathe the word *defeat*—let alone admit it.

The wind shifted, blowing enough snow off the tail of Colby's beloved—and now busted—De-Havilland Beaver to validate Brody's hunch.

"Yeah, baby!" he shouted, already using his lightweight shovel to dig out Colby and his passenger. "One more hour and they'd have been buried till spring."

"Think they're alive?" asked Tanner.

"Hope so. Never much cottoned to dead fish in a can—not even packed in oil."

Tanner grimaced. "Love you, Brode. Always the poet."

"Not!" called out Sergei Koyck, one of the founding members of the crew.

"All right," Brody said. "Let's quit the chatter and dig. It's damned cold out here. Once we find Colby and his fare, I can't wait to sink my teeth into that Christmas ham I smelled cooking at the lodge."

Twenty minutes later, the beams from their headlamps cutting weak yellow paths through blowing snow, the four-man crew located the plane's windshield and then dug around to the door. The temperature must've been dropping a few degrees every minute, 'cause Brody felt as if his ice-crusted eyebrows were crinkle fries.

"Got it," he finally said, digging out the handle, then kicking away the remaining snow to yank open the door. It would have been faster to bust a window, but if either Colby or his fare were unconscious just on the other side, Brody didn't want them cut by glass. "Someone wanna give me more light?"

Tanner offered a powerful flashlight from his tool belt.

"Thanks," Brody said, peering into the gloom. At first glance, the plane appeared abandoned, but then he shone the light into the cargo area. "They're here," he called back to the guys, "but I can't tell if they're still alive."

He climbed in, slicing the light through his foggy breath toward the lumpy mound.

No blood. But no signs of movement, either. And no appendages peeking out to at least give him a clue.

Damn, he hoped they weren't already gone. That'd be a really crappy ending to an already crappy day.

He and Colby went way back. Not that he'd go shouting it from the rooftops, but Brody loved Colby like a brother.

Steeling himself for the worst, praying for the best, Brody jerked back the covers to find a sight even more shocking than two dead bodies.

Two very much alive and buck-naked bodies.

Snuggled together cozy as a couple of squirrels all tucked in for winter were Colby and his fare— both in a deep sleep.

Hmm, their ordeal must've been exhausting, all right—in a *good* way!

Colby's fare was a pretty little thing, decked out in nothing but his goofy Santa hat. Judging by the pink tones of their bare skin, both parties looked to be in excellent condition.

Tossing the cover back over the juicy parts, Brody cleared his throat, then shouted, "Got 'em, boys!"

Tanner popped his head through the open door. "Colby okay?" His lips curved into a wide grin. "Oh heck, yeah. From the looks of it, I'd say he's doing a damned sight better than the rest of us."

COLBY SAT STRAIGHT UP, cast a sleepy look at his grinning friends, and said, "Hot damn. The elves put a rescue crew in my stocking." He couldn't stop smiling—until he noticed not just his naked chest, but the naked woman beside him.

Whitney.

Sweet, beautiful, innocent, almost virginal Whitney. After the night they'd just shared, she'd officially become an ex-almost-virgin.

Oh, man, he thought, rubbing his stubbled jaw.

Man, oh man.

Never.

Never, in a million, trillion years would his buds let him live this down. They'd hound him till the end of time, at which point they'd follow him straight to hell to start all over again.

Drawing the covers over himself and his still-sleeping companion, Colby groaned.

What had he done? Oh sure, chances were Whitney wasn't pregnant, but what if she were? There'd be no question about his marrying her. He would. Period. No child of his would ever grow up without his or her dad.

But he was putting the cart before the horse. First off, odds were that she wasn't pregnant. And second, even though he was attracted to Whitney, they weren't anywhere ready for a lifelong commitment.

"Yo, Colby?" Brody said. "You two ready to get the hell off this mountain?"

"Yeah," Colby said, putting his hand to his suddenly aching forehead. "Just give us a sec, will ya?"

"Sure thing, bud. Just come on out when you're ready."

After his friend had left, closing the cabin door behind him, Colby said to the warm curves beside him, "Knock, knock? The coast is clear. You still under there?"

The woman he'd just spent the best hours of his life with poked her mussed head out from under the covers. She wasn't smiling.

"You okay?" he asked, smoothing his fingers over her hair, releasing the subtle, clean scent that had driven him wild all night long. Just the silk of her hair against the palm of his hand renewed his hunger for her.

She nodded but wouldn't meet his gaze.

Slipping his fingers beneath her chin, he forced

her to look at him. "Those guys are cool," he said. "They might come off a little rough around the edges, but trust me, not a word of your part in this will ever be mentioned once we get off the mountain."

Nodding, she swallowed hard.

"Hey then, what's wrong? I know being found in the buff was awkward, but sweetie, we're going to live. That's a good thing, right?"

"Yes, of course. It's just that…"

"What?"

"This…us—all of it—was just so out of character for me. Don't get me wrong, I loved it. Being with you. I wouldn't trade what we've just shared for the world. But while on the outside nothing's changed, in here—" She touched her hand to her heart "—I'm scared to death that nothing will ever be the same."

"What do you mean?"

"Beats me," she said with a shy smile. "Maybe just that I thought I had my whole life figured out, but now, I'm not so sure."

"Well, hey," he said, lacing his fingers through hers. "How about letting me help you figure it out? My hours are pretty flexible. Over the next few weeks, we could get to know each other under less stressful circumstances."

"That sounds nice," she said. Her wistful expression squeezed his heart. "But I don't think so."

"Why?"

"It would just never work."

"What wouldn't? I'm not talking lifelong commitment here—just sharing a bottle of wine over a good meal. I'll even cook."

"Thank you," Whitney said. "I appreciate the offer. In fact, I appreciate everything you've done for me. You're a super pilot for getting us through this alive—and an even better friend—but I think that's where it should end."

That's where it has to end, because as incredible as it seems, over the course of one night, I've fallen for you, Colby Davis. Hard. The problem is, what we shared wasn't real. It was a magical night based on the fact that we both thought we were going to die. We both said and did things we never would've under ordinary circumstances. How do I know the man you were last night is the real you? How do I know the feelings you evoked in me were real?

Bottom line, Whitney thought, as she clutched the covers higher around her neck, was that the depth of her feelings for Colby was scary. The easiest way to avoid having to explore those feelings was to ignore them.

She'd return to her world. Colby would return to his. And, with any luck, the two of them would never meet again. As painful as that might be, it was the only sane thing to do.

For very sound reasons, she'd distrusted men for most of her life. Why on earth would she trade that wealth of emotional knowledge for one idyllic night, that under ordinary circumstances, would never have happened?

"Women." Reaching for his shirt, Colby shook his head. "If I live to be a hundred, I'll never understand you people."

Rolling her eyes, she grabbed her own top. "Likewise."

Colby finished dressing in silence, then said, "I'll wait outside for you to get your clothes on—but you might want to hurry. The weather's not getting any better."

"Okay, thanks. Oh—Colby?"

"Yeah?"

"I'm sorry."

"Me, too."

After they'd loaded Whitney's luggage and junk food into Brody's Cessna—he'd put skis on it for the winter—the trip to the Global Oil site took just under an hour.

Dot, the only woman on Global's crew, showed Whitney to her room. A few minutes later, Whitney returned and thanked Colby again, along with the rest of the guys. Then, without so much as a hug, she claimed exhaustion and went to bed.

Beside a roaring fire in Global's rec room, with *Christmas Vacation* blaring on the big screen,

Colby clinked beer bottles with Brody. "Thanks again, man. I wasn't looking forward to becoming a human Popsicle."

Brody cracked a smile. "Didn't look like you were in too much danger of that, judging by the heat you and Miss Chicago were radiating."

"Man…" Colby snorted. "Talk about a failure to communicate. There was one point during the night when I actually thought she could've been the one. I mean, we were…" He shook his head. "Then once you guys got there—poof—it was like the woman I met had been a dream."

"She's a dream, all right," Brody said, sipping his beer. "Definitely too good for the likes of you."

"Thanks, man. Appreciate it."

"You bet." Brody slapped Colby's back. "Just doing my part to keep you real."

WITH THE WIND HOWLING outside her beige cell of a bedroom, Whitney tried losing herself to sleep, but it refused to come. Over and over her mind kept flashing back to Colby and the wonderfully wild time they'd shared.

She closed her eyes and caught glimpses of him freeze-framed in her own private movie. His square-jawed face and sea-green eyes. Those biceps and washboard abs. She'd loved just staring at him and running her fingers along his rippled stomach and the tree trunks he called arms. He'd probably earned his strength by chopping wood and maintaining his plane—the one now stuck forever at the top of a mountain.

What would he do without it? Undoubtedly, he had insurance. But still, having been through one minor auto accident that had required her to submit a claim, she knew the next few weeks didn't hold much fun for him.

Her throat tightened.

In a perfect world, she'd want to be there with him, helping him through his frustration. But if there was one thing she'd learned in her twenty-six years, it was that as beautiful as the world often was, it could also be cruel.

Her own parents—even friends with failed relationships—had shown her that a girl like her would be playing with dynamite to entertain, even for a second, the notion of staying with Colby.

In the first place, how did she know he'd even want her to stay? And in the second, she *couldn't* stay.

I'm afraid of falling for him. Of opening myself up—I could get hurt. And what about my career? I've worked so hard to get where I am.

She curled onto her side beneath a pile of wool blankets and hugged Colby's Santa hat, which still smelled of him. Lulled by off-key carols and the faint male laughter drifting in from the rec room, she felt drowsiness overtake her. From the sound of things, quite a few guys were still awake. It wasn't any old masculine voice catching her attention, though. Only Colby's.

Had it really been less than twelve hours since all his laughs had been for her?

Squeezing her eyes tight, for what she promised herself would be the last time, she imagined herself with him. Maybe in Global's festive rec room? Or that cozy cabin of his he'd talked about? Shoot, since it was her fantasy, she even tried imagining him in her ultra-feminine Chicago apartment. But try as she might, she just couldn't see brawny Colby Davis at home on her turf.

No, he belonged up here in the wild. Alaska suited him. Just as she knew deep in her heart that it didn't suit her.

With a sigh, she returned to her fantasy of Colby's cabin. She was back in front of a crackling fire, back in the circle of his arms. They'd share a few beers, a few jokes, a few still-warm Christmas cookies, and most of all…a few more spellbinding kisses.

"WELL, GUESS THIS IS IT," Colby said to Whitney well over a month later in mid-February, not sure what else to say in the few minutes before she had to go through security and board her commercial flight. When she'd called and asked him, in a painfully polite voice, to fly her from the oil site to

Anchorage, he'd agreed—against his better judgment. After picking her up in a rented Aviat, he'd spent an awkward couple of hours trying his damnedest not to brush his arms against hers or to inhale the familiar scent of her shampoo.

At the Anchorage airport, she hadn't wanted him to escort her to the security gates, but he'd insisted, needing to make sure she made the short trip safely.

His conscience twinged.

Yeah, right, what he really needed to do was make sure she once and for all left him in peace.

With her finally back in Chicago, he wouldn't have to worry so much about his downright spooky attraction to her. That attraction had done its fair share of keeping him up late at night, dreaming of her. Of the sexy cinch of her waist easing into lush hips, of the rush of tenderness that swept through him when he just whispered her name.

"Thanks," she said, pausing in front of the metal detectors to hold out her right hand for him to shake.

He took her slight hand in his and gulped.

How could one simple touch bring back so many steamy memories?

The smoothness of her skin. The heat of her breath on his lips just before he kissed her. The heavy swell of her warm breasts in his hands as her nipples hardened against his palms.

He shook his head. This had to stop.

For whatever reason, the lady didn't have the hots for him like he had for her—or, correction, *had* had. His momma didn't raise no fool. Ever since Whitney had given him the cold shoulder the night of their rescue, he'd warned himself to stop thinking about her. And the instant she set foot on her flight, forgetting her would be a whole lot easier.

She'd be back in Chicago. He'd be back at work. And with any luck, he'd never, *ever*, have to see her again.

"Thanks for what?" he managed to ask, barely able to breathe through the storm of emotions crashing through him. What was wrong with him? Why couldn't his body take the hint that no matter how good the two of them had once been, whatever chemistry they'd shared was over?

She shrugged before turning his insides to mush with the sweetest, saddest grin.

Were those tears shimmering in her eyes?

She swallowed hard. "Thanks for just being you, Colby Davis."

For a second, he thought she was going to follow that cryptic statement with a hug, but she didn't. A guy in a fancy suit gruffly asked if he could cut past her in line. And just like that, the moment was gone, and so was she.

Watching her slight form disappear among the

other travelers crowding the concourse, Colby tucked his hands into his jeans pockets, then muttered, ''Goodbye, Whitney.'' Finally he turned away from her and headed back to his life.

Chapter Four

Colby used the tail of his red flannel shirt to wipe sweat from his abs, but then figured, what the hell? Days like this were a gift from the Alaskan gods, so he went ahead and took his shirt off, tossing it onto the dock. The hot July sun warmed his chest as he buffed the left wing of his new girl, Janine— a 1999 Cessna Caravan he'd gotten an outrageous deal on due to the previous owner's divorce.

Reason? The usual. Poor guy's wife hated Alaska.

Hated eternal sun and bugs in summer, eternal darkness and snow in winter.

Too bad she hadn't stuck around to see today.

Not a cloud within five hundred miles. A hint of a breeze sighing through the spruce, stirring the lake just enough to shoot diamonds off choppy waves lapping the underside of the stubby dock.

And the smell.

Sweet holy Mary, there was nothing quite like

the smell of Kodiak Lake baking in the sun. The musky, mossy, fishy blend made his mouth water just thinking about all those trout he planned on catching next weekend. Of course, since today was Saturday, his much-anticipated weekend off was still another whole week away. He put his back into buffing the finish his new owner's manual called Jet-Glo Snow White.

From across the lake flashed a glint of white sun on glass. A dust cloud billowed behind a fast-moving red pickup. Henry. With luck, he was delivering that box of reworked parts Colby was supposed to fly out to the Global Oil site this afternoon.

Kneeling to slap the lid on his can of wax, Colby eased his lips into a smile. It was good to be back in his routine. Transporting tourists to the best fishing spots. Bringing supplies and mail to the Global site and to the smattering of Kodiak Gorge citizens who lived on the edge of civilization but still had an occasional hankering to read the *Miami Sun Herald* or eat Virginia ham.

Back on his feet, heading for his office, Colby noted that Henry was nearly there—not that the chug-glugging of his cantankerous old Ford hadn't already announced that fact. Every winter, Henry tucked the truck into his shed till spring. And every spring there were bets on whether or not the heap would start back up.

This particular winter being so harsh, Colby had been among those betting that this would be the year the old truck finally gave up the ghost. But to the contrary, much like Henry himself, it had come back louder and smellier than ever. Smoking and belching, the vehicle startled a flock of geese into honking flight as it rounded the swampy area at the lake's south end.

Colby grinned.

Yep, it'd been a long winter, but summer had finally come, along with an end to all his waiting.

Waiting for insurance money to come through. Waiting for his mom to stop calling every day to make sure he was okay. Waiting to find a new plane. Worst of all, waiting for the guys around town to lay off with the wolf whistles every time he strode into sight.

Okay, so he'd been caught with his pants down, but it wasn't like ninety percent of the gang hanging out at Kodiak Lodge wouldn't have done the same had they been stuck in a similar situation.

After all, Whitney was beautiful, intelligent and funny. She had the most luxurious black hair, and her nose crinkled when she laughed. And those eyes—big and brown—were shot with intriguing amber flecks even his dim flashlight had picked up.

After the guys had rescued them, she'd had about the same initial reaction he'd had—jubilation at first, then embarrassment, then shock. In the hour it had taken to deliver her and all her junk food to the oil site, they'd said a whole five words.

She'd chosen a seat well away from him on Brody's plane, making it painfully clear that what they'd shared—whatever it was—wasn't only over, but that it never should've happened. That only made him grumpier, since she was the one who'd practically begged him not to let her die an almost-virgin.

When he'd left her at the airport, he'd felt as though the least he should do was wish her well with a friendly hug, but she'd stood ramrod-stiff.

Lucky for him, he reminded himself with a sharp breath, was the fact that she was thousands of miles away from him and presumably busy with her Chicago life. Right where she belonged. Right where, though he'd never admit it, he hoped she'd stay. Not that he'd given their encounter much thought.

After all, it had just been a night. An ordinary night. Crash a plane. Make love five or six times. Nothing too earth-shattering there.

Oh, yeah? Then why was he getting hard just thinking about her? Not to mention his last time seeing her?

HENRY BLARED the red Ford's horn, jolting Colby from his downright unacceptable memories. Fanning himself with a box flap, he blamed the day's sunshine for dredging up all that heat.

Shrouded in a cloud of dust, the truck stopped a mere two feet from the lake's edge. The sun's glare on the Ford's tinted windows prevented Colby from seeing most of the car's interior. "How're things?" Henry shouted out the open driver's side window with a wave of his beat-up fedora.

"Couldn't be better." Colby set his box filled with waxing supplies on a dock post. "Been to the clinic yet about your arthritis?"

Henry shooed off the question.

"You do know they have medicine to help?"

"Damned horse pills. Save your mothering for someone who needs it."

Colby grinned. Looked like he'd be taking Henry to the doctor himself. "You bring those parts for Global?"

"What parts?" Henry turned off the engine, then eased open his door.

The geese that had only just settled down about a quarter mile down the road started honking again.

"What do you mean, what parts?" Colby asked, shrugging into his shirt. "Global hired you to re-work them two weeks ago. You promised to have them to me no later than today—coincidentally, the same day I promised them to Global."

Henry waved him off. "What I brought is way more fun than some old parts. Got dropped off at the lodge last night. Think that fella Vic, out of Anchorage, was the one making the delivery."

"Oh yeah?" Hand to his forehead, shading his eyes from the glare, Colby said, "Unless you happen to have a million bucks stashed in there with my name on it, I'd just as soon have Global's parts."

Henry turned to the truck and hollered, "You ever plannin' on getting out?"

The squeal of the rusty passenger door sent the geese into such a commotion that they took off for the far end of the lake.

"Come on over," Henry shouted. "I promise Colby won't bite."

WON'T BITE?

Actually, now that Whitney had a second to think about it, yes, Colby had taken a few lusty nips that steamy December night. Not that she'd thought about their time together since then—unless, of course, those thoughts concerned her current situation. And in that case, thinking of him was not only understandable, but advisable.

To a certain extent.

Forcing a deep breath, tucking her long hair neatly behind her shoulders, she pushed her considerable mass off the truck's seat and onto the ground, trying to be swanlike but feeling more like a one-legged loon.

She took her time stepping out from the shield of the truck's door, unprepared for the impact of what seeing Colby again might do to her—and what his seeing her might do to him.

Sooner than she would've liked, she was struggling to conquer her runaway heart and sweating palms. And all because Colby Davis stood backdropped by a blazing blue sky, looking way better than any mental image she'd ever even dreamed of conjuring up.

Tall and lean and tan and…oh my.

She licked her lips, willing her fingertips to stop tingling as she remembered running then up and down his abs.

Forcing her gaze higher, she landed in serious trouble. Trouble tinted Gulf of Alaska green. He was staring at her as though, rather than your average *very* pregnant woman, she was a creature beamed down from a galaxy far, far away.

Easing her lips into a smile, she said, "Um, hi, Colby. Long time no see, huh?"

He grinned as if laughing at a private joke, then shook his head, looking down while kicking the gravel at his feet.

She took a few tentative steps forward, left hand on her seven-month-pregnant stomach, the other smoothing windswept hair off her cheek to tuck it behind her ear. "How have you been?"

"Oh, no," he said, taking equal steps back, warding her off with outstretched hands. "Don't tell me I'm—I mean, we, I mean—" There again went that brilliant, white-toothed smile. The one she'd replayed a thousand times in her head—strictly for informational purposes. After all, she did need to periodically apprise herself of her unborn child's future dental health. "Wow. Guess I'm not quite sure what I mean. I mean, of course, I must be your baby's…why else would you be here?"

Whitney turned to Henry. "You can go ahead and leave. Looks like this might take a while."

"You sure?" the wiry old guy said. "I don't mind stayin'. This here's way better than anything happening on my soaps."

Whitney felt silly for having to swallow back tears.

What had she expected? Harps playing in the trees and little blue booties falling from heaven upon her arrival?

It wasn't as if she'd returned to Kodiak Gorge looking for a husband, or even a father for her child. All she'd wanted to do before she got too far along to travel was inform Colby that he was going to be a dad.

Period.

He could handle the news as he pleased—just as long as beyond developing a mutually agreeable visitation schedule, his actions had nothing to do with her or what ultrasounds promised was her son.

After all, she'd determined around about her

mom's fifth wedding that marriage would never be for her. And now that her career was going strong, Whitney was entirely self-sufficient.

Sure, it would take some adjustment to fit a baby into her hectic schedule, but that was okay. She'd already interviewed several excellent nannies, and once Talbot Livingston Foster II—she'd decided to name him after her mother's father—got old enough, he could happily spend his toddlerhood at her company's in-house day care. It was top-notch.

Whitney parked herself on a rough-hewn log bench paralleling the dock while Colby followed Henry to his truck, mumbled a few choice-sounding yet unintelligible phrases, then just stood there, hands in his pockets, watching his friend drive off.

He turned back to her just as a breeze whipped up off the lake, catching the flaps of the box sitting on a dock post.

By the time it occurred to Whitney that the box didn't look all that stable, it'd already tumbled into the water.

"Oops," Whitney mumbled, looking forward to the day when her reactions once again matched her thoughts. As efficiently as possible, she pushed herself off the bench and knelt on the edge of the dock, hoping to snatch one of the flaps before the whole thing sank.

"Here, let me get it," Colby said, jogging onto the dock.

He beat her to the box, but just as he grabbed it, she grabbed it. Before she could find her center of gravity, she'd begun a free fall into the water.

A screech prefaced her splash, and while she wasn't at risk of drowning because she knew perfectly well how to swim, she was shocked by the water's icy chill.

A second later came another splash, as Colby jumped in after her, which was ludicrous, since she'd only landed in water barely up to her neck. Still, when he wrapped his arms around her to tow her to shore, she didn't complain.

"Thanks," she said as he helped her slosh onto the grass, the padded insoles of her black pumps squishing. A picnic table sat beside a boulder that had bright blue forget-me-nots blooming from every crack and crevice. "T-t-hat's p-pretty," she said, teeth already chattering.

Colby unfastened his jeans to reveal black boxers dotted with gray airplanes.

"W-what are you d-doing?" she asked.

"What's it look like I'm doing? Taking off these jeans so I can go inside and put on new ones. You're doing the same with that uptight business suit."

"Really, Colby, I'm fine. It's such a nice day. I'll just dry off in the s-sun."

He shot her stomach a look. "We made…a baby

together, and now you're worried about me seeing some skin?''

''The baby—it's a boy.''

Looking to the sky, he swiped his fingers through the glistening spikes of his hair, then shook his head while his face erupted in a huge smile. ''A son? I'm having a son?''

''Well…to be technical, *I'm* having a son.'' She grinned.

''Sure, but me, too. Wow. At first I was—hell, I mean heck, I didn't know what I was feeling. But to think that inside you is a little kid with maybe my momma's eyes and my cravings for flapjacks with extra butter and syrup, and my love of basketball, and—'' He looked to where she stood shivering by the water's edge. ''Would you listen to me,'' he said, ''rambling on like a gossipy old woman when you and my son are standing there freezing? Come on, woman, take off those clothes.''

''I don't think so.''

''Oh, come on, it's not as if we haven't seen each other before. By the end of the day we'll be walking down the aisle together. Don't turn prude on me now.''

''Considering how bossy you've become, I wouldn't walk down the road with you, let alone any aisles!'' She shivered, at which point he took the matter out of her hands by scooping her off her feet and into his arms. "What are you doing?" she shouted.

"Getting my son into a hot shower."

IN THE GLORIFIED toolshed-turned-office where Colby occasionally crashed after returning from late flights, he found Whitney a new outfit, complete with thick white socks. He offered her a pair of dry boxers, but she'd politely declined before locking herself in the bathroom.

Dressed in dry jeans and a green Kodiak Lodge T-shirt, Colby sat on a stool at the counter of his kitchenette, glowering toward the tiny bathroom.

The shower went off, and in his mind's eye he saw her all steamy and fresh-scrubbed, breasts full, stomach ripe with his son.

His son!

He couldn't wait to teach his kid to fly and fish and play ice hockey and—well, granted he'd have to get the kid out of diapers before trying any of that, but now that Whitney was moving back, there'd be plenty of time to hash out the already bustling schedule of his son's life.

The bathroom door opened, and his future bride moved into the triangle of light spilling through, looking better than he ever had in a pair of his gray sweatpants and a navy-blue T-shirt with a big bulge in the middle. She'd towel-dried her long hair and the inky spirals left the T-shirt's shoulders damp.

Even from this distance, he could tell she looked tired, so he got up from his stool and guided her to the recliner he kept in front of an old black-and-white TV that on sunny days picked up one channel.

"I can walk, you know," she said in a voice as chilly as the lake.

"Yeah. You also get an A plus in cranky."

"Sorry," she said, expression sincere. "I'm hungry—and I left my suitcase of snacks back at the lodge."

He laughed.

"What?"

"You and your snacks. I'll be sure to stock up for you by the time you get to my house."

Fingering her hair, she said, "What do you mean, get to your house? For the next week, I'll be perfectly fine at the lodge." She paused. "I never planned to stay that long but the airfare was much cheaper."

"Sure, you'll be fine," he said, reaching into a cabinet for a box of crackers and a can of squirt cheese. "For tonight, anyway. I imagine it'll take at least that long to get a marriage license, but by tomorrow night you'll be living with me."

"Excuse me?" She froze.

He held out her goodies. "What don't you understand?"

"How about every word out of your mouth?" she said as she took the food items.

He reached for the recliner's side handle and flung her back, causing her to cry, "Colby!"

"Sorry. You shouldn't be on your feet."

"I'm not. In case you've suddenly gone blind as well as crazy, I was already sitting down."

"Yeah, but you should be lying down, after falling in the water and traveling and all."

She sighed.

"Oh, hey, give me those," he said, snatching back the crackers and cheese. "Where are my manners?" In seconds, he'd prepared three crackers, each piled with a perfect spiral of cheese. He held one to her lips. "Eat."

He could tell her first instinct was to bat his hand away, but evidently hunger got the best of her as she jumped at his bait like a rainbow trout after one of his best flies.

"Thankwou," she said around chewing. She swallowed, then nailed him with an amber-flecked glare. "Colby, as nice as all this invalid treatment is, you do understand I'm pregnant and not dying?"

He shrugged. "As far as I'm concerned, I've missed enough of my son's life. I'm not going to miss a second more." *My dad left me and I'll be damned if I let anything get between me and my boy—even his mom.*

"Yes, well." She dropped her gaze. "That's just it. You seem to be under the impression that you have a choice in the matter, and the fact is, you don't."

Chapter Five

Colby blinked. "Okay, let me recap. You show up, seven months' pregnant by my calculations, then tell me it's my baby. I'm cool with that. Granted, it's a shock, but the more I think about it, the more I figure the three of us are going to lead a great life."

"True—only we'll be leading those lives apart."

He frowned. "Come again?"

"Baby Talbot and I, we'll be in Chicago, while you'll be—*ooh!*" Her cheeks took on a flushed glow, and her eyes sparkled.

"What?" he said, on his knees beside her. "Are you all right? Does bickering hurt the baby?"

She grinned and took the other two crackers from his open palm, popping one into her mouth and setting the other on her chest. Then she reached for his hand, curving his fingers around the peak of what he'd already dubbed Mt. St. Nick in honor of the fact that the little guy had been conceived on a mountain on Christmas Eve. "What?" he asked again.

"Shh," she said. "Feel."

"Whoa!" Tears sprang to Colby's eyes. "Was that what I think it was?"

She nodded. "That's my son."

"Don't you mean *our* son?"

"Well, technicallwy," she said around the last cracker. "But here's the deal. I didn't come here wanting anything from you. I just thought you might want to know you're going to be a father."

"And the thought never occurred to you that I might want to do more for my kid than send him a few postcards of grizzlies and the Northern Lights?"

She wriggled her sock-clad toes.

He reached for her chin, gently turning her to face him. "Answer me."

"I can't."

"Why not?"

"Because the idea of you being a full-time dad is so far outside of the realm of possibility it never even crossed my mind. I mean, I've reserved a nanny, and a slot in my company's day care, and…"

Her tone implied that since she already had all of those logistics worked out, her son didn't even need a dad.

Colby took a deep breath.

Maybe he was going about this all wrong. He'd never liked being told what to do. Could he blame Whitney if she didn't, either?

Taking her hands in his, he said, "I'm sorry if it seemed like I was ramrodding my agenda down your throat, but work with me here. You've had seven months to adjust to this and I've had about twenty minutes. I just, well, I assumed you were here to get married."

"I can see where you would," she said, "and I suppose in the case of other women, you'd be right in that assumption, but…" She blinked fast a couple of times. "The whole marriage thing—it's just not for me. Besides which, there's my job to consider. Not to mention the not-so-little matter of us practically being strangers. Anyway, sorry I snapped at you. After my snack, I'm feeling much calmer."

"Good," he said, nodding while patting her stomach, hoping for another feel of his wriggling son. "Calm is good. Okay, so here's my take on the matter…. No son of mine is growing up without his father."

While she'd been in the shower, he'd scoured the place for an engagement ring, but the only thing he'd come up with was a large nut—the metal kind, not a walnut or pecan. He fumbled getting it out of his jeans pocket.

Clink. It hit the hardwood floor before rolling beneath Whitney's chair.

Colby groaned.

She peered over the edge of her seat and said, "Look, if you're about to do what I think you're about to do, you might as well save your breath."

Grunting, he shoved her chair a good fifteen inches back, causing her to exclaim yet again.

When the chair lurched, she grabbed the top of his head, but her pulling his hair didn't hurt—at least not physically. Emotionally, though, it reminded him of *that* night, and the way she'd plunged her fingers into his hair every time he'd brought her to—

"Found it," he said, wishing he could as easily find a fix for the fire raging beneath his fly.

He blew on the ring, buffed it across his T-shirt to make sure it had a sort of pretty shine. Since he was already on his knees, he figured at least that "down on bended knee" thing was taken care of. He cleared his throat, then reached for Whitney's left hand, but she'd already clenched it into a fist.

"Come on," he complained. "How am I supposed to propose if you won't even let me see your ring finger?"

"Simple. You're not proposing. I already told you I didn't come up here to find a husband, but solely to fulfill my moral obligation and offer visitation rights."

At that, he had to laugh. "Oh, and you don't think you have a moral obligation to see to it your baby grows up in a loving, two-parent home?"

"Who said anything about love? All I see is some guy on his knees, holding up…what is that thing?"

"A nut. And so you're turning me down just because I'm not offering a three-carat rock?"

"No. Not at all. I'm turning you down for one reason."

"Okay, let's hear it."

"I'm *never* getting married. Please understand—it's nothing personal. You're a great guy. But I made the decision a long time ago and I plan to stick to it." Not only had her own parents proved an excellent case study to back up her choice, but so had countless friends with their failed marriages and relationships. And if those weren't enough, she'd also read hundreds of work-related files on divorce.

Colby needed to face facts.

No matter how romanticized marriage had become in their society, Whitney believed the concept of a man and woman living happily ever after was as rare as siblings without rivalry.

"Yeah, well, I can be just as bullheaded, and I say we *are* getting married."

"Aren't."

"Are."

"Aren'—"

He stopped the mother of his son midprotest with the mother of all kisses. At first, she stiffened, but then he slipped his hand beneath her tangled, still-damp hair. That only made him want more, so he moved closer, close enough that he was almost sharing the recliner with her. But then baby Nick was getting in the way, so Colby had to finagle himself into an even more awkward position. The recliner lurched, squeaking and creaking before shattering into a half-dozen splintered sections.

"Colby!" Whitney laughed. "Are you trying to kill us?"

"Nope," he said, drawing her into another kiss. "I was just trying to create a good excuse for putting a recliner at the top of our list when we register for wedding gifts down at Schlump's Hardware, Furniture and Jewelry."

"Mmm," Whitney said, popping the last bite of prime rib sandwich into her mouth. Sensing a stalemate back at Colby's so-called office, she'd convinced him to return her to Kodiak Lodge.

While he'd waited for their dinner order to arrive, she'd waddled upstairs to smooth her hair into a crude French twist, then change into business attire. The straight-lined black dress, flats and hose had fit better when she'd been at five months, but the scratchy linen blend made her feel more in control than she'd felt cocooned in the soft cotton and all-too-familiar scents of Colby's sweats.

"Now see?" she said, finishing off her garlic toast. "Doesn't a nice hot meal make everything better?"

Colby grunted.

"What's that supposed to mean?" she asked, fanning herself while moving her chair back from the crackling fire. Granted, it was a little chilly outside, but this was ridiculous.

"You hot?"

She nodded.

He frowned, got up, grabbed her milk and plate, and set them on a table beside the long bank of picture windows overlooking the sun-kissed lake. When she made no move to get up, he said, "Want me to carry you?"

Rolling her eyes, she struggled to her feet, then crossed to the new table. After taking her seat, she gulped her milk and wished it was a large, caffeine-laden Mountain Dew.

Nugget, the lodge's owner, must've eyed them through the kitchen pass-through. Big as a lumberjack and wielding a meat cleaver as efficiently as any ax, he ambled their way, his expression as fiery as his red hair. "What's the problem?" he asked. "Don't like that table?"

"She's hot," Colby said.

"You gonna clean both messes?"

"If it's a problem," Whitney said, "I can move back." She snatched a menu from between the salt-and-pepper shakers to use as a fan.

"Ladybug." Nugget placed his meaty hand on Whitney's shoulder. "It's not a problem for you—just him. Oh, here, let me refill this for you. A woman in your condition can never drink too much milk." He shot Colby a look, then snatched Whitney's empty glass, returning with it full to the brim.

"All right…" Colby sighed, eased back in his chair and crossed his arms. "Let's have it, Nugget. What's in your craw?"

The lodge owner eyed him a good long while with a merciless beady blue stare. "You wanna know what's in my craw, Colby Davis? Then I suggest you head on down to the library and bone up on the Kodiak Gorge history of deadbeat dads."

Colby pressed his lips tight.

It wasn't like Nugget to play dirty. Obviously with that deadbeat dad reference, he was referring to Colby's own dad—how he'd up and deserted his wife and son. Yeah, Colby could've let Nugget in on the truth of the matter—that he was all set to marry Whitney, only she wouldn't have him. But what was the point in explaining, seeing how until he put a ring on her finger, everyone in town seemed hell-bent on thinking the worst of him?

Nugget all but growled before stalking back to his lair.

"What was that all about?" Whitney asked, leaning forward as much as Baby Talbot would allow.

"Take a wild guess."

"I wouldn't have a clue."

He snorted.

"What? How am I supposed to know?"

He leaned forward, too, enough so that the lingering scents of prime rib and sour cream combined with the scents that on that long-ago snowy night, she'd come to know as him. Sweat. Leather. Airplanes, and the sexy speed that they implied.

It took her a second to regroup before she'd even realized he'd been talking. "Excuse me?" she said.

"What part about the fact that my good friend Nugget thinks I'm a world-class jerk didn't you understand?"

"All of it." She smiled.

Leaning back, he sighed. "Look, he obviously thinks what any other sane person—including me—would. That the only reason you came back here was to claim a husband for you, and a father for your baby. And rightly so. Hell—I mean—heck, I'm prepared to make an honest woman of you just as soon as we can get the license, but—"

"But I'm being stubborn as a big ole Alaska-sized mule, right?" She'd adopted what she hoped was an appropriate back-country twang.

"This isn't a joke, Whitney. We're talking about a child here—*my* child."

"Correction—*my* child."

"Okay," Colby said, easing back in his chair. "For the sake of the argument, let's agree to address Nick as *our* child."

"Fine. Only his name is going to be Talbot."

"Over my dead and bloated body."

"Mmm…that's a mighty tempting proposition that I—" She leaned forward to add emphasis to her upcoming point.

Splash!

Whitney's freshly poured milk tipped, sloshing all over her and the table and the floor and her dress and—

"You were saying?" Colby flashed her a grin.

"Here's napkins," Nugget called out as he hustled from the kitchen. To Colby, he added, "What're you doing just sitting there, you big oaf? Can't you see the lady needs help?"

The trio of men who'd been sitting in the corner eating burgers also leapt to her assistance. "Let me help, ma'am," the biggest said.

"I'll help her, Stanley," Colby said, pushing back his chair, napkin in hand. He parted the crowd to pat Whitney's soaking lap. "After all, she is about to be my wife."

"Then you already asked her to marry you?" Nugget asked, releasing a gush of air. "Thank heavens. I was afraid you'd taken the same path as that no 'count—"

"I'm not," Colby said, cutting Nugget off. It wasn't anyone's business but his own what his father had done. Continuing with his task, he ran the napkin across regions of Whitney's lap he hadn't touched since...

He looked up just in time to see her cheeks glow.

"In fact," he said, dabbing the soggy napkin up her inner thigh, "for the past hour we've been hammering out the details of our upcoming ceremony, haven't we, sweetie?" His lowered tone, gritted teeth, and squeeze to her knee implied that, for whatever reason, he wanted her to play along with his delusion, but Whitney was having none of it.

"No, *sweetie,* if you'd ever stop arguing long enough to listen to reason, you'd have heard me patiently explain that in today's society—"

Lips pressed into a dangerously thin line, right in the middle of her latest speech, Colby slapped the sodden napkin to her almost-empty plate, then stormed out of the lodge. And hey, she'd still had a baked potato skin left that she'd been planning to dip in ketchup!

How dare he not only ruin her potato, but walk out on her like that? Leaving her alone with four gaping strangers *and* the bill.

"You really oughta marry 'im," said a squat man with a big red nose and even bigger black cowboy hat. "Elsewise, there'll be no livin' with him."

The burly guy Colby had called Stanley removed his worn brown UPS hat to swat the shorter guy on the back of his head. "Damn straight there'll be no livin' with him. Colby'll move to wherever she lives."

"What if that's Texas? You know how he hates Texas."

"Well, then, he'll just have to deal with it when the time comes."

"Yeah, well, what if she's from some fool place like California, huh? Then what's he gonna—"

The graying man, who up to this point had stayed out of it, dropped to one knee in front of Whitney, removing his Kodiak Gorge Auto Repair ball cap to tuck it beneath his left arm. "Ma'am," he said, boldly grasping her hand, "if Colby out there won't marry you, I will."

Nugget started swatting all three of them with the dishrag he'd brought in from the kitchen. "Oh, hush up and leave her alone. For pity's sake. You'd think none of you'd ever seen a woman before."

"None pretty as her," the graying man said.

To Whitney, Nugget said, "Go on upstairs and change. We'll see about cleaning up this mess."

"Thanks, but no," Whitney said, swishing yet another napkin through the largest white puddle. "I can't let you do all of this." She tried getting up, but her belly caught the edge of the table, shifting it just enough to knock the ketchup bottle onto the polished wood floor. "I'm so sorry," she said, cheeks warm. "The baby's growing so fast. I guess I'm not used to being so big."

All four of them had stopped bickering to stare.

"What?" Whitney asked.

Nugget shook his head. "You need looking after."

Now it was Whitney's turn to thrust back her shoulders. Looking after? The man acted like she was a child, instead of about to have her own child. "I'll have you know I've been self-sufficient for quite some time now—not to mention the fact that I graduated in the top two percent of my college class."

Laughing, Nugget said, "That's book smarts. What I'm talkin' about is common sense. The kind of sense that if you had even a smidgen of, you'd be using to run right out that door and ask Colby to marry you."

"But I barely even know him," Whitney explained. "We live thousands of miles apart." *Besides which, I'm doing just fine on my own, thank you very much, which is why no matter how sweet or handsome or determined to marry me Colby happens to be, I'll never marry him—or any man.* "Why would we even want to get married?"

The three stooges gravely shook their heads and turned back to their table.

With one last snort, Nugget pushed through the swinging kitchen door.

AFTER NUGGET SHOOED her out of the dining room, Whitney trudged upstairs to change from her stained dress into comfy stretch-waist jeans, a white Hillborough College sweatshirt and her extra pair of dry sneakers.

In her charming room with its gabled ceiling and surprisingly feminine yellow-and-blue calico bedspread and curtains, she eyed the bed longingly. But she figured it would be best for the baby if she worked off some of the negative energy still zinging through her from her time spent with Colby.

What was it about the man, she wondered, taking her time navigating the wide lobby staircase, that one minute had her utterly fascinated and the next utterly frustrated? Just thinking about the look on his face when he'd placed his big, warm hand on her even bigger tummy to feel Baby Talbot wriggle…

Ugh. She fanned away instant tears.

This was no time to get mushy.

She was headed outside for a workout, not a blubber-fest!

Resolutely pushing her way out the lodge's front door, she stepped onto the still sunny porch—a fact that would take some getting used to, seeing how it was past nine at night. One bonus of all that sun, though, was that it was still a perfect temperature for her walk alongside the lake.

She'd just breathed in the sweet smells of fish and soaring spruce and windswept water when a clunk came from the far end of the porch.

"Colby," she said, hands to her chest. "You scared me." He sat in a rocker and had had his feet crossed at the ankles upon the porch rail, but the clunk she'd heard was his hiking boots hitting the floor. "What're you still doing here?"

He laughed. "Thinking about what I'm going to do about you."

Hands resting on her stomach, Whitney strolled his way. "I'm sorry about acting all snippy in there. You kept going on and on about us getting married, and all I wanted to do was eat, and…" She dropped her gaze, scuffed the tip of her sneaker against a raised nail on the wood plank floor.

"And?"

Did he have any idea how handsome he looked? How sexy that dimple was on his right cheek? How thick and touchable his dark hair was and how broad his shoulders were and how late at night, whenever she allowed herself to think of their time together, her insides went all quivery and weak.

She remembered skimming her hands along his chest, wondering at the strength just beneath his skin, imagining a life in which she woke up next to him every morning, secure in the knowledge that he didn't view her as a trophy or cook or chauffeur, but as a partner.

An equal in life and love.

Ha. Whitney had seen enough of her mother's and friends' awful marriages to know the only good marriage was one that had never taken place!

"And?" he prompted again.

"And, well…" She flopped her hands at her sides. "I was looking forward to us having a nice, civil conversation, that's all. While I can't foresee ever getting married, I do think it'd be best for my son if I'm at least friends with his father, don't you?"

"There you go again. Your son? Come on, Whitney, you act as if you made him all by your lonesome. Seems to me, I was there, too."

She opened her mouth to retort, but nothing escaped but a high-pitched squeak. She spun on her rubber soles, abandoning her earlier plan for a walk in favor of lounging in bed watching satellite TV.

"Oh, no," he said, broad hands singeing her shoulders as he turned her around. "Don't even think about running off on me. At least not until you admit I did most of the work in conceiving my son."

"He's my son, and what do you think I'm doing

now? Do you think lugging around this two-ton kid of yours is fun?''

"Ha!" he said. "There you go, you admitted it."

"Admitted what?" she said, trying awfully hard to slow her pulse. Colby stood close enough that his belly grazed her belly, and his warm breath fanning her lips smelled of the mint Nugget used as a garnish on his iced tea.

"That the baby's mine."

"Hello?" She rolled her eyes. "That fact has never been in contention. That's why I'm in town. To tell you my baby is yours."

"Well, then…"

"What?"

"I've had it with you," he said, releasing her to swipe his fingers through his hair. Stomping off the porch, he mumbled, "I can't imagine why I ever even slept with you. I mean, yeah, you had that almost-a-virgin sex kitten thing going—not to mention the fact that I was gonna die, but that mouth of yours is—wo-oooooh—"

Chapter Six

Colby tripped.

Not any ordinary catch-yourself stumble, but a fall of mammoth proportions all the way down the front porch stairs.

"Colby!" Whitney cried. He heard her scuttle across the porch and down the stairs. "Oh my gosh," she said, from somewhere closer to him on the gravel path. He felt one cool hand on his forehead and the other on his cheek. "Are you okay?"

He eased open his eyes.

"Thank goodness," she said with a relieved sigh. "I don't know what I would've done if something had happened to you."

Groaning, he said, "That's funny. I figured you'd be relieved to see me knocked off."

Tears shone in her eyes. "H-how could you say such a thing? Do I really come across as that heartless?"

Though every bone in Colby's body ached at that

moment, his heart ached more. He was sorry for bringing those tears to her eyes, but dammit, she hadn't exactly been playing nice.

"No," he finally said. "Here, give me a hand up, then I'm calling it quits—at least for the night. Maybe all these accidents are a sign that you're right and we shouldn't be together." Already heading toward his black Jeep, he glanced at his gravel-ravaged hands.

"You're bleeding," Whitney said, chasing after him. "Let me drive you home, then I'll bandage those up for you."

"Are you kidding? After everything you've already done, you expect me to hand you the keys to my Jeep?"

"If you do," she said with a wide smile, "I promise to at least consider your proposal. Sort of."

"Really?" he asked, raising his eyebrows.

She nodded.

He tried to reach for his keys, but she quickly caught on to his problem.

"Let me," she said, sliding her hand deep into his front pocket, setting off all manner of sparks. Luckily, once she realized his distress, she finished her task efficiently and without any cracks about him having a flashlight in his pocket.

BENEATH HIS CABIN'S soaring cathedral ceiling, Whitney dabbed Colby's fingertips and palms with a peroxide-soaked cotton ball.

They sat across from each other—Colby on the couch with his hands over a towel she'd folded on the coffee table, Whitney perched on the edge of an overstuffed armchair.

She'd expected his house to be the quintessential mountain man's digs. But while it wasn't exactly neat as a pin, the open living room with its loft, which she assumed was the master bedroom, and the roomy country kitchen made the house as welcoming as any home she'd ever seen.

Honey-hued logs rose to the polished plank ceiling, providing a suitably impressive backdrop for the river rock fireplace. She could all too easily imagine warming herself beside it on blustery winter nights....

Colby's furniture wasn't so much about style as it was about comfort. It was big and overstuffed, upholstered in a navy-and-forest-green plaid that managed to be manly yet inviting. He didn't have knickknacks gracing tabletops, just a few pictures. Most of those had been taken with a woman Whitney assumed was his mom. Other shots of him and his friends showed Colby hanging one-handed off the edges of cliffs, skiing, hamming for the camera during a skydiving free fall.

Whitney frowned, accidentally pressing harder than she'd intended on one of his deepest cuts.

Good thing Baby Talbot would be growing up a safe distance from his adrenaline-junkie father!

"Ouch," Colby said with an exaggerated wince.

"Sorry," she said, "I'm trying to be gentle, but for someone who looks like such an adventure-seeking stud in all these pictures, you squirm more than a six-year-old."

"This how you're going to treat our son?" he asked. "All gruff and businesslike without even a kiss to make him better?"

She rolled her eyes.

"Here I am in pain—light-headed and downright dizzy—and you're not healing me, you're roughing me up."

"Am not!" she protested.

"Oh yeah? Then prove you have a tender side hiding somewhere behind those soulless brown eyes."

"Soulless? Did you just call my eyes soulless?"

He grinned.

"Oh, I'll give you soulless, right in your..." What she wanted to give him was a good tongue-lashing, but thinking up a suitably insulting response would take too much energy—especially since that disgustingly handsome grin of his already had her out of breath.

Maybe a better approach would be showing him just how tender she could be?

Raising his hand to her lips, she rained hot, soft

kisses all around his wounds and right on up to the pulse points on his wrists.

He had a minor scrape on his right cheek, too, so she leaned forward, taking on the perilous task of kissing him while at the same time trying to keep her belly from grazing his.

Only she failed miserably—and on way more points than bumped bellies.

Whitney had meant her sexy ministrations to affect only him—and to prove only that she was the most tenderhearted person she knew. But when she paused, hoping Colby was ready to apologize, he was quiet and she felt strangely addled.

"How's that?" she whispered into his right ear.

He gulped. "Better. Thanks."

"Sure you don't need additional medicinal kisses?"

He shook his head.

"All right then." She eyed the latest bulge in his pocket, wishing she could forget the night when she'd grown intimately acquainted with that particular part of his anatomy. "That's, um, probably good. Now, quit whining and let me get on with my nursing."

Five minutes later, she'd applied antibiotic ointment, gauze and tape to Colby's scratches. When she placed the small square of gauze on his cheek, a twinge of guilt rippled through her. He looked so sad. If she hadn't been running off at the mouth, he wouldn't have been running down those steps to escape her.

"Can I get you anything?" she asked.

From his perch on the sofa, with his long, lean legs propped on the coffee table, he said, "There's sun tea in the fridge. Think you could pour me a glass?"

"Sure."

Heading to the kitchen gave Whitney a much-needed breather. What was it with him constantly invading her personal space?

Oh, right, like it'd been him kissing you?

There went her cheeks again.

She'd only kissed him because he'd called her soulless. What else could she have done?

Reaching into the fridge for the tea, she lingered in the blessedly cool air.

Must be some baby hormone thing turning up her thermostat. Without a crackling fire in sight, the only other thing that could be causing such unbearable heat was her frustration with Baby Talbot's father.

Right. You're frustrated, but way more because of all that time spent apart *from Colby than with* him.

Scowling, Whitney slammed the fridge door hard enough to rattle the pickle relish and olive jars.

Setting the jug on the green slate counter, she rummaged through various cabinets for a glass, finally finding one to the left of the sink. The sink held five dirty glasses, a cereal bowl with a few Cheerios still floating in it and another bowl wearing what she guessed to be the remains of last night's chili supper. Before she left for the night, Whitney decided she'd wash Colby's dishes for him. With his hands all cut up, he shouldn't get them wet.

She wasn't sure why she cared. Probably it went back to her generally kind nature—not that he cared about that.

She marched back across the room to the side-by-side stainless steel fridge, which had an ice and water dispenser in the door. Slipping the glass beneath the ice nozzle, she said over the mechanical tinkle and crunch, "You've got a great house."

"Thanks."

"I take it Alaskan pilots make a nice living?"

He shrugged. "I do all right. Guess I usually just go for the top of the line in most things. It's a bear getting appliances or electronics up here, let alone repaired. So I'd just as soon pay extra for quality goods, then not worry about them breaking down."

Whitney nodded. She respected his good financial sense. With luck, her son would exhibit the same sort of logic.

She poured Colby's tea, then delivered it to him.

"Aren't you having any?" he asked.

She shook her head. "After the milk incident, I'm not thirsty. I am hungry, though."

"I've got plenty of snack food in the pantry." He set his glass on the coffee table. "This time, I'll serve you."

"No," she said, pushing him back down. "You're the wounded one, remember?"

Grinning, he shook his head. "All right, Miss Independence, help yourself."

"Thank you, I will."

If he'd added a TV, Colby's pantry was so big it could've doubled as a den. A dazzling array of boxes and bags and cans contained everything from flour and canned green beans and yams to cookies and chips and—yum, more squirt cheese!

Whitney snatched a can of bacon and cheddar cheese along with a box of crackers, then headed back to the living room. "I also like your taste in snacks. Squirt cheese isn't the sort of thing I'd buy myself, but—"

"But you don't mind wolfing down mine?"

There went her stupid blazing cheeks.

"It's okay," he said. "There's plenty more where that came from. I buy in bulk."

"Gweat," she said with a happy, cheesy sigh. Mmm, squirt cheese ought to have its very own section on the food pyramid her baby books were always yapping about.

She downed another and another, having fun

making pretty patterns on the cracker tops. "What?" she asked when she caught him eyeing her. "I'm hungry."

"I see that." He grinned, and the sight of his green eyes and adorably mussed hair squeezed her heart.

Would Baby Talbot look like him?

Oh, she hoped so. God had never created a more beautiful man. Not that she was admiring Colby for her own benefit; she was merely making note of it for her son's sake.

"So," he said after a long spell of awkward silence during which all she could hear was herself chewing. "Ready for that talk on marriage?"

That brought her appetite to a screeching halt.

She swallowed her last cracker, then snapped the plastic lid on the cheese can and methodically crinkled the cracker bag shut before slipping the cardboard tab into its slot on top of the box.

"Well?" he asked again.

"I did promise to discuss it, didn't I?"

Leaning forward, resting his elbows on his knees, he nodded. "After everything that's happened today, you can see why it's imperative we get this wedding on the road. We're not much for hothouse flowers up here, but I can at least pick you a pretty forget-me-not bouquet, and Nugget'll bake us a cake. We've got a historic chapel Preach can do the ceremony in—or, for that matter, we can do it at the lodge or even right here. It doesn't matter much to me. I always figured that'd be the kind of detail better left up to my bride. Oh, you'll need a dress. I'll have to think on that one. Guess if you feel up to it, we could hop on over to Valdez or maybe down to Yakutat to buy you something lacy and white.''

"You sound as if you've got this all thought out."

"Sure. Waiting for you back at the lodge gave me a lot of time to plan." And then there was the part of him that felt as though he'd been waiting his whole life to get married. To start a family. Demonstrate to his father how marriage was done. How being a great dad was done.

Colby had come damned close to sealing the deal with Margot, but with the benefit of hindsight, he figured things had worked out as they did for a reason. Margot was a Texas girl, used to the finer things in life. Looking back on it, he realized she wouldn't have lasted through the first week of an Alaskan winter. But Whitney, hell, she'd already been through the worst Alaska had to offer, and she was back for more.

"Mmm." She fiddled with her fingers on her lap before turning her warm brown eyes on him. "In all that planning, did you ever think about what marriage truly means?"

He scratched his head. "I don't get the question."

Duh. Of course, he knew what marriage meant. *Forever.*

"That's my point." She sounded a little choked up. "Marriage is supposed to be a lifetime commitment, right?"

"It will be for me."

"Okay, but here's the deal. True, we shared one unforgettable night, but other than knowing we're compatible in bed, what else do we have? We're strangers. Do you really want to marry a stranger?"

He shrugged. "Don't take this personally, but this isn't so much about me wanting to marry you as it is about me *having* to marry you."

"Who says? Nugget and those nuts down at the lodge?"

"Hey," he said, raising his tea to empty it in a few refreshing swigs. "Those nuts happen to be my friends."

He stood, turning toward the kitchen for a refill. Whitney stood, too.

"And even after taking them out of the equation, I'm going to marry you because of my son. No matter what you say, I know he'll be better off in a two-parent home." He curved his bandaged hand around her stomach, igniting a slow flame before heading to the kitchen, leaving behind those distracting waves of heat.

She chased after him, stopping beside him where he gripped the edge of the sink, staring out the window at the view that never failed to calm him. From this vantage point, a good twenty feet back and above a narrow portion of Kodiak Gorge, the jagged gray rock canyon looked impenetrable.

Hand on his shoulder, she gently turned him to face her. "Do you think your son would want to grow up in a home filled with strife?"

He felt a muscle twinge in his jaw.

"Because face it, Colby, that's what the two of us would share. Do you honestly think I'm ready just to give up my career? The life I've created for myself? If we can hardly get two words out of our mouths without bickering now, what happens when mutual resentment sets in? What kind of message would that send to a child? With me, in Chicago, Talbot will not only have love, but friends. A top-rated play group and a doting mother and nanny. The finest schools and clothes and cultural opportunities most kids only dream of. Does that sound like such a horrible life?"

He grunted. "Now, who sounds like she has it all worked out? All except for what you're going to say when *Nick* gets old enough to ask about his daddy. *Where is he?* he'll ask. *Why doesn't he love me enough to be with me?*"

Whitney crossed her arms and turned away. "I

refuse to have this discussion. The issue of Talbot's father may never even come up.''

''I wouldn't be so sure.''

''Why not? How could you possibly even know?''

''How? You wanna know how?'' He gripped her by her shoulders, dragging her perilously close. ''I damn well know how, Whitney, because I learned firsthand what it feels like to grow up without a dad. And as long as there's breath in my body, you can be damned sure I'll never bring my own son that kind of confusion and pain.''

Chapter Seven

Back at the lodge, Whitney stepped away from the window, with its spellbinding view of the sun just now setting over the lake. She should have been enchanted by the postcard-perfect scene, but all she really felt was tired and cranky. She was sick to death of trying to make that bullheaded man not only understand her point of view, but agree with it.

Backing up to the bed, she grabbed a strand of strawberry licorice before falling onto the downy comforter and pillows. She closed her eyes, sighed, chewed.

The last time she'd slept on down had been—

Okay, false start. Time to think about something else.

Anything else.

Classic TV trivia. Who would've been hotter together? Greg and Marcia from the Brady Bunch? Or the Professor and Mary Ann?

I'll tell you who was way hotter than either one of those match-ups. Colby and Whitney.

Grr. She furiously chewed the rest of her licorice.

Okay, so how many times had she been over the whole night spent in the wrecked plane? They'd both thought themselves on the brink of death. What they'd shared *ought* to have been hot. Given a choice, who wanted to die in a flurry of so-so passion?

But now, they were both very much alive.

In a way, it had been like being on vacation, when everyday stresses seem nonexistent. But they somehow always manage to reenter your life around the time you're packing to go home—to remind you that your vacation really is over.

That was how things were with her and Colby. Over.

Excitement like that couldn't last forever. It burns itself out. Kind of like her mom had burned out after all those bungled marriages. What marriage was she on now? Number seven? Or was it eight? Who could keep up?

Her most recent spouse was Neil. He owned a used car lot in Berwyn. Made a truckload of money at it, and spent every dime on his hobby of collecting railroad memorabilia. Dining-car china, silver pieces, porters' uniforms, monogrammed bed linens, signal lanterns. If it had to do with trains, he collected it. He even wore a conductor's cap to

work every day, and used an old Pullman car as
his office. Eight of the ten rooms in his house were
dedicated to his love of trains; so was every weekend.

Whitney had nothing against trains. If anything,
she found the whole era of train travel fascinating
and romantic. Her problem was with the way her
mother had assimilated Neil's love of trains. During
their weekly mother-daughter calls, pretty much all
she talked about was which new piece they'd
picked up.

If it'd only been this one case, Whitney wouldn't
have been worried. But with Haywood, her mom
had taken up sailing. Lyle did golf. Vincent had
seemed more in tune with his four dachshunds than
with her mother, who, on Whitney's last visit to
their happy home, had lovingly trailed after the
wriggling pack, scooping up dog biscuit crumbs
and a trail of shredded socks.

What was it about all of those relationships that
made her mother lose herself? Or for that matter,
had her mother ever been on her own long enough
to even recognize who she really was?

"THERE YOU ARE, sugar biscuit," Nugget said as
Whitney meandered into the lodge's crowded, sun-
flooded dining room at 6:00 a.m. "I wondered
what'd been keeping you."

Keeping her? Did no one around here ever sleep? "Morning, Nugget."

"Sleep well?"

Practically falling into a chair at the table beside the one she'd shared with Colby, Whitney groaned.

"I'll take that as a no," Nugget said, slipping a menu onto the table. "I'll be right back out with a nice glass of milk."

Blech. "Could you please just bring me a cup of decaf coffee?"

"I would, honey bun, but I never have understood that whole business of how they take the caffeine out of the coffee. Seems downright unnatural. Highly unsafe for the baby."

Okay. "Well, my pediatrician understands the process fairly well, and she says it's safe, as long as I don't overdo it."

Nugget shook his head. "Nope. I don't think so." He flashed Whitney a wide smile before heading for the kitchen. "Be right back with that milk."

Crossing her arms on the table, Whitney dropped her head into them and groaned.

Great. Another fun day in paradise.

"Oh good, I didn't miss you." Colby slid into the empty seat at her table, then snatched up her menu.

Whitney slowly raised her head. "Miss me? Where else would I be at this hellish hour? And where are your bandages?"

"I'm all better—see?" He held out his hands, and the gashes that had made her queasy the previous night had faded into no big deal. Maybe they *hadn't* been that big a deal to begin with—at least not in the real world.

In her mind, though…

She took a deep breath. The thought of his being hurt—no matter how small the injury—didn't sit well with her.

"And as for where else you might've been," he said, "you could've been doing just about anything. Fishing, gold panning, hiking."

"Hiking. You honestly think I look ready to hike?"

"Maybe. I know if I was a moose, I'd get a kick out of watching you waddle down the trail."

"Oh no," she said, slapping her palms onto the table. "Did you just say I waddle?"

"Darlin'," he said with a charming grin. "I've seen it—and I think it's adorable."

Talk about stealing her thunder. "Well…"

"For that matter, the head attached to that waddling body of yours isn't so bad, either."

"Um, thanks. I think."

"You're welcome. Oh, before I forget…" He eased out of his chair and knelt beside her, "Good morning in there, Nick," he said to her stomach, molding his fingers against it. "This is your dad. I just wanted to make sure you're getting an all-right start to your day.'' He shifted his hand lower, only to plant a quick kiss on the spot where his palm's heat still lingered—just in time to feel his son's response. Deep inside her, Talbot gently rolled, easing his foot in a wide arc all the way across her stomach.

Colby stared in wonder. ''Was that…?''

She nodded. For some crazy reason, tears lodged at the back of her throat.

''Well, I'll be damned…'' he said, eyes suspiciously shiny as he stumbled back into his seat. ''I mean darned. My kid already likes me.''

''He does that all the time,'' Whitney said, toying with a plastic tub of grape jelly. ''It doesn't necessarily mean anything.''

''Don't,'' Colby said, his eyes suddenly cold.

''What?''

''Deliberately set out to downplay what was for me a very big moment. Like it or not, Whitney, I am your baby's father. No matter how hard you try to reason that fact away, you can't.''

''I-I wasn't trying to.'' *All I was doing was trying to make sense out of the feeling that shot through me when you talked to our son.*

Our son.

Was that the first time she'd thought of Baby Talbot as anything other than all her own?

''I've got to make a run up to the oil site.''

''But you haven't eaten.''

His eyes brightened. "That mean you want me to stay?"

She hesitated, then said, "Ah, sure."

"Oh boy, now there was a warm welcome if I've ever heard one." Pushing his chair back from the table, he stood, pressed another quick kiss to her stomach, then sauntered out the lodge's front door.

With all eyes in the room on her, Whitney felt her cheeks flame. What? What did these people want from her? She'd done the right thing in coming up here to even tell Colby about his son. She hadn't *had* to. She could have just kept Talbot a secret, and Colby never would have known.

No, you couldn't. Not for a second could you have kept that man from knowing he had a son. It wouldn't have been right.

Lips pressed together, Whitney reached for the menu and snapped it open. Who cared what these people thought of her? It wasn't as if she was ever coming back up here again.

If those adrenaline-junkie pictures she'd seen at Colby's house were any indication of the kind of father he'd be, she was right to keep Talbot far away.

Good grief, Colby would probably celebrate their son's first birthday with a baby bungee jump off the rim of Kodiak Gorge!

"Ready to order, cupcake?" Nugget set a full glass of milk on the table.

Whitney looked up at him. "I don't suppose you've reconsidered bringing me a decaf?"

"Nope. But how about some nice eggs scrambled with ham, tomatoes and cheese?"

"I was thinking pizza sounded good. Or maybe some powdered sugar donuts."

Nugget grinned. "Ham-egg scramble it is then. I'll have it right out to you, doll."

Whitney sighed.

It was going to be a long week. Why had she chosen now to be frugal over the cost of an airline ticket?

COLBY TOOK A SEAT at one of the six round tables in Global Oil's newly decorated mess hall, then frowned. A couple of months back he remembered hauling a lot of paint over here, but yellow? Who the hell'd ever heard of painting an all-male mess hall yellow?

Of course, Dot lived there, too. But she fit in so well with the guys, no one even thought about her being a woman.

"Hey, Colby," Todd Fulmore said. The master welder set his tray on the table before easing into a seat. He winced.

"Back still giving you trouble?"

"Yeah. Though I gotta say, those new mattresses we got have made a difference—and the recliners in the game room. Heaven. That little woman you brought up here did one helluva a job in making our lives a whole lot nicer.''

"You mean Whitney?'' Colby took a bite of his roast beef sandwich, trying his best to look uninterested.

"Yeah, that was her name. At the time, we didn't have a clue what she was doing, but now I want her back—getting us some improvements to this food.'' He eyed his grayish slab of meat loaf. "Heard the two of you were an item. See her lately?''

Colby nearly choked on his latest bite. "Uh, yeah, you might say that.''

"Mmm, I smell a story,'' Dan Dascoll said, taking another empty seat at the table. "It's been a slow week. Spill your guts.''

"Yeah,'' Todd said. "Because, believe me, you sure don't want to hear what old Dan here's been up to.''

Rolling his eyes, Colby said, "I already know. Word travels fast when it involves a five-foot-six, stacked, blue-eyed blonde.''

Dan leaned back in his chair, rubbing his jaw. "Yep. Last weekend was undoubtedly one of the happiest of Heather's life.''

Todd pitched his roll at Dan's wide grin, but Dan just caught it midair and took a big bite before flinging it back.

Todd made a face before shooting from three-point range into the trash.

"Out with it, Davis," Todd said. "If I have to hear about his wild nights with Heather one more time, I might just have to—"

"Take a cold shower?" Dan winked.

"All right." Colby finished off his chocolate milk. "Dan, you remember that dark-haired looker who spent a couple of months up here last winter?"

"Shoot, yeah. I made a play for her, but she was all business. Real cold, even though I heard rumors 'bout you and her gettin' real hot that night in your plane."

"Can it, Dascoll. She now happens to be the mother of my son."

In unison, Todd and Dan whistled.

"Damn," Todd said. "That was fast work. Congratulations."

"Thanks." Colby sat a little straighter. Yeah, his little guys had been pretty strong swimmers.

"So?" Dan asked. "She call you wanting child support?"

"Not exactly."

"Wait—let me guess. She wants you to get your ass down to the lower forty-eight and marry her ASAP."

Colby had to laugh at that. "I wish—except for the lower forty-eight part."

"She wants to marry you and move lock, stock and barrel into your place?"

"Since you're never gonna guess, I might as well tell you. According to her, all she came up here to do was tell me I'm gonna be a dad."

"And…" Dan stared, apparently dumbfounded.

"That's it. She just wanted to tell me, then she planned on leaving town. But I'm having none of it. There's no way in hell my son's growing up without his father."

"I can see your point, man, but she's a cool customer. One of those career women with no time for guys like us."

Nodding, Colby said, "You hit the nail on the head with that assessment."

"So? What're you gonna do?" Todd asked.

Colby shrugged. "I'd like to think there's a peaceable way out of this. Hell, I offered to marry her last night."

"But she turned you down?"

"Uh-huh."

Dan shook his head. "All I can say is good luck, man. Sounds like you're gonna need it."

COLBY HAD ALMOST FINISHED the preflight check on his plane for the return trip to Kodiak Gorge when his friend Dot sauntered up the dock. She stood about six-two, always wore her lucky red Oklahoma State hat crammed over a mess of salt-

and-pepper curls, and was renowned for the best dirty jokes in a five-hundred-mile radius. Today, though, Dot wasn't smiling.

"I heard you were up our way," she said.

"Yep, brought Pitkins a box of gaskets."

"Heard that's not all you brought."

"S'cuze me?" Colby wasn't sure he liked her tone.

"You heard me."

"Sure, but why don't you try telling me what's behind it? Something bugging you?"

"In a manner of speaking."

"Well then, spell it out." Colby stuck his head back under the cowling to check the oil.

"Okay. I heard you're gonna be a father."

"Uh-huh."

"You gonna do right by that little gal?"

"Gonna try."

"You'd better do a damned sight better 'n that."

Colby stepped out from under the cowling and wiped his hands on a rag. "We've been friends for years, Dot. I would hope in all that time you've come to know me as an honorable man."

"I *used* to think so."

Colby gritted his teeth. He'd had just about enough of being labeled the bad guy where he and Whitney were concerned.

"See, one snowy night a while back," Dot said, "I talked Whitney into knockin' back a few root beers, and she opened up like a bloomin' flower. Told me how she thought she might be pregnant, and how the only person who could be her baby's daddy was you, but how she didn't see the two of you ever gettin' much further than you already had."

"Uh-huh. And that's pretty much the way she still feels."

"You tried changing her mind?"

Colby laughed.

"You're gonna have to treat her with kid gloves. The little girl's been hurt."

"She's hardly a little girl, Dot. She's a full-grown woman with a head full of so-called progressive ideas that'd scare off a grizzly."

For the first time since his arrival, the woman cracked a smile, but far from being her usual guffaw, it was more of a wistful chuckle. "That's my girl. Got enough big-city notions to scare off a whole pack of grizzlies, but that's just it, Colby. It's all show. Inside, that girl's feelings are tangled like snagged fishing line."

Colby shrugged before pulling down the cowling and fastening it closed. "I'm real sorry to hear it, but since she's not exactly opening up to me, there's not much I can do."

Dot put her hands on her hips. "I'll tell you what you can do—*make* her marry you. 'Cause after the kind of example she's seen set by her momma, that's the only way she's gonna do it.''

"Again," Colby said, "seeing how she hasn't mentioned any family trouble to me, I fail to see that it's any of my business."

"It's your business because that baby she's carryin' is yours, and I'm assuming you want to keep that child here in God's country where he or she belongs. Am I right?"

Colby's heart pounded. "It's a boy. Her baby— *our* baby. And yes, I'd very much like to keep him in Kodiak Gorge, but his momma's stubborn. Short of kidnapping her, nothing else is gonna make her stay."

"I know. I heard all about her crazy idea of raising this baby alone. Even back before she knew for sure she was with child, the one thing she did know was that she wasn't ever gettin' married."

"She say why?"

"Her momma. Fancies herself a Liz Taylor. Been married seven times. Each time worse than the last. Our Whitney said she doesn't ever plan on ending up like that."

"Can't say as I blame her," Colby said, jaw tight as he winced at the sun shining off the lake.

Our Whitney.

A long time ago, back before their disastrous airport goodbye, he'd thought of her as his. He'd fantasized about what it might be like for the two of them to end up together. But there was a damned big difference between the vulnerable beauty she'd been that night up on the mountain and the all-business ice queen she'd been with him most of the time since.

As late as this morning, he'd held out hope of the two of them reaching an amicable agreement where their son was concerned. In other words, she'd agree to marry him on a friendly basis for now, and see where their friendship might lead.

He'd been prepared to give her one hundred percent of everything he held dear, including his heart, but she'd turned him down cold. As far as he was concerned, they'd now reached the point where the only person who could fix their dilemma was a good attorney. One who dealt with child custody situations. Because Colby no longer wanted to share their son.

He opened the plane's door. "Been nice talking to you, Dot."

"You heard me, didn't you? She's hurt. You gotta take a different approach with her type. You know, use some finesse."

"Finesse, huh?" Colby shot his old friend a broad smile. "Why don't you try that on your man, then tell me how it works?"

AFTER WATCHING Colby take off in that snazzy new ride of his, Dot picked up the control room phone and dialed a familiar number.

"Kodiak Lodge," Nugget answered.

"It's me."

"You get the job done?"

"Tried."

"That's not good enough."

"Nag, nag, nag."

"Don't you sass me. Doggone it, I'm practically that boy's daddy, and I'll not have any grandson of mine being raised in some backward town like Chicago. Probably don't have a decent steak in the entire state of Ill-noise, and who knows where a granddad can take his grandson to teach him how to properly snag a trout."

"You want me to launch Phase Two?"

Nugget sighed. "Let's give 'em one more night on their own, but if she hasn't accepted his proposal by then, it's time to pull out the big guns."

Chapter Eight

Colby rubbed his eyes to make sure that what awaited him at the end of the dock wasn't a mirage. Granted, with the tricky head wind, the flight back to Kodiak Lake had taken longer than usual, but he didn't feel tired enough to have conjured up an unbelievable sight like this.

Seated pretty as you please on top of the boulder that had forget-me-nots growing out of it, wearing jeans and a pretty pink top, was Whitney, her dark hair glinting in the late-afternoon sun.

"Hi!" she called out with a wave and smile that wiped out all his carefully made plans to tell her that if she didn't marry him, he was calling an attorney.

He couldn't do that to her.

He wasn't that kind of guy, and seeing her now, he knew she wasn't a hardball kind of girl. Just like Dot had told him, she was a softie on the inside, and it was high time he started treating her like one.

Especially since she wouldn't have come all the way out here unless she had a very good reason—like telling him she had finally agreed that marrying him was not only the right thing for their son, but for her.

Filled with a sudden calm at the notion that his whole life was about to take a welcome turn for the better, Colby took a deep breath.

Time to meet his bride.

Oh sure, technically they knew each other, but something about the sparkle in her eyes told him they were about to meet again as if for the first time.

"Hi, yourself," he said, shutting and locking the plane door before slinging his flight bag over his right shoulder. Hands in his jeans pockets, he headed for the end of the dock. "Nice day, huh?"

"Gorgeous."

"What'd you do today?"

"Bit of this, bit of that," she said, standing, then meeting him halfway. She held her hands behind her back.

"What've you got?" he asked, touched that she thought enough of him to have gotten him an apology gift. Whether she was hiding a bouquet of handpicked flowers or a candy bar from the drugstore, he'd love it. Not for the gift itself, but because she'd finally accepted the inevitable.

They were meant to be a family.

"Oh, not much," she said, still wielding that pretty grin.

God, she looked beautiful carrying his child. Complexion radiant, eyes bright. At that moment, he knew he'd never seen a more gorgeous woman.

The two of them, crazy as it seemed, were right.

"Out with it," he said. "What'd you get me?"

"Get you?" Her grin faded.

"Yeah, you know. Isn't that a gift you're hiding behind your back?"

"Um, well, I suppose you might say that."

"Oh, I get it. You want me to guess? Draw out the suspense along with the fun." He liked this new playful side to her personality. It reminded him of the woman he'd met all those months ago in his dearly departed Beaver.

"Well…"

"Let's see. Is it bigger than a bread basket?"

"Colby, I—"

"Duh. Since it fits behind your back, I'm guessing that's a no. Sorry. Stupid question. Okay, give me a second to regroup."

"Colby—"

"No, really. I'll get it this time. You brought me a—"

"Colby, would you just *listen* for a second? You and me—we're strangers. What I brought *is* a gift. A gift I had my lawyer draw up that guarantees your financial and emotional freedom from any future claim I might make on you in your capacity as my child's biological father.''

As her words—her poison—sank in, Colby's blood ran cold. At first, his heart thundered, but then it slowed to dull, furious beats. God, how could he have been such a fool? She'd played him like a damned fiddle. Sure, in a moment of anger he'd thought about suing for custody. But there was a *huge* difference between thinking about it and actually following through.

He swiped his fingers through his hair.

''Here,'' she said, holding a crisp legal-sized envelope bearing his name and address. ''At first, my attorney suggested I just mail these—to keep everything tidy. But I wanted to present them face to face. You know, make the whole thing more personal.''

Hot tears pricked Colby's eyes and he hated himself for not having seen this coming. All his life, he'd held tight to the Pollyanna image of being the perfect dad alongside his perfect wife. They'd love each other, deeply and forever. The three of them—hell, maybe even the four or five of them—would be a force to be reckoned with. Their loving bond, their *family* bond, could never be broken. But just as he'd seen how futile that dream was with Margot, he was seeing it again with Whitney. But knowing she already carried his son made the pain that much worse.

He looked at her, at the silent tears streaming down her cheeks. "Tell me," he said, swallowing with difficulty. "How the hell can you stand there so...unmoved, when I see this is hurting you as much as it is me?"

She wiped her cheeks. "Yes," she said, "it's hurting me, but not for the reasons you think."

"Oh, reasons like you're condemning our son to life without a father before he's even come out of the womb? What other reasons could there be?"

Whitney turned away—not because her decision to raise her son alone was wrong or somehow invalid, but because she couldn't stand seeing the hurt her decision had inflicted on this obviously strong, loving man.

What had she done?

Her lawyer had been right. She never should have come here—not if she expected to start her journey into motherhood with a clean conscience.

The truth of the matter was that she'd read all the books. She knew how important having a father was to a boy—but she couldn't let Colby do it. Fears that he'd pull some stunt like baby bungee jumping weren't fueling her determination to cut all ties. Truthfully, she just couldn't bring herself to make the same mistakes her mother had, over and over again.

Marriage wasn't for her. Her disaster with Rocco had been enough. She couldn't sign her life over to a man—not even a man who seemed as wonderful as Colby.

Deep inside her lurked the certain knowledge that, as far as she was concerned, if Colby turned out to be as rotten a father as her own had been, her son would be much better off never knowing him. She was saving her son years of costly therapy and pain.

"Please sign these," she said, clearing her voice. "It'll make things much easier for everyone."

He took the papers. Stared at them. A muscle ticked in his throat as his fingers slowly tightened around them.

"Colby? Did you hear me?"

"Oh, yeah," he said with a harsh laugh. "Loud and clear." He stepped closer and closer until she smelled his trademark scent of airplane and leather and sweat. He stepped nearer still, and she felt his radiated heat. And then he was there, in her personal space, daring her to flinch.

"Now, it's time for you to hear this." Never looking away from her, he ripped her papers in half, then flung them into the lake.

COLBY HAD FIGURED that after a good four or five hours, he'd feel better about the afternoon's events. But as he sat on the rough-hewn log bench tucked into the curve of Kodiak Lodge's stairs, he still felt nothing but confusion and contempt for the mother of his son. And that hurt. Granted, they hardly knew each other, but he'd been prepared to offer the woman his very heart on a silver platter. And oh, she'd taken it, all right. Taken it off the platter to shred it into a zillion tiny pieces.

And what was *he* doing?

Sitting here like a damned fool, knowing he had to yet again swallow his pride for the sake of his child.

After showing her in unambiguous terms what he wanted her to do with those papers of hers, he'd driven her back to the lodge, where she said she planned to take a nap. He'd done the same himself. When he woke up, he felt that same old familiar lead chunk where his heart used to live.

The bottom line was, he wanted his son—not just for a few weekends out of the year, but every morning. He wanted to smell his child's tiny SpongeBob jammies sticky-sweet with syrup. To feel his chubby hands twining round his neck as he carried him in from the car after he'd fallen asleep in his car seat. He wanted all the quiet times. The intimate moments part-time dads never got to see. Hell, he'd even been looking forward to sharing his son's moments with Whitney—the first time she breast-fed him or gave him a bath in the sink.

They could have shared all those special times.

Why couldn't she see that? How could she possibly think her way was best? For whom? Surely not for their son?

That was why he was back at the lodge for a last-ditch effort. He had to talk some sense into the woman. He knew she was book smart. Now was the time to see if she was common-sense smart, too. Because that was all this situation needed. Some good old-fashioned common sense.

He heard a commotion above him and stood. At the top of the stairs, Whitney—who looked twelve months' pregnant—had bumped into a side table. In the process, she'd knocked over Nugget's set of *Reader's Digest* condensed books and a few knick-knacks he kept on hand because he said they made the place more homey for his guests.

Colby had just mounted the first step to help his son's accident-prone mother, when a couple of the guys—and a gal—from Global walked in the front door.

"Hey there, Colby," Dot called out, Todd and Dan right behind her. "Long time no see, huh?"

"How'd you guys get over here?" Colby asked.

"We, um, had an unexpected cargo shipment late this afternoon. Cutty Milborn brought it in from Juneau. We, um, hitched a ride back with him."

"Okay, that explains how you got from the site down to Juneau, but what're you doing *here?* His rig can't land on this lake."

"Damn, Colby, what's with all the questions?" Dan said. "Can't you just be glad to see us and leave it at that?"

Head aching from his constant worrying over how to keep his son, Colby grinned. "Sorry. Guess I'm just itchin' for a good fight." To show Dan there were no hard feelings, he patted him on the back before the threesome tugged him along to the lodge's bar. What the hell? What would one beer hurt? If nothing else, it would buy him a little time to compose his thoughts before his talk with Whitney....

WHITNEY HURT, and not just because that solid brass moose had fallen on her toe.

The afternoon with Colby couldn't have gone worse. She'd had the whole speech worked out in her head for months. How most men would be thrilled to be relieved of the burden of an unplanned child. And how she'd actually be doing him a big favor by agreeing to sole custody—giving him visitation rights if he wanted them, of course. The one thing she hadn't counted on was the fact that Colby would be the best father any child could ever imagine.

He didn't just want his son. He was *fighting* for his son.

And if she'd even said her next thought aloud, her friends would consider her mad. But lately, she was beginning to think she felt her son pulling toward Colby. Whenever she was around him, Baby Talbot became extra active. Kicking and rolling, arching as if reaching for his first hug.

Probably all of that could be attributed to gas, or the effects of too many fatty foods on her already thin nerves. But still, what if there *was* something to it?

She stacked the last of the books back on the table at the top of the stairs.

What if she was wrong about her son not needing a father? Even worse, what if—

"There you are," Nugget hollered from the foot of the stairs. "I was just coming to get you."

"What's up?" Whitney asked, smoothing her hair, which she'd secured in a tight chignon at the base of her neck.

"Oh, I'm just coming to wag a little fresh-baked pot roast under your always-hungry nose."

"Mashed potatoes?" Whitney asked, stomach already growling.

"Absolutely, along with plenty of gravy, a nice green salad, sugar-glazed baby carrots and, for dessert, hot apple pie."

"Mmm, I should've been down here an hour ago."

Nugget laughed. As Whitney reached the bottom step, he held out his hand to lead her into the crowded dining room.

"Aren't there any women in this town?" she asked, eyeing the all-male crowd of about twenty.

"Sure," Nugget said, bringing Whitney to her usual table beside the bank of windows overlooking the glistening lake. "But they're all home with their families."

"Oh."

"I hear you don't go for that sort of thing."

"Family? Are you kidding? My best friend back in Chicago has a huge family. I eat over there a lot. Her mom's a great cook and has so many kids, she never notices an extra person sneaking up to the table."

"Ahh, so then you do plan on settling down with a good man someday? Maybe having more little ones?"

Whitney narrowed her eyes. "If this is your way of asking if I've accepted Colby's proposal—the answer's no."

"Gracious," he said, eyes wide, hands on his barrel chest. "I wouldn't dream of asking such a personal question. That sort of thing should be left up to Colby himself. And speaking of that dear boy... Look, here he comes. Hey, Colby! Over here!"

Whitney skimmed the faces in the small male mob to see only one.

Even though all Alaskan men seemed to grow taller and more muscular than others, her baby's father was in a class all his own. Even with his dark hair ruffled and a shadow of growth on his cheeks, his green eyes were mesmerizing. The look he cast her way filled her with shame for the cavalier way she'd handed him those forms.

He'd deserved better. At the very least, a heck of a lot more tact.

''What a nice surprise,'' Nugget said, patting Colby's back.

That easy camaraderie sparked a curious bolt of envy in her. She didn't realize how much she missed simple human closeness.

Waking up after having made love, she'd found the air in the plane painfully cold, yet inside their cozy down nest, Colby's naked skin had burned against hers. How well she remembered turning to him while he still slept, feeling free to touch him, outlining the silhouette of his shoulders and chest in the darkness, pressing close to drop kisses on his whiskered cheek, loving the sharp sensation of stubble against her lips.

Her leisurely exploration had awakened him, and he'd drawn her into his arms, growling like a lovable old bear as he'd playfully rolled on top of her. He'd supported just enough of his weight so she didn't feel crushed, yet he'd rested on her in a way that let her know he was all man. He'd sheltered her, yet at the same time—

"Care to call a truce?" Colby said, drawing out the extra chair at her table.

"Sure," she said, flashing him what felt like a wobbly grin.

"Can I bring you both the pot roast?" Nugget asked.

"Sounds good to me," he said, raising heat in her cheeks with his concentrated stare. "Whitney?"

"P-please," she said, somehow having forgotten just how appealing Colby could be when he tried. Or was he always this appealing, and she'd just been so focused on keeping him out of her life that she'd forgotten how much fun life could be with him?

Stop it, she told herself. Thoughts like these had landed her mother in seven failed marriages.

Nugget made his way back to the kitchen, stopping to shake hands and slap backs at each table along the way.

It didn't matter that the two of them were surrounded by people; suddenly Whitney felt as if they were, once again, alone.

"I like your dress," Colby said.

"Thanks." She glanced down at the simple blue-and-white cotton toile dress with its empire cut. It was her favorite of all her maternity clothes—the one item she still felt pretty in, despite her ever-growing girth. "Colby?"

"Uh-huh?"

"I'm sorry."

"Me, too. I shouldn't have thrown your papers away like that."

"No. I mean, yes. Yes, you should have. I mean, we're both adults here, and even though I can't see myself ever getting married, I didn't mean to come across like some baby-making robot."

He shrugged.

She gave him a halfhearted smile. "I'll take that to mean I was as callous as I feared."

"Well…" He took her hands and gave them a gentle squeeze.

Warmth eased through her, and when the baby kicked, she gasped at the intensity.

"You okay?" he asked.

"Yeah. Our, uh, little slugger here must be ready for dinner. He's raising quite a fuss."

"Do you mind?" he asked, releasing her hand to reach across the small table.

Assuming he meant to curve his fingers and palm to her big belly, she guided his hand, then covered it with her own.

Baby Talbot rolled, and Colby's eyes lit up. "I think he likes me."

"Much as I hate to say it, I think you're right."

"You don't have to make it sound like such torture."

"Sorry," she said. "Again. It seems like all I've done since I got here is apologize."

"And I feel like that's my fault."

"No. Not at all. Here I'm supposed to be trained in helping people improve their lives, yet my own life is a mess."

"I wouldn't go that far. You've been blessed with my baby, haven't you?"

"My, aren't you the modest one."

He winked, and her resolve to close her heart against the memories of the magic they'd shared melted a bit more.

After dinner, when Nugget automatically brought Colby a coffee, Colby politely declined in favor of a glass of milk.

"You didn't have to do that, you know."

"Sure I did." He forked up the last of his hot apple pie. "What you're going through—it has to be tough. You need to know you're not alone."

What she would've given to hear those words during her first trimester. The mornings she'd been sick. The nights she'd lain awake confused, wondering if she could handle being a single mom. Knowing sadly that in light of what she'd learned about marriage, she had no other choice.

You're not alone.

It was a lovely sentiment, but aside from her son, she *was* alone, and always would be. For the fleeting moment she glanced up, only to lose herself in

Colby's luminous gaze, the knowledge causing her a pang of sadness.

Then she reminded herself that loving someone hurt. She'd given love a try with Rocco, and look where that had led.

No, she was smart to stick to her resolve. It was one thing to be lonely. It was totally another to be consumed by soul-crushing pain no amount of aspirin could ease.

At a loss for words, Whitney looked down at her pie.

It had been much easier to convince herself that she was doing the right thing back when Colby had been so obstinate. This charming side, the side she'd first been attracted to when he'd shared his grape Bubble Yum, was a definite drawback.

"What's your favorite movie?" Colby asked.

Pleased by the lighter tone of their conversation, Whitney sighed. "I don't know. You go first. There are so many, I'll need a second to think."

"Okay. Let's see… On any movie list, *Terminator* and *Independence Day* would have to be high, along with *Alien* and *Aliens,* but the last two in that series?" He shook his head and grinned. "Your turn."

"I'm still thinking. I've spent so much time studying, and then working, I haven't seen that many movies. You go again. It's fun hearing what you like."

"Hmm, to show I'm not all action and do have a sensitive side, *Last of the Dogmen* and *Sleepless in Seattle*."

"Whoa. Even I've seen that one, and it's definitely not your average shoot 'em up action flick."

He shrugged. "What can I say? I'm a well-rounded guy, fully qualified to make a great dad and husband."

"Colby," she warned. "This has been such a nice night. Please don't start."

"I'm not starting anything—just putting in a plug. You know, like a five-second campaign speech." The little-boy grin he shot her way somersaulted over her every objection, sending her pulse racing and her attraction meter spiking.

What was she going to do if her son had the same ability to melt her heart with just one glance? How was she going to spend the next eighteen years separating him from his father, when every look reminded her of the man she was trying to avoid?

"You all right over there?"

She looked up, straight into his worried eyes. "I'm fine."

"You sure?"

Swallowing hard, she nodded. Oh, why had she ever come here? Colby was a good man who'd make a great dad, and maybe he'd even make someone a great husband—just not her. "I think I'm ready to call it a night."

"Sure," he said, standing to help her out of her chair. They'd long since paid the bill. Or rather, he'd paid the bill, even though she'd insisted Nugget charge their meal to her room. "Sorry. I should've noticed you were getting tired."

"I'm a big girl, Colby. Please stop acting like my well-being is your responsibility."

His large hand deliciously warming the small of her back, they walked out of the considerably less crowded room. Only two other tables were occupied, by sportsman types wearing outfits fresh off the pages of an L.L.Bean catalogue.

In the shadowy cove of the stairs, he paused to take her hands in his. "Look, Whitney, what you just said, about not being my responsibility? You've got that all wrong."

The warmth in his eyes made her mouth feel dry.

"You see, from the moment you first climbed on board my plane, you *became* my responsibility. Your life was quite literally in my hands."

"Yes, but in case you haven't noticed, we've landed safely."

"Have we, Whitney?" He drew her closer, easing her hands behind her back, fitting their bodies together like two puzzle pieces. She licked her lips. "Look at me," he said.

Helpless to do anything else, she did.

"Do you think for one second that anything about this situation is safe? For god's sake, Whitney, we're talking about a baby. My baby—yours. You act as if this is some kind of game you're determined to win, but it's so much more. A whole life is at stake, and—"

"Sixty-seven bottles of beer on the wall, sixty-seven bottles of…"

Colby groaned. Through the lodge's front door tottered ten or so very drunk Global Oil guys with Dot and Dan at the helm. Brody, Tanner and Sergei followed close behind.

"There's our man," slurred Dan. "And look, he's got his bride-to-be with him, too."

"Excellent," Tanner said.

From out of the dining room stepped Nugget, along with Henry, Stanley, and all three cooks and dishwashers.

"What's going on?" Colby asked as the crowd came closer. He slipped his arm around Whitney.

"What do you think is going on?" Dot asked.

"I-I'll just be heading on up to bed," Whitney said with a funny little giggle as the crowd of at least twelve or thirteen men and her friend Dot surrounded them. At least ten more people streamed in from the bar.

"Sorry, sugar bun," Nugget said, "but this here is an Alaskan intervention, and you'll be going nowhere but where we send you."

"Oh, no," Colby said. "You're not really going to—argh!"

Too late for protests, he and Whitney had already been hefted off their feet and propelled toward the door.

Chapter Nine

"Let me out of here!" Whitney shouted, banging on the delivery truck's metal door. Outside, a lock clicked into place.

"Good job, boys," Nugget said, his voice muffled but chipper. "Dot? Brody? You two grab the coffee I packed for the ride, along with that milk for our expectant momma?"

"Yessir."

"Let me out!" Whitney screamed. "Are you people *nuts?* This is kidnapping! *Double* kidnapping!"

Colby, drawing Whitney onto one of the comfy pillows lining the truck's floor, said, "Wouldn't that be a triple kidnapping, or don't I count?"

"Grr," she said, eyes flashing in the oddly romantic light of at least fifty green glow sticks. "Tell them to stop, Colby. This isn't funny."

"Hey," he said, holding up his hands in surrender. "You see me laughing? I'm just as much a

victim here as you. And look on the bright side.''
He pointed to a heart-shaped basket filled with a
bottle of sparkling cider, crackers and Whitney's
favorite squirt cheese. ''At least they gave us
snacks.''

She made a good show of frowning, but couldn't
quite hide the twinkle in her eyes when her gaze
landed on the cheese.

The truck engine started. From outside, Nugget
hollered, ''Don't you two worry about a thing.
Brody and Dot were just pretending to be drunk.
They're both sober as preachers on Judgment Day.
They'll get you where you're going, nice and
safe.''

Colby groaned, spotting boxes of what he
guessed were supplies in a corner.

''Okay, hit it!'' On Nugget's command, the truck
lurched forward, flinging Whitney against Colby's
chest.

He shook his head. ''Sometimes I wonder if all
the isolation up here isn't throwing a few people
off their rockers.''

''This thought just now occurred to you?'' Whitney asked. ''Aggh!'' A tooth-jarring pothole left
her holding on to Colby for dear life.

''Hey!'' Colby shouted toward the truck's cab.
''You two fruitcakes mind slowing down?''

They did, and thankfully, although the ride was
still bumpy, the bumps became easier to bear.

A few minutes later, Whitney realized she was still clinging to Colby, her arms around his neck, her cheek pressed against the warmth of his chest. She knew she should let go, but didn't want to. He was not only a safe harbor in this bizarre storm, but a comfortable one.

"We're gonna be all right, you know," he said, stroking her hair. She nodded against him. "This is what my so-called friends consider an Alaska-sized therapy session."

"Yeah, but where are they taking us, and what do they hope to achieve?"

She felt him shrug. "Probably some cabin out in the woods. Most of us have places out in the boonies we use to just get away."

At that, she leaned back and cast him a grin. "Oh—like the stress of being around all two hundred or so occupants of this town can be a strain?"

"Hey, try over a thousand occupants. Kodiak Gorge is a happening place."

"Sorry."

"You should be." He tweaked her ear.

"What was that for?"

"Sass. Now, where was I?"

"Explaining why your high-stress lifestyle requires you to get away."

Shaking his head, he said, "You're incorrigible."

She laughed.

"Anyway, I imagine they're planning to leave us wherever they drop us off until we either bicker each other to death or agree to marry."

"They have to know we can't be manipulated like that."

Back to stroking her hair, he said, "Oh, I don't know. When Nugget gets a hankering to do something, there's no stopping him. He did this to my friend Tanner and his wife Jenny when they announced they were getting a divorce."

"So? What happened? Are the two of them still married?"

Sighing, Colby said, "Guess they fell under the category of bickering each other to death. I have to confess to being in on that kidnapping, though. After their time together, they never spoke to each other again."

"Wow."

"Yeah. That's kind of how I felt."

On that note, Colby cradled Whitney closer, glad when the steady rise and fall of her breathing told him she was asleep.

There weren't many roads leading out of Kodiak Gorge. Two, to be specific—Old Gold Road and New Gold Road. And Old Gold Road should've been downgraded to Old Gold Mule Trail about twenty years back. Judging by the increase in bumps, Colby guessed they were on the trail.

The one that led straight to his fishing cabin.

Dammit, he knew Nugget and the rest of the gang meant well, but having Whitney in his town was hard enough. Why in the world would they believe he wanted her up at his sanctuary? Especially since every time he cast out his fly rod from now on, he'd be thinking of what quiet joy could be found in having his towheaded son standing right there beside him, proudly holding up his first fish.

The strange thing about that image was the absence of little-boy-Nick's mother. Did the fact that Colby couldn't imagine her in his future mean he was destined to only see his son part-time?

No. The very idea was unacceptable. He snuggled his son's mother close, settling in for a long, bumpy ride—both emotionally and physically.

"WHITNEY, HON, wake up." Colby eased her from his chest, grinning at the tiny wet spot in the middle of his dark green shirt where she'd drooled sometime in the night.

"No," she said, snuggling closer. "It's too early."

Moving her off him and onto one of the dozens of pillows lining the truck's floor, he tried the door, and it slid right open. Hand to his forehead, shielding his eyes from the blinding sun, he was treated to the sight of one of his favorite places on earth— his log fishing cabin in all its rustic glory, nestled among towering Sitka spruce, mountain hemlock and cedar.

Between the trees the lake glittered.

As far as Colby knew, the lake didn't have a formal name. He'd always just thought of it as his lake. Although now, oddly enough, he was looking forward to sharing it with Whitney.

Usually, he flew in, and the aerial view of his private paradise always filled him with quiet pride, but the place was just as sweet from this angle. Even though Whitney was a big-city girl, he couldn't imagine her not forming an instant attachment.

Turning to her, he knelt, sweeping her thick hair back from her ear so he could whisper, "Wake up, sleeping beauty. We're home."

Still lying beside her from when she'd needed a late-night snack was a can of squirt cheese. Knowing she'd be wanting another hit soon, he put it in his pocket for later.

"Yoo hoo…sleeping beauty. Time to rise."

She swatted at him. "I already told you it's too early to wake up."

"Mmm," he said. "Judging by his momma, our son's gonna be a bear to wake up for school every morning."

"He'll go to night school," she said, eyes still closed, a grin tugging the corners of her mouth.

"That's all well and good," he said, taking her

hands in the hopes of making her sit up. "But last I heard, Kodiak Gorge didn't offer late-night kindergarten."

"They would for our boy—he'll be special."

Colby's spirit soared. "That mean you've rethought your plan to head back to Chicago?"

Her eyes popped open, and she bolted upright. "What?"

"What you just said—you know, about our son being special, and how Kodiak Gorge would open a kindergarten just for him. That mean you're sticking around?"

"No—absolutely not. I was half-asleep. I wasn't in my right mind after not getting a moment's decent rest."

"That's funny," he said with a wry laugh. "Most of the night, your snoring kept me up."

"I can't help it," she said, scrambling to her feet. "All this dry air up here messes with my sinuses."

"Oh."

"It does."

He hopped down from the truck, then held out his arms to help her.

"Thanks," she said, "but I can do it myself."

"By all means," he said, stepping aside. "I wouldn't dream of interfering."

"Thank you."

Using the side of the truck for support, Whitney

started to jump down, but the truck floor looked to be a good two feet off the ground, so she opted for another approach, figuring she'd squat, turn around, then hop down backward.

But considering how her belly got in the way, that wasn't working, either.

"Need help?" the know-it-all standing beside her inquired, laughter in his tone.

"No," she muttered from between clenched teeth.

"Sorry. Just asking."

"Yeah, well, don't."

She next tried a forward squat, but when she felt queasy, she turned around again, thinking it was just a matter of—"Oooh!"

Colby snatched her from behind, briefly cradling her before setting her on her feet.

"I said I could do it," she barked.

"You're welcome."

Hands on her hips, she glared at him. But facing that handsome, warm-eyed mug of his, all whisker-stubbled and kissable like it had been on that snowy night, she couldn't hold onto her anger—especially since she would have had to resort to asking for his help eventually. "I'm sorry," she said. "I do appreciate your assistance."

He shrugged. "It wasn't a big deal."

"It would've been in about five minutes if I hadn't got to a bathroom." She grinned. Hand to her forehead, she looked around, then said, "This place is straight off the pages of a storybook." A few seconds later, she added with a wince, "A nice, happy storybook, if you'd kindly show me to the facilities."

"Sure. Right there," he said, pointing to a crude path leading off into the trees.

"What? Is this cabin like a storage shed, and the real house is down that trail?"

"No, I just mean the bathroom is down the trail."

"Oh—like you've got a bathhouse," she said, already on her way. "That's cool. A bubble bath would feel fantastic."

"Just keep walking," he said. "I want it to be a surprise."

She flashed him a smile. "Mmm… Maybe this whole kidnapping thing won't be so bad after all. Kind of like a spa weekend."

"Just keep walking," he said. "You can't miss it."

With a perky wave, she rounded a bend in the path. Leaning against the truck, arms folded, Colby crossed his legs at the ankles, then counted. "Five…four…three…two—"

"An outhouse! Your only bathroom is an outhouse?"

Dot and Brody came charging up the other path that led to the lake.

"What's the commotion?" Brody asked. "There a grizzly?"

Colby let out a snort. "Oh, there's a grizzly, all right. A big old momma grizzly who just found out there's no flush toilet."

"That's my cue to beat it," Dot said, hopping into the back of the truck to grab a box Colby presumed held supplies. "Brody, help me out. I want to be gone before she comes back."

"For crying out loud," Colby said. "You're not really planning on leaving us here, are you?"

"If we don't," Brody said, "Nugget told us he wouldn't serve us for the next year."

"And you two actually believe that?"

Brody had already dumped one box onto the dirt at Colby's feet and was going for another.

"Aw, don't leave me up here with her. She scares me."

"Yeah, well you shoulda thought about that before you—"

"Speed it up, Brode—this here's the last one." Dot hefted the last box off the truck, yanked the back door down and secured it, then hightailed it around to the cab.

Brody followed hot on her heels.

Colby wasn't far behind them. "Come on, guys," he wheedled. "You know how well this worked with Tanner and Jenny, so what in the hell makes you think it would work with—"

They'd shut and locked both cab doors.

Dot started the engine, grinding it into first gear.

"Hey!" Colby pounded on Dot's door, chasing the truck out of the cabin's yard. The place used to have a driveway, but since he'd never used it, sometime over the years it had blended with the forest—a fact made only too evident when a birch sapling whipped his left cheek. "Ouch. Dammit."

In the time it took him to mutter a few more curses, his two supposed friends and their truck vanished behind a dust cloud.

Raking his fingers through his hair, Colby muttered, "Behold, the power of Nugget's home cooking on a bachelor and an old married woman who between them can't open a can of soup."

"Where's the truck?" Whitney asked, eyes wide. "All the squirt cheese was back there—and those yummy little crackers with the—"

"Do you like trout?"

"What do you mean?" she said, eyes narrowed, hands on what was left of her hips. "They just went off for a quick bite to eat at a restaurant down the road, right? After that, they'll be back in a couple of hours?"

He sighed.

"Colby? They will be back, right?"

"In a few days."

AFTER WHITNEY GOT OVER the initial shock of realizing she wasn't going anywhere, Colby planted her on a comfy rocker on the cabin's screened porch, then hauled in the supplies. There were lots of them, including her suitcase and toiletries from the hotel.

She'd offered to help, but he still seemed under the impression that just because she was pregnant, she was also helpless. Normally, she'd have delighted in proving him wrong, but—she yawned—this was one time when she was happy to abide by his macho request that she rest.

Granted, the outhouse thing was a real drag. And instead of a proper stove, the kitchen had a wood-burning monstrosity that looked as though it had been hauled up here in gold rush days. But sitting as she was now, gazing out at the view, she was surprised that she couldn't think of anything she'd rather be doing—and that included working at the job she loved.

The control freak in her should have been railing. Instead, Whitney felt an odd sense of peace. If pressed, she couldn't have even explained why. For whatever reason, this cabin was where she needed to be.

The diamond-shot lake was ringed by spruce. At the far end stood aspen in a field of wildflowers. Behind those was a snowcapped mountain. In the patch of enchanted forest serving as a yard, a woodpecker had his way with a half-dead cedar, and from over the lake came the occasional honking of geese.

The sweet smell of wood smoke hung in the air. Colby must've gotten the stove to work. He'd explained earlier that he couldn't light a fire in the rock fireplace because a bird family had moved in for the summer.

"You cold?" Colby asked, strolling through the cabin's open door with a fuzzy red blanket.

"Maybe a little," she said, cuddling into it when he tucked it over her lap. "Thanks."

"You're welcome." He pressed a tender kiss on her forehead before heading back inside.

The baby kicked. "Colby?" she called out.

"Yeah?"

"Despite our differences, let's try to have a nice time up here—for however long those so-called friends of yours decide to leave us."

"Sounds good to me. Anything you need?"

"Other than that bath I was wishing for, along with a snack, I'm pretty much content."

"You really want a bath?"

"It'd be nice, but I'm guessing that the only shower or tub up here is the lake, right?"

He winked. "What do you want for a snack?"

"Colby? What? Do we not even get the lake to bathe in? Is it infested with ultra-hardy piranha or flesh-eating arctic bacteria?"

"Snack?"

"Pizza?"

"How about baby carrots and ranch dip?"

"Yum."

Yet again avoiding her hygiene question, he disappeared inside the cabin.

Wrapping the blanket around her shoulders, she followed him, only to be pleasantly surprised by what he'd done with the place in the past thirty minutes. On her first trip through, the sofa and few chairs had been shrouded in old muslin dustcovers, as had the bed, giving the whole cabin the appearance of ghost central.

But now...

Now it was a cozy haven with a gently worn red sofa and chairs, and a big wrought-iron bed, fluffy and inviting with its mounds of pillows and cheery, red-plaid spread. Above the rock fireplace hung an uncannily accurate watercolor rendition of the lake.

Colby caught her appraising the room and reddened.

"What's wrong?" she asked, admiring the red-calico curtains with their pretty lace trim.

"What's wrong?" he asked with a slight cough. "I'd forgotten how girly this place is. My mom painted that," he said, pointing to the picture Whitney had just admired. With any luck, their son would inherit her artistic flair. "I used to spend so much time up here that she redecorated the place for my twenty-fifth birthday. Guess she thought I could use it for a love nest.''

Now it was Whitney's turn to redden. ''Well?''

''What?''

''Did you? Use it as a—you know.''

He looked sharply away.

For a second, Whitney couldn't figure out what would make Colby react that way, but then understanding dawned. As much as she wanted to believe he'd never been with any woman but her, she wasn't that naive. ''You came up here with Margot, didn't you?''

He nodded.

''And knowing how well that turned out, you're figuring the same is about to happen with me.''

''Actually,'' he said with a half laugh, ''I was thinking more along the lines that at least with Margot I'd had a fighting chance, but with you...''

''Oh—you think I should agree to give up my entire life—my work and friends? Just because you want me to?''

''No, because our son needs you to. He's a kid. Can you imagine what a kick he'd get out of coming up here? Fishing, camping, learning how trappers and miners used to live off the land.''

''Getting bitten by mosquitoes,'' she said, slapping at a little sucker about to tear into her arm.

''God help him if he's even half as bullheaded as you.''

"Why am I bullheaded just because I know what I want?"

"Because you're so caught up in knowing what you want, you can't even see what our child needs."

Chapter Ten

Whitney should've been enjoying herself.

Here she sat in a steaming copper tub, complete with berry-scented bubbles. Not only that, but perched pretty as you please on a table beside her was a tray of snacks—the squirt cheese she'd feared long gone in the truck, and those little round crackers she'd come to adore. Sweet grapes and slightly tart apple slices. Best of all, a tall glass of sweet herbal iced tea Colby had cooled by sticking the whole plastic jug of it in the frigid lake.

Cheese cracker in one hand, tea in another, the rest of her immersed in sinfully warm water, she should've been content. But from just outside the window came the sharp whack and ker-thunk of Colby splitting logs in two, then the halves hitting the ground.

From the moment they'd stepped out of the truck that morning, he'd been working while she lounged. Never in her life had she felt so useless—

unless it came to making her mother listen to objections concerning her latest marriage.

Her mother's experience had shown her what an all-around disaster marriage would be. Cooking, cleaning, watching nothing but sports on TV. Always having to put your needs below someone else's. Of course, Whitney would do all of that and more when Baby Talbot came into the world, but until then—no siree, Bob. She wasn't about to go turning her life upside-down for some man she hardly knew.

Oh no—of course not. Especially when it's so much easier just sitting around on your tush letting him do all the work for you.

Whitney squeezed her eyes shut. From outside came another thwack and ker-thunk, then whistling. It was cheerful whistling, even though he still had to have a few painful places left over from his fall down Kodiak Lodge's front stairs.

"Baby," she said, curving her hands around her belly. "Your father's a workaholic, and your mom's turning into a whine-a-holic."

Her only answer was the occasional plip-plop coming from the old-fashioned hand pump beside the sink.

Colby was a good man. Judging by what her single friends said, a really good man was an increasingly tough breed to find in this day and age. He was handsome and loyal and honorable and hardworking. And here she was grousing about how she'd never marry anyone, let alone a man like him, when he was working so hard to make her time at the rustic cabin enjoyable.

Okay, so she'd established the fact that she was behaving like a spoiled brat, but what was she going to do about it? There was no way he'd let her help cut wood.

Maybe there were other things she could do? She could cook or dust or pick berries, or whatever else mountain women did to help their men keep food on the table.

Not that Colby was *her* man.

Scrambling out of the tub, Whitney hastily dried herself on the fluffy white towel Colby had been thoughtful enough to provide, then dressed in black warm-up pants, a white T-shirt, and the matching warm-up jacket. After adding thick white socks and comfy shoes, then securing her ponytail, she headed outside. To her surprise, Colby wasn't at the neatly stacked woodpile where she'd thought he'd be.

"Colby!" she shouted, swallowing a twinge of panic. What would she do if he'd been eaten by a bear or had fallen down some rotted old mine shaft?

"Over here!"

With relief, she spotted him at the lake's edge, fluidly casting a fly rod in and out. He'd changed into a navy-blue T-shirt, and with each cast, the muscles of his shoulders and back flexed. Remembering only too well the feel of those muscles beneath the sensitive skin of her palms, Whitney licked her lips.

Carefully making her way down the dirt path, she called, "Catch anything?" *Besides my heart?*

"One. But I figured since you probably want to eat, too, I might need to catch a few more."

"A *few* more?"

"Hey, it's not your fault that kid of mine is always hungry."

Having reached him on the shore, she reached up to tweak his ear.

"Hi." He sent her a quick grin before once again casting out. "I thought you were relaxing in the tub?"

"I was," she said, plopping her behind on a smooth-topped boulder, wincing when the cold seeped through the thin fabric of her pants. "But then I got thinking about how hard you've been working ever since we climbed out of that truck, and I started feeling guilty."

"Aw, this isn't work," he said with another cast and another grin. "This is as close to heaven as I figure I'm gonna get on this earth."

"You like fishing, huh?"

"Yep, always have."

"When did you learn?"

He shrugged. "Seems like I've always known. But I guess, looking back on it, I used to tag along with my friend Brody and his dad. He was a pretty cool guy—half Athabascan Indian. Died of a sudden heart attack a few years back." Colby threw out another cast. "Anyway, he taught us to tie our own flies, and he was a real stickler for not catching more than we could eat. We must've fished every river and lake round here for a couple hundred miles."

"Wow, I'm impressed. Sounds like I'm angling with a pro."

His expression took on a wistful glow. "I'll never forget my first big catch—a forty-pound king salmon. Man, did he fight. Toward the end, I was beginning to wonder if that sucker was bigger than me. Brody's dad put it on ice for me till we got home, so I could show it to Mom. I wanted to save it, but we didn't have the money to take it to a taxidermist, so Mom thought she'd try tanning it by scooping out the insides, then hanging it on the clothesline." Still wearing that far-off expression, he chuckled. "After it dried, she moved it to the shed to try making it into a pillow or something, but whatever she'd done didn't work, and the thing started stinking. One morning I went out to the shed before school to look at it, only to find the shed door had been busted in, and a black bear was munching my poor fish for breakfast."

"Oh, no!" Whitney said, hand to her mouth to hide her horrified smile. "What did you do?"

Grimacing while throwing another cast, he said, "Truth? Flat-out bawled. Mom let me stay home from school sick."

"She sounds sweet."

"Uh-huh."

"She still happy with her new husband?"

"Uh-huh."

"Please tell me if I'm overstepping the bounds here, but you told me your dad left the two of you. How old were you?"

"Six. He took off the day before my birthday. Mom and Nugget held this great party for me down at the lodge. All the town kids came. My friends Brody and Tanner. Streamers, balloons, cake. But through the whole thing, I stood at one of the lodge windows, just waiting for my dad to get there."

"How awful."

"Yeah, well, crap happens."

"But you were just a little boy. Did he leave a note, or at least call, or what?"

"None of the above. One day I thought we had this perfect little family. The next, he was gone."

"Wow. I'm sorry." Whitney swallowed hard, thinking back to the day her father had left. There'd been nothing mysterious about it. Thanks to the volume of her parents' fights, she'd known he was moving in with his secretary, then filing for divorce. From that time on, he'd sporadically taken Whitney on trips to the Brookfield Zoo. He probably figured he'd done the best he could by her, but somehow it'd never been enough. She'd wanted so much more. His opinions on her art projects. Time watching a TV show together. The chance to play the cakewalk game together at school carnivals.

Sometimes she'd wished he'd vanish.

She'd always thought it would've been easier never having known him at all than knowing he was out there, living just a few miles down the road. So close, and yet far too busy to waste his time on her.

And now here was Colby's story of his own messed-up father, which proved that even if her dad had just disappeared, it wouldn't have been any easier.

So how did that affect her convictions about raising her son without a father? It left her more confused than ever.

"Don't be sorry, Whitney. I'm over it. And anyway, it's not like it's your fault."

"I know, but—oh, look! You caught one!" Whitney's animated cry echoed all the way across the lake.

"Come here," he said, edging toward her with the pole. "Reel him in."

"Oh, no—you do it."

"Really," he said, one arm around her shoulders urging her to her feet, flooding her with warm awareness of his size. "It's high time you learned how to catch your supper."

She stood and he put his arms around her, awkwardly shuffling the rod into her hands. His hands cupped hers, making sure she held the rod tight and away from her stomach.

"Okay," he said, "start reeling."

She did. When her tingling fingers slipped, he was there to catch the reel, starting her again. "Pull back," he urged.

Laughing and breathless, she did.

On the lake's sparkling surface, the trout leapt, landing with an impressive splash. "Look at him!" she said. "He's huge!"

Laughing along with her, Colby said, "I'd offer to make him into a pillow for you, but…"

"That's okay, but thanks for the thought."

Tugging hard on the rod, he said, "You bet."

They stood there together, reeling in the fish, for what felt like the longest time, when it had probably only been minutes. He was still fighting as Colby unhooked him, then added him to an antique basket.

"That was fun," Whitney said once he'd rinsed his hands and was again standing beside her.

"I'm glad you enjoyed it. I wasn't sure."

"What do you mean?" she asked, shading her eyes from the sun.

"Just that, you being a city girl and all, I thought you probably wouldn't get a kick out of something as mundane as fishing."

"Nothing about that was remotely mundane," she said, helping him gather his pliers and a khaki-colored vest covered in more fishing flies. "Though I have to admit that this is the closest I've come to hunting up my own dinner—unless you count picking a lobster out of a tank."

"Nope." He carried the rod and basket of fish in one hand, resting his free hand on the small of her back.

Not only did his touch warm her, but it made her feel safe and secure, as if she was someone to be looked after and cherished.

It was a lovely feeling and quite unexpected.

Soon, she thought, she'd have an entire new life to care for, in the form of a child, at least for the next eighteen or so years. But then what? She wasn't about to saddle her son with one of those needy mothers who expected him to dedicate his life to her. What happened after he left the nest? What happened when she was once again on her own with nothing to warm her but memories of perfect days like this?

"You're awfully quiet," Colby said, slipping his

trout rod into a hollow log holder on the cabin's porch.

"Mmm…just thinking."

"About the baby?"

She nodded. "How did you guess?"

"When you think about him, you have this funny protective way of holding your stomach."

Lips curved upward as she followed him to the small fish-cleaning station at the porch's far end, she said, "I've never noticed, but I guess you're right." She looked down to find herself doing it again and laughed. "Oops."

"Don't sweat it. It's cute." Scaling her fish, he added, "Besides, I like knowing you're already watching out for the little guy—even if you do hit the squirt cheese a bit too hard."

Leaning against the porch rail, she grimaced. "Guilty as charged. Need any help?"

"Nah. Why don't you go on inside and take a nap? I'll wake you when lunch is done."

"Colby, I'm not an invalid."

"Did I say you were?"

"No, but…"

"You've already put in a full day lugging my kid around."

"Are you for real?" she asked with a shake of her head.

"What do you mean?"

"I mean, you're flawless. You're like some textbook example of the perfect guy. Don't you ever loaf around doing nothing? Or burp real loud, or leave your clothes all over the floor?''

"Sorry to disappoint you, but what good would any of that do?''

"I don't know, I just…'' She tugged her sweat suit zipper up and down. "Part of me feels like you're too good to be true. There's got to be something about you that's bad.''

"Why?''

"I don't know. Just because.''

"Let me guess,'' he said, filleting the bones out of the fish. "If I'm not some womanizing chauvinistic creep, you don't have a convenient out.''

"Excuse me?''

"You heard me. If I'm a bad guy, then you're the good guy by default. You're not only right in keeping me away from my son, but you're noble. You're taking the high road, while I'm a few thousand miles away where you can forget all about me. Then you can tell our son anything you want. But you wanna know something, Whitney?''

Swallowing hard, she raised her chin.

"Whatever you say to him, you're going to know the truth. Whatever you decide at the end of the week, you're gonna know I *am* a good guy. I'd be a caring, considerate husband to you, and a damned good father for our son. So hey, if you decide at the end of this week that none of it matters and that you'd be better off sailing this family ship all on your own—well, you can just take that up with my lawyer. But in the meantime, I want you to know what you're passing up.''

''Are you done?'' she asked, swiping tears from her cheeks with the backs of her hands.

''Not hardly.''

''Great. Then I guess I'll take you up on that offer of a nap.'' Turning her back on him and his speech, Whitney stormed into the cabin and threw herself on the bed.

Chapter Eleven

"Smooth move there, bud," Colby mumbled under his breath a good twenty minutes later as he eased a blanket over Whitney's sleeping form, tucking the fringed edges around her toes. He'd wanted to chase after her right away, but since he'd been covered in fish guts, it had felt all wrong.

Why had he spouted off at her like that?

After getting over the initial shock of being kidnapped, he'd actually sent up a silent thanks to his friends. They'd realized that all it'd take to convince Whitney that both she and their son would be happy up here was a few days alone in the true Alaska. Once she saw the majesty of the land surrounding the cabin, not to mention what an excellent provider he could be without a supermarket, she'd have no choice but to concede that he was right—the two of them should get hitched. As for her job, he wasn't all that clear on exactly what she did. But if she'd worked here once, why couldn't she do it again?

Could it really be that simple? Suddenly he wasn't so sure.

Here he'd been working his butt off for her, yet nothing he did seemed good enough. And he was starting to get the feeling that nothing he'd ever do would be good enough. Particularly since she'd already made up her mind to leave.

With a resolute sigh, he headed into the kitchen to stoke the fire in the old woodstove.

Cooking was always a challenge up here, but the food tasted so much better that it was worth the extra effort—extra effort he was now doubly determined to make in the hope of making Whitney forget their latest argument.

As he melted pats of the butter Nugget had packed, then added chopped garlic cloves and the trout fillets, Colby's mind wandered to the time he and Whitney had met.

Their first night had been so…incredible.

How had everything else gone so wrong? What was he missing?

He tossed a box of ready-made pilaf into butter simmering in another pan, then sliced off the rough ends of a bunch of pencil-thin asparagus.

This last run he'd made to Global, Dot had let him have it. Telling him he'd better treat Whitney with kid gloves. She'd rambled on about what a rough childhood Whitney had had, and how that mother of hers had set such a rotten example.

Stirring the pilaf, then adding water, it occurred to Colby that a part of him was tired of the fight. Tired of always being the one making concessions.

But then he remembered the ultimate prize.

A son.

How long had he dreamed of becoming a father? Forever.

And if he was even half the man he'd professed to be out on that porch, then no matter how many times he had to suck up to Li'l Miss Independence, he'd do it. This wasn't just about him, but also about his son.

"THIS IS DELICIOUS," Whitney said, swallowing her last bite of trout before sipping lake-chilled sparkling cider. "Thank you."

Across the candlelit table, their glances met, and she hastily looked down. What had happened out on the porch still felt too real. Too raw.

"You're welcome. Any ideas as to what you want to do tomorrow?"

"What're my options?"

He forked up a bite of fish. "Since we've already established that hiking is out, I've got a boat. We could row around the lake."

"That'd be nice."

"Good."

"Good."

Whitney bit her lip hard as tears welled up.

She hated this...this feeling of stiff formality between them.

Worst of all, he'd been right.

Every word he'd said out on that porch was true, but that didn't make any of it easier to bear. Okay, so he was the one guy in a million who might make a great dad or husband. That didn't mean she could simply blink and forget all the painful memories of her own absentee dad, or the disasters her mom and assorted divorced friends had made of their lives.

Yes, it would be so easy to believe that if she gave marriage a chance, her life might turn out differently than her mother's or her friends'. But what if she was wrong? It wouldn't be just her own life she was messing up, but her son's. From where she stood, she didn't think taking that kind of risk was an honorable thing to do.

"*E.T.*," she said a few minutes later, sick of the silence.

"What?"

"*E.T.* You asked me the other night what my favorite movie was. That's it. *E.T.* I cry every time I see it."

He sighed, obviously as fed up with their awkwardness as she was. "What do you want to do, Whitney? 'Cause we can't keep fighting. It isn't good for you or the baby."

"I know," she said, bowing her head, hating the fact that yet again he was right.

"Don't look away from me," he said, reaching across the small table to tuck his fingers beneath her chin.

"Why not?"

"Because you're beautiful. I want to see you."

She glanced up with a faint smile. "How come, no matter how determined I am to distance myself from you, I feel like we keep getting closer?"

With a shrug, he said, "I'm guessing it has something to do with my cooking."

Tears still clinging to her lashes, she sniffed before laughing. "You're probably right."

"Of course I'm right. I'm damned good-looking, too. Our kid's probably going to be the next Brad Pitt."

"You think?"

"Oh heck, yeah."

They shared an impromptu toast of cider.

"*The Parent Trap*—both versions," she said. "I'm a sucker for anything Disney."

He glanced over his shoulder as if checking to see whether anyone else was listening. "Me, too. But what kind of man admits to getting a kick out of kid flicks?"

A good man. An even better father.

"That damned *Pocahontas*. I was baby-sitting a couple of Brody's nieces, and the first thing they did was pop in that flick. I swear, by the end, they'd run off outside to play football, and there I was sitting in the living room bawling my eyes out.''

"Quit," Whitney said, laughing so hard that she was tearing up all over again. "You're going to make me pee."

"Oh? And that's a bad thing? Like my bathroom accommodations are lacking?''

"They're lacking, all right—lacking a flush toilet!''

"That's it," he said, shoving back his chair to storm over to her side of the table. "Now you've done it."

"Colby! What—agh!" He hefted her into his arms, heading out the back door. "What are you doing?" she asked, breathless from laughing.

"You said you had to pee, didn't you?"

"Yeah, but in a real bathroom."

"Oh—so now my sweet little outhouse isn't even real? Would you prefer going behind a nice, tall spruce tree just like the bears?"

"No, I…" He'd carried her midway down the outhouse trail. With her arms wrapped around his neck, her lips inches from his, she was aware of him as she hadn't been since all those months ago, when they'd been forced together in a cramped cockpit. He was hard yet soft, and he smelled of butter and garlic and trout.

Before she could stop herself, her fingers had

wandered to the back of his head, easing into his coarse hair, urging him to press his lips to hers.

Leaning against a tree, he settled her deep in his arms, groaning as she opened her mouth, searching for his tongue. This was lunacy, yet she felt powerless to stop. This undeniable attraction had brought them together. Now, with his baby growing inside her, part of her wanted him back.

She kept telling herself they were strangers, but that now seemed a lie. At this moment, she knew him as intimately as her next breath.

"Whoa," he said, pulling away, breathing hard. "What're you doing, Whitney?"

"I don't know," she said, resting her forehead against his chin. "Does it matter?"

"Heck, yeah, it matters. I can't just turn all of this on and off. Not now. With the baby, it goes much deeper than sex between us."

"I know."

"Do you?" he asked, setting her on her feet, forcing her gaze to his.

She wrenched her chin from his hold, throwing her arms around him in a hug—not a sensual hug, but a confused one.

"Talk to me," he said, hugging her fiercely in return. "Tell me what you're thinking."

"I don't know," she said against his chest. "That's the problem. Just when I think I'm doing the right thing by heading back to Chicago, something reminds me of that night—of the way you made me feel. Safe. Like as long as you held me in your arms, nothing could ever go wrong."

If you became our son's full-time father, would he feel protected, too?

"I'm glad I made you feel that way, Whitney, but it's nothing I can sustain. Something in life always goes wrong. I can't prevent that. I'm just a man. All I can promise is that whatever rough patch we hit, we'll get through it together."

She nodded.

"Still have to go to the bathroom?"

"Yeah."

He reached for her hand, interlocking their fingers. "Come on, I'll walk you the rest of the way."

LATER, BACK INSIDE, Whitney asked, "How long does it take to get used to the fact that it's always daytime?"

"Don't know. I've never known the sun to do anything but what it does here." Colby glanced up from his task of putting fresh-smelling sheets and a blanket on the sofa. Whitney had changed into pink silk pajamas.

"We're both adults," she said, slipping a red flannel pillowcase onto his pillow. "We could share the bed without incident."

"You so sure about that?" He winked.

She reddened, plumping his pillow before dropping it at the end of the sofa.

"Come on, then, let's get you settled in for the night."

"I can put myself to bed, you know."

"Uh-huh." He pulled back the red down comforter, and she climbed in between navy-blue sheets. Once she'd settled her head on the pile of pillows, her dark hair fanning around her, he tugged the covers back, tucking them tight around her toes.

"You're spoiling me."

"Uh-huh. Good night," he said to her belly.

"Good night."

He blew out the three candles that had been lighting the room, but even with the shades drawn, at a few minutes past eleven, it wasn't completely dark.

"Brr," he said, climbing into his own makeshift bed. "Sorry about there not being a fire."

"It's okay. It's not like we could evict the bird babies."

"True."

Whitney pulled the covers up to her neck. "Thanks for a nice night."

"You're welcome."

"And next time we play checkers, I'm beating you."

He laughed. "Dream on."

Funny that he'd use the word *dream*. Aside from

their one war of words, the rest of the day had been as perfect as a dream. Catching the fish. Sharing Colby's delicious meal. The mock battle on the way to the outhouse that had ended in an epic kiss. Warm and funny conversation over three games of checkers.

Throughout the day, she'd drawn contrasts between him and her mother's men. Whitney had complained that her mother had constantly bent over backward to serve her husbands, but with Colby, the case was completely opposite. As much as Whitney had wanted to help out, he wouldn't let her, claiming she needed to rest.

Without him she would've been lost in this wilderness setting, but with him, she felt happy and secure.

Trouble was, none of this was real. It was a vacation. In a few days, their kidnappers would return them to Kodiak Gorge.

In a couple of months, Baby Talbot would be born, and she'd no longer be so clumsy and vulnerable. There'd be no need for Colby to watch out for her. Doubtless that was when his true colors would show.

"Tell me a story," she said, for her child and for herself. She wanted to collect memories of the way Colby was now, instead of the way he'd inevitably turn out to be.

"'Bout what?"

"Surprise me," she said, her voice reaching out to him in the eerie almost-dark.

"When I was a kid, my mom worked hellacious hours at the lodge. It wasn't that she wanted to, but I guess she had to. After school, she used to haul me back down there, and I'd get bored. I resented her for not just letting me stay home alone."

"How old were you?"

"Nine. Ten. Somewhere in there. Brody's mom ran the grocery store, so she was never home, either, but Brody got a choice of either staying on his own, or going out with his dad on welding jobs. Mom said I was all she had left, so she needed to keep me close."

He rolled over and sighed.

"I knew she was doing her best," he went on, "but I remember this feeling of suffocation. Like I had to get away."

"But you were so young," Whitney said, rolling onto her side to face his voice, resting her cheek on steepled hands.

"Yeah, but once my dad left, I matured fast. Mom tried being brave, but I used to hear her crying in the middle of the night. I'd go into her room, you know, just to tell her everything was gonna be okay, and she'd grab hold of me, squeezing so hard sometimes I thought I was gonna break. I wanted to help her, but I couldn't."

"What'd you do?"

"Ran away. Nugget took me and Brody and some other guys up here on a camping trip once. It used to be an old fur trader's cabin, but over the years it got run down, and pretty much anyone who wanted to use it did. I'm still not sure how she did it—maybe through the state *Homestead Act*—but Mom gave it to me for my eighteenth birthday."

"Okay, but wait. You were nine or ten, and just ran away up here?"

"Uh-huh."

"But it's so far! How long were you gone? Your mom must've freaked."

"I left her a note."

Panic welling in her throat over what she'd do if her son ever tried such a stunt, Whitney said, "So I'm assuming some sort of rescue crew came out for you the next day?"

"Nah," he chuckled. "In the note, I'd told her where I was going. She already knew Nugget had taught me how to live off the land."

"And…"

"And she climbed into the family Jeep, brought me all my schoolwork for the week, then told me she'd check back on Saturday."

"And you were nine?"

"Maybe ten."

"Wow."

"What?"

"She sounds like an incredible woman."

"She is. I'd like you to meet her one of these days."

Slipping out from under her covers, Whitney winced when her feet hit the cold hardwood floor. Then she hustled over to the couch to give Colby a big hug.

"What was that for?" he asked, yanking off the back sofa cushion, then tugging her down beside him, drawing the covers over them both.

"I feel sorry for you."

"Why?"

"I don't know. You were just a little boy. I wish you'd never been put in the position of feeling you had to run away."

"Oh, I don't know. I think it was probably good for me and Mom. I got my space, and she learned to trust me and rely on herself."

"Still…"

"What?" he asked, pushing strands of her hair over her shoulder.

"You were just a baby."

He laughed. "I was a baby the day before my sixth birthday. By the day after, I'd been forced to grow up."

"Oh, Colby." She hugged him again, only this time, her heart went out not only to him, but also to her unborn son. What was she doing, dooming him to a childhood like Colby's, without a dad? But on the other hand, hadn't he just pointed out that after a few growing pains, he'd essentially been fine?

She kissed him on his whisker-stubbled cheek, then said, "If you could snap your fingers and bring your dad home, would you?"

"No."

"That was fast."

"It's the truth. From the second I realized the bastard wasn't coming back, I didn't care. It was like a light switch flicked off inside me where my feelings for him were concerned."

Whitney's training had taught her it couldn't have been that simple. "There had to be more to it than that," she murmured.

"Nope."

"Oh, come on," she said, wishing the room were brighter so she could see his expression. "Weren't you scared? I mean, didn't your mom try looking for your dad? You know, thinking he could've been hurt?"

"Can we please change the subject?"

"Sure, but—"

He silenced her by moving his hands to her cheeks, then kissing her. Hard at first. Urgently. Then softly, making her limbs sluggish and weak.

He shifted, wrapping his hand around her belly. She angled into him, overcome with emotions raised by his kiss and by having him so close to their son.

As intensely as she'd tried pretending this baby was solely hers, she could no longer do that. This man, this soon-to-be father, was real—and growing more so by the moment, as he flooded her mind and body with memories of the night they'd made this miracle growing inside her.

"Take me back," she said.

"Where?"

"To that night. The way things first were between us."

"Why?" he asked, his voice hot in her ear.

"Because it was good. Fun."

She edged up, reached under his shirt, pulling it off. She wanted his bare skin against hers.

She wanted to feel safe, the way only he had ever made her feel. Even if it was just for one more night or, if she was lucky, the rest of her brief time in Alaska.

Crying now, for reasons she couldn't begin to fathom, she dragged her own shirt off. "Just make love to me. Make me feel like you did that night."

"Whitney, no," he said, his breath warm and moist on her collarbone where he'd just pressed an openmouthed kiss. "You don't know what you're saying."

"Yes," she whispered, raining kisses down his chest. "Yes, I do."

Hands gripping her shoulders, he pushed her back. "Then tell me why."

"Because I…" She bowed her head.

"I'd like to flatter myself by assuming it's because you love me, but since you keep refusing to marry me, I'm guessing that's not it."

Silence.

"And, sure, maybe it's just because you're hot for me, but since the woman I know isn't the type for casual sex, that's not it, either."

Silence.

"Bringing me to the granddaddy reason of them all. You feel guilty about your plan to leave here with my son—but somehow, I don't even think that's what this is about. I think it's deeper, even more selfish than that. I think you want to have raw, mindless sex with me because, just like that night up on the mountain, it'll make you forget. That night, you wanted to forget the fact that you very well could've died." He shook his head. "So let's hear it, Whitney. What're you trying to forget tonight?"

"That was uncalled for," she said softly.

"But you don't deny it's the truth?"

Escaping to the bed, she muttered, "Can we please just get some sleep?"

"Sure, Whitney. Let's sleep. But if you think you're going to wake up in the morning with this whole thing behind us…you're wrong."

Chapter Twelve

Long after Colby's soft snoring told Whitney he'd fallen asleep, she lay awake, cursing him yet again for being right.

What was he doing? Reading her mind?

Yes, she had been trying to forget.

Trying to forget she'd ever met Colby Davis.

Meeting him had been akin to catching a most pleasant virus, one she hadn't been able to wipe from her system. He was noble and caring and funny and a good listener and cook. And now she was carrying his son. And he wanted to marry her, but she couldn't marry him because she refused to give herself up. She refused to abandon her career.

And that was her right.

She didn't have to marry her baby's father if she didn't want to.

The only problem was, the more time she spent with Colby, the more she feared that maybe, just maybe, there was a part of her that did want to marry him.

What did that mean?

She'd only been back in his arms for a couple of days now, yet she felt as though they'd never been apart. With a few well-aimed verbal arrows, he had the uncanny knack of slicing straight through her every charade. Yet his words, however naked they left her feeling, were meant to be thought-provoking rather than cruel.

After this last go-round on the sofa, he'd actually shifted out from under her, then scooped her into his arms to carry her to bed. After tucking her in, he'd placed a tender kiss on her forehead, then quietly whispered good-night.

Why didn't he ever thunder and rage? Why was he always such a gentleman? Why did he always have to be the perfect embodiment of the kind of man she'd dreamt her son's father would be? Why couldn't he be rude or overbearing or obnoxious?

If I'm a bad guy, then you're the good guy by default. You're not only right in keeping me away from my son, but you're noble. You're taking the high road while I'm a convenient few thousand miles away where you can forget all about me.

Was that what she wanted? To forget him?

Did she never want to see his easy smile again? Or remember the way he smelled of sun and sweat and airplanes? Did she want her son growing up in the city, or learning to live off the land like his dad had done at such a tender age?

When Whitney was ten, she'd spent a lot of time worrying about her mom, but she'd also played with Barbie dolls and friends. She'd have had no more thought of running away than of flying to the moon.

For all her grousing about how tough it had been when her folks split, she'd still managed to have a pretty normal childhood, all things considered. Colby, on the other hand, felt he'd become a man at the age of six.

Maybe that was why she was so devastatingly attracted to him? Because he was truly a man in every sense of the word? He provided not only for her physical needs, but her mental ones. She was tired. And a part of her selfishly wanted someone else to help her with life's daily grind.

But then maybe, in its purest sense, that's what marriage truly was? A melding of emotions and lives and responsibilities that, if done right, would indeed be a wonderful thing? But countless case studies—as well as her own mother—proved that making marriage a partnership instead of a dictatorship was a near impossible task.

Armed with that knowledge, why would Whitney even want to try?

Maybe because being married to a great guy like Colby just might be worth the effort?

DETERMINED TO GIVE her brain, fogged by all these questions, a much-deserved day off, Whitney woke bright and early the next morning vowing that today she'd show Mr. Perfect a thing or two about cooking—namely, that she was every bit as good as he was.

Although to see him now, one leg hiked over the sofa back, one leg on the floor, covers askew, snoring loud enough to wake a hibernating bear, one would doubt he was a master of back-country cuisine.

Not wanting to wake him, she straightened his covers, covering his poor cold toes on the floor.

After struggling to dress herself in a fresh jogging suit, then jogging on out to the so-called bathroom, she stood in front of the kitchen stove, wondering what to do next.

Having been a big fan of the *Little House on the Prairie* books and TV show when she was a kid, Whitney knew the first step was starting a fire in the beast's belly.

Colby, being the efficiency guru that he was, already had a galvanized aluminum bucket standing by with twigs she assumed he used for kindling. Also readily available were extra-long kitchen matches and small logs.

Okay, so all the necessary equipment was there. Now all she had to do was make a fire.

Ha! Famous last words.

Thirty minutes later, she had a fire all right—a raging inferno that had turned her sunny-side-up eggs into charcoal briquettes!

Coughing and blinded by smoke, Whitney reached for the cast-iron frying pan, but forgot to use a pot holder and jumped back in pain. By the time she'd grabbed one of the oven mitts hanging from a rack on the wall, the toast she'd thought was browning burst into flame.

"Colby!"

In seconds, he came running to her aid. "What the—"

"Help! My breakfast is on fire!"

"I see that," he said, calmly reaching beside the stove for a fire extinguisher, then putting out her meal. That done, he opened the window and used a cookie sheet to fan the smoke. "You should get out of here," he said. "It can't be good for you or the baby to be breathing all this smoke."

"But, Colby, I—"

"Out," he said, hands over her shoulders as he marched her out of the room. "Ugh, it's smoky in the living room, too. Okay, time for a new plan."

"What?"

He snatched his blanket off the sofa, wrapped her in it, then gave her a gentle push toward the paned door leading out to the screened porch. "Go. I'll bring you some tea."

"But I wanted to cook breakfast for you this morning."

"How about you settle for eating a good breakfast for me?"

"Ha ha."

He pressed a sweet kiss to her forehead, then opened the door and nudged her outside.

Whitney huffed her way into a comfy chair, put her feet up on the porch rail and glared at the breathtaking view.

Brilliant blue sky, sparkling blue water, woodpecker at it again, yadda, yadda, yadda.

The place was gorgeous.

She got it.

What she also got was that never in her whole life had she felt like such a klutz.

How was it that for twenty-six years she'd managed take care of herself just fine—better than fine, judging by her last raise—yet out in the woods she couldn't survive ten minutes on her own? Talk about an ego blow.

Even worse was the fact that, not fifteen minutes later, the resident mountain man carried out a tray loaded with two plates of steaming hotcakes and sausage!

"Mmm, that smells good," she said, unable to fathom how he'd managed to prepare the feast in such a short time. "Where'd you get the meat?"

"Nugget packed a bunch of perishables on dry ice."

"Nugget's good," Whitney said through her first sinfully delicious bite. "You are, too. This tastes decadent. I'm talking major caloric sin."

"Thank you—and yep."

"Is there nothing you *can't* do?"

"What can I say? Unless a guy wants to be at Nugget's mercy for food, he's gotta learn to fend for himself."

"Or find a wife."

"Nah." He winked. "In my case anyway, I figured why should I burden myself with a wife when I can already do everything for myself?"

"Everything except bearing a son?" The syrupy taste in her mouth turned sour. Here, all along, she'd been under the assumption that like the men who'd married her mother, Colby would expect her to conform to his every wish and command. Maybe he truly did want just her son. Once he legally had him, Colby wouldn't care whether she stayed or left.

"That was a joke," he said, nothing the least bit funny about his tone. "You know that, don't you?"

She nodded. Of course she knew he'd been joking. What was wrong with her? She was starting to sound out of her mind. Colby was a wonderful man—of that she was sure. He wanted his son near him because, even though the baby wasn't even born yet, he already possessed a deep love for the boy. As for marrying Colby, it was the best solution for sharing their son.

Whitney knew the solution was logical, but how could she know it was right?

"Aw, man," he said, setting his plate on the porch rail, then taking hers to do the same. "I wasn't going to let on I knew this, Whitney, but when I was up at Global the other day, Dot—"

"No. Don't tell me she told you about my mom."

He nodded. "Look, I can see where watching your parent go through so many failed marriages would be enough to scare anyone off. But you've gotta understand that if we were to do this thing—get hitched—" He went down on his knees in front of her chair, clasping her hands. "I'd want to do it right. And I'm not just talking about the ceremony, but the life. I don't want a forced marriage, but a real one. I'm not looking for a housekeeper or nanny for my son, but a companion. A best friend. Not someone I can share chores with, but someone I could *love*."

Giving his big, warm hands a squeeze, Whitney dared to raise her gaze to his, and what she saw took her breath away.

Beyond his rugged good looks was a burning intensity telling her that not only did he fully intend to fight for what was his, but that he also intended to win.

She dared to ask, "That woman you just described. That friend you want to call a wife. You think you might've found her in me?"

When he bit his lower lip and looked away, her heart sank. Of course he didn't love her. He'd only said that with time, he *could*.

"If you don't love me," she said, her voice small against the breeze whispering through the spruce, "why do you keep asking me to marry you?"

"Because it's the right thing to do."

Holding on to him for dear life, she asked, "But just because something is morally right in the eyes of society, how do you know it's right in here? Where it counts?" Releasing him, she pressed her palms to her chest.

He shrugged, molded his hands to her stomach. "For whatever reason, Fate brought us together all those months ago. And now, because of the life we've created, we might be meant to come together again. I guess there are some things you just have to take on faith."

Faith.

Now there was something she hadn't had in a while—if ever.

If she were raising her son alone, faith could come in handy. Faith in a lot of things. Faith in his teachers to do a good job. Faith in his friends not to lead him astray. Faith in him to always do the right thing.

Raising her son alone.

The thought was daunting. But after Whitney's father had left, her mother had refused to do anything on her own, even raise her child. That had led her straight into seven unhappy marriages.

"I DON'T KNOW about this, Colby. Are you sure it's safe to hike right up to them?" She cast a worried glance over her shoulder, not seeing that she was close to tripping over an exposed root.

"Of course," he said, guiding her past the obstacle, then shooing a mosquito from her back. "And this isn't really a hike, but a scenic stroll." Colby took her hand, slowing her down so he could watch where she was going as their footsteps fell silent on the thick layer of spongy spruce needles.

This trail with its pungent conifer smell and tunnel feel had long been one of his favorites. Sun slanted at lazy angles through the trees' enormous branches, spotlighting giant ferns at their feet. As a kid, it'd been easy to imagine himself roaming among dinosaurs in this place. This far inland, it was a natural oddity, and as an adult, he'd learned to appreciate how special it truly was.

"Believe me," he said, "once we get there, you won't be sorry. I've been watching bear families here since I was a little kid, and I'm still alive to tell the tale, aren't I?''

"Yeah, but I read on the flight up that, statistically, people are more likely to be killed by a bear in Alaska than by a taxi in New York City.''

He stopped her in the middle of the trail to kneel in front of her belly bulge. "Did you hear that?'' he said to his son. "You're not even out of there yet, and already she's trying to squash our fun.''

"Hey, someone has to be the grown-up here.''

"And who was the grown-up this morning who set the toast on fire?''

"Oops.'' She shot him a sheepish grin. "That was different.''

"Right. Meaning, if you mess up, all is forgiven, but if I do—''

"Whoa,'' she said, palms flat against his chest. "Does that mean you're admitting you messed up by bringing me here? 'Cause if so, I'll be happy to get back in the rowboat. All that rowing was nice and peaceful, but—''

He put his fingers to his lips. "Shhh. Look.''

A good twenty yards off the trail, in a grassy clearing, a momma black bear fished for dinner from a gurgling stream, while her two cubs frolicked in tall grasses.

"Listen to their little growls,'' Whitney whispered, eyes wide and shimmering. "Oh—and look at their mom, turning back to give them a scolding look.''

Guiding Whitney a few yards further down the trail, he gestured for her to sit on the rough-hewn log bench he'd constructed when he'd been a teen. ''Black bears rarely stray more than five miles from where they were born, so I probably watched that momma play when she was a cub.''

Whitney wrapped her arms around Colby in a hug.

''What was that for?'' he asked.

''For bringing me here. At first I thought this was crazy. I mean, who actually goes looking for bears? But this was exciting—way better than seeing them in a zoo. Thanks. You were right. It was definitely worth the walk.''

''So all I get for hauling your behind up here to see a spectacle that most city girls only see at the zoo is a measly hug?''

''Well…''

The size of her smile toppled his heart, making the thought of her returning to Chicago in just a few short days incomprehensible. She and baby Nick had to stay here. They just had to. His son needed to see bear cubs play every summer weekend. He needed to know this trail as well as he knew the route to school. And to know that rose hips were delicious, but baneberries—like the ones within reach from this bench—were poison.

"I suppose just this once I could part with more—assuming, that is, that when we get back to the cabin you'll start dinner."

"We just had lunch."

"Yeah, like an hour ago."

He fished a granola bar from his jacket pocket. "Here. Don't say I never gave you anything."

"Likewise," she said, planting her hands on his clean-shaven cheeks for a kiss.

Sweetly, she pressed her lips to his, coaxing his mouth open with her naughty tongue, slipping her inquisitive fingers around his neck and up into his hair.

When she groaned, he hefted her onto his lap, his hand pressing her closer.

Why couldn't she see that here, now, what they shared was human perfection? Life just didn't get any better than this, especially with their son between them.

When she eventually pulled back, breathless and dazed, they looked up to see the momma bear frozen midstream watching them, ears perked. A few seconds later, she gathered her troops, chasing them into thick woods.

"Oops," Colby said, tucking flyaway strands of Whitney's long, dark hair behind her ears. "Guess she only wants her cubs watching G-rated tourists."

"Hey," she said, swatting his chest. "Who are

you calling a tourist? I've got half a local growing in here.'' She patted the baby.

Feeling high on entirely too much fresh air and sunshine and kisses, Colby tossed out, ''You know, it wouldn't be too hard to make you a local, too.''

''I know.''

''Does that mean you're at least thinking about staying?''

The tremulous look she cast his way gave him cause to hope. ''Raising our son among all this would be nice, wouldn't it?''

The mere thought had Colby swallowing tears. Since his emotions had swelled to the point that he feared he'd be unable to speak, he nodded.

''Hey,'' she said, brushing back the hair from his forehead. ''You okay?''

''Um, sure. Heck, yeah.''

''I don't believe you.''

''Okay, then, I guess I'll come right out and say it. I want my son to have all of this as his back-yard—not just as his once-a-year, week-long va-cation.''

''I don't blame you,'' she said. ''This place, it's gorgeous, but—''

''Wait. If I'm going to be one hundred percent truthful with you, Whitney, you've gotta know that I want you here, too. There's so much I want to share with both of you.''

"Oh, Colby…" She raised her hand to his cheek, and he leaned into her touch.

"I'm not even sure how it happened, but I'm getting to like you—a lot. I want to be with you. All the time. You've become like…a pet I want constantly by my side."

"Gee, thanks…I think."

"God," he said, smacking himself on the forehead. "That came out all wrong. I didn't mean that you were like a dog or cat, I meant—"

She put her fingers to his lips. "Shh. When I was a girl, I had a Yorkie. His name was Samson, and he went everywhere with me. He was my very best friend, and to this day, sometimes when I'm lonely or confused, I wish I had him around. You know, as an impartial ear to bounce off my nuttier thoughts and ideas." She took a deep breath, wiping at a few stray tears with the backs of her hands. "Jeez, what is it about you, always making me cry?"

"I don't know, but I guess if a guy told me I looked like a dog, I wouldn't be all that happy." He grinned, and she kissed him again.

"I loved Samson—a lot," she said, close enough for him to feel the heat of her words on his lips. "So when you compare me to a favorite pet, believe me, far from taking it as an insult, I took it in the true spirit in which I suspect you meant it— as a high compliment. Thanks."

He kissed the tip of her nose. "You're welcome."

Taking her hands, he helped her off his lap and onto her feet. Once he'd stood, as well, he took her right hand in his, then led her back down the trail.

"You like spaghetti?" he asked once they were almost back to the boat.

"Sure. Why?"

"Nugget put Italian sausage in our supply pack, along with a big tub of red gunk I'm guessing is his famous sauce."

"Yum."

"I'll even let you cook the pasta."

She glanced over her shoulder to stick out her tongue.

They'd walked a little while longer in companionable silence when she said, "Um, Colby..."

"Yeah?"

"Remember when you showed me how to tie that knot for the boat?"

"Yeah?" His stomach sank as he saw sun flash off the rowboat's aluminum hull.

The hull that, instead of resting on shore as it had been earlier, was now bobbing merrily in the dead center of the lake.

A stiff breeze had come up since they'd left, and the once glassy lake was now dotted with whitecaps. Just beyond Frazier's Peak, the snowcapped mountain in front of the cabin, storm clouds loomed.

"Sorry," Whitney said, nibbling her lower lip. "Looks like I might need another knot-tying lesson."

Lightning cracked and thunder rumbled in agreement.

Colby just stayed silent.

Chapter Thirteen

"Do you think the boat will ever come back?" Whitney asked from the comfy rocker that Colby had placed in front of the kitchen stove. Blessed heat radiated from the ugly beast, leading her to suspect that if it continued playing nice, they might one day be friends.

"Eventually," he said, stirring the fragrant sauce that had her hungry stomach growling. Shooting her a wink, he said, "Don't sweat it. It's not that big a lake. I'll hike around in the morning to get it once it washes ashore."

Outside, thunder rolled as rain pummeled the cabin's tin roof.

"The lake sure felt big, hiking around it in this storm."

He shrugged. "I've been caught in worse jams—like, say, that time we crashed our plane into a mountain. Ring any bells?"

Twirling a lock of her still-damp hair, she made a face.

"You look awfully comfortable over there. I thought you were making the pasta?"

"I was, but then you starting poking fun at me, so now I figure I'll just sit here and watch you make the pasta."

Already at the sink filling a large pan with water from the well, he said, "I can see it now. If we do end up hitched, I'll spend the rest of my days at your beck and call."

"Only if you want more babies," she said, tucking her red blanket around her still-nippy toes.

"Do you?" he asked, putting the pot of water on to boil, then pulling out a chair at the small table.

"I don't know. I've been so busy with work, I guess I've never much thought about it. I mean, I always wanted at least one child, but I guess, yeah, it might be fun for Baby Talbot to have a little brother or sister to play with."

He winced. "Could you please stop doing that?"

"What?"

"Calling *my* son Baby Talbot. His name is Nick."

"I hate to rain on your parade there, fella, but—" Judging by the stern set of his lips and jaw that he was no longer teasing, Whitney said, "I'm sorry. I can see that helping pick our baby's name might be important to you.''

"You think?" He sprang to his feet, then crossed the kitchen and began furiously stirring the sauce.

Whitney pushed herself up from her chair, letting the blanket fall to the floor.

At the stove, she stepped behind Colby, sliding her arms around his waist, resting her head between his shoulder blades. With their baby nestled between them, if it weren't for the rigid set of Colby's back, all would have been right with the world.

"I'm sorry," she said, giving him a squeeze. "Nick it is. It is cute, in light of the night he was conceived. And anyway…it's the least I can do." After all, Colby probably wouldn't be seeing his son for a long time. The very thought made her always-healthy appetite fade.

How was she going to do it? Just walk away?

What she'd felt for her dog Samson was nothing compared to what she feared she was beginning to feel for this intriguing man.

Still, no matter how much she'd come to enjoy Colby's company over the past few days, she had to remember that their bond was only temporary. Her own mother had proven that the percentage of marriages that were real was minuscule compared to the ones destined to end in divorce. And what about her friends in college who'd married only to quickly get a divorce? And those were just the people she knew. How about all of those bickering couples on *Dr. Phil?*

Whitney didn't want her son going through the kind of pain she had when her folks broke up. Shoot, for that matter, Colby himself had suffered the same fate, and he hadn't thought it was any more fun than she had.

And look what had happened between her and Rocco. Now, there was a full-on relationship disaster!

Shielding their son from future pain was the right thing to do.

The responsible thing.

The *only* thing.

Turning to face her, Colby kissed her hard, making her mind and heart spin. "Marry me," he said. "And not because of the baby, but because of what the two of us share."

"I can't," she said.

"Of course you can. All it takes is a short little ceremony and voilà—we're husband, wife and baby."

And it really would be just that simple. The only problem was that, in her heart, she'd be forever bound to him. How did she know he'd feel the same? She just couldn't risk it. There was too much at stake. Not just her own emotional well-being, but that of her son. What if she said yes, and then Colby turned out to be less than wonderful after all? What if, like his own father, he got tired of the whole family thing and moved on to greener pastures? Yes, there was no doubt in her mind she could take care of herself and son all on her own, but how would she mend the hole that Colby's leaving would make in their little boy's spirit? On her soul?

"I see that mind of yours working a mile a minute," he said. "Remember our talk about faith?"

She squeezed him for all she was worth.

"That's it. Lean on me. I promise you that, together, we can make this thing work."

I PROMISE WE CAN MAKE this thing work.

Friday afternoon, Whitney was back in her Kodiak Lodge room, gazing across the lake. Cold rain pelted the windows, and the gloom suited her mood.

Rubbing her belly, she crossed the room to ease onto the bed, flipping through channels with the remote.

When Dot and the man she'd been introduced to as Colby's friend Brody had arrived back at the cabin to pick them up bright and early that morning, she'd actually been sad to pack up and let the place go. She'd expected to be angry with her kidnappers, but on the contrary, she was grateful to them for allowing her that wondrous, all-too-brief time with the father of her son.

Still full from a late hearty breakfast of ham and eggs and what had felt like gallons of milk pushed on her by Nugget, Whitney flipped off the TV. Maybe all she needed was a nap. But that didn't work, either, as she missed the wind whispering through towering spruce and Colby's gentle snores.

Their last night at the cabin, he'd shared the big bed with her. That had been the best, having him hold her just as he had that long-ago night on the snowy mountain. Being in his arms again had been a dream she hadn't even known she'd wanted to come true.

Hugging Colby's Santa hat—her guilty souvenir of their first happy night—she grunted as she rolled onto her side, toying for what felt like the gazillionth time since her arrival with the idea of throwing caution to the wind and marrying Colby.

He was warm and funny and handsome and smart.

He was everything she'd ever wanted in a father for her child, and everything she'd never dared hope for in a husband. Back when she'd sat around with her girlfriends giggling late into the night about guys, a man with all his qualities was what she'd claimed to be holding out for. So now that she had him, why couldn't she keep him?

Because there was no such thing as *keeping* a husband, as her mother had all-too-painfully learned. For that matter, even keeping a boyfriend was tough, as Rocco had shown her.

True, but if what she and Colby shared was different? Better? After all, they had the common bond of a child.

Oh—as if her parents hadn't had a child when they'd divorced?

Like Colby's parents hadn't had one when his dad left town?

Scooting up in bed, Whitney tucked Colby's hat under her pillow and switched the TV back on.

She found a repeat of *Trading Spaces,* and reached for her trusty can of squirt cheese on the bedside table. It was empty, as was her bag of licorice.

Arms crossed, legs crossed at the ankles, she'd resigned herself to spending the afternoon rating Frank and Doug's latest designs when a knock sounded at her door.

Startled, she put her hand to her belly, then smoothed her hair into a neat ponytail. ''Who is it?''

''Me.'' Colby.

Hooray! Now there was some entertainment.

As fast as possible with a stomach the size of hers, she crossed the room to open the door, then pulled him into a hug. ''I thought you had to fly to Global this afternoon.''

''I did. I went fast, so I could get back to you.''

"How sweet. Thank you."

"You're welcome," he said, kissing her full on her lips while cradling his hands on either side of the baby. "So? You ready?"

"For what?"

"Your grand tour?"

"Of what?"

He kissed her again. "What do you think? Kodiak Gorge."

"COLBY!" Whitney complained on the tenth dusty stair of Schlump's Hardware. The creaky old staircase was dark and musty—downright spooky. She found it odd that the hardware store was on the town tour, but Colby insisted she had to see the supposedly haunted building.

She sneezed.

"Bless you."

To use him as both protection against ghosts and a tow line, she tucked her fingers into his back pockets. "I'm exhausted. Are we almost there?"

"Just a couple more steps." At the top, he stood aside to make room for her, then said with a flourish of his hands, "Ta-da!"

All she saw was an equally dusty, dank and gloomy hallway, at the end of which creepy pale red light spilled through a stained-glass window. She flinched when something scurried into the room two doors down from where they stood.

"This isn't funny," she said. "People catch diseases from places like this."

"Oh, quit complaining," he said. "Where's your sense of adventure?"

"Back at the lodge. I think I smelled home-baked peanut butter cookies—and you know how much Nugget wants me to drink milk."

As he took her by the hand, Whitney caught him rolling his eyes. "That man's poured enough milk down you to open a dairy."

"Colby!" Reddening, she swatted his behind.

"Is it just me, or have you been doing an awful lot of butt touching on this trip?"

"No!"

"Not that I'm complaining, but…" Leaning against a wall that had been papered in old newspapers, he slipped his hands around her waist, lowering his mouth to hers for a delicious kiss.

"Mmm…" she teased. "This tour is definitely looking up."

"Any idea where you are?" he asked.

"The perfectly dreadful second story of Schlump's Hardware?"

"Nope." He kissed her nose. "You happen to be standing in a piece of Kodiak Gorge history."

"Oh?" She raised her eyebrows, trying not to breathe for fear of contracting some rare form of lung disease from all the dust.

"This very spot happens to be the infamous Dot's Bordello."

Whitney choked on her saliva. "Dot? Our Dot ran a bordello?"

"Nah, her great-grandmother."

"Oh, cool! Dot's grandma was a lady of the night. A shady lady."

"And in this room right here," he said, dragging her into the same room the scurrying thing had vanished into, "Schafer Kingsley shot Barnabas Riley in cold blood for sleeping with Felicity Holmes."

Whitney grimaced, taking a backward step, but Colby pulled her alongside him. Driving rain hit the room's only window.

Whitney shivered.

"The event was in all the papers from Anchorage to San Francisco. Schafer shot the poor bastard straight through his family jewels. That night, Felicity hanged herself off the second-floor balcony."

"What happened to Schafer?"

"He was publicly hanged a week after that."

"And you brought me here why?" Whitney asked, walking deeper into the gloom, the soles of her sneakers cracking broken glass.

"Well, first off, because the place is famous. It's been on two Travel Channel ghost show specials and starred in its very own History Channel documentary on untamed Alaska."

"Oh."

"Still not impressed?"

"Well… It's more than sad, Colby, it's—"

"Tragic," he said, tucking his arms around her. "If you come here at, say, 2 a.m., folks say you can still see Barnabas and Felicity dancing."

Baby Nick kicked, and Whitney jumped slightly.

Colby grinned. "Somebody's enjoying himself."

"That's because he doesn't know any better. What kind of tourist town is this? Don't you have any fudge or ice cream shops?"

"Rough customer, are you?"

"Yes. I paid a lot for this tour."

"What? One measly kiss?"

"I think we're up to two or three now, thank you very much."

"Yeah, well—"

A cold breeze blew through the room, skittering three yellowed newspapers across the wood floor.

"Harvey?" Colby called out, assuming the store's owner must have opened a window. When the chubby proprietor didn't answer, he winked, then said, "Let's get out of here."

"THIS MORE TO YOUR LIKING?" Colby asked a few minutes later, as he led Whitney into the ethereal glow of the town's chapel. The building had been constructed of native stone mined from the gorge, and the pews carved from Sitka spruce. Red carpet, which he'd heard had been a gift to the church from

Dot's great-grandmother, lined the center aisle, and several candles flickered on the altar. Outside, rain still fell, hammering the tin roof.

"It's beautiful," Whitney said.

"The steeple was carted all the way from San Francisco on mules."

"The whole way?"

"Well, not the whole way. I imagine part of the journey was by ferry, but still."

"Do you ever attend services here?"

"Occasionally. I used to come more, when Mom was still in town. She dragged me every Sunday when I was a kid."

"I think it'd be nice being part of a church like this."

Colby caught a wistful edge to Whitney's simple statement. "Your family never went to church?"

"My dad's a philosophy professor. He's also an atheist."

"For real?"

Walking a few steps ahead of him into the hushed place, she nodded.

"Wow. How 'bout your mom?"

"She's never much said one way or the other."

Hence Whitney's problems with the whole faith issue? How could she believe in letting a higher power work things out for the best if she didn't believe in said power at all? "And you?"

"I spent a summer helping out a Peace Corps

friend of mine in Senegal. Pretty standard stuff. We helped build a village clinic. When it was done, people from miles around came to see the doctor. Little kids with strange growths coming out of their backs and heads. Old people blind from cataracts that here in America would be fixed in a routine outpatient procedure.'' Staring straight ahead, she ran her fingers back and forth along the smooth back of a pew. ''I saw a man in his prime die from an infected wound on his ankle. I saw a woman die of old age, surrounded by those she loved. I saw three babies born, and those births, more than anything else, made me see what a miracle life is. A crazy, happy miracle none of us have any idea how to control.''

''Yeah, but you can do your dead level best to guide it.''

''You think?''

''Yeah, I do.''

''Okay, so what happened to us on that mountain—who could've predicted that? You yourself checked the weather before we left and said it was safe for flying. We both thought we were going to croak, yet we lived. I never would've dreamed I'd become pregnant practically the first time out of the gate, yet all of it happened.''

''Your point being?''

Shaking her head, she grinned, sliding onto the pew beside him. ''I guess that *is* my point—that there's no rhyme or reason to any of what we go through."

"If that's the case, why fight it? Why not just go along for the ride?"

"Because I can't. I have to be in control."

"Why?" He took her hand, rubbed the tender spot between her thumb and forefinger.

"I guess because, growing up, I never once felt secure. Not until I'd entered college and could follow my own set of rules."

"Which included no men, because men hurt you."

"Yes."

He gave her hand a squeeze. "Not all men, Whitney. Not me."

"I know," she said. "That's what makes this decision over whether or not to marry you all the harder. Yes, after the time we've spent together, leaving you would be one of the hardest things I've ever done. But if I marry you, and if we have ten happy years together before our relationship falls apart, that just might be more than I can bear."

Leaning forward, he tried to say *forever* with his gentle kiss. An eternity later, he pulled back, and he whispered, "Marry me, Whitney Foster, and not just for the son I love, but because I love you."

Chapter Fourteen

Whether Whitney believed him or not, Colby meant what he'd said back at the church, and he hoped here, now, in the loft bedroom he'd helped construct with his own hands, he could again use his hands and his heart to build on his relationship with the mother of his son.

"I love you," he said, unzipping the pale blue jacket of her latest jogging suit.

"I love you, too," she said, arching her head back when he kissed her throat. "But I don't know why or even how you could love me. I've given you nothing but grief since I got here."

"True," he teased, easing her jacket off her shoulders and down her arms, letting it fall with a barely audible sound to the carpet. "But every time you annoy me, you have this uncanny knack of reeling me back in." Outside, rain still fell. Inside, he gently drew her white T-shirt over her head, then kissed a trail along the outline of her pretty pink bra. "I loved the way you cared for my cuts after I fell down the lodge stairs."

"I thought you said I was a bad nurse."

"I lied. You were the best. Tender and caring, just the way I'd want you to be with my son." He hooked his thumbs into the waistband of the jogging pants that matched her jacket, tugging them slowly down, letting her use his shoulders for support when he lifted her right foot out, then her left. "I love the way you got so excited over catching a fish, yet you didn't go all squeamish when it came time to eat him—unless I count those tears I saw in your eyes when you thought I wasn't looking. But I will count them, 'cause they tell me you understand Alaska on a basic level—that, up here, nature is a gift to be used but also respected."

"Know what I love about you?" she asked, tugging off his navy-blue T-shirt.

He shivered from the sensation of her cold fingertips on his chest. "You're freezing," he said. "Let's get under the covers."

"I'm fine," she said, planting butterfly-soft kisses along his collarbone and throat. "I love the way every time I turn around, you're wondering if I'm cold. All the time getting me blankets. Tucking in my toes."

"They're cute toes."

"Thanks."

Undoing the top button of his jeans, then another

and another, she knelt before him, kissing each inch of his black cotton boxers that she bared. "I wasn't going to mention this," she said, glancing up at him, eyes sparkling. "But since I'm here, I love how you still wear boxers with stuff on them. These little dancing bears are adorable."

"Yeah, just so long as we keep them a secret just for you."

"Scout's honor," she said, solemnly looking up before bursting into another grin. "Okay, so where was I? Oh—I love the way you didn't yell at me when I let the boat get away."

"That was pretty boneheaded," he teased.

"Oh—and I suppose you could've done better? In case you forgot, right after my knot lesson, you gave me a refresher course on kissing. Could I really be blamed if your second lesson overrode the first?"

"Oh, in that case, I guess you're forgiven."

She gave his jeans an extra hard tug.

"Let's see, I also love your cooking, and the way you forgave me for nearly setting your cabin on fire."

"Nearly?" He choked back a laugh. "Seems to me you were well on your way, darlin'."

"Do you want to hear this?"

"Only if it's truthful."

After tugging his jeans the rest of the way off, she stood. "How's this for truth?"

They'd shared many kisses over the week, even more during their wild night in his plane, but none came close to rocking him the way this one did. It was not only the first time they'd kissed with their true feelings exposed, but the first in broad daylight with her big, bare belly rubbing his.

What a turn-on. He'd done that.

He'd made a baby—well, not entirely on his own, but he had played a big part in his son's creation.

Falling to his knees, he kissed the miracle inside his wife-to-be's stomach. While she clung to his hair, he pulled her pink cotton panties down, helping her step clear. Then he was fumbling at her back to unhook her bra and wishing he was more of a ladies' man when it came to removing lingerie.

"Dammit," he said. "Why the hell don't they make these things with an emergency release?"

She laughed, parking his hands on her full breasts before reaching back to accomplish the task herself. "You know," she said, "I think you actually did a better job of that in the dark in the cramped cargo area of your plane."

"You're right. Probably felt more like the backseat of a parked car."

"Oh, so you were one of those guys, huh?"

He laughed. "I wish. There were four kids in my graduating class—all four of them guys. My friend Brody's girl, Raven, was a junior, but she'd been pretty much taken since the all-school picnic back in sixth grade.''

''Bummer.''

''My thoughts exactly.''

''Well, you big stud—finally, here's your chance to have your way with a naked, willing woman.'' Grinning, she held out her arms. Laughing right along with her, he tried smoothly getting her into bed, then positioning himself on top of her, but the task proved tougher than he'd planned.

Lying on his side, his hand in the hollow of her hip, he said, ''Okay, is it just me, or does Nick make for a logistical nightmare in, um, certain adult areas?''

Bunching pillows under her head, Whitney said, ''Seems to me you'll just have to get more creative to reach our goals.''

''I will, huh?''

She winked. ''After all, you're the one who got me this way.''

''Woman, are you always going to be sassy?''

She took a second to think, then said, ''Uh-huh.''

''Okay, then, guess I'll just have to learn to live with it.''

And learn he did.

He started by hushing up that smart mouth of hers, making it impossible for her to speak, only to moan.

''Colby, I—''

"*Shh,*" he said, tucking his head between her knees to have a little fun.

"*Ohhh.*" She braced her fingers in his hair, tugging so hard he winced. He repeated that trick with his tongue—the one that had gotten her hot even in driving snow. Judging by how much harder she was now pulling his hair, he guessed she still liked that particular move.

Whitney squirmed, but the magician between her legs held her in place, nipping her inner thighs, kissing that little—"*Ohhh!*" She wanted him to stop, but at the same time never stop. The sensation was maddening.

He tried shifting on top of her, and she tried making way, wanting nothing more than to let him complete the job he'd started, but there was no getting past her belly.

"Um, let me try something else," he said, shimmying free of his boxers before going for another position. But that didn't work either, and they landed in a tangle of sensation-flooded limbs right back where they'd started.

"What're we going to do?" she asked, by this time feeling more than a little desperate. The things that man did with his tongue!

He sat up and raked his fingers through his hair. "Okay, let's think. We're two reasonably intelligent adults, surely we can—aha."

"What?"

In wickedly sexy, straightforward terms, he spilled his plan in her ear. When she'd thoroughly reddened, he asked, "Think it'll work?"

She showed her approval with another kiss.

EVEN THOUGH HE WAS exhausted from the second wild night he'd shared with Whitney, Colby still couldn't sleep. Around 6:00 a.m., he quit trying in favor of making his future wife a big breakfast.

Funny, but when he'd first gotten home from the cabin, he'd taken a quick shower then headed back out, not wanting to be alone. But now that he had Whitney and his future son with him, the place felt like home again, and he never wanted to leave.

Figuring Whitney would be extra hungry, he whipped up a batch of waffles and link sausage, accompanied by some cantaloupe Henry had left on his doorstep, with a note explaining it had been on sale at the town grocery.

Once he'd assembled two plates on a tray, wishing he had a daisy or something to make it more romantic, Colby grinned. Yep, to be thinking of daisies at this hour made it official.

He had to be in love.

Whistling his way through the sun-flooded house, he took the stairs two at a time, anticipating the view at the top. And he wasn't disappointed to find his very own sleeping beauty still snoring away, gorgeous bare legs tangled in sheets.

Setting the tray on the nightstand on his side of the bed, he slid back under the covers beside her, taking a moment just to drink her in. God, she was beautiful, with her long hair fanning around her pillow and her complexion golden from all their time spent up at the cabin in the sun.

She rolled over, baring her full left breast, and the little boy in him couldn't resist having a little more fun.

AN HOUR LATER, while Colby was in the kitchen nuking the waffles and sausage, Whitney lounged in his great big whirlpool tub, munching on sweet, cubed cantaloupe.

What an incredible night—and morning—she thought, gazing out the wall of windows overlooking the rugged gorge. The first time she'd seen it, she'd thought it intimidating, but now she saw it as a challenge. Just like she'd conquered her fear of being with this intoxicating man, one day she might conquer Alaska.

One day.

Her latest bite of cantaloupe turned sour in her mouth, making it hard to swallow.

Her heart lurched, and she feared she might be choking.

Oh—she was choking all right.

Not on the fruit Colby had so lovingly prepared, but on her own stupid fears. *One day,* meaning she still wasn't quite ready to commit. *One day,* maybe, but certainly not today. That would be all right. Colby was an understanding guy. She'd go back to Chicago, have their son, and just as soon as he had some free time, he could hop over for a visit.

For that matter, once Nick was big enough to travel, the two of them could come up for visits, and then—

"Here you go."

She lurched, splashing water onto the fluffy red rug in front of the tub.

"Sorry," he said, setting the food tray on the wide red tile ledge. "I didn't mean to sneak up on you."

"I know," she said, swallowing back tears. She didn't want to discuss this. Not now, when everything between them was so right. Her plane left Anchorage that evening, so she still had plenty of time before she'd have to hightail it to the lodge to pack. Until then, she wanted to enjoy the precious hours they had left.

"What's wrong?" he asked, taking his plate, then sitting on the ledge beside her. "You seem upset."

"Let's not talk about it now. I just want to enjoy breakfast. It smells wonderful. Your mom and Nugget did a great job teaching you how to cook."

"Thanks, but back to the subject—what's up?

Are you sick? Did we overdo it last night and...
hurt the baby?''

"No, of course not," she said, her hand on his
forearm. "I've never felt better."

"Then why the sad eyes?" He set his as-yet un-
touched plate back on the tray.

"You can probably guess," she said. She looked
down. "Think about it. My flight leaves tonight."

"Y-your what?" It was a damned good thing
Colby hadn't had a bite of waffle in his mouth, or
he'd be dead from sucking it down his windpipe.

Had the woman lost her mind?

Surely he'd misunderstood.

"My flight. I have to get back to Chicago tonight. I still have plans to finalize for the birth and
arranging for the nanny to start full-time after my
maternity leave. I have bunches more stuff to buy
for the nursery. Oh—and I thought I'd pick up one
of those— What?"

Jeez, had she just now noticed the anger in his
expression?

Smacking his palm against the wall, he said,
"Please tell me I didn't just hear you say you're
still going to have this baby in Chicago."

"Of course I am. You didn't think I could have
it here, did you?"

He hardened his jaw. "If you're worried about
not having a doctor, we have a great one. Remember that TV show where the town paid for the doc-

tor's med school if he'd agree to spend a chunk of time practicing there? We did the same thing. Doc Meadows is nice. You'd like her. I'll get you her number and you can make an appointment.'' On his feet, arms crossed, staring out at the postcard-perfect view, he said. ''If you don't want to get married, that's…fine. Just please—don't go.''

He looked back to see tears streaming down her cheeks as she awkwardly tried getting out of the tub. She almost slipped, but caught herself. He wanted to be the one catching her, holding her, toweling her dry, but he guessed it was time he realized she could take care of herself.

''Colby…'' He held out a thick green towel. Her lips curving in a sad half smile, she took it and wrapped it around herself. ''I'm so sorry, but—''

''You're sorry?'' He choked on a bitter laugh.

''I can't stay. I can't marry you.''

When he turned away from her, clenching his fists, she stretched out one hand and turned him back.

''I'm not saying I might not some day change my mind, I just need more time to study the dynamics of the whole marriage thing. My favorite area of study has been group dynamics under extreme conditions. But I'll for sure take an extra look at marriage. You know, to see just how many of them work. I've looked into dysfunctional relationships, but I'll check into the positive side as well.''

"So that's all the thought of marrying me is to you? Just one more case study?"

"Think of the baby, Colby. Do we really want to subject him to us breaking up, if in a couple of years—or maybe even months—from now, we decide our relationship isn't going to work out?"

"Fine, Whitney. I give up." So furious he doubted he could even be civil, Colby started to walk out, but before he left, he had one more thing to say. "I thought last night—hell, this whole week—was magic, but then what do I know, right?" He laughed. "I'm just some country boy you picked up on one of your field studies. As for our son, I'm sure you'll see him as just a convenient little study package, too."

"Colby, I—"

"Don't," he said, the cords in his neck tight. "Don't you dare spout some highbrow academic explanation for your cowardly behavior. And that's just what you are, Whitney Foster, a great big coward too damned afraid to start off on what could've been the best trip of your—no, both of our—lives."

"Please, Colby," she said, crushing his T-shirt in her hands. "Please try to understand. A long-distance relationship won't be so bad. We can work this out over the phone."

Nostrils flared, eyes cold, he said, "The only thing left to work out is our custody agreement. Get

dressed, and I'll take you as far as the lodge. After
that...I'll see you in court.''

THE RIDE FROM COLBY'S once-enchanted home to
the lodge had taken an eternity. Packing in front of
a grim-faced Nugget had been another eternity. But
now that she was finally on board the charter flight
she'd arranged to take her to Anchorage, Whitney
knew she was doing the right thing.

The mere fact that it'd been so rough saying
goodbye to all these people told her staying
would've been unhealthy. It couldn't be good to
form such immediate attachments—and she had
formed attachments to every coot who'd appeared
at the lodge to say goodbye.

Henry, still wearing his tired old fedora, hugging
her so tight it hurt, tucked a bag of his sweet-
smelling pipe tobacco in her pocket—just in case
after the baby was born she wanted to take up
smoking. Stanley, bringing her a bouquet of forget-
me-nots that only served as a reminder of the
flower-dotted boulder beside Colby's dock. Nugget,
sending her off on her journey with a still-warm
plate of foil-wrapped peanut butter cookies and a
thermos filled with nice, cold milk.

''You all buckled in back there?'' the pilot
asked. This was far different from the time she'd
flown with Colby. The plane was bigger, and she
sat in a seat two behind and to the right of the

middle-aged, balding pilot, whose matter-of-fact concern reminded her of carpooling with one of her friends' fathers. Nothing about him was remotely similar to Colby, and as her new pilot rambled through the standard commercial flight safety pitch, Whitney's throat ached from missing the man she loved.

The pilot glanced over his shoulder. "You okay?"

"I'm fine," she said, silent tears streaming down her cheeks as he revved the plane's engine. She'd long since taken Colby's Santa hat from her purse. Gripping it like a lifeline, she was still crying as the plane's floats clacked over Kodiak Lake's choppy water.

You a virgin?

Crying, grinning, peering out over the rapidly fading view, she touched her fingers to the small oval window.

Nope. She was officially no longer even an almost-virgin. But since she knew no man would ever come close to giving her what she'd cherished in Colby, she also knew she'd probably never make love with anyone else.

"Want anything to eat or drink?" the pilot asked over the engine's dull hum. "I've got some pop and pretzels in a cooler behind the back seat."

"No, thank you." *I'm never eating again.*

"Sorry it took me so long to get over here. Had

to repair a busted fuel line. Damnedest thing. We've had a mouse problem back at the hangar. Looks like one of the little buggers must've chewed right through it.''

''That's okay,'' Whitney said, knowing full well nothing would ever be okay again. What had she done?

Oh, she knew from the crushing pain in her chest that she'd made the right decision in leaving. It was coming here in the first place that was now causing her doubts.

Just like her lawyer had said, she should've informed Colby via mail that he was going to be a parent. It would've been clean, efficient. No fuss, no muss.

Oh, so that's what this week was to you, Whitney? Fuss and muss?

Even with a few squabbles, this week had given her a glimpse of familial heaven—a place she'd never even dreamed existed.

Wiping away still more tears, she straightened in her seat.

This was crazy. For the sake of Nick, she had to pull herself together.

Nick. Ugh, even thinking her baby's new name brought on a surge of grief over having to say goodbye.

If leaving was so right, how come it was turning out to be so hard?

Up in front, she noticed a lot of tapping on the controls. Remembering what'd happened after Colby had done the same thing, she asked, ''Is everything all right?''

''Yep.'' He frantically flipped a few more switches before the engine sputtered and died.

Pale pink fluid streamed across Whitney's window.

Fuel?

''Mayday! Mayday!'' the pilot shouted into the radio.

Whitney, eyes wild, hugged her belly, bracing her feet.

No, no, no.

This couldn't be happening again!

What were the odds of a person surviving two plane crashes?

Nil.

Absolutely nil.

Ironically, the same odds of ever finding a more perfect husband for herself or a more perfect father for her baby than the very man she was trying to escape.

Oh, dear God, what'd she done? She never should've left. She never should've—

''Hold tight, ma'am! We're going down!''

Chapter Fifteen

"Hey, man, how you doing?"

Colby glanced up from the beer he'd been nursing at the lodge's bar to see his old pal Brody standing there wearing a sympathetic look. "News travels fast round here, huh?"

"What do you mean?"

"Oh, come on," he said. "The news about me being dumped by Whitney. Guess you and I are destined to be bachelors forever, huh?" He raised his long-neck beer. "Let's toast—to bachelorhood."

Brody took the beer, and slid it down the bar. "I'm sorry about your girl, but we just got an emergency call. You sober enough to fly?"

Colby rubbed his eyes, forcing himself instantly alert. "Yeah. I've just had half of this one."

"Cool. Let's rock and roll."

After standing, then leaving a few bills on the bar, Colby asked, "Who's in trouble? Lost hiker?"

On their way out of the bar's gloom and into the lobby's obnoxiously bright light, Brody shook his head. "Downed plane."

"YOU DID A GREAT J-JOB landing," Whitney said, unable to stop her teeth from chattering despite the warm sun and two blankets. Why hadn't she worn a nice practical jogging suit and sneakers instead of this stupid black linen dress, black leather pumps and black panty hose now sporting a run?

"Relax." The pilot, seated beside her on a flat-topped boulder on the lake's shore, patted her back. "We're fine. Help is already on the way. On a clear day like this, shouldn't be but twenty or thirty minutes till we get another ride."

"You're sure?"

"Absolutely," he said, giving her one more fatherly pat.

After the repaired fuel line had apparently broken again, he'd landed the plane smoothly on a small lake that reminded Whitney of the one facing Colby's cabin, only without the snowcapped mountain. Pretty as you please, the plane had drifted to shore, and the pilot had jumped out, towing it the rest of the way in before helping her off. She hadn't even gotten her feet wet.

Then why was she so cold?

Same old song.

Fear.

Only now, it was fear that Colby wouldn't take her back. Although the so-called crash landing had turned out to be no big deal, those moments of wondering whether she'd live or die had seemed more like hours. Through it all, the one topic on her mind was regret. She deeply regretted not handling things differently with the man she now knew she loved.

Yes, she wanted a sweet little wedding attended by all her new friends. Yes—she wanted a three-tiered cake and a forget-me-not bouquet, and a wedding dress hand sewn from Kodiak Lodge T-shirts if only it bound her to Colby forever.

She'd been a fool. Hiding behind fear.

Ironic how it was fear that'd finally shaken her free from her doubts about marriage. On the verge of dying, she finally realized that in loving Colby, she wasn't losing her heart, but gaining her soul.

Faced with death, she'd found faith.

Faith that whether she'd lived or died, she'd loved and been loved. But just the knowing wasn't enough. Now that she was very much alive, she wanted the joy of living.

From the east came the buzz of one plane, then two.

"We're saved!" she said, tossing off her blanket to crush her pilot in a hug.

He cast her a *told you so* look before she awkwardly climbed down from the rock, teetering up and down the shore on her stupid heels, waving her arms.

Wincing from the sun's glare on the broad expanse of water, Whitney put her hands to her forehead, heart pounding at the view. There were two planes—the first she recognized as the one Colby's friend Brody had flown the night of the blizzard. The other belonged to none other than the man she hoped would be her husband within a matter of days—hours if they could find a willing preacher. She didn't need any fancy cakes, dress or flowers. All she needed was him.

As if performing in a precision air show, the approaching pilots landed their planes in tandem before smoothly gliding the rest of the way across the lake. The closer they came, the more she smelled exhaust from their engines mixing with the rich scents of the fishy-smelling water and pungent spruce.

Though her heart was still racing, her spirits soared.

Those scents were Colby's scents, and the first thing she planned to do when she saw him was give him a fiercely apologetic hug.

With the engines off, all fell quiet on the lake, save for the breeze shushing through the trees and small, lapping waves rolling ashore.

Brody stepped out onto his plane's float. "Some excitement, eh, Vic?" he shouted to her pilot. Vic.

She'd been so terrified thinking she'd never see Colby again she hadn't even asked the man's name.

Colby's friend Tanner also climbed out of Brody's plane.

"Yep," Vic said. "It was touch and go there for a few minutes, but the old girl did me good."

"I'll say," Brody said, tying his plane to a fallen tree, then crunching along the pebbled shore to help Vic inspect his engine.

He hadn't even looked at *her*.

Hadn't even said *hi*.

What'd you expect? It's probably no big secret that you ran off with his best friend's son!

Chest tight, throat aching from a fresh round of approaching tears, Whitney pressed her hands to her baby, then set off across the shore to Colby's plane.

At the same time, he climbed out.

Sergei followed, but when she approached, he cast her an arctic look before heading over to Vic.

Ignoring him and his cold shoulder, she waddled the rest of the way to Colby, throwing herself into his arms. Tears followed in an uncontrollable gush. "I'm so glad to see you," she said against his chest, loving his strength and smell and sheer breadth. "Yes, I'll marry you," she cried. "I'm so sorry to have been such a fool back at your house this morning. W-when I thought we were going to die—I-it was horrible, Colby."

"I can imagine," he said, awkwardly patting her back instead of murmuring comforting words into her hair. Instead of lifting her up for the reunion kiss she'd spent the past endless minutes dreaming about.

"Colby?" She slowly unclasped her fingers from where she'd clenched his T-shirt, which was still damp from her tears.

"I'm thrilled that you and the baby are safe," he said, "but…"

"But what? Didn't you hear me? You don't have to be mad at me anymore. I've seen the light—literally," she added on the heels of a nervous laugh. "You were right—about everything. Oh, Colby, we'll make a beautiful family, and I do trust you, and love you, and our life is going to be just great."

A muscle ticked in his hardened jaw, and instead of their usual warm sea-green, his eyes had grown stone cold.

"Now that we know you're okay," he said, "Brody's gonna ferry you and Vic back to Anchorage so Vic can grab some parts, and you don't miss your flight."

Her heart thundering as though an entire sled dog team was racing through her chest, Whitney gave another nervous laugh. "Yeah, but didn't you hear? I'm not going to Anchorage. To heck with catching my flight." She threw herself at him in another hug, but just when she'd gotten comfortable, he gripped her shoulders, lightly pushing her away.

"Yes, Whitney. You're leaving. Now." He whistled and Brody looked in their direction. "Vic, whenever you're ready, Brode's gonna ferry you back to get a new line."

Vic nodded, then knelt to gather the few tools he'd already spread on the ground.

"Colby?" Whitney began to tremble all over. "Colby, please. Didn't you hear me? I want to marry you. I love you. Look—I even have proof." More than a hint of desperation in her tone, she ran as best she could the short distance to her purse to get Colby's hat. "Look," she said, waving it on her short trip back to his side. "I know I shouldn't have, but I took this the night we were rescued. I was wrong, Colby—about everything. I loved you then, only I was too afraid to admit having fallen for you in only one, incredible night."

"My hat? That's your so-called proof?" He laughed. "While I'm flattered I was a good enough date that you wanted a souvenir, some corny Santa hat doesn't mean you love me, Whit. You could've died. You were understandably scared. But scared doesn't equal love—not after that proper little speech you delivered just a few hours ago back at the house. In fact, I'll bet if you think hard enough, you could even come up with a label to identify your sudden change of feelings. Maybe some kind of Stockholm Syndrome thing."

"How can you say that? You don't know what's going on in my heart!"

Toying with the tether rope to his plane, he said, "Better than anyone, Whitney, I do know what's going on inside you, and it ain't pretty. Emotionally, you're a scared ten-year-old living in a grown woman's body. You have this academic view of the world, neatly assembling every emotion and person into textbook-perfect case studies—but you know what? I don't want to fit into one of your studies. I want to be the *only* study. I wanted to be your whole life, just like I offered to be yours. But you turned me down one too many times and now I rescind the offer." Stepping onto the float, in front of Sergei and Tanner, he said, "Somehow, we'll reach an equitable custody agreement, but as for the two of us being a couple—we're history."

"Yo, Whitney!" Brody shouted. "Your ride's back here!"

One trembling hand on her baby, she put her other over her mouth, not caring who saw her tears.

How could he do this me? How could he be so cruel?

Stupid questions considering how often she'd been cruel to him. Belittling his desire to raise his son. Not trusting him to be a kind and caring husband to her. Yet again, he'd been right in his biting words, only now there was nothing she could do to repair the damage she'd done.

She lowered her hand from her mouth to try apologizing once more, but it was too late. By the time she figured out what to say, he was already back in his plane, waving at her to step back.

When she refused to budge, to break her stare, Brody slipped his arm loosely about her shoulders, guiding her to his plane. "I'm real sorry," he said. "You two would've made a good team."

"Then talk to him, Brody. *Please*. Make him understand that—"

"Shh…" Brody squeezed her shoulders. "It's over," he said while Colby started his plane's engine. "You gotta face facts. It's over."

"But I love him!"

"Really?" he asked, even as Colby backed his plane away.

"I think I do." Swallowing hard, she added, "Isn't that enough?"

Brody laughed sadly, guiding her the rest of the way toward his plane. "For Colby, nope. *Thinking* isn't anywhere near enough. He's your basic all-or-nothing kind of guy."

THAT NIGHT AT THE LODGE BAR, Colby stared at the tall-neck beer in front of him. It'd been staring back at him for going on nearly an hour now, but he still hadn't taken a drink.

Some drunken fool had put about twenty bucks' worth of my-wife-left-me-and-took-my-'57 Chevy-with-her country music on the jukebox, and Colby's head throbbed in time with the blinking neon Coors sign behind the bar.

Brody should've been back by now.

What an afternoon—hell, he might as well go a little further and include the whole damn week.

The way that woman played him ought to be criminal.

She'd played with his heart like a dog with a rawhide chew toy. And then saying some goofy hat proved she'd changed her mind and loved him. That was crazy. Just plain nuts. People didn't change all of a sudden. They just didn't. And if anyone should know that, it was Whitney. After all, she was the one with all those damned book smarts.

"How you doin'?" Tanner asked, easing onto the stool beside him.

"How do you think?"

"You ever gonna drink that beer?" he asked. "Polnick says that's the last one, then we're gonna have to switch to tap 'til he gets another shipment."

Polnick was the bartender currently shoveling his way through a plate of Nugget's lasagna.

"Take it," Colby said. "Guess I'm not in the mood for drinkin'."

"Wanna fly down to Cordova, then? See if we can score?"

"Jeez, Tanner." Colby scowled. "Way to go on the sensitivity there, bud. No wonder Jenny left you."

"What? Because she left, I'm supposed to be a hermit?"

"You made a lifelong vow to be faithful to her, remember?"

After taking a long swig of his newly acquired beer, he said, "She's the one who left me. I'd say that pretty much cancels any and all agreements."

Colby shook his head. "I'm outta here. Catch ya later."

Tanner grabbed Colby's sweatshirt sleeve, yanking him back. "You know what your problem is, Davis?"

"Why don't you tell me, McCormick." Colby steeled his jaw. Closed his hands into fists.

"You're just too damned loyal. Like a big old hound dog, just waitin' around for a pat on your dumb, blind head."

"You're wasted," Colby said through gritted teeth, "so I'm gonna pretend you didn't say that."

As if sensing a fight, the guys in back stopped playing pool to watch.

"Pretend all you want, bud, but that girl played you like a fiddle. Hell, she's probably back in Chicago right now, chatting up some guy she met in the airport lounge. Hell, how do you even know that baby she's carrying is yours? What if she's not even pregnant? Like she's just messin' with your mind? Like some UFO conspiracy thing, that—''

Smack.

Colby hit his so-called friend hard and fast, right across the jaw.

In slow motion, Tanner fell off the stool, cracking the back of his head on the bar.

Colby was ready to give him another blow at the first smartass comment out of his mouth, but a bunch of guys stepped in to stop him.

"Let him be," somebody said.

"He's just drunk. He didn't mean anything."

"You'll be all right." Someone patted him on his back.

No. No, Colby knew he wasn't anywhere near all right, and he feared he might never be again. Jeez, he'd just hauled off and slugged one of his best friends.

Colby held out his hand to Tanner to help him up, but Tanner batted it away.

"I was just tellin' you the truth," Tanner said, spitting blood on Colby's right hiking boot.

"Yeah, well, next time, keep it to yourself."

"Come on, there, big fella," Polnick said to Tanner, helping him to his feet.

Tanner wobbled for a second before regaining his footing, then took one look at Colby and swung.

The fight was back on.

"WELL, KID," Brody said, standing at the security gate for Whitney's flight. "Guess this is it."

The strength of her sudden hug in the midst of a human river of traffic moved him to the point that after she let go, it took him a few seconds to regain his composure.

After dropping off Vic, she'd had three hours to kill before her flight, so he'd taken her to a hole-in-the-wall beer joint that served good burgers and even better onion rings. They'd talked for every minute of those hours, and she'd told him the whole story, right down to the secret she'd only just told Colby—she'd fallen hard for him that first night they were together, but was too afraid of losing him to ever claim him in the first place. She'd also told Brody that in the back of her mind she wondered if she hadn't returned to Kodiak Gorge to do exactly that—claim her man. Her baby's father.

Standing here now, watching her blink back tears, Brody knew his heart couldn't take it a minute longer.

He'd known Colby literally all his life, so he figured if anyone had a right to interfere in that life, he was the one.

Grasping Whitney's small, cold hands, he asked, "You like surprises?"

The hope lighting her face transformed her from a sad little girl to a full-on gorgeous woman. Brody's chest tightened. If she weren't already carrying his best friend's baby, he'd have made a play for her himself.

She nodded.

"Then come on. We've got a lot of work to do."

Chapter Sixteen

"Thank you," Whitney said to Brody around mid-night when he stopped his truck in front of Colby's house. "For everything."

She slid across the seat to throw her arms around him in a warm hug.

"It was my pleasure." Pulling away, he laughed. "I just wish I could be around to see the look on Colby's face when you show up at his door."

Whitney nibbled on her lower lip. "Do you think he'll take me back?"

"Remember, you're in Alaska now. Time for you to assert yourself. This isn't a matter of giving the man a choice, Whitney, it's telling him how it's going to be."

"You're right. I'm in control." She fumbled with the door's handle, then felt her old familiar fears return. "Funny," she said, finally shoving the door open. "If I'm in control, how come I feel faint?"

Laughing again, he climbed out to carry her bags to the porch, then they walked back to his truck.

"You'll be fine," he said, climbing behind the wheel. "Now get out of here so I can go home and get some shut-eye."

With one last hug, Brody was gone, save for the faint smell of exhaust hanging in the air, and the glow of his taillights through the dirt road's dust.

Well, this is it, Whitney thought, straightening her shoulders for the march up to the house that— if all went well—would soon be her home. Either Colby would take her back, or she'd spend the next couple of days out here sleeping with the bears, because one thing was for sure. She wasn't leaving until Colby hadn't just given her an answer, but the *right* one!

Her footsteps sounded abnormally loud on the porch steps when the only sounds they had to compete with were the whining bugs. In the airport rest room, she'd changed out of her black dress and heels into a comfy pair of maternity jeans and a pink sweatshirt. She'd never realized sneakers could clomp so loudly.

Her stomach growled.

Even that was noisy!

Heart pounding, mouth dry, she knocked at Colby's door.

There were no lights on inside, just a faint blue glow. She guessed the TV was on in the loft. She knocked again, and when there was still no sign of life, she tried the door, only to find it open.

Terrified, excited, ready to burst into tears at the first sight of the man she loved, Whitney eased the door open and stepped inside before closing it silently behind her.

Her tennis shoes were, thankfully, quiet on the hardwood floor.

From upstairs spilled the laugh track and bouncy music of an old *Seinfeld* episode.

Taking the stairs slowly, she forced herself to breathe, praying Colby was awake since she didn't have the heart to wake him. But she doubted her nerves could stand not knowing his reaction to her return until morning.

At the top of the stairs, she released a deep sigh before approaching the bed. "Colby?" she asked softly.

She crept closer, closer—except that he wasn't there.

On TV, *Seinfeld* faded into a cat-food commercial.

Meow, meow, meow...

If he wasn't in bed, where could he be? She checked in the master bath, but found that empty, too. She deliberately avoided looking at the tub where she'd made the worst decision of her life.

Creeping back downstairs, she glanced at the

couches, thinking he might've fallen asleep there, but nope.

He wasn't in the kitchen, either.

Her stomach growled again, and on her way past the pantry—the pantry that, if all went well, would soon be hers—she opened the door, flipped on the light, then foraged for a can of squirt cheese and a box of her favorite crackers. There they were. Yum. One mission accomplished.

She flicked off the light and was backing out the door, arms loaded with snacks, when from out of the darkness a familiar male voice said, "Stop right there, and put down whatever the hell you're stealing 'cause I'm in no mood to deal with a thief."

"Colby, it's me."

He flicked on the kitchen light, blinking at the sudden glare. "Whitney?" He set a baseball bat on the counter, his shoulders sagging. "What the hell are you doing? I might've hurt you."

"What does it look like I'm doing? I'm fixing a snack."

He shook his head as if to clear it. "Okay, let's back up. Why are you fixing a snack in my house? I thought you'd be in Chicago by now."

Calmly putting her treasures on the counter beside the bat, she flipped open the cracker box, taking a whiff of salty, tangy, spicy goodness. "Mmm...I've been craving one of these all day."

Stepping to the counter to pop the lid on the

cheese, then squirt out a circle atop her cracker, he said, "What're you doing here, Whitney?"

He handed it to her, and she popped the whole thing in her mouth, closing her eyes while she chewed. "Mmm…this is so good."

He rolled his eyes—one of which she now noticed was black. The left side of his jaw was swollen.

She gasped, touching her hand to his bruised cheek. "What happened?"

He flinched from her touch, pushing down her hand. "Nothing. It's no big deal."

"Yes, it is. You've been in a fight."

He shrugged.

"Colby? What happened?" She reached out again to touch him, but again he flinched away.

Oh, boy. She took a deep breath.

Looked like this was going to be tougher than she'd figured. Maybe she should just save all her questions about his fight for another time, and proceed to the next item on her agenda.

Digging into her pocket, she said, "Brody and I had a nice day. He took me out for the best cheeseburger I've ever had, and then we went shopping."

"You and Brody?" Colby nearly choked. First Tanner had been trashing her, and now his friend Brody had been making moves on her? What was this world coming to when not a single one of his friends could be trusted?

"Uh-huh. We went ring-shopping because, just as you've pointed out so many times, this baby of ours is going to need a father."

"Oh. Let me get this straight. Since I turned you down, you went running to Brody and he snapped you up?" Colby didn't think he could feel any more furious than he'd been at the bar, but this...

Snatching up the baseball bat, he stormed to the front door. When he got his hands on that so-called best friend of his, he was going to—

"Colby, wait!" Whitney ran after him, catching him at the door by clutching the back of his shirt. "You misunderstood. It wasn't like that."

Jaw clenched, fingers gripping the bat, he spun around. "Tell me what it was like then. I'd really like to know."

Never had Whitney seen him so enraged—not even the time she'd pulled out those custody papers she'd had her lawyer draw up. Could the fact that he was so insanely jealous at the mere thought of her hooking up with Brody be a sign in her favor? That he still felt *something* for her?

She licked her lips, unsure where to begin.

"I'm waiting," he said, right hand on the door.

His left hand held the bat, so she worked it loose, leaning it against the corner. His hand free, she grasped it, fumbling with his ring, but eventually slipping it on. "Brody took me shopping for your ring—and mine," she said, holding up a matching band. "We can have a proper ceremony tomorrow, but tonight, I want us to have one all our own. I want—"

For the longest time he stood there staring at her, his gaze searching her face for any indication that what she'd said might be another one of her games. But then he must've recognized that she was tired of playing games. All she wanted now was for the two of them to be together—forever.

Colby crushed her in a hug, burying his face in her hair. "I was so scared," he said. "When Vic's plane went down, I kicked myself for not forcing you to stay—for not locking both of us in my pantry and throwing away the key."

"I like it in there," she said with a teary, sniffy giggle.

"I know." He felt shaky. Weak. Rage fell away, making room for the shimmering waves of love he felt for this woman and his child.

"When we came to get you and Vic," he said, "I wanted to take you back right then and there, but my so-called friends told me to let you go. Tanner—he's still so bitter about Jenny leaving him. He told me to forget we'd even met, but I couldn't. I love you."

"I love you, too," she said when he lifted her up for the kiss she'd rehearsed a thousand times in her head. She wrapped her legs around his waist.

He crushed his mouth to hers, almost afraid to

believe she was really there. "I'm sorry I left," she said, her breath hot and moist in his ear.

"No," he said, his fingers buried in her soft hair. "I'm sorry I pushed you. Jeez, of course, you'd have qualms about marrying some guy you've only known a week."

She kissed him again. "I feel like I've known you forever. I think that was the scariest part. Everything we've shared—it's so different from what I thought love should be."

Between them, he felt his son kick, and he set Whitney down. "I didn't hurt the little guy, did I?"

"No," she said with that tinkling laugh he loved. "I think he's just saying hello."

Colby knelt to kiss her belly. "You're gonna have a great life," he said to his son. "We're gonna fish and hike and I'll teach you how to fly."

"What about me?" Whitney asked, her fingers in his hair. "Don't I get to do any of that fun stuff?"

"Fishing and hiking—yes. As for the flying... Woman, I'm never letting you near a plane again."

Epilogue

"Colby, good grief, would you leave the tree alone, and come sit with us by the fire?"

"I want everything perfect."

"It is. Your mom and stepdad and the whole crazy crew is going to love what you've done."

"It's not their opinion I'm worried about," he said, scooping his pride and joy from his momma's arms. "Nick, here's, got to learn how Christmas is done. After all," he added, removing his bedraggled Santa hat to settle it on his son's small head, "conceived like he was on Christmas Eve, he's a real live, Santa Baby."

"Hey," Whitney teased, standing beside him. "I thought I was your Santa Baby?"

He kissed the top of her head. "Can't a guy have two?"

"What are we going to do when we have a daughter one of these days? Maybe another son?"

Their gurgling three-month-old between them,

Colby pulled her into a hug. "Then I guess we'll have a house full of Santa babies. But hey, I thought you wanted a few more years to get your consulting business off the ground before we try for any more?"

"I do, I'm just saying that when the time comes, you'd better watch out."

"…Better not pout?"

Wagging her finger at him, she grinned. "You'd better not cry I'm tellin' you why…"

"Santa Claus is comin'…to town."

They were still laughing and singing carols an hour later when the doorbell rang, and in spilled Colby's family and Vic, who'd flown them in for the occasion.

Whitney's mother and stepfather were coming for a nice, long visit over New Year's. Whitney was looking forward to many fireside chats with her mom, during which, hopefully they could once again learn to be close.

After a buffet meal of ham and turkey and all the trimmings, Colby's step nieces and nephews took baby Nick into the TV room for movies.

Whitney excused herself from the boisterous crowd laughing and sharing stories in front of the fire to make a fresh batch of eggnog.

She jumped when Colby stepped up behind her, but then he eased her into his arms as he placed a string of kisses around her neck, kisses that followed the form of the gold necklace he'd given her the day Nick was born. It had a beautiful gold-and-diamond snowflake charm. "Mmm...I love you," he said.

She turned to face him. "I love you, too."

"It's snowing again."

"And..."

"So, I know the white stuff's been lucky for us, but I'm wondering if next year you want to go somewhere warm for Christmas? Hawaii?"

"Nope. I like it right here in Kodiak Gorge—snow and all." She fingered her charm.

"Yeah, but I was thinking..." He gave her another kiss.

"About what?"

"Well...since I'm in charge of decorations, and Nick and I are sharing the family Santa hat, and since he's now our official Santa Baby—I don't want you feeling left out."

"I don't. I was just teasing about—"

He silenced her with another kiss. "I figured as much, but still..." He released her to dig in his back pocket. "Just so there's no family squabble, I bought you this—only it might be a little cold here for you to truly enjoy it, which is why next year Hawaii might be a better place to spend the holidays."

Whitney raised her eyebrows.

The only thing in her husband's hand was a scrap of red satiny fabric with a teeny bit of green attached. "Um, thanks," she said, "but what is it?"

He beamed. "A Santa baby bikini."

0910_NEW VOICES

Do you dream of being a romance writer?

Mills & Boon are looking for fresh
writing talent in our biggest
ever search!

And this time…our readers have
a say in who wins!

For information on how to enter
or get involved go to

www.romanceisnotdead.com

All the magic you'll need this Christmas...

When **Daniel** is left with his brother's kids, only one person can help. But it'll take more than mistletoe before **Stella** helps him...

Patrick hadn't advertised for a housekeeper. But when **Hayley** appears, she's the gift he didn't even realise he needed.

Alfie and his little sister know a lot about the magic of Christmas – and they're about to teach the grown-ups a much-needed lesson!

Available 1st October 2010

1010/26/MB307

Spend Christmas with
NORA ROBERTS

Daniel MacGregor is the clan patriarch. He's powerful, rich – and determined to see his three career-minded granddaughters married. So he chooses three unsuspecting men he considers worthy and sets his plans in motion!

As Christmas approaches, will his independent granddaughters escape his schemes? Or can the magic of the season melt their hearts – and allow Daniel's plans to succeed?

Available 1st October 2010

www.millsandboon.co.uk

10/24/MB312

FIVE FABULOUS FESTIVE ROMANCES FROM YOUR FAVOURITE AUTHORS!

A Christmas Marriage Ultimatum by **Helen Bianchin**
Yuletide Reunion by **Sharon Kendrick**
The Sultan's Seduction by **Susan Stephens**
The Millionaire's Christmas Wish by **Lucy Gordon**
A Wild West Christmas by **Linda Turner**

Available 5th November 2010

www.millsandboon.co.uk

M&B

1210/09/MB318

Four fabulous, festive, sparkling romances

SUSAN MEIER
BARBARA WALLACE
PATRICIA THAYER
DONNA ALWARD

Christmas Wishes

& MISTLETOE KISSES

Baby Beneath the Christmas Tree by Susan Meier
Magic Under the Mistletoe by Barbara Wallace
Snowbound Cowboy by Patricia Thayer
A Bride for Rocking H Ranch by Donna Alward

Available 19th November 2010

www.millsandboon.co.uk

A Christmas bride for the cowboy

Two classic love stories by bestselling author
Diana Palmer in one Christmas collection!

Featuring

Sutton's Way
and
Coltrain's Proposal

Available 3rd December 2010

www.millsandboon.co.uk

WEB/M&B/RTL3

Discover Pure Reading Pleasure with

**Visit the Mills & Boon website for all
the latest in romance**

- **Buy** all the latest releases, backlist and eBooks

- **Find out** more about our authors and their books

- **Join** our community and chat to authors and other readers

- **Free** online reads from your favourite authors

- **Win** with our fantastic online competitions

- **Sign** up for our free monthly eNewsletter

- **Tell us** what you think by signing up to our reader panel

- **Rate** and review books with our star system

www.millsandboon.co.uk

 Follow us at twitter.com/millsandboonuk

 Become a fan at facebook.com/romancehq